"WHAT ARE YOU DOING?" SHE GASPED. HER EYES WIDENED AS SHE STARED AT HIM IN ALARM.

"I'm going to make love to you." Plunging his arms into the water, Nat encircled her body at the waist and fastened his mouth on hers. Her lips, hard and tight, softened under his. Her bosom, slippery with soap, pressed sensuously against his chest. He slid one hand down her back while the other cupped one elusive breast.

Deep inside her, some part of Melanie stood in appalled recrimination at the rapid numbing of her defenses; then, with a silent scream, it died forever as Melanie matched Nat's urgent desire.

At that moment, she *hated* Nat . . . she *loved* him. . . . But, most of all, she *wanted* him!

1.50

SHADOWS
ON THE
WIND

Rita Gallagher

A DELL BOOK

Published by
Dell Publishing Co., Inc.
1 Dag Hammarskjold Plaza
New York, New York 10017

Dell ® TM 681510, Dell Publishing Co., Inc.

ISBN: 0-440-18042-2

Printed in the United States of America

First printing—May 1982

To my first love,
Uncle Cam,
and
To Hank,
whose tender care
taught me, at last,
the true meaning
of love

PROLOGUE

JUNE—1850

___

The heavy carved door slammed shut and words spoken spitefully, in clipped, New England tones, rang in Nathaniel Larimore's ears . . .

She is Mrs. Jared Hardy now, the old aunt had said, eyes gleaming with malice. *She has a child, and expects another, come midwinter.*

With sinking heart and the realization that Laura was lost to him forever, Nat turned away to begin the long downhill trek.

Massachusetts basked in late afternoon sunshine and New Bedford harbor resembled a brilliant blue sapphire accented by diamondlike whitecaps at the mouth of the bay. The hills of the town rose sharply from the water's edge and lofty mansions, parks, and gardens were opulent. Long avenues of gold and green maples vied for attention against brightly flowered terraces rising, staircase fashion, up the steep slopes.

Descending slowly, Nat gazed down at the wharves in the distance. Mountains of empty casks, piled side by side, awaited oil from the depths of returning whalers. A few merchantmen were berthed among the whaling ships, loading or unloading, and from the holds of some issued the sound of carpenters repairing and refurbishing. The smell of pitch overrode the rank whaling odors as coopers blended their noises of fires and forges in preparation for new voyages.

Halfway downhill, Nathaniel paused to lean

against a tall tree. His startling deep blue eyes stared
vacantly into the distance as he sought to absorb the
knowledge imparted by Laura's aunt.

There were few passersby on the hill. At this hour
only housemaids were about, returning from late
market or rushing off on last-minute errands for dila-
tory mistresses. For those who saw him, however, a
glance was not enough. Footsteps lagged while eyes
rested overlong on the handsome blond man brooding beneath the huge elm and many a maid blushed
unseen, yearning for his notice.

A tall Nordic man he was, with broad shoulders
and wide chest tapering down to narrow hips and
lean, muscular legs. His sandy hair was thick, sunstreaked golden blond. His nose, large and hawklike,
betokened a sensual man with a lust for living. A
firm, stubborn jaw jutted a shade too much and the
rugged features lacked symmetry. But taken as a
whole, Nathaniel Larimore was a vigorously masculine man whose stalwart body exuded an irresistible,
magnetic virility. There was an air about him; an un-
mistakable stamp of authority. Those observing him
now felt the impact of his very presence; that indefin-
able, nebulous charisma defying description and
possessed by a privileged few. They had no way of
knowing, in that brief glimpse, that the full-lipped
mouth could curve in a broad smile, exposing large,
perfect teeth, while deep-set piercing eyes could hold
one mesmerized.

For a long time Nat stood there. He was only
vaguely aware of the steady murmur of voices floating
on warm winds from the streets surrounding the
docks, where foreign sailors, oddly dressed, spoke with
strange tongues and gestures, jostling the unwary and
frightening the fainthearted.

Nat's gaze sought his own ship, the *Mirimar*,
berthed at the far end of the dock. Sails furled, she
thrust three tall masts toward the bright blue sky

while his men, scurrying like ants in the distance, carried heavy boxes and sailcloth bags into her bowels, returning with empty arms to roll kegs and barrels up the gangplank. She sailed again within a fortnight.

The beauty of the scene below escaped Nat. His thoughts were on the last evening he'd spent with Laura, three years ago . . .

"You are a flirt!" he'd accused. "A tease! Were it not for your high birth, you could easily be a woman of the streets! These past two months of our separation have taught you nothing! I warned you, Laura, an inconstant woman is not for me! You lead men on! Then, in the unreasoning way of women, expect me to defend your honor."

His burning gaze had stabbed angrily down into her laughing green eyes as they stood, incongruously, over the fallen man between them.

"You're jealous!" Laura had crowed. "If you want to keep me from other men, then seal the guarantee by marriage!"

"I would not wed one of your ilk!" Nat retorted heatedly. "I find such as you in all ports, on many a dock . . . and in every seaman's tavern."

His cheek stung with her slap.

"And you, fine captain! Are you so noble; so chaste? You admit to bedding wenches in seaports across the world! Yet, you condemn me for gazing with favor upon another man!"

Nat did not answer.

He'd bent down, nudging the stunned man with his foot.

"Get up, cur! I do not blame you for following her lead; I chastised you for believing she could be accosted in my company."

He stood tall again, and his eyes met Laura's. They stared at each other for a long moment.

Then, softly, she'd murmured: "Marry me, Nat. And there'll be no more of these scenes."

"You're a fever in my blood," he'd answered. "But you are not the woman I want to wife."

"Who, then?" Laura whispered, sidling into his arms.

And his heart echoed the words: *Who, then?*

He'd sailed away the next morning, vowing to put her out of his thoughts forever. But he had not succeeded.

Laura stood beside him on deck with the wind blowing her long red hair. He felt her warm hand in his through dense fog and sudden squalls. And at night, her body, warm and supple, melted against him, matching ardor for ardor, hunger for hunger.

Now, three years later, standing on the hill just below her former home, Nat wondered.

If he did not love Laura enough to wed, why this pain, this longing, this agony at finding her life closed to him? For one mad moment, Nat thought of rushing up to Jared Hardy's house and crushing Laura in his arms, husband or no. But sanity returned, and he resolved once more to end his yearning.

So, in the days that followed, he busied himself with ships and shipments—to forget Laura. But he knew, as long as he must remain in New Bedford, he could not refrain from raising his eyes, twenty, fifty, one hundred times a day, to the hill where she lived. He looked for her in the shops . . . on the street . . . in the park. His restless gaze searched passing carriages while he walked aimlessly through the town. Perhaps, one day, they would meet face to face . . .

Possibly, he reasoned, *if I saw Laura once more, her ghost would be banished. If I became friendly with Jared, or even old Ephraim, I might be able to wangle an invitation, and accomplish my purpose.*

Nat knew Ephraim and Jared Hardy by sight,

though had spoken not more than a dozen words to either of them when they met now and then at the auctioneers. He knew the Hardy reputation as businessmen; both of them honest and unswerving in their integrity. Nat remembered Jared as quiet, reserved, but an astute and sharp-minded tradesman, following in his father's footsteps in everything but love for the sea.

And so, Nat searched his mind for a reason to visit the Hardy warehouse, eventually coming up with a weak excuse which, he hoped, would hold under scrutiny. He decided to think on it for a while and went about his business in the meantime.

He had brought a cargo of tobacco from the southern states and, stopping at the tobacconists' to confer a special tin upon him, saw a dainty, wide-eyed young lady whose femininity attracted him. When she blushed becomingly and rushed from the shop, he realized she had unwillingly responded to his masculinity. Intrigued, he questioned the shopkeeper. He was even more intrigued to learn she was Melanie Hardy; Jared Hardy's sister, Ephraim Hardy's daughter, and more important, Laura Hardy's sister-in-law.

Thoughts of Laura once again rushed to mind, and no matter how busy he kept himself, he could no longer dismiss the yearning to see her.

On a bright summer day a week or so later, Nat walked by the Hardy warehouse and impulsively decided to pay a visit. He had no valid excuse, but figured that conversation might ultimately point the way for some sort of intercourse between them, thus bringing him closer to Laura without jeopardizing her position as Jared's wife.

After a short wait in the entry room, he was escorted into the presence of Ephraim Hardy. Nat felt as though he were being impaled on a well-honed blade as Ephraim's bright black eyes pierced through him.

"What can I do for you, Mr. Larimore?"

"I would like some conversation, Mr. Hardy. If you have the time."

"I've been expectin' you," Ephraim answered laconically.

"Expecting me?" Nat's astonishment was evident.

Ephraim nodded.

"Why?"

"Why are you here?"

"To discuss certain matters . . ."

This conversation wasn't going at all as Nat anticipated, and he had not yet formulated his plan perfectly enough, he realized, to fool a man like Ephraim Hardy.

He took a deep breath and plunged on: "I have a shipment of tea from Ceylon—" he began.

Ephraim interrupted him with a knowledgeable smile.

"Mr. Larimore. You are a shipowner, so you don't need my ships. You are a merchant, so you are not in need of my services. I understand you have warehouses in Boston and Maine, so you don't need my space."

Ephraim paused, puffing a pipe and observing Nat's discomfort through amused, dark eyes.

"I know why you have come, Mr. Larimore. It is to request permission to call upon my daughter, Melanie, is it not?"

Nat dropped his eyes. His face was inscrutable and he maintained the mask for the moment it took to evaluate Ephraim's words.

It would be dastardly unfair to Melanie to lead her to believe anything could come of their relationship. On the other hand, if he called upon her, he would satisfy his all-consuming desire to see Laura once more.

"Melanie has a suitor, James Talbot, who sails his own ship," Ephraim continued. "It is said you shared the same father."

"We did not!" Nat said explosively.

"Perhaps not." Ephraim answered, ignoring his ire. "But there are those who insist he is Jonas Marfrey's son."

"Jonas always said 'nay' to that; and I believed him," Nat answered, more quietly.

"In any case," Ephraim went on, "I have not discussed with my daughter her feelings in the matter, but young Talbot approached me for permission to call upon Melanie shortly before his present voyage to the Indian Ocean. As to whether or not your suit would be welcome, I cannot say at this time. If my daughter loves young Talbot, your courtship would be futile. I will advise you of the situation at a later date."

He waved a hand expansively.

"Sit down, Mr. Larimore. Be comfortable. Remove the ledgers from that chair and put them on the floor by the window." He shook his head. "My son and his wife are touring Europe, and I must say I can't wait for his return. Things have piled up during the six weeks he has been away."

Nat absorbed this bit of information while he did as he was told.

"When do they return?" he asked, seating himself in the recently vacated chair; hoping his tone was as politely casual as any stranger making inquiry about people unknown to him.

"Within two months, I believe. My daughter-in-law is expectin' and has no business gaddin' about a foreign country!" There was an edge to his voice, and Nat rightly guessed old Ephraim was not too fond of his son's wife.

Ephraim reached for the wide-bottomed captain's decanter on his desk and poured two jiggers of rum.

"How is it that you expected me?" Nat asked, accepting a glass. He anticipated the answer, but wanted to make certain.

"Mr. Larimore," Ephraim said with a chuckle, "New Bedford is a small town; under twenty thousand people. There isn't much that goes on without someone becoming aware of it." He emptied his pipe ashes into a bowl on the desk. "I know you made inquiry about Melanie from the tobacconist, who is a friend of mine."

How like Ephraim Hardy and all I've heard about him! Nat thought.

Straightforward and honorable himself, Ephraim assumed no gentleman would make inquiry about a lady unless his intention was to court her.

"I have looked into your reputation and finances," Ephraim informed an outwardly composed and inwardly shaken Nathaniel. "I have been told you are your own man, with principles and integrity in business. You have a way with the ladies, but I assume, at thirty years of age, you are looking to settle down with a woman of quality to bear your children." Ephraim cocked an eye at him. "Are my assumptions as correct as my information?"

"I assure you, Mr. Hardy, my intentions are honorable." Nat realized there was nothing else he could say. "However, if Melanie is in love with Talbot, why did you take the trouble to investigate my affairs?"

His eyes locked with Ephraim's for a long moment, as he waited for an answer.

"Because I believe young Talbot would be an indifferent husband at best, for my daughter," Ephraim said at last. "I have not discussed him with Melanie, for I want to present an alternative suitor. I prefer entrusting the life of my daughter to a man of your stature and obvious business acumen."

Nat inclined his head.

"I appreciate your preference for me, Mr. Hardy; but ultimately, it will be up to Melanie to choose, will it not?"

"Ultimately, perhaps," Ephraim answered tersely.

"I am due to leave the country within a week," Nat told him. "I go to Boston tomorrow to arrange my affairs with my business manager."

"A Mr. Paul Lanier, I believe. He handles your accounts, signs your cargo manifests, and hires your minions. He must, indeed, be trustworthy, for you are gone much of the time and your finances have not suffered in your absence."

Nat was uncomfortable. Obviously, Ephraim had made an extensive and thorough inquiry into his circumstances. For a fleeting moment, he felt incensed at the gall of the man.

"I apologize for what some might consider prying into your business, Mr. Larimore," Ephraim said, astutely reading his mind. "However, Melanie is my only daughter. Should you have a girl one day, you will understand my feelings about the man she marries."

"I understand your feelings, Mr. Hardy. But since I had not yet expressed my interest, I do feel your investigation was somewhat premature," Nat answered quietly.

"Am I to assume," Ephraim queried with surprise, "that your intentions were misinterpreted by my friend, the tobacconist? And your presence here in my office does not confirm his perception of your interest?"

Embarrassed, Nat leaned back in his chair and took a long swig from his glass.

"Of course not, Mr. Hardy. I was taken with Melanie, and I did so express the fact to your friend. I apologize for my testiness, but when a man's affairs are so thoroughly probed into as you seem to have done, it is a bit unsettling."

"Again, Mr. Larimore, my only concern is for Melanie. I beg your forgiveness."

"Done!"

"Shall we shake hands on it, then?"

Ephraim's hand was small in Nathaniel's, but the grip was that of a man twice his size.

"How long is your voyage to last?"

"A year—possibly two."

"Whaling?"

"No. I sail on one of my merchant vessels, the *Mirimar*. I leave Boston with a shipment of cotton goods and leather for the Orient, returning with silk. On the way home, we put in at Brazil for coffee, and possibly, the Spice Islands."

"Many things may happen in a year or two. If, by the end of your voyage, Melanie has still not married, perhaps we shall make plans then."

"Perhaps."

"Why do you not send one of your captains on this voyage?"

"Because I train my captains on several voyages before I turn over my ships." Nat smiled pointedly. "Entrusting a ship to a man is somewhat like entrusting a daughter. You must be certain he knows how to avoid reefs . . . and ride out storms!"

Ephraim acknowledged the barb with an appreciative smile.

As the afternoon wore on, Nat found himself liking Ephraim Hardy and felt a growing respect for his mind and his business judgment.

Ephraim told of his impending voyage, one to which he had looked forward since the death of his wife, eight years ago.

"There is no ship like a whaler," Ephraim said, eyes lighting up as he touched on his favorite topic. "And no life exciting as a whaleman!"

They spoke of ships and voyages and all things pertaining to the sea.

Sunlight slanted low through the leaded windows when Nat rose to say good-bye. It had been a pleasant afternoon, and Nat felt he'd made a true friend. As he left Ephraim, his handshake was warm and his promise to call upon Melanie when he was next in port, sincere.

Nathaniel Larimore could not know that when he again sailed into New Bedford harbor, Ephraim would have settled his debts with his Maker in a far-off ocean, leaving the memory of a warm handshake, a twinkling eye, and a sincere heart, with the man he had chosen to become his son-in-law.

CHAPTER ONE

NEW BEDFORD, MASSACHUSETTS
FEBRUARY 1852

Nathaniel Larimore was coming to dinner. He had visited her brother at the warehouse for permission to call upon her and Melanie Hardy had been on the verge of vapors ever since. Though the thought of marriage to Nat was somewhat frightening, Melanie realized time was passing swiftly. Unless she accepted the proposal she was certain would come, she faced a life of maiden aunthood in the home of her harried brother, Jared, and his hostile wife, Laura.

With mixed emotions, Melanie, in chemise and waist cincher, surveyed her image in the cheval glass. During all of her nearly twenty-three years, she'd thought of herself as plain. On this very important night, however, looking objectively at her reflection, Melanie could not deny that she was attractive.

She was a small woman, but her carriage and the proud way she held her head gave an illusion of height. Thick chestnut hair was drawn back into a fashionably large coil at the nape of her neck. Little ringlets at the temples drew attention to wide, unusually large, velvet brown eyes. A minute drop of belladonna into each one heightened the color and added sparkle to rare moments when innate shyness dissipated enough to permit a direct gaze. A flush of excitement gave a rosy glow to delicate cheekbones, enhancing her smooth, olive complexion.

The sudden cries and voices of children were distracting. Melanie stood uncertainly in the center of the bedroom staring at her *café au lait* satin gown lying across the bed. A full, flounced skirt cascaded to the floor, and the décolleté neckline, tiny, cap sleeves, and tight bodice to the hips, must be complemented with proper jewelry. Moving to the dressing table, Melanie pored through her jewel box, growing increasingly annoyed at the shouts of three-year-old Jared, Jr., and the piercing cries of baby Eliza. Underlying her vexation was a nagging sense of guilt. It wasn't that she didn't love the children, and she certainly loved her brother. Laura, however, was a different matter. It seemed to Melanie that the children, though infants still, reflected their mother's antipathy toward their maiden aunt.

Melanie believed Laura's resentment was because Ephraim Hardy had chosen to leave half his fleet of New Bedford whaling ships as dowry for his plain, unmarried daughter. The rest of his wealth, including this house on the hill, had gone to his only son.

Despite the fact that Jared's inheritance provided more than enough for Laura and their two children, Laura's heart had not softened toward Melanie.

She wants it all! Melanie told herself. *During the past year since Father's death, her bitterness has grown. Laura's grudge cannot touch Father, so she has turned it against me!*

Her nephew's scream reverberated through the closed door as he ran past and down the long hall with his nurse in hot pursuit. Moments later, scolding all the way, the woman ushered him back toward the nursery to sup with his sister.

In the sudden silence that followed, the grandfather clock in the hall below stairs chimed the hour of seven.

There is plenty of time, Melanie told herself sternly. *Nathaniel isn't due until eight.*

A log in the fireplace flared and sputtered, throwing diminutive sparks against the screen on the hearth. The sound was familiar and brought back a flood of childhood memories here at Halcyon House. Raising her head from the jewel box, Melanie gazed about this room that was her last refuge in the only home she had ever known. The thought of leaving it made her heart ache.

The white three-storied Halcyon House perched high on a hill overlooking the terraced streets of New Bedford. Hearing the February wind howling outside the windows, Melanie recalled the winters of her childhood, realizing with a start how long it had been since she took pleasure in winter snows and summer breezes.

Maturity dulls perception, she thought, *blinding the senses to all things but those affecting the heart or the purse.*

She remembered ice-covered trees glittering in cold, clear air and congealed frost, five inches thick, on the windward side of the doorposts. She heard again the crunch of snow beneath her sled as she rode breathlessly downhill, slowly coasting to a halt near the gable-ended Whaler's Inn. The sign, swinging over the door, had creaked forlornly in the wind, while the sketched image of a whale, with its tall, straight jet of misty spray, was covered with ice. There had been a stillness about those long-ago winter afternoons, as if Jack Frost had laid a hoary hand on sounds and voices, lest the brittle air shatter into minute fragments.

And when darkness covered the land, dim lamps and firelight had played shadows on the walls of her room. Sitting on the bench before the fire, with her feet barely reaching the warm hearth, she would listen to the bitingly cold night wind howling in anger and frustration at being held at bay, while shades and phantoms gathered round the casements, peering in at her. In her secluded, third floor bedroom, with fire burning low in the grate, she would feel a loneliness, a growing void too deep to describe, even to herself. Someday it would end, this childhood, and she feared its ending.

All this before she was thirteen years old, with her mother and father in the room below, and her brother, Jared, across the corridor.

Now, the halls of Halcyon House rang with the sound of Jared's two children, and in the fall there would be a third. This long year since learning of her father's death, Melanie had withdrawn from the over-stuffed, overfilled rooms. The home she had known was no more. It was a house of strangers; an uncongenial sister-in-law, preoccupied brother, noisy nephew, and crying niece, attended by assorted servants. Only Kate and Lawrence, housekeeper and butler, remained constant; gentle reminders of how it was when Father was alive. The thought of Ephraim Hardy brought tears to Melanie's eyes.

A small statured man he was, wiry and quick. Through grit and hard work he had built his empire, and having accomplished his goal, died. Melanie pondered this thought a moment. Was this what life meant? To flare and flame like a candle, momentarily giving heat and light, then to flicker and perish, leaving only melted wax and smoke to remind the world of what had been?

She shook her head, remembering her father's death far from home with none of his blood to see, nor to sorrow. It had been months before the news reached New Bedford. Melanie sighed, and recalled her brother's words. *He would have wanted it this way,* Jared said. *Since Mother's death when you were thirteen, he has longed to join her. Something of himself went with her when she left us, and he turned to his second love, the sea. It is fitting, I suppose, that he went as he did, hunting the whale in a far-off ocean.*

Ephraim Hardy was sixty-three years old when he and five members of his crew were towed out of sight by a harpooned whale near the Isle of Desolation off Patagonia. The remaining crew of his ship, *Orion,* searched for a day and a night, until a raging storm forced them to abandon hope. It had been his first voyage since his wife's death. He had promised her then that he would remain at home until Jared completed his education and Melanie was grown.

He had wanted to go. Melanie thought of their conversation that last night as they waited for dawn. She could see him now, standing before the great fireplace in the kitchen, sipping strong black coffee laced with rum. His shadow flickered larger than life, reaching across the room to make spasmodic efforts at climbing the pantry wall as the fire in the grate rose and fell.

The talk that predawn morning was strange, for Ephraim was a taciturn man, not given to maudlin meanderings nor easy confidences. And as he talked, Melanie filled her eyes and her heart with him. Something deep inside must have told her this would be the last time.

"There is mortal peril in the life of a whaler," he'd said, puffing his pipe with a far-off look in his eye. "Death comes suddenly, with no time for preparation. It's an abrupt, hearty shoving of a man into the hereafter. And what then? I think, what they call my shadow," gesturing at his black, wavering silhouette, "is more real than this body wherein I dwell. It is, mayhap, the essence of my soul, my better being . . ."

In the boots and pantaloons of a whaler, his large, deep eyes fiery black, he showed glimpses of a daring spirit fortified by the staunch belief that death is but a pause in the ongoing journey of the soul. He was confident that, for him, all things in life were possible and would remain so, until his eyes closed for the last time on this earth.

He had spoken again, still staring into the fire . . .

"A man must meet death on his own terms; on land, sea, or in his own bed. How much better to die doing! I've had my fill these past years of desks and books and dry, musty warehouses. I want to explore the vast oceans again, feel the wind and storm on my face. A man must do what he must, and I have a need to hear ropeyarn tingle like wire, see the plunging bowsprit as we run into the wind, and with bursting lungs and reeling senses crawl under the path of the boom and spar! My life was like that once, and by God, I want to live it again before I die!"

Lost in the vivid imagery of his words, eyes wide, barefoot, huddled on the hearth bench, Melanie had been mesmerized by her father. Jared also, though twenty-four and father of two, had silently and worshipfully fastened his gaze on Ephraim's face, uttering not a syllable since his greeting an hour earlier. He'd left his sleeping wife and infants twenty minutes away to climb the hill to Halcyon House; walking each step under bright stars and wondering at his old father who would leave solid land for the heaving, spasmodic sea.

Ephraim faced his children.

"Should I not return from this expedition," he said, "there are certain things I would discuss with you." His eyes fell upon Melanie. "I know you await young Talbot's return from his voyage and hope to be wed. He has spoken to me of this, but it was some time ago, and never mentioned since." He puffed his pipe slowly, while Melanie's heart flipped topsy-turvy. She never knew James had the thought, and he had kissed her only once, on a summer's day beneath the oak tree atop the hill and never did so again.

"But, I am not certain, Melanie," her father continued, "whether the lad spoke out of love for you, or the realization that my ships would be a handsome beginning for a young, ambitious seaman who hopes to make his mark in the world." His bright dark eyes softened. "Though I don't mean you are not a comely lass! There's many a man would be grateful for a smile from you, were you not so shy."

Then, seeing the protest in her eyes, and glancing at Jared, he went on. "Yes. I know there are those who would say you are plain. Not many though. And those who do are jealous and wish they could be like you. Don't listen to them, child, for they are like gnats in a rising wind."

And Melanie knew that he meant Jared's wife, Laura.

"Should James Talbot prove to be false, however, there is one other I would have you deem eligible. He will make himself known to you, since he has spoken to me not too long ago. You have not met him, but he has seen you and would like to be considered as a husband. I have told him I believe your heart lies elsewhere and I love you too much to force you into a loveless marriage. He has agreed to bide his time and, all things being equal, give you the opportunity to know him. His name is Nathaniel Larimore. He is a man of proven stature in his finances and, while some nine years older than you, he looks for a wife of grace and quality to provide heirs for his estate. Though 'tis said he is brother to James Talbot, in my opinion they vary greatly in character and outlook!

"He is a handsome devil and it is hard for women to leave him alone. His recent inheritance of Jonas Marfrey's wealth makes him all the more attractive, though had it been otherwise, I'm convinced he would have made a fortune on his own. He has the drive and determination necessary for acquisition and, I hear, becomes richer as time goes on. Whalers and merchantmen sail under his insignia, but it is not his wealth which recommends him. It is the man himself. He is a strong man in all ways, with a sharp, keen mind and forceful, fearless will. He has a way with women, but I believe he tires of sowing wild oats and perhaps a woman like you could break him gently to the tether.

"At any rate, he seems true and earnest and belongs completely to himself. He is not a man easily led and his companions, while few, reflect his image. Despite gossip spread by women of the church, he is not a womanizer. He drinks a man's drink, but is not a drunkard. He is not a churchgoing man, but there's many a God-fearing man never stepped foot inside the brick and mortar where mealy-mouthed hypocrites would have us believe God dwells."

He paused for a long moment, looking into the fire.

"I don't say he will make you happy, child. That only you may judge. I do say that if things don't work out between you and young Talbot, Nat Larimore should have a chance to present himself. If you find it in your heart to consider him, I believe you could smooth out the rough edges and make him worthy of yourself."

Melanie held her breath. So many things went on around and about her of which she was unaware! She had, indeed, heard of Nat Larimore! The girls and women of the church choir where she went each Tuesday evening spoke of him often. The giggling young girls, breathless and excited, told of his flashing blue eyes, golden-blond hair, and the rippling muscles that showed under suntanned skin as he worked, alongside his men, on the ropes and sails of his ships. They told of his deep, resonant voice as he called, giving orders and cursing roundly, feeling perhaps that those who watched so close to the wharves were not ladies enough to deserve consideration in his speech.

And the older married women jealously wished they were young enough to catch his eye, while at the same time, those with daughters feared for them.

They said he was a rounder, a seducer of young girls, and pirate of neglected wives. They said he was a golden Viking devil, to be shunned, not favored with seductive feminine glances.

Melanie had seen Nat one summer day as she went to the tobacconers for her father's pipe. She had known him instantly from the description of her friends, and when his bold, blue eyes fastened upon her, she blushed from the tips of her toes to the roots of her hair, feeling suddenly naked and exposed to his penetrating gaze. She fled the shop swiftly, without asking for the pipe, and walked rapidly around the corner with the sound of his voice in her ears and her body aching and shamed at its response to his manhood.

Her mind had wandered while her father addressed himself to Jared. Now again he directed his words to her.

"Melanie, I have provided for you, whether or not you find yourself a husband. Jared will continue to do as he likes best, namely, run the business and keep far from the sea. He knows prices and ledgers and, as your brother, will see to it that you want for nothing as long as you live, regardless of your status as maiden or wife.

"As far as a husband is concerned, it is my wish that you be happy, since our passage through this world is brief, at best. Follow your instincts in choosing. A man may seem to be many things, but ultimately, he cannot hide his soul. You, with your large brown eyes and quiet ways, will discern the cowardly liar from the stalwart man and will recognize the soul of your husband before you make him so."

He'd kissed her then and held her close for a moment.

"God be with you, my daughter, for He loves you, as I do."

Then, shaking hands with Jared and clapping him

on the shoulder, he walked out the door into the first light of dawn, to perish without a grave in the dispassionate sea, which allows no record but memory . . .

Shortly following the news of Ephraim's death, James Talbot sailed again into New Bedford harbor. He brought with him a foreign wife, whom he proudly presented to the town, and Melanie's hopes of leaving her brother's house suffered a near-fatal blow.

Now, Nathaniel Larimore was coming to call upon Melanie as he had promised her father. And Melanie wondered if she could, indeed, fathom the soul of this man; and if so, would she blind herself to his true nature because of her need to marry and have a home of her own?

Again, Melanie reminded herself of her father's evaluation of Nathaniel; and the giggling observations of her friends. Then, she recalled an incident several nights ago at the evening meal when Jared announced Mr. Larimore's request to visit Melanie.

"You mean, Nathaniel Larimore?" Laura's tone had been incredulous.

"Yes," Jared had answered, fastening sharp brown eyes on his wife's obviously agitated countenance. "Are you acquainted with him?"

Jared had always been shy and retiring. The mysterious comings and goings of the town's society had never piqued his interest but now, momentarily, he wondered if there was something in Laura's past of which he was unaware.

"No! That is, of course not, Jared! However, I have heard of him. Several years back . . . after he inherited . . . his reputation with the ladies was quite notorious."

"I am aware of that."

"Then, surely, you would not want your sister . . ." Laura stopped.

"Mr. Larimore made an agreement with Father just before his last voyage," Jared said softly.

Laura's large green eyes had widened: "Your father betrothed Melanie to Nat Larimore?" Her voice shook with agitation.

Jared's eyes did not leave Laura's face.

"He gave his consent; if Melanie is so inclined." Jared's voice had lowered and Melanie's knowledge of her brother told her that he was disturbed.

The rest of the meal had been consumed in silence.

Later, querulous voices had wafted up the common chimney to Melanie's room from the master suite directly below. With the flues at proper angle, only loud voices were ever heard, but then, even Laura's tones, placating, almost pleading, were carried on the drafts.

Puzzled, Melanie had climbed into bed, shutting her ears against the murmurs. Gradually, silence had settled in, broken now and then by an occasional sound that might have been a sob, or the February wind soughing through the pines outside the windows.

Now, the grandfather clock chimed the half-hour. The sepulchral tones roused Melanie from her reverie.

She sighed and hurried into her many-layered petticoats. She wanted to be ready when Nat arrived.

CHAPTER TWO

Kate answered the bellpull summons.

After helping Melanie into her gown, she fastened myriad tiny buttons beginning below the waist and climbing to a spot beneath her shoulder blades.

"Ye're beautiful, child!" the old servant enthused with an admiring gaze when the task was complete. "Ye outshine all I iver laid eyes on!"

Melanie turned to face the mirror and looked searchingly at herself. "Including Laura?" The unexpected question surprised Melanie more than it did Kate.

"Laura!" Kate scoffed. "Niver could she compare to ye in looks!" She turned Melanie about to face her. "I've watched ye grow from a shy, lonely child to a lovely, gentle lady." She stroked Melanie's cheek as she did long ago at the death of her mother. "It ain't without misgivin's that I saw yer brother bring Laura Callaghan here to live. Yer life has bin blighted by that woman iver since! Irish I am, and Irish she may be; but 'tis sorrow I felt fer ye whin the likes o' her took over this house! Orderin' ye about as she does! Whin she ain't fit to wipe yer boots!"

Kate's voice was rising along with her temper, and Melanie knew she must call a halt before her words wafted down the chimney to Laura's ears in the room below.

She placed a gentle hand over the old woman's lips.

"You're prejudiced, Kate," she said with a tender smile. "Thank you for being so."

Kate frowned.

"I know I should be mindin' me own business. I speak me mind too frank!" she said in quieter tones. "But ye do yerself no justice comparin' yer looks to Laura's. Ye have a softness about ye that Laura Callaghan niver had! Ye have true beauty, child! An' soul beauty, as well! We all agree on that. Ye should hear the go'in's on 'bout the table whin the help sets down to eat!"

And Melanie knew her suspicions were correct. Laura's oftentimes unreasonable demands made her unpopular with the servants.

Kate sighed: "Ag'in, I may be steppin' outta me place, but, if 'twas what I wish fer ye, 'twould be James Talbot callin' on ye tonight and not Jonas Marfrey's favored son!"

Melanie felt a twinge of pain, remembering that golden day when James kissed her atop the hill above Halcyon House.

Dashing, devil-may-care, he'd stood there looking at her through heavy-lidded, soft brown eyes with a glint of amusement in their depths. His shoulders were broad and he cut a dashing figure in sailor's breeches and loose, silk shirt slit to the waist in front, while his thick, wavy brown hair ruffled in the wind.

She recalled the hope as she waited for him—and the hurt when he sailed home with a beautiful Polynesian wife.

"James is a married man," Melanie answered gently.

"Not fer long, is what I hear! His frail little wife is ailin' bad with th' fever from 'er outlandish island!"

Melanie was surprised: "That news has not reached my ears!"

"He took 'er to th' big house at Marblehead, is why! Home to th' Neck, I went las' week an' learned Ol' black Sadie's takin' care o' her, jist as she cared fer 'is mither. James comes ter New Bedford 'cause 'is paw bided here, but when it comes ta' mendin' th' hurts, it's ol' Black Sadie 'e runs ter!" She shook her head. "Poor lad! Seem's 'e's cursed! His mither bein' what she was . . . an' 'is father denyin' 'im, then grudgin' a bit o' land an' a ship; whilst handin' 'is half-brother, Nathaniel, all else!"

"There is much doubt about who really fathered James."

"An' Nat, also!" Kate retorted. " 'Tis true, though. James's mither was a wharf wench. She 'bided with many a sailor in 'er time, but James favors Jonas about th' eyes, an' if Jonas didn't b'lieve 'im 'is own, why hand 'im anythin'; much less a whalin' ship an' th' big house with land? Conscience gifts, that's what they was . . . an' all the rest to Nat!"

"What is it you dislike about Nathaniel Larimore, Kate?" Melanie's eyes met the woman's earnest blue gaze in the mirror.

Kate hesitated. " 'Tis not that I dislike 'im, child; fer he too was born on the wrong side o' th' blanket! 'Tis that he's been given all on a platter, 'n his half-brother has naught but what 'e can scratch fer 'imself."

"You have known James a long time, Kate. You are prejudiced toward him, also."

"Since he was a wee lad a'beggin' on th' docks in Marblehead," Kate answered, refusing to acknowledge she might be biased. " 'Twas glad I was to see Jonas Marfrey finally pay the divil's due an' set the lad 'n 'is mither up in the big house. 'Though Jonas did not much else! Thin splittin' that Marblehead land down th' middle, half to each o' them; settin' the brothers agin' each other! They neither one will iver 'bide happy there!"

"He educated them well, Kate."

"In England!" she scoffed indignantly. "Furrin' schools, ta' keep James from 'is mither 'til she died! Furrin' schools niver did no good fer nobuddy!"

She picked an invisible thread from Melanie's shoulder, then stepped back with an admiring glint in her eye.

"Ye're sure a beauty, Melanie Hardy! An' none to be found anywhere to match ye!"

Melanie smiled and leaned over to kiss her wrinkled cheek.

"Changin' th' subject, are ye?" she mimicked.

Kate grinned.

"I know whin I've said enough," she answered, and with a satisfied gleam in her eye, turned and left the room.

For she knew Melanie would give thought to the information she'd imparted, and should marriage to Nat fail to materialize, Melanie would then, perhaps, turn her mind back to James Talbot's direction, when he was a widower and needed consoling.

Compliments were rare in Melanie's life and Kate's praise rang in her ears as she moved lightly downstairs from the third floor. The soft rustle of her satin gown made her feel like a butterfly just emerging from a cocoon.

On the second floor balcony, Melanie gazed up at angels, frozen in flight over the frescoed cathedral ceiling above the entrance hall and prayed Nat would see her as Kate did. She glanced over the balustrade. Lawrence was placing tall urns filled with delicate varicolored silk flowers, new from the Orient, on either side of the towering double doors. He straightened, flipping his butler's coattails, and spied Melanie, slowly descending.

The staircase, sweeping from the second level, broadened, curving gracefully downward to the white

marble floor. Almost halfway in her final descent,
Melanie paused while the grandfather clock chimed
the three-quarter hour.

"You look lovely, Miss Melanie," Lawrence said in
proper tones when the last, echoing chime had faded.
His old eyes glistened and she knew he was remembering her as a child. "How I wish your father could
see you tonight."

Melanie sighed: "Perhaps he does, Lawrence," she
answered softly.

At that moment, the heavy knocker sounded at the
great doors.

Poised as in flight, Melanie could not move. One
hand held the polished mahogany banister, the other
fluttered to her throat. She riveted large brown eyes
on Lawrence, who went to answer the summons.

The tall, frosted glass portal swung open. From her
lofty position, Melanie saw Nathaniel Larimore enter
Halcyon House, fifteen minutes earlier than expected.
He did not immediately see her, and she had a moment to observe him, unnoticed.

Elegantly resplendent in a dark blue, double-
breasted cape, he was unbelievably handsome. He
seemed taller; his shoulders were wider than she
remembered, and though he was clean-shaven, he
wore long sideburns in the fashion of the times.

As the door closed behind him, Nat removed his
tall, brushed beaver hat and Melanie saw his thick
sandy hair streaked pale gold by a tropical sun. Short,
crisp tendrils curled over the edge of his turnover collar as, assisted by Lawrence, he was divested of his
outer garment.

He wore a dove gray, lightweight wool frock coat
with narrow, dark velvet collar. A brilliant sapphire
stickpin sparkled against the white satin background
of a wide, wrapped cravat. Dress trousers, exactly
matching the coat, fit tight across muscled thighs and
long, well-formed legs.

Lawrence turned toward the guest closet, and Nat stopped him to retrieve a linen-wrapped bottle from the cape pocket. As he did so, he lifted a surprised gaze to Melanie, immobile as a statue on the staircase.

The impact of his penetrating blue eyes engulfed her.

They stared at each other for a long moment.

Nat broke the silence. "You are even lovelier than I remembered!" he said, taking a step toward her.

Then, turning back to Lawrence: "I took the liberty of bringing some excellent Madeira acquired on my recent voyage. I expect my host and hostess will approve." He thrust the bottle into the butler's hand.

Nat didn't wait for nod or comment. He turned once more to Melanie. In a few quick strides, he reached the staircase and stood two steps below her, thus placing them at eye level with each other.

He took her hand.

"Melanie." His tongue seemed to savor her name. "Melanie. A beautiful name. It fits you."

The timbre of his voice sent thrills running down her spine. And when, still holding her hand captive, he placed one arm at her waist and gently led her down the rest of the stairs, his touch set her heart to fluttering and she struggled to control her breathing.

I must say something! Melanie thought in panic. *Else he will think me mute!*

"Let us go into the parlor, Mr. Larimore." Her voice sounded overly prim to her own ears. "My brother and sister-in-law will be down directly."

With a pang of regret, she gently disengaged herself and led the way, beckoning him to follow.

"May I offer you a brandy?" she asked as they entered the room.

Nathaniel nodded, taking in plush Persian carpets and a roaring fire on the hearth.

As Melanie went to the sideboard, she saw him in

the mirror. He was standing uncertainly in the midst
of Laura's new, Victorian furniture. She stifled a
quick, nervous smile, realizing Nat was trying to decide on a place to be seated. The delicate, spindly
legs of the nearest group of chairs had been inspected
and found wanting. Then, decisively, he walked
toward the fireplace to a small love seat, gingerly testing its ability to hold his weight.

Nat's presence made the large parlor seem suddenly
diminutive. This was a man whose rooms and fur-
nishings must match his size and powerful personal-
ity. He brought with him an air of fresh breezes and
the tingling, spine-chilling excitement of storms and
raging seas.

More than six feet tall, Nat towered over most
men, but it was his air of overwhelming interest in
and zest for living that made everything else recede
into the background.

With hands only slightly shaky, Melanie poured the
brandy and placed it on a small silver tray. Walking
toward him, she was aware of his eyes, evaluating,
speculating, and silently she prayed he could not see
beyond the decorous facade to her fluttering heart.

He stood up and took the glass, while his other
hand sought hers in a firm grip. His steady gaze was
hypnotic.

"You are a distractingly lovely woman, Melanie,"
he said huskily.

During that brief moment, Melanie felt the surging, shocking contact between them. She turned away
quickly, pulling her hand from his grasp.

"Thank you, Mr. Larimore," she said primly.

With stiff propriety, she walked to the love seat on
the opposite side of the fireplace. Facing him across
the low table, she deposited the tray and imperiously
motioned him to be seated. He complied and an awkward silence filled the room. Melanie tried in vain to

think of something to say and, inwardly shaken, reviled herself for her stupidity.

Then, Nat rose slowly to his feet. His eyes were fastened on the doorway behind her, and Melanie noted with pain in her heart that his entire being was concentrated on what he saw. As far as Nat was concerned, Melanie might as well have been on the moon.

"Mr. Larimore . . ."

It was Laura's voice, and Melanie was instantly defeated. She'd seen that look on men's faces before. She'd faded into the woodwork on numerous occasions when, in the company of her sister-in-law, males were mesmerized to the exclusion of anyone else. Why now, of all nights, did she have to experience this feeling of ineptitude, this failure to live up to expectations, when Nat was her life . . . her future . . . her only salvation . . . her escape?

Laura swept into the room.

Melanie raised her eyes and all her worst fears were confirmed. Laura was breathtakingly beautiful! It was still too early for her pregnancy to show, and in a gown of pale green satin, her voluptuous figure was a vision to arouse the most celibate of men. Her graceful neck and wide, smooth shoulders were fashionably bared and a small ruffle at mid-upper arm held the low décolletage. An inch or so of incarnadine lace rising above the bodice cupped firm, full breasts, exposed almost to the nipples, beguiling the eye in quest of demarcation between lace and creamy flesh.

The satin clung like a smooth second skin from rib cage to hips, accentuating her tiny waist. Beneath the ballooning skirt were at least five petticoats, and Melanie knew one was heavily quilted, stiffened with inserted rounds of whalebone, while others were of prettily decorated flounced muslin. Pale pink Chantilly lace backed by stiff tulle peeped out from under the artfully gathered draping of her skirt, and when she turned, the hem of her gown raised slightly, giving a glimpse of the latest Paris evening fashion, white satin ankle boots with baby French heels.

A mass of thick red curls cascaded down the back of her head and long ringlets at the temples and behind her ears emphasized the emerald earrings Jared had given her as a wedding gift. Wide-set green eyes with dark, thickly fringed lashes held a sultry look under winged, delicately arched brows as Laura stared boldly into Nat's raptly attentive face.

"I trust Melanie has seen to your comfort." The voice, low, husky, implied much more than the banal words.

Nat did not immediately reply.

Watching him, Melanie saw that he searched Laura's face, almost questioningly. Narrowing his eyes, he looked away, then quickly back again.

Suddenly, he turned to envelop Melanie with the same questing gaze and after a moment she was warmed by the light in his blue eyes.

"She has seen to my comfort," Nat added belatedly. *And opened my eyes as well!* he thought.

For he saw in that moment that Laura's beauty was only skin deep. In a sudden rush of memory he'd compared Laura of old with Laura today. Though married, mother of two children and expecting another, her sultry, flirtatious demeanor had not changed.

She is frivolous as ever! he thought in astonishment. *Her role as wife and mother should have brought some depth!*

Gazing from Laura to Melanie, he was struck at the contrast.

The one is genuine, he realized. *And the other, though brilliant, is like cut glass beside a diamond!*

As Nat looked once more at Laura, it was with the knowledge that the ghost that haunted him these past five years was forever banished from his heart.

When he turned back to Melanie, his eyes softened

and a warmth pervaded his being; a yearning firing of his blood that would always manifest in her presence.

Jared entered the room then.

The greeting between the two men was warm and friendly.

"Let me formally introduce you to my wife and sister," Jared said, always properly decorous.

Introductions were acknowledged all around, but Melanie, observing Laura and Nat, realized somewhere deep inside that this was not the first time these two had met.

One of the household maids appeared with hors d'oeuvres and remained to serve drinks. Melanie and Laura sipped sherry as the men discussed the subject uppermost in the politics of the day: the growing opposition of the North to the slavery of the South.

Laura conducted herself as a polite hostess, but now and then Melanie detected a light in her eyes when she looked at Nathaniel that could not have been born of one hour's acquaintance. No matter how hard she tried to believe otherwise, Melanie felt these two had met before this evening, and known each other well.

Puzzled, shaken by Nat's initial response at sight of Laura, Melanie raised her eyes to the large portrait of Ephraim Hardy gazing down upon the gathering from above the fireplace.

Is he here because of me, Father? Or is it because he was once caught in Laura's spell and cannot forget her?

Ephraim's eyes seemed fastened upon his daughter; soft, reassuring. She could almost hear his voice *. . . Be patient, my girl! All will be well!*

In sonorous tones, Lawrence announced dinner. Melanie took Nat's proffered arm and they followed host and hostess into the dining room.

Irish linen tablecloth and napkins, crystal wine and water goblets, Spode china and Danish silver took on a luster of their own in the soft light of tall beeswax tapers held by an ornate silver candelabra. On either side of the polished rosewood buffet, whale-oil lamps of brilliant crystal cast their glow, reflecting in the mirrored wall opposite. A centerpiece of the colorful silk Oriental flowers, part of a recent cargo on one of Jared's ships, added a finishing touch.

The conversation was a continuation of that begun in the parlor, with Laura now and then interposing an opinion, skillfully steering away from Nat's open antislavery point of view and Jared's equally adamant contention that northerners should maintain a policy of nonintervention.

There was a temporary lull as the main course was served. Melanie, wondering about this handsome man whose name she hoped to bear, leaped with sudden resolution into the breech. "Tell me, Mr. Larimore, are you a New Englander by birth?"

There was a long silence, while she strove to calm the butterflies in her stomach.

Melanie's soft voice fell upon Nat's ears and he realized she was repeating her question. His thoughts had been far away. Looking at her flushed face and anxious brown eyes, he saw what an effort it was for her to begin a conversation.

He smiled gently at her and took a sip of wine before answering.

"I was born in a little town in Denmark, but I never knew its name. As a small child, I was taken by my Danish mother to Plymouth, in Devon, England. A few weeks after our arrival she died of a fever at the inn where we stayed. I was only four years old at the time. After her death, I was placed in an orphanage."

He paused, then, after a moment, went on. "My mother was a comely maid, as I recall. 'Though it is possible that my memory made her beautiful when in reality she may not have been. Perhaps all small boys believe their mothers to be angels of loveliness, since they are the first love of their lives, and in some cases, the only love."

The serving maid stood at his side with platters. Helping himself to generous portions, Nat was aware of the rapt attention of his audience.

"And your father?" Laura asked.

"I have no idea. I recall only that she told me he was a mariner and we went to Plymouth when she'd heard he might put into port there. My mother died without ever seeing my father again; for I remember we met each ship at the quay, and after searching many faces, my mother and I trudged back to the inn alone.

"I am completely ignorant as to whether or not I am a bastard, since my mother never mentioned marriage and, at four years old, it never occurred to me to ask.

"Whether the Larimore name belongs to my father, or my mother, I have no way of knowing." He continued, after a long pause. "Some years ago, when I captained my first ship, I sailed to Denmark hoping to find something of my past, or possibly my family. But there was no village name to remember and no one recalled the name Larimore in any of the hamlets and towns I visited. I decided then and there to draw my own conclusions; to begin life in the here and now, with no ancestry and no record or memory of the past. A clean slate, as it were, henceforth. Whatever I do, and whatever my children do, the future Larimores must live with and accept . . . for better or worse, in pride or in shame . . ."

"Then, Jonas Marfrey did not father you, as many believe?" Jared interrupted.

"If he did, he took that secret to his grave," Nat answered quietly. "For many years I questioned him,

and received neither confirmation nor denial." His
voice took on a musing tone.

"I was nine years old when Jonas Marfrey came to
the orphanage bringing food and clothing as, I was
told, he'd done for many years, off and on. He was
committed to the place, since he'd been raised in that
same foundling home. There was an instant bond between us and that afternoon he took me away with
him. We sailed on a whaling voyage to the offshore
waters of Newfoundland. Old Captain Marfrey, without wife or kin, raised me as his own; educated me
and taught me all he knew about the sea. When he
died, he left me the bulk of his fortune."

"And what of James Talbot? Is he truly Jonas's
son?" Laura pursued.

Nat shrugged: "Jonas always denied it; though he
felt sorry for James, and did what he could to provide
for him."

Laura smiled. "I have said for years that you two
could not possibly be brothers, nor even half-broth-
ers! You are nothing alike in looks, or in tem-
perament!"

Jared shot Laura a look of astonishment.

"How could you possibly know that, my dear? I was
unaware that you were acquainted with James Talbot; or, for that matter, with Mr. Larimore, before
this evening."

Flustered, Laura dropped her fork, which landed
on her plate with a loud clatter.

"I met James Talbot quite a few times at Mrs.
Hoffman's soirees, Jared, before you and I were ever
acquainted! And, of course, I have heard of Mr. Larimore . . ." Her voice quavered.

She is nervous! Melanie thought, taken by surprise.
*So, I am right in surmising they have met before
tonight. And quite possibly, known each other well!
But why are they hiding the fact?*

After a lengthy silence, Nat went on in a pensive mood.

"Jonas left me five whalers, three fishing schooners, and three merchantmen, along with a small house in Bangor, Maine; a stand of timber on the Kennebec, and a point of land just north of Marblehead. Through trading, whaling, and other interests, my holdings have increased."

He looked at Melanie, who quickly dropped her eyes.

"I am now ready to take me a wife and settle down," Nat continued. "I want to anchor on that little point of land. I want to build me a house and fill it with children. A man tires of wandering after a time, and wants to put down roots, warm his hands at his own hearth fire, and bed his own woman."

Nat's resonant voice had dropped to a low, thoughtful tone, and underlying his words there was a yearning of which he seemed totally unaware.

CHAPTER THREE

On the Sunday next, following their meeting, Nathaniel Larimore attended services with the Hardy family. Nodding heads and wide-eyed whispers went, apparently, unnoticed by Melanie as she walked up the aisle on Nat's arm in the wake of Jared and Laura, to be seated in the family pew. Later, they mingled with the churchgoers at a box luncheon held in the meeting hall.

In the days that followed, Nat's calls at Halcyon House were frequent and welcomed. Before the end of the month, Melanie had accompanied him to a play given by a road company newly arrived from Boston; they'd dined at the elegant new hotel restaurant high on a hill overlooking New Bedford harbor, and, bundled against the cold, joined the young people's choir group on a moonlight, horse-drawn sleigh ride.

As time went on, Melanie began to relax in Nat's presence. He did his best to make her comfortable—drawing her into conversation, listening attentively to her rare comments and infrequent offers of opinion.

Melanie told herself she must have imagined Nat's response to Laura's beauty that first evening. Surely, there had been nothing between them. She attributed it all to her overly active imagination and inferiority complex where her sister-in-law was concerned.

March came in like a lamb. There was a hint of

spring in the air and the sky reflected peerless blue on the harbor. Melting rivulets of snow ran down hills and along the roadside gutters.

Gazing from her window at bright morning sunshine, Melanie smiled happily as she prepared for a fitting at her dressmaker's. In a flurry of haste, she had delivered bolts of cream-colored silk and chocolate brown velvet to Mrs. Goulet, commissioning her to begin a ballgown for the most important event of the season: Mrs. Hoffman's Ides of March soiree.

Following the custom, all proper marriageable young ladies, the cream of New Bedford society, would be paraded there for the inspection of every young, eligible bachelor available. Mothers and daughters excitedly whispered, plotted, planned; fathers and sons argued, for matrimony, they all knew, was the basic reason for the spring soiree and many a fainthearted lad sought excuses to evade the noose and the net. Then again, some bachelors with wine tastes and ale purses hoped to snare a pretty pigeon with paternal wealth before the state of their finances became general knowledge.

Riding downhill in her phaeton, listening to the clip-clop of horses' hooves on the cobblestones, Melanie hugged herself in a sudden spasm of joy. Nat made such a difference in her life! Like the fairy tale princess, she'd been asleep, adrift for many years. Now, with the arrival of her prince, she'd awakened into living. Excitement, and an enthusiasm she'd never before known, encompassed her being and she loved every minute of it. Every hour of every day was an adventure. She greeted each morning with thoughts of Nat, and never knew when a package, a small trinket, or treasure would arrive from her love; or indeed, when he, himself, would show up at her door. Sometimes, a messenger brought a note, telling her in advance of his arrival to squire her to a dance, to the theater, or to dine.

That she was deeply in love with Nathaniel, Melanie had no doubt. She'd fallen in love with him that long-ago day at the tobacconist's. But until now, she'd been frightened, insecure, afraid to admit, even to herself, that she loved. She'd been deeply wounded by James Talbot's offhanded treatment of her, and living in the shadow of Laura's stunning beauty had made her even more insecure and frightened. Nat's attentions had caused Melanie to blossom. Since he had come into her life, she walked with a spring in her step, a light in her eyes, and a glow in her cheeks, remarked upon by her friends.

Ultimately, she would become Nat's wife. The thought thrilled Melanie beyond measure. He had not yet declared his love, nor she hers; but when Nat touched her, when she felt his arm about her waist while entering or alighting from a carriage, or dancing the new waltz, Melanie was so filled with happiness she could scarcely breathe!

Even Jared teased her one morning as they sat alone in the breakfast room.

"Love becomes you, my pretty sister," he'd said, gazing at her with approval.

"Thank you, my dear brother," she'd answered, coquettishly making him a curtsy.

"Has Nat declared himself yet?"

She'd looked at Jared in surprise.

"Would he not ask your permission first?"

"He requested and received Father's permission to call upon you nearly two years ago. Since I, in turn, recently gave mine, I assume he will now press you for a wedding date," Jared answered, placing another sausage on his plate. "However, it is still early in the courtship . . . not quite three weeks, I believe?" He raised his eyebrows questioningly at Melanie.

She nodded.

Three weeks! Could life change so drastically in just three weeks? It could! It had!

* * *

Melanie's carriage drew up to Goulet's Dressmaking Establishment across from the midtown park. The circular drive was crammed with vehicles arriving and departing. Fashionable carriages with liveried coachmen and sleek, prancing horses discharged exquisitely gowned ladies, the upper echelon of New Bedford society, for their fitting appointments. The place buzzed with activity. Since Melanie's childhood, her own and her mother's gowns had been beautifully fashioned by this fine seamstress.

The whaling industry had taken over New Bedford these past fifteen years and the nouveau riche wives and daughters of shipowners, captains, and merchants had become more and more demanding. Debutantes, rich widows, and elegant but shady paramours, as well as wives basking in the glory of their husbands' wealth and position, all descended upon Goulet's with copies of *Harpers New Monthly Magazine,* the latest Paris periodical, *Magazin des Modes,* and *Godey's Ladies Book.*

There were other seamstresses and dressmakers, of course. But, none of Mrs. Goulet's standing. Only Goulet's could faithfully reproduce original Paris creations or modify them without duplication, while maintaining chic style and couturiere design to the continuing satisfaction of a demanding clientele.

Mrs. Goulet's modest home had become too small to meet the demands of her clamoring customers, and her own two hands could not fly fast enough to meet their needs. So, she took several young seamstresses in training and moved into a large, renovated house in midtown. Even proper Bostonians had heard of her talent, and gladly traveled the long day's journey to avail themselves of her expertise.

Thoughts of Nat had caused Melanie to tarry too long in dressing this morning, so upon arrival, she was forced to wait in the elegant parlor for an available fitting room. Melanie, smiling to herself, felt no impatience at the delay. The background hum of feminine voices interspersed with giggles and now and then a matronly laugh fell pleasantly upon her ears. Fashion magazines were placed about on piecrust tables beside chaise longues and more formal Victorian settees and sofas. Unaccustomed happiness filled her entire being as she leafed idly through the fashion plates.

Then, from over the planter-lined, three-quarter wall, came the familiar voice of an older woman.

"Bold as brass, she walked aboard his ship! In broad daylight, mind you! Uncaring who was to see."

The voice was that of Mrs. Simon Carstairs, wife of one of the town's leading merchants. With three married daughters living beyond her meddling reach in Boston, and an abundance of maidservants to do her bidding, Minnie Carstairs occupied her time exercising a sharp, caustic tongue. She was fast gaining a reputation as New Bedford's chief gossip.

"Perhaps it had something to do with her husband's sister," a vaguely familiar voice answered.

"It would be charitable to believe so." Mrs. Carstairs's voice came again. "However, I'm certain I'm not the only one scandalized several years back by her brazen chasing after Jonas Marfrey's heir."

"She was young then, and perhaps somewhat rebellious," the unknown voice answered. "But she certainly married well. Jared Hardy, like his father, is a model husband and parent."

There was silence for a moment, then the vaguely familiar voice went on.

"Minnie, you place more emphasis than deserved upon her visit to his ship. He seems very attached to the Hardy girl, and I hear tell that he plans to marry her; 'though it has not yet been announced."

"If he does marry her," Mrs. Carstairs answered, "it

will only be for the reason he has not yet recovered from his infatuation with Jared's wife!"

Clutching *Godey's Ladies Book* with a fierce grip, Melanie's knuckles went white. It was all she could do to keep from tearing the pages. The voices moved on and she sat there in the parlor, flushed, painfully aware of her naiveté.

And I told myself I'd imagined his reaction to Laura that first evening. What a dunce I am! Everyone knows Nat's reason for courting me!

Melanie's embarrassment knew no bounds. Later, after the initial shock, she would realize that Minnie Carstairs's reputation as a vicious gossip was not unearned; despite what she had put into words, there was still room for doubt, as the unknown champion pointed out.

For the moment, however, one phrase rang over and over in Melanie's mind. *Bold as brass, she walked aboard his ship!*

So Laura had visited Nat's ship! Why? What could possibly possess a married woman, almost three months pregnant with her third child, to visit a man . . . alone . . . aboard his ship; most likely in his private quarters?

Quietly, Melanie arose from the chaise longue and spoke to the girl at the tiny French desk near the door.

"I will return again for my fitting. Please remove my name from the list until tomorrow. At the moment, I am feeling suddenly unwell!"

And she walked outside into the unseasonably warm March day. But, the sunshine was lost upon her now. For all Melanie knew, the sky was dark and overcast, with storm clouds threatening upon the horizon.

She had sent the carriage on and told her driver to return at the end of two hours. Now, uncaring, she walked blindly across the park and through the town toward the hills. Then, moving swiftly, she began the ascent to Halcyon House.

For the next two weeks, Melanie was downcast, introspective; a source of puzzlement to Nat and of annoyance to her brother and sister-in-law.

"Whatever is the matter with you, Melanie?" Jared asked. "You've changed suddenly from a happy, pretty young lady to a sober, morose old maid!"

"As she will be, if she doesn't come out of this sulk!" Laura's sharp voice chimed in smugly. "Nat responds to laughter and gaiety! Like most men, he has never been attracted to dullness and sobriety!"

Jared's piercing glance in his wife's direction was not lost upon Melanie.

"Your knowledge, my dear, of Mr. Larimore's preferences, is of course, assumption on your part?"

Laura paled.

"Certainly, Jared! I am only pointing out, for Melanie's good, that men are not drawn to downcast faces!"

The discussion was dropped immediately, to Melanie's relief. She had no predilection for airing her grievances to Jared, thereby causing his unhappiness. But she realized then that Jared was not unaware of Laura's previous acquaintance with Nathaniel Larimore, and admired her brother the more for his conduct in the presence of his possible future brother-in-law. As for Laura, Melanie felt an antipathy bordering on hatred.

Mrs. Hoffman's stately mansion was ablaze with light. A stream of carriages lit by side lanterns glowing like fireflies in the night slowly climbed the hill to converge upon the Georgian manor.

Melanie, seated next to a garrulous Nat, stared quietly out the carriage window. Opposite her, Jared, with a strained smile, commented occasionally at a quip from Nat, or an animated Laura, but for the most part he too rode in silence.

The carriage reached the Hoffman drive and fell in behind others in the line. Torches lit the winding driveway, and runners with hand flares guided skittish horses through trees bereft of foliage and lawns spotted with the last snows of winter. They drew up under the porte cochere where liveried footmen placed carpeted steps at the carriage door and assisted them to alight.

A black Italian marble floor in the vast reception hall echoed the blaze of hundreds of candles in crystal and silver chandeliers. Mrs. Hoffman, sparkling with jewels, greeted her guests at the entrance to the enormous ballroom. The mayor of New Bedford, his wife and daughter, as well as several judges, civic leaders, and their wives, were also in the receiving line.

The ballroom was breathtaking in splendor. Huge, bronze-branched candelabra and enormous, cranberry glass whale-oil lamps reflected in mirrored walls, bathing the room in brilliance. The dance floor was polished to a watery depth and at each end of the room, on a royal blue carpeted dais, musicians played stringed instruments and horns in perfect harmony.

The furniture edging the floor was dark, heavy, and highly glossed. In a far corner stood a great Oriental teakwood cabinet displaying an abundance of Wedgwood, porcelain, and Dresden china. The pale blue ballroom ceiling, three stories high, had a gathering of angels; winged cherubs with round, pink cheeks peered down upon the mortals from behind puffs of scattered white clouds.

Along one side of the mirrored wall, a lengthy linen-covered buffet table held dishes, platters, and chafing pans filled with food; roast beef and turkey, pork loin and hams, pheasant, capon, fish of all kinds; jellies, relishes, vegetables, pastries, and sweet-

meats of every description; and in the center of it all
stood an enormous punch bowl. Various exotic fruits,
shipped in ice from warmer climes especially for this
affair, floated in the amber liquid, and in their solid
state were placed in bowls scattered temptingly
throughout the bounteous repast.

Waiters in red jackets carried wide silver trays and
platters skillfully among the crowd, serving champagne, wine, rum, and other beverages. The guests
had only to request and their every wish was fulfilled.
Mrs. Hoffman's soirees were well known for opulence
all along the New England coast, and she never failed
to maintain her reputation.

Flanked by Nat and her dazzling sister-in-law, Melanie felt like an ugly duckling betwixt a pair of
swans. Ostensibly admiring Laura's and Melanie's
gowns, women gazed at Nat in wide-eyed fascination
and looked away blushing when he turned in their
direction. Others, more sophisticated, sent him enticing smiles and long, simmering glances through half-
closed eyes; or contemplated him slyly over bare
shoulders as they waltzed with their partners.

On the other hand, Laura was intermittently surrounded by men who, deliberately or not, turned
their backs on Jared in an attempt to capture his
wife's attention.

Melanie stole a look at her brother's troubled eyes
and strained smile as he spoke quietly to a friend.

*And this must be endured for the next five or six
hours!* she thought, with rising panic.

"Melanie!" The voice, deep, male, held obvious
pleasure.

She turned, as did Nat.

Then, amazed at the sudden fluttering of her heart,
Melanie met the delighted gaze of James Talbot.

Truly, he was a handsome man. While he had not
the breadth of shoulder nor the heights of Nathaniel,
he exuded the same vigorous energy reminiscent of

winds on stormy seas and swift, decisive action. He
cut a pleasing figure in dark blue tailcoat and
trousers. A white satin tie between the lapels of a
gray velvet waistcoat added elegance to his appearance. He was clean shaven. His countenance, under
thick, wavy brown hair, was handsome, though
more effete than the rugged features of his half-
brother. Long familiarity and close observation might
apply ruthlessness to what a friendly observer would
term a strong jaw and stubborn chin.

James's soft, brown eyes engulfed Melanie and she
blushed under his deceptively languid gaze.

She smiled, genuinely happy to see him.

"It is nice meeting you again, James," she said, realizing the inadequate words only vaguely expressed
her pleasure at sight of him.

"You are beautiful, Melanie!" The deep intensity
of his voice sent a rush of heat through her body, and
she knew the unbecoming flush was reddening her
complexion.

They were silent, staring at each other.

When her heart had slowed to a normal beat, Melanie was startled to recognize beneath James's tran-
quil exterior a burning tension, barely controlled and
all-consuming.

Nat had been speaking with an acquaintance while
keeping an eye on Melanie's interaction with Talbot.
Now, in a voice tinged with annoyance, he broke the
spell between them.

"We are missing our waltz, my dear."

Melanie opened her lips to excuse herself, but totally ignoring Nat's presence, James said in a quietly
sympathetic tone, "I was sorry to learn of your father's passing, Melanie. He was a fine man. We had a
long talk one day and discussed you at length."

Melanie was reminded of the enmity between the
two men when she saw Nat's scarcely veiled hostility.

"That discussion did not prevent you from taking a foreign wife!" he said, biting his words.

Raising cold eyes to Nat's icy gaze, James Talbot, with a twisted smile, spoke softly, with the deadly sibilant tone of a serpent.

"I believe that is none of your business."

"I am making it mine!"

With a boyish grin, James turned to Melanie.

"Enjoy the ball, my dear, despite your peevish escort!"

Then, giving her a slight bow, he turned his back and walked slowly to the other side of the ballroom.

Melanie allowed Nat to lead her to the dance floor. In silence they took their places for a cotillion and she was startled to see storm clouds in Nat's eyes as he looked at her across the space between them. Surely, he was not angry because of the interchange between herself and James? Melanie shrugged that notion away, telling herself Nathaniel cared naught about her affections, previous or present. No, she decided, it was just the hatred between the two men that had fired Nat's rage.

She searched her own heart, realizing that, since her father first spoke of James Talbot, she'd wondered what it would be like to see him again. But beyond the initial shock, her affections were not involved. Despite hurt, anger, and humiliation, Melanie was forced to admit to herself that her love belonged to Nat, and no one else.

The meeting with James was still on her mind, however, as they finished the cotillion and Jared swung her away in a waltz. Upon reflection, she decided it was the change in James Talbot that both fascinated and repelled her. He seemed a man driven by some inner demon. Something gnawed at him and shone through the light in his deceptively candid eyes. She wondered about his wife and if she still malingered in the house at Marblehead. Kate had said no more about her and Melanie was certain, had the situation changed, she would have been so informed by her old servant.

As she finished the waltz with Jared, James approached her to request the next dance. Because her card had been filled earlier in the evening, she quickly tucked it into the tiny beaded evening bag attached by a gold chain to her wrist.

"I just happen to have this one open," she lied, praying the portly judge whose name had been scrawled opposite this number would conveniently forget . . . or, seeing her swept away over the floor in James's arms, might understand and forgive her own lapse of memory.

Unexpectedly, Nat's eyes were on her most of the evening. When they danced, he was complimentary, concerned, and tried to draw her out—but, as avidly as he pursued, she withdrew.

When she danced again with James, she laughed easily, uncaring that Nat watched from the sidelines. James was fun. He made her laugh, and his attentions, though having no impact on her heart, soothed her wounded soul, made her feel less an ugly duckling, and more an assured, lovely woman.

The ball was in full swing and Melanie was suddenly tired. Reasonably certain no one observed, she slipped between two tall potted palms to a tiny balcony outside. She closed narrow French doors then stepped out of the light to lean against the cold brick wall.

It was a frosty, moonless night. Stars, diamond pinpricks in a black satin sky, winked spasmodically through the icy pall of this frigid March evening. The wind felt good on Melanie's hot cheeks, and there was a smell of snow, signaling that winter was not yet over.

Nat was so attentive, so concerned for her welfare! At times, she wanted to shout at him; tell him she knew the reason for his concern, and make him aware that she was not as naive or as stupid as he obviously believed. It had been difficult to paste a strained smile on her face while his arms held her as they danced and his lying eyes and lips paid token compliments to her beauty. What a deceitful man he was, to court one woman for love of another!

Nat! Her heart wrenched at his name, and the fury that had built up since that day at the dressmakers' drove the knife deeper into her wounded feelings.

So busy was she with her thoughts, it was with a jolt she realized the voices floating upward were those of Mrs. Simon Carstairs and Jared! She peeked over the low railing and saw that they stood on the wide balcony, just below.

"I'm sorry, Mr. Hardy!" Minnie Carstairs was saying. "I felt you would want to know before you gave your sister in marriage to this man."

"Indeed!" Jared's voice cut like steel through her last words. "Mr. Larimore requested the presence of both my wife and myself to make the decision as to the betrothal gift. Since I was otherwise occupied, I sent my wife in my stead." His tone was sure, and firm. "I will thank you, Mrs. Carstairs," he continued, "to never again jump to conclusions concerning my family!"

Jared turned abruptly on his heel and entered the ballroom, leaving Minnie Carstairs shivering with the frostiness of his exit as well as the cold night air. A moment later, she too returned to the ball.

Melanie's heart pounded. So Nat had requested Laura's visit and Jared's to choose her betrothal gift! Her heart sang.

I was right after all! Nat does love me!

Laura's visit to Nat's ship did concern Melanie, as the strangely familiar voice had suggested that day at Goulet's. With a start, Melanie realized she had heard that voice tonight as she entered the reception hall.

Her champion was none other than Mrs. Hoffman, herself! Melanie smiled. Of course! Mrs. Hoffman; friend to her mother in the golden days of her childhood. Since her mother's death, Melanie had seen her infrequently, at the spring soirees and a few other parties at the Hoffman home. But shy Melanie went out only when she had run out of excuses, so she'd missed much that went on in the growing town these past few years.

The cold wind blew stronger and Melanie, heart surging with newfound happiness, once more entered the ballroom. Her eyes swept the crowd in search of Nat. She wanted to make up to him for her morose silence and sulky ways these last two weeks.

A dance had just ended. People surged toward tables and crowded near open doors for a breath of air. Suddenly, across the polished floor, Melanie beheld Nat from a new perspective. These six weeks of their courtship, he was always at her side; now, she studied him at a distance—this man she would, hopefully, marry.

He stood with Mrs. Hoffman, the mayor, and his lady. Several other women crowded about them with the pretense of speaking to their hostess, but Melanie noted without surprise that their eyes strayed irrepressibly to Nat. They became effervescent whenever he deigned to glance in their direction.

Nat's gaze met Melanie's across the room.

Looking into those startling blue eyes, Melanie realized that beside Nat, every man in the room faded into insignificance. Handsome, heir to the ships of Captain Jonas Marfrey, and well on his way to making another fortune on his own, Nat was the most sought after bachelor in New Bedford. There were handsomer, wealthier men in the large ballroom, yet Nat's powerful magnetism commanded all eyes. Women of every age gazed in fascination and the men watched too, puzzled, doggedly intent upon discovery of the reason for the attraction.

But it was none of those things that made Melanie's knees weak and her heart nearly jump out of her breast. It was the sudden realization that there was a chemistry between them; a strange force that drew them irresistibly to each other, no matter what the circumstances—over the heads of a crowd, or alone in a quiet room.

Melanie stood waiting beside the potted plants. Nat's eyes pinned her to the spot as he made his way toward her. When he reached her side, the orchestra struck up again.

"You're cold!" he said, leading her to the dance floor. "Have you been walking outside?"

"Yes," she answered softly.

She looked up at him, eyes glistening with love and unshed tears. Her smile was tremulous, and though she wanted to put her apology into words, she could not.

Nat was puzzled. What had happened, he wondered, to change her again? He marveled at the vagaries of women. At first, in the beginning of their courtship, she'd been shy, but certainly not averse to his attentions. Then, unaccountably, nearly two weeks ago, she'd become cold, silent, and moody. Now, within fifteen minutes of their last dance, when she'd pulled away at his touch and given terse answers to his attempts at conversation, she had changed again! He wondered if it had anything to do with James Talbot.

His brows knit and he looked down at her with puzzled eyes.

"Melanie, we must talk! I'll get your wrap and we'll walk in the garden."

He guided her to the edge of the ballroom, near the reception hall. She waited. In a few moments, he returned and draping the fur cape over her bare shoulders, guided her downstairs to the foyer. They stepped out onto the large balcony recently occupied by Jared and Mrs. Carstairs. Crossing the balcony, they went down wide, curving steps to the walk circling the garden. There were no flowers. Trees thrust stark limbs skyward while patches of snow still lay across most of the brown frozen lawns. An icy March wind whistled through bare branches, but Melanie's heart sang with joy.

Nat took her gently into his arms.

"Something has been wrong between us these past two weeks, Melanie. You have not been yourself. Tell me what troubles you."

She smiled, unconsciously nestling against him, her head on his shoulder.

"Nothing is wrong, Nat. Nothing troubles me now."

"Has it to do with Talbot?"

"No!" she answered. "It had to do with us, but it is resolved now, and I am happy." She reached up, touching his cheek. "I am sorry, Nat, for my moodiness these past two weeks."

"You'll tell me about it . . . someday?"

"Someday."

He kissed her then. Their first kiss. And Melanie's spirits soared to the heavens. She returned his kiss with all her heart, surprising Nat, as well as herself. She felt safe in his embrace. She felt she belonged there, and all her doubts and fears vanished when his lips touched hers.

Nat did not question further.

Delighted at Melanie's response, he had to remind himself that she was innocent, virginal, and did not realize the impact her soft, desirable body had upon his senses. He drew away gently.

But, reaching up, Melanie put her hand behind his head and raised her mouth to his with the simple eagerness of a wanton child.

Despite himself, Nat kissed her thoroughly. His head spun while his body pressed urgently against her.

"Melanie . . ." he whispered hoarsely, "I have dreamed of kissing you . . . holding you . . ."

His mouth moved, kissing her throat. Then, he brought his lips to the snowy, upper curves of her breast, cupping it with his hand. His tongue wandered slowly toward the edge of the décolleté bodice.

Melanie drew in her breath with a little cry, trembling with ecstasy. She was powerless to stop him. In Nat's hands and presence, she was like soft clay . . . a reed, bending to his will.

"No, Nathaniel!" she managed to whisper. "No . . ."

He raised his head. Drawing her to him with a vise-like grip, he rained kisses on her hair, her face. His hands circled her slender waist, holding her pinned against him.

Melanie, throwing caution to the winds, responded with her entire being. His lips were burning, tantalizing fire on her flesh, demanding . . . urgent with desire.

In a voice filled with passion, he whispered:

"Ah, my love! How impatient I am to teach you the ways of loving . . ."

Pulling slightly away from him, Melanie held her breath, attempting to quench the fire he had kindled in her veins. She waited. Surely, now, he would ask her to become his wife!

"When we are married, my dearest," Nat continued, pulling her to him once more, "we will explore all the thousands of pleasures known only to lovers. You are a beautiful, passionate woman, and tonight you have set my fears at rest. I truly believed my touch repulsed you. Now, you have shown me otherwise, and I am filled with happiness."

He kissed her again, gently this time.

"Will you marry me, my sweet Melanie . . . soon?"

I will never forget this moment, no matter what the future holds! she thought with a sudden flash of insight.

"Oh, yes, Nat," she murmured against his lips, "I will marry you."

His hand slipped under her bodice, cupping one breast, teasing the nipple to erection, while his lips sought hers again in avid passion. Desire consumed her like a flame, and she only knew she could not live without him.

Stars exploded in the heavens while Nat pressed Melanie back against the trunk of a leafless tree, his body welded against hers. Every nerve in her being tingled with longing. She felt his manhood, frighteningly large, pushing against her, and wantonly wished there was less clothing between them.

Oblivious to the cold wind, they remained there in the darkness while his mouth sought every part of her exposed flesh. She felt the tugging of his lips on her breasts . . . his warm hands . . . and she knew only that she desired him with a passion she'd never known possible. His hands, his mouth, raised her to a height of sensuousness beyond reason. And Nat, in a frenzy of passion, brought her to a crescendo of ecstasy.

Then, as suddenly as he'd begun, he stopped.

"My God, Melanie! You are to be my wife! I cannot compromise you in this manner. I apologize, my beloved. But you make me forget myself and everything else, in longing for you!"

He straightened her décolletage, smoothed her gown, and held her gently about the waist while she rearranged her hair.

"Let us go back to the ball, my Melanie," he said. "And announce to the world that we will be wed before spring is out."

"Nat, it is now March!" she said. "There is much to be done!"

"June!" he answered with a grin. "My house at Marblehead will be nearly completed then. I can wait no longer! Let us marry in June, my love!"

"June . . ." She breathed in acquiescence, and could say no more, for Nat's lips once again claimed hers. . . .

The next hours were the happiest Melanie had ever known. Jared made the announcement and everyone at the ball gave congratulations. Everyone except James Talbot. In the midst of the flurry following the announcement, James drew her aside and gazed anxiously into her eyes.

"You will be miserably unhappy with him, Melanie! He is not for you! Surely, you are aware that it is Laura he loves?"

She shrugged and turned away, determined not to let his words affect her happiness. Riding on clouds of delirium, she joined the others, oblivious to conjecturing or envious faces. She thought she had buried James's warning forever, but his words came rushing back to haunt her sooner than she would have believed . . .

It was past three in the morning when they returned to Halcyon House. Thoughts of Nat, and all that transpired between them in the garden, filled Melanie with rapture as she drifted off to sleep.

Then, Laura's voice, high-pitched, near hysteria, flew up the chimney. Sharp words with the impact of bullets propelled Melanie abruptly back into the world of reality.

"Jared! It was nothing! I met him while shopping. He asked me aboard to look at antiques from the Orient for his Marblehead home . . ."

Through shattered illusions and broken dreams,

Melanie stared into the darkness and recalled her brother's firm, positive tone as he lied to Mrs. Carstairs; as easily as Nat lied convincing Melanie of his love!

All men are liars! she told herself. *And never again will I play the fool!*

CHAPTER FOUR

As the carriage rushed over the Post Road toward Boston, Laura and Melanie stared silently out of their respective windows.

Summer nudged spring this beautiful May morning. Meadows were green in the countryside and there was a smell of fresh-turned earth. Birds sang in new-leaved trees; cows munched in pastures; and bright yellow butterflies, testing their wings, fluttered over the landscape. Daisies and buttercups sprinkled hills and valleys, while lush green grass carpeted the lawns of passing towns.

Jared and Nat had left for Boston the previous week to lay plans for setting up a spermaceti candle factory on Nantucket Island. Their whaling vessels produced the necessary sperm oil, and demand for the candles, which burned brighter than whale-oil lamps, outdid the supply.

Only yesterday, Melanie and Laura had received invitations sent by messenger to join them for a few days aboard Nat's ship, the *Mirimar*, docked in Boston harbor.

"If you are feeling up to the day's journey," Jared had written his wife, "perhaps the change will do you good. Shopping usually cheers you and Boston merchants offer items not always available in New Bedford."

Laura clutched desperately at the hand strap beside the window as the carriage lurched around a bend in the road. Five months along in her pregnancy, she felt every bump of the wheel. The child within her shoved back angrily, and the ceaseless rocking of the carriage added to her discomfort. Upon arising at dawn this morning, she'd felt queasy, which was rare, for usually Laura had a fine sense of well-being during quickening. She fought down another bout of nausea and reached into her reticule for crackers her maid had given her to nibble during the trip. She was so looking forward to this holiday! It was just what she needed to chase away the boredom she'd been feeling lately.

Through midmorning sunlight and shadows, the carriage rushed past an ever-changing panorama. Quaint old hillside graveyards held slate headstones that were ancient when Boston was but a hamlet. White-steepled churches lifted an admonishing finger over quiet villages and now and then, a gilded weathervane sparkled in momentary illumination.

They rolled past rude garrison houses, rambling frame buildings with oddly assorted windows on different levels, standing cheek by jowl with eighteenth-century homes whose Georgian ornamentation, pilasters and scrolls with fanlights over double doorways, proclaimed elegance. Pre-Revolutionary saltbox houses looked over shaded lawns and trout pools dozed beneath arched, graceful elms.

The carriage lurched again and when it steadied, Laura glanced at the pendant watch pinned to her bosom. It was nearly nine of the clock; not yet two hours of travel and she longed to stop at the roadside to regurgitate. If only she could hold down the nausea until they reached the Toll House. They were to lunch there and change horses for the final leg of the journey. At this moment, however, food was definitely unthinkable.

Laura looked at Melanie's exquisite profile and fought down the urge to fly at her. Since they'd climbed into the carriage, Melanie had turned her head toward the window and remained immobile as a statue, barely answering when Laura made a comment or two this past hour.

How like a small brown wren she looks! Laura thought, wondering if a man like Nat could really be attracted to this tiny, fragile woman.

She gazed searchingly at Melanie's thick chestnut hair, drawn back into a fashionably large coil at the nape of her neck, and saw no beauty in the proud way she held her head.

Melanie's tucked, brown silk bonnet, swathed in pink tulle, had a modish broad brim with two small red roses holding it all together at the crown. She'd left the ribbons untied to enjoy the cool breeze on her neck, and little ringlets over her ears peeked beneath the sides.

Laura's bile rose at the recollection of how Nat had sought out Melanie, going to Jared and insisting he be allowed to call upon her. But, she comforted herself that he had called upon her aunt while she and Jared were in Europe two years ago. So, he had not forgotten!

You should have seen his face! Aunt Judith had said, gleefully, *when I told him you'd married. Serves him right, for draggin' his feet! He might have known he couldn't keep a beauty like Laura Callaghan dangling while he made up his mind!*

Now, mind you, she'd continued, *he seeks out the Hardy girl only to see you again. He will never marry her! Mark my words!*

But now, it looks as though he will! Laura thought, glancing again at Melanie.

Laura's critical gaze traveled over Melanie's lightweight merino dress of pale tan, accented with brown velvet trim. Narrow pleats on the bodice fit smoothly over small, rounded breasts and the elongated waist accented her petite figure. The demure neckline had a wide velvet collar, matching the cuffs on long, cling-ing sleeves. Her skirt, bell-shaped in the mode of the day, fell gracefully from just above the hip, and when she was seated, dainty brown kid slippers peeped out from under the hemline.

Grudgingly, Laura admitted to herself that the girl had excellent taste in dress. She turned away then, to stare blindly at the passing scene.

Since Nat's appearance at Halcyon House, Laura's emotions had been erratic . . . soaring to the skies . . . and plummeting to the depths.

He sought her out because of me! she told herself that first night. *He loves me . . . and Melanie is the key to unlocking the door between us!*

Then, as the evening wore on, uncertainty set in. Watching Nat's eyes on Melanie, Laura began to doubt. She wondered if his virility was attracted by Melanie's delicate femininity.

At first, Laura rejected the idea of Melanie's mar-riage to Nathaniel. Then, realizing future opportu-nities to be with him after her child was delivered, she feared Melanie would somehow destroy Nat's evident determination to join the family. In truth, Laura had no conscience about cuckolding Jared. After her pas-sionate romance with Nat, her husband's lovemaking left much to be desired. She looked forward to the day when Nat would lust after her again. Since she determined it would be so, she did not doubt her wish would become reality.

Laura was accustomed to having her own way!

She was three years old when her mother died an hour after delivering a stillborn son. The following year, her father, a wealthy shipowner, drowned in a storm off Cape Hatteras on the maiden voyage of his Baltimore clipper ship. Laura's maternal aunt, wife to a wealthy New Bedford merchant, took her to raise. Childless themselves, the elderly couple spoiled and coddled her, providing everything Laura demanded and much she never thought of, or even wanted. An heiress in her own right, they dotingly showered more wealth upon her.

Laura's beauty brought others into her web as well, and she soon learned that what might be initially denied could be acquired by proper scheming under the guise of innocence. As she grew up, she presented a beautiful face to the world, but when crossed, a spiteful meanness showed itself and disappeared as quickly as it surfaced when her wishes were granted.

When Laura was eighteen, she had her choice of men. However, a driving need for attention and reassurance and a tendency to flirt outrageously muddied her reputation somewhat. Daring, unconventional for the Victorian age, Laura's escapades kept the staid upper echelon of the town supplied with constant gossip. In truth, Laura was a narcissist. What pleased Laura was of prime importance, and if, in the doing, it pleased others, well and good; if not, it was of no consequence.

On a dare, she'd gone to the docks with friends, eager to see the handsome heir to Jonas Marfrey's wealth. The fact that Nathaniel's half-brother, James Talbot, was in the group had added impetus to the adventure. The vendetta between the two was a well-known fact, and it was said part of the fun was to watch the animosity that never failed to spark when they were in close proximity to each other.

Nat, astride the deck of the *Mirimar,* was clad only in white cotton breeches, rolled to the knee. His sandy hair had sun-bleached flaxen streaks and muscles rippled under the bronze skin of his back and shoulders. Laura saw him as a tall Norse god come to earth for the express purpose of rescuing her from suitors who paled into insignificance beside his own golden splendor.

He totally ignored his half-brother, and James Talbot, engrossed in watching the byplay between Nat and Laura, could have been just another onlooker.

When Nat's startling blue eyes rested upon Laura, she'd stared back like a common trollop and smiled flirtatiously. He'd tested her then, sending forth a string of curses at his men for some minor infraction, while watching her wide green eyes for signs of dismay. She'd smiled boldly, invitingly. He grinned back at her and against the remonstrances of her friends, she'd accepted the challenge in his eyes and gone aboard.

He'd kissed her in his quarters and his hands on her body, his lips on her mouth, were a pleasure she refused to deny herself. An hour after she boarded his ship, Laura lost her virginity and regretted it months later, only when faced with the realization that Nat had no intention of marrying her.

He'd been angry upon discovering that she was virginal and told her in no uncertain terms he would not be obligated.

"Your bold actions and knowledgeable ways led me to believe otherwise," he told her. "You were begging to be deflowered; but do not look to me for promises, financial or otherwise!"

"I am not in need of your gratuities, Mr. Larimore." Laura had answered, coolly arranging her clothing. "I am Laura Callaghan—an heiress in my own right!"

Staring out the carriage window, Laura smiled, remembering Nat's expression when he recognized her name; and the dawning realization of the enormity of his transgression.

Without another word between them, he'd escorted her from the ship. The next evening, drawn irresistibly, Laura was back. With astonishment in his eyes, Nat watched her come aboard. As silently as they had parted, they walked side by side to his quarters.

They'd had three months together, of lovemaking and laughter. And fighting; bitter, angry fights when

Nat denounced her venomously, attacking her devious, flirtatious ways.

The town watched with interest as the spoiled social butterfly and Jonas Marfrey's handsome heir apparently conformed to the mores of the times in a whirlwind courtship. But society matrons and others in the elite upper echelon were not fooled for long. Gradually, the true state of affairs became obvious. Early conjectures about their possible marriage soon deteriorated into discreetly raised eyebrows and whispers behind gloved hands when Laura flirted outrageously at various functions, while her escort brooded in livid silence on the sidelines.

When Nat had had enough, he turned his back and ended the affair.

Angrily, Laura set out to bring him to his knees. Having tasted her charms, she reasoned, certainly Nat would not long resist her siren call.

But, she was wrong.

After the breakup, they were separately invited to the same festive gatherings. But Nat steadfastly refused to notice when Laura showed up with myriad suitors in a vain attempt to force his attention. Aside from politely acknowledging her greetings, he showed not the slightest sign of softening his attitude.

Laura found herself competing with the plainest wallflower for Nat's favor. Now and then, to save her embarrassment, he would dance with her, or bring her a glass of sherry or champagne. But it was apparent his ardor had cooled. In the eyes of their social set, Laura's feverish pursuit of Nat and his now obvious disinterest was a source of amusement. Her high-handed self-confidence and stunning beauty had won victory over many men and earned the enmity of those women not so well endowed. They were delighted now to observe her downfall in her campaign to irrevocably snare Nathaniel Larimore.

The night before Nat sailed on a voyage that was

to last three years, Laura appeared on the deck of his ship.

"For old time's sake, Nat!" she wheedled. "Let's have a sip of wine and close the gulf between us. We loved once; surely we can love again?"

Staring down at her thick, red curls and the fetching décolletage of her fashionable gown, Nat had fought an overwhelming urge to crush her to him.

"Friends, Laura," he said in loud, deep tones. "But that is all! There will be no seduction in my cabin and no storming of the bastions of my heart. It is over, Laura; and best for both our sakes."

Laura agreed; then coaxed and promised to behave if he would take her to a tavern near the wharf. Finally, against his better judgment, Nat gave in.

Accustomed to opulence and manners, Laura observed the coarse brawling tavern folk with fascination and after a few glasses of ale, threw herself wildly into the melee. Before Nat could roughly pull her aside, she had joined in the singing and dancing. Drunken sailors, enticed by her beauty and abandonment, pulled and shoved at her in an effort to embrace, or kiss her. By the time Nat reached her side, her bodice had been torn by obscene hands and long red hair fell wildly about her shoulders. She was laughing as he wrapped her cloak about her and swiftly propelled her outside into the night.

A sailor followed them from the tavern and Laura sent taunting glances over her shoulder, egging him on with a swing of her hips and a toss of her waist-length hair. When he took up her invitation, attempting to lay hands upon her, she became frightened and clung to Nat.

Nat felled the man and sent him on his way, then turned to Laura, answering her bid for marriage. First, he had insulted her; then coldly, bitterly, spoke the words she remembered now as clearly as if they were engraved upon the back of the carriage seat opposite.

"I care not for a wife I must watch. There is more to marriage than bedding a woman!" He'd brought his face close to hers, and she remembered his hands, grasping her upper arms painfully as he forced her to listen. "It is not in my nature to love without respect. I cannot marry you, Laura, for despite your background, you are a lying, cheating wench! The mother of my children will be honorable and cause me no worry when I am halfway 'round the world!"

"Then love an honorable woman!" Laura spat. "But, on cold nights when you lie beside her, your loins will course with longing for *me*! And it will be *your* honor then, at stake!"

He'd turned away without answering and left her standing there beside the docks, to make her way home alone.

The next morning, from her balcony, she'd watched his ship sail out of New Bedford harbor. When it had disappeared over the horizon, she had gone back inside to plan her life.

Laura's reckless, madcap ways damaged her reputation and she had known her chances for marriage were growing slim. So she set about looking for a husband, settling upon Jared Hardy as her choice.

The church held a box lunch picnic the Sunday following Nat's departure, and Laura contrived to have her number drawn by Jared. Never mind what gyrations and strings she had to pull to do so; she made herself most charming to Jared and by the end of the day, he was completely under her spell.

If Jared Hardy was puzzled and dumbfounded at sudden attention from the town beauty, he was also pleased. A quiet, unassuming man, content to bury himself in the whereabouts of his father's far-flung ships and the books and business of family warehouses, he never took time to seek out feminine companionship. He was disinterested and usually oblivious to the advances of scheming mothers with eligible daughters believing him to be, and rightly so, a good catch.

Old Ephraim, shrewd and sharper-eyed, held his tongue and his own opinion, knowing his son was being baited for the hook, but knowing also that was probably the only way Jared would ever marry.

During their courtship, Laura felt decidedly uncomfortable in the presence of Ephraim Hardy. It was as if the man looked straight through her, knew what she had in mind and, without condoning, tacitly accepted her manipulations.

Two months after their courtship began, an opportunity presented itself, and Laura deliberately seduced Jared. They had been driving in the country in Jared's new phaeton, when a sudden rainstorm forced them to seek shelter in a nearby barn. Soaked, shivering, they sought the warmth of the hayloft, away from the animals below.

Knowing exactly what she was doing, Laura contrived to fit her body lengthwise against Jared under the guise of seeking warmth. His kisses, tentative at first, became bolder as Laura responded with rising desire. In reality, Laura surprised herself. She was unaware that, having been aroused by Nat, her passion had matured and needed only the kindling of an amorous and attractive man to burst into flame once more.

Innocent Jared, carried to heights of desire heretofore unknown, followed his instincts and consummated a sexual fantasy envisioned from the moment he first set eyes on Laura. When the summer storm had passed, Jared's passion went with it. Sober and contrite, he begged Laura's forgiveness and proclaimed his love. After abjectly declaring himself undeserving, he requested her hand in marriage. Laura, apparently in shock at her own moral laxity, assured

Jared that indeed, she would marry him, and in view of the circumstances, the sooner, the better. Jared concurred and vowed that whatever arrangements she desired were his desire also.

In the flurry and excitement of those few weeks before marriage, Laura rarely saw Ephraim Hardy. However, at the wedding reception in the gardens of her home, Ephraim found the bride beneath a spreading elm. His wise black eyes looked deep into her own and she knew his astute mind had fathomed the fact that she had seduced his son. When he conferred a fatherly kiss upon her fevered brow, Laura felt he had bestowed the laurel wreath of victory.

So Laura settled down to become Jared Hardy's wife. Actually, she was fond of Jared and after their first child was born, her fondness grew into love—all the love of which Laura was capable, as long as she found it convenient, and there was no necessity to forgo any pleasure her narcissistic nature demanded.

And so things would have remained, had not Nathaniel Larimore come back into her life to turn her limbs to jelly and set her aflame with desire at the mere sight of him.

She looked again at Melanie. Surely, this delicate, tiny creature was no match for the fiery Nathaniel Laura remembered! She studied Melanie's face and her body, and decided when the time was right, Melanie would be no hindrance to her plan to once again have Nat as a lover.

Suddenly, as if reading her mind, Melanie turned to confront Laura straight on, with big searching eyes so like Ephraim Hardy's.

"Tell me, Laura, when did you first meet Nat Larimore?"

Laura stared in astonishment.

"You remember . . . the night he came to call upon you. Last February, I believe."

"The truth, Laura! I know you were in hot pursuit of him some years back!"

"Upon what authority?"

"Gossip, Laura. But gossip usually has some basis in fact."

"Lies!"

Laura could feel agitation rising from the pit of her stomach and her face flamed nearly as red as her hair.

"I met Nat the night you met him and that's a fact!"

"That's a lie!"

Impulsively, Laura raised her hand and slapped Melanie's face. The sound seemed to echo above rumbling carriage wheels rushing over the rough road. They stared at each other for a long moment, while Melanie's cheek turned pink from the blow.

"You've just answered my question, Laura," she said quietly.

It was past midday when they reached the Toll House. Not another word had passed between the two women since the shock of Laura's slap. They lunched in silence. Laura, stomach churning, ate very little, while Melanie, apparently deciding to ignore her sister-in-law, ate heartily of the famous cuisine. She ended her meal with the renowned cookies, some of which she took to savor the remainder of the journey.

The horses slowed as they climbed the blue hills of Milton, and cresting the summit, the women beheld Boston Bay and the harbor beyond. Sails sparkled brilliantly under bright blue skies, as brigs, schooners, sloops, and all manner of vessels, large and small, crowded the waters of the port. Melanie searched for the *Mirimar*, but the distance was too great to make a distinction. Then, rolling downhill again, the harbor was hidden from view as they traveled steadily toward the coast.

They smelled the water before they saw it. It was after three o'clock when a swift salt breeze blew inland, reeking of seaweed and lobster pots drying in the sun.

Following the coastline, they rode down a long slope. They dipped into the lowlands, passing through desolate salt marshes, clay pits, and scrub where the smell of the sea enfolded them, strong and rank. They rode past workers filling in the shoreline coves and bays, creating land for future warehouses, fisheries, and other activities connected with the bustling business of ships and shipping.

Moving up Commercial Street, the coach made its way with difficulty through the crowds. Hawkers, workers, sailors, and merchants swarmed the narrow road.

"Here's potatoes, beans . . . peas, cucumbers . . . cabbage! Here's onions!" The loud, raucous voice belonged to an old bonneted woman sitting in the midst of the walkway, surrounded by her wares.

A whale-oil man bumped the side of the carriage with his wooden shoulder yoke. From each end hung a long string holding a can with a spout full of oil.

A chimney sweep, apparently a free Negro, pushed through the mob crying in a deep, ringing voice: "Sweep! Sweep-O! Sweep! Sweep-O!"

They passed a stand where lemons and oranges glistened in the sunlight and a gaunt scarecrow of a man called: "Frooot—very fine! Very cheeep! From the wa-a-a-rrmmm countries!" Farther down the street, a pretty fish maid salted quahogs and called her wares for a cent or two apiece.

The women pitched forward as the coach stopped abruptly at the foot of Commercial Wharf. They heard the driver call and there was a rumble of male voices while he directed a messenger to the *Mirimar*, berthed in the harbor beyond the last pier.

They waited.

A steady flow of people passed the windows. Some glanced unseeing into the interior; others stopped, gawking at the women inside until sent brusquely on their way by the vigilant coachman. The hum of voices rose and fell with the breeze and a fly buzzed against the cushioned seat opposite.

Glancing at her watch, Laura saw that slightly over thirty minutes had passed since word of their arrival was sent to the ship. Each second seemed an hour. It was warm and stuffy in the carriage and she felt the need of ventilation to fight the nausea again.

"I'm going for a breath of air," she told the coachman as she stepped outside.

"There are cutpurses and worse walking this street, mistress," the driver cautioned. "I shouldn't venture far, were I you."

Laura didn't answer.

The cool breeze entering the carriage as Laura alighted tantalized Melanie. She, too, stepped outside and with a nod to the coachman, strolled a short distance behind her sister-in-law.

She lingered at a flower stand nearby, debating whether to buy pansies for the shipboard cabin. Moving along, she passed a butcher's stand displaying red meat, thick with flies; then paused to examine with interest the silk scarves shown by a gypsy woman.

The gypsy's eyes were hooded, and her long fingernails, painted an unbelievable blood red, quickly untied knots in a wide silk scarf while she observed Melanie. Then, nodding her head in Laura's direction, she whispered, "She will take from you if she can. Be wary of her!"

Astonished, Melanie could only stare.

Laura, a few paces away, turned startled eyes on the gypsy. Melanie couldn't be certain whether or not she had overheard. Coolly, the gypsy's eyes went to Laura's waist with a knowing look.

"You will not have the child, missus!" she said, in a sibilant voice. "It is not meant to be!"

Laura backed slowly away from the woman.

Engulfed by a sudden chill, Melanie gripped the side of the rickety booth to steady herself. Just then a rough seaman shouted.

"Runaway!"

A string of curses spilled from his lips as he grasped Laura's shoulders from behind and shoved her abruptly against the gypsy. Screams rent the air and terrified people scurried on both sides of the narrow street as a runaway horse, pulling an ice wagon, missed Laura by inches. The arms of the gypsy broke her fall when she sank into a dead faint. The rough seaman disappeared into the crowd.

Jared and Nat appeared out of nowhere. Melanie stood frozen, still clutching the side of the booth as both men rushed to Laura, now prone on the ground with her head on the gypsy's lap. Jared reached Laura's side first. Ineffectively, he attempted to revive her, speaking softly, chafing one wrist. But it was Nat who decisively took over. Slipping out of his coat, he laid it over the cobblestones and gently lifted Laura from the woman's arms. He stretched her flat upon the ground and calling for salts, took the water-soaked scarves the gypsy proffered, placing them on Laura's forehead and wrists.

"Melanie . . ." Nat's sharp voice brought her out of her stupor. "You must have smelling salts in your reticule!"

Nodding, feeling like a simpleton, Melanie reached into her purse and held them out to him. Nat passed them under Laura's nose. She turned her head, frowning, then opened her eyes to gaze about in confusion. Nat raised her to a half-sitting position.

Melanie observed jealously that he held Laura a

shade too close and rightly suspected she was enjoying the embrace. The thought crossed her mind that it was incongruous to see Jared the onlooker while another man ministered to the needs of his wife. Then she realized Nat's superior strength made him the one most likely to lift Laura in her delicate condition.

With Nat's assistance, Laura struggled to a sitting position. Melanie bent down beside her to retrieve her reticule and froze at the voice of the gypsy.

"Your souls entwine . . . yours and this one!"

She looked up. The woman's hooded eyes rested on Nat, but Melanie was uncertain whether it was Laura's soul or her own, to which the gypsy referred.

Melanie stood straight again.

"Well, let us get her aboard! Apparently, she will have to be carried!"

Was that her own voice—sharp, biting, and so unlike her? Astonished at the conflicting emotions that impelled her outburst, Melanie endured a surprised glance from Nat and a momentary stunned expression on the face of her brother.

Nat lifted Laura to her feet. Jared took her other side and Laura walked trembling, between them.

"A shallop awaits us at the foot of the wharf," Jared said reassuringly to his wife.

Melanie fell in behind them but was halted, when the gypsy placed a restraining hand on her arm.

"Be careful, miss, that your own vengeance does not turn itself back upon you!"

The voice was low, meant only for Melanie's ears. Piercing black eyes probed deep into hers for a chilling moment. When the woman released her, the eyes became hooded again, reptilian. A cold sense of foreboding swept over Melanie. Turning swiftly, she ran to join the others who had reached the steps. At the platform below, the shallop waited, four oarsmen at the ready.

Seated in cushions, the women opened parasols to

protect delicate complexions from the sun's slanting rays. The bustling wharf receded as the oarsmen bent to their task. In late afternoon, ships in the harbor sent long shadows over the water. The wind was freshening. Screeching seagulls wheeled and soared, pure white against the darkening sky. Now and then a gull dipped beneath a nearby wave and with one swift movement passed overhead, a tiny, struggling fish in his sharp beak. Beyond the last pier, a vision of beauty in steel blue waters, the *Mirimar* rode at anchor. Her three masts glinted in the final rays of the sun and furled sails rivaled whitecaps tipping swells near the mouth of the bay.

Melanie tried not to notice Nat's concerned glances at Laura, pale and beautiful, leaning back among the dark cushions.

CHAPTER FIVE

Upon arrival aboard the *Mirimar,* they were ushered into the salon where Mahmoud, the Hindu manservant Nat had inherited from Jonas Marfrey, served refreshments.

"We have all week to dine at Revere House and anywhere else you wish," Jared told his peevish wife as they sipped a cool drink. "You have had enough for one day."

"But Jared," Laura pouted, "I have so looked forward to dining in Boston this evening."

"My dear!" her husband replied firmly. "You fainted from excitement and exhaustion. It has been a long journey and we must take no chances with your health. Tonight, you will rest!"

As Nat's betrothed, Melanie was to occupy the commodious master cabin while Nat took a smaller berth amidships. Soon after their arrival, however, Melanie's quarters were utilized by Mahmoud for the purpose of unpacking and pressing the women's wrinkled gowns. So, despite Melanie's aversion, she was forced to endure Laura's company a bit longer while they changed dusty garments and performed their ablutions in the first mate's cabin, assigned to Laura and Jared.

They supped that night aboard ship under the excellent ministrations of the Hindu, whose inscrutable face, carefully observed by Melanie since their arrival, gave no evidence of recognition when Laura appeared.

They played cards until ten o'clock when the women excused themselves and left the men discussing business. Once on deck, Melanie and Laura parted as they had spent the day, in silence.

Melanie stepped over the threshold of the master cabin and closed the door. She stood with her back against it, surveying these warm, intimate quarters she would soon share with Nathaniel on their South Seas honeymoon.

The L-shaped bed-sitting room bespoke Nat. Pressed glass whale-oil lamps in ornate bronze holders were fastened at intervals to paneled walls, reflecting a warm glow on heavy polished woods and brass accoutrements. Several unlighted ship lanterns swung from thick black beams that curved darkly against a white ceiling.

To Melanie's left, charts and maps hung above a carved cherrywood desk and behind a louvered door was the captain's bathroom and water closet. Nat's pipes rested in a wall rack next to the desk. An aroma of sandalwood emanated from several wooden tobacco cannisters on a low teakwood table beside a great leather chair and ottoman.

Melanie walked across the polished plank floor to stand at the edge of a thick Persian rug intricately woven with a pattern of ruby red roses and dark, forest green stems that seemed almost three-dimensional against a background of palest blue. A wide, tiered berth, made to fit against the curve of the ship, nestled beneath a huge round porthole framed in brass. Moonlight pouring through the double glass sent an iridescent path across the dark blue satin coverlet. Just beyond the foot of the bed, shafts of light poured through the single thickness of two smaller portholes, also circled in brass.

A short distance away, a diminutive rattan table

stood between two cane-woven oriental chairs, whose convoluted, fanlike backs were as tall as Melanie. One, a mandarin butterfly chair with large, spreading-wing design, held a little red velvet cushion in its center. The scrolled, semicircular pattern of the other proclaimed it to be one of the famed peacock chairs.

And on the inner wall stood a large armoire with high chiffonier beside it. When Melanie opened the doors, she saw her gowns there in perfect state, without a wrinkle. Her portmanteau and trunk had been unpacked and the drawers of the chiffonier, lightly scented with her own sachet, held her underthings in neat stacks and nightdresses carefully laid out.

Melanie gazed about this room where Nat slept and lived, wondering if Laura had been here. This cabin, she reminded herself, must have heard laughter and lovemaking. Somehow, the picture of Nat making love to a nameless, faceless woman was unimportant—but Nat making love to Laura was a painful, unbearable thought!

She sat down suddenly in the mandarin chair, her pleasure in this beautiful cabin marred by the shadow of suspicion. She tried to rid herself of the vivid tableau her imagination conjured, but no matter how she fought to exorcise the ghosts, she saw Nat with Laura, in all her seductive charm, on this wide berth that was destined to become Melanie's wedding bed. She recalled the night in Mrs. Hoffman's garden when he asked her to be his wife—and wondered if Laura responded to his touch with the same abandon.

Leaning her head against the high back of the chair, she closed her eyes, reminding herself that Nat invited Laura aboard this ship not too many weeks ago.

She sat up suddenly, as a new thought struck her. Perhaps he did not invite her aboard! Perhaps Laura invited herself! Melanie knew in her heart that Laura and Nat had been acquainted before Laura's marriage to Jared; and she knew her sister-in-law lied this morning. If she lied once, she could lie many times.

Perhaps, Melanie now told herself, *it is Laura who seeks out Nat, and not the reverse!* She sighed. *And perhaps, I am wishfully thinking!*

Melanie knew her changing moods had confused her betrothed these past weeks. He'd attempted to draw her out, to tear down the barrier between them. But Melanie, having tried, convicted, and condemned him, could not speak of her fears about Laura.

Her heart lurched at the image of hurt and puzzlement in his blue eyes and love for Nat overwhelmed her.

I will give him the benefit of doubt! she told herself, disrobing for sleep.

But she took back that promise almost immediately, remembering how gently he'd held Laura this afternoon while she recovered her senses . . . and his concerned gaze as she reclined in the shallop on the way to the ship.

The night was warm, the cabin stuffy. She pulled the pins from her hair, letting it fall to her waist, and began brushing it fifty strokes. Then, in her lightweight batiste nightgown, she padded barefoot over the Persian rug, across the plank floor to Nat's desk. Standing on tiptoe, she swung the whale-oil lamp toward her, turned the wick, and extinguished the light. She did the same to the other lamps, then went to the small portholes near the foot of the bed. Unfastening the brass locks, she opened them wide. A soft ocean breeze ruffled her hair, cooling her face and shoulders.

Impulsively, she slipped the nightdress from her shoulders, letting it fall about her ankles. She stood there, nude, bathed in moonlight. Reveling in cool wind on her naked flesh, she knew total freedom from restraint for the first time in her life. And somewhere deep inside, she was shocked at the hedonistic pleasure of this unforeseen moment.

Since Nat's first touch on their betrothal night, Melanie had been aware of her body in a manner she'd never dreamed possible. He had awakened something within her that was at once thrilling and frightening. With one flowing movement, she stepped out of the circle of her gown, swept it from the floor, and draped it across the coverlet at the foot of the bed. Then, she slipped between the sheets.

The cool silk caressed her skin. Melanie was not surprised at Nat's weakness for such Sybaritic sensuality. She reclined luxuriously, moving her feet and legs in delight, feeling the smooth expanse of satin, slippery on her nude body.

Closing her eyes, she imagined Nat beside her, his arms drawing her close, covering her mouth with his.

Lost in the memory of his kiss, Melanie drifted in that ethereal world between sleeping and waking. Her body, responding to fantasy, became languorous . . . haunted by the impress of Nat's hands and mouth.

At first, she was uncertain whether the knock was real, or just part of her dream. The knock was repeated. The door opened, and Melanie struggled slowly back to reality.

Through heavy eyelids, Melanie saw Nat standing beside the bed. Startled into wakefulness, she sat up, pulling the silken sheet about her nude body, conscious of her long hair falling in disarray down her back.

Moonlight spilling through the large porthole beside the berth gave Nat's eyes the look of live coals as he drank in her beauty.

"I'm—I'm sorry, Melanie." His voice was husky, his breathing quick, as though he'd been running. "I . . . I . . . needed a pipe, and thought you might yet be about . . ."

She was immobile, staring up at him through large,
eager eyes filled with the memory of her erotic
dreams.

Suddenly, Nat sat on the berth and drew her to
him. He ran his hands down the long, thick mane of
hair, then lifted it to caress the silken skin of her bare
back. Every nerve in Melanie's body responded to his
touch. Brushing aside the satin sheet, Nat fastened his
mouth on the rosy nipple of one breast, while tenderly massaging the other.

Melanie gasped, closed her eyes, and gave in to the
passion sweeping over her like a tidal wave.

The moon blazed a silver pathway across the
waters straight to Melanie's bridal bed, outlining
with a bright aura Nat's flaxen head bent to her
bosom. His strong, surprisingly gentle hands; his seeking, voracious lips and tongue were all in the world
Melanie was conscious of; nothing else existed—nothing else was important! There was only Nat . . .
his body . . . his touch on her flesh; and her love,
her totally consuming love for him.

Time stood still while Nat explored the virginal
body of his bride-to-be. Every curve, every soft, tender
spot, his searching hands and mouth touched eagerly,
yet slowly, as a man traveling in the desert ap-
proaches water; with avid longing, but cautiously
aware that slaking thirst too much, too soon is just as
deadly as the fiery sun.

Was it Laura's laugh floating on soft breezes and
moonbeams through the porthole, or only an echo
carried on the wind? In any case, the spell was broken. The sound chilled Melanie. Something deep inside recoiled as the ghost stirring in this bed arose
once more to haunt her.

Melanie said not a word; she did not even protest.
She merely stopped responding to Nat's touch.

He lifted his head; gazed into her eyes.

"What is it, my love?"

"It is Laura," she answered simply. "You knew her before you came to call upon me last February." It was a statement, not a question.

"Yes, I knew her."

"Why did you conspire to keep your acquaintance a secret?"

Nat shook his head: "I have no idea! I merely followed her lead, believing perhaps she had a good reason. Then, it became too late to rectify . . ."

"You were in love with Laura?"

"No."

"You *thought* you were in love with her?"

"No."

Melanie lapsed into silence, absorbing his answers.

He had moved up, half-sitting, half-reclining on the large pillows. She was lying in his arms, her head on his shoulder; her hand in his.

"Nat." Her voice was almost a whisper and she held her breath, not certain she wanted to know.

"Did you invite Laura aboard this ship a week or two before proposing to me at Mrs. Hoffman's soiree?"

"I have never invited Laura aboard my ship," he answered. Then, after a long pause, he repeated, "Never."

The last seemed to be rumination on his part, and his voice held an element of surprise, as though he had not previously realized the fact. But that rumination was not noted by Melanie until much later. For the nonce, she was content that Laura had not come aboard at his invitation.

"Did she invite herself then, Nat?"

He was silent for a time before answering, and she sensed the tension in his body at her question.

"Laura does as she pleases," he said noncommittally.

"Why, Nat? Why did she come aboard?"

He sighed.

"Melanie, whatever Laura's reasons, they have

nothing to do with us. She is married to your brother. We are to be married; and our happiness is independent of theirs. Do not belabor Laura's reasons for doing whatever she wishes."

He sat up then, and pushing her slightly away from him, held her by the shoulders and stared into her face.

"Is her visit the reason you placed such distance between us since the night of our betrothal?"

"Yes. I believe you loved her once. I cannot abide the thought of being a go-between for your liaison."

"Melanie!" Nat's voice broke with emotion. "It is you I love! As you undoubtedly notice, I find it difficult to keep my distance until we are wed!"

"I am told," she replied primly, "that lust has naught to do with love and one is not to be confused with the other!"

Nat's eyes twinkled in the moonlight as he raked her nudity with a yearning gaze.

"You are absolutely adorable!" he said, chuckling. "You sit there with the air of a moon goddess, long hair running riotously down your back, nary a stitch on your seductive body, and speak with all the propriety of a nun in Sunday school!"

They both collapsed in a burst of laughter.

A knock at the door startled them into silence.

Melanie froze.

Nat, with the quick agility of a man accustomed to dealing with the unexpected, slipped into the shadows behind the wardrobe.

"Melanie! Are you there?"

It was Laura's voice, low, husky, and urgent.

"One moment, Laura."

Melanie reached for her nightgown at the foot of the berth and donned it on the way to the door. Before she reached it, however, Laura stood at the threshold.

"I thought I heard voices," she said, as her gaze swept the cabin.

"If there were voices in here, Laura," Melanie said coolly, "it would be none of your concern."

"But it is my concern. Your wedding is in four weeks. As your sister-in-law, it is my duty to insure that you go to your marriage bed virginal," Laura answered, sweetly. "Or I would be derelict in my obligation to Nat."

She stopped. Her large green eyes widened as Nat stepped into the center of the moonlit room.

"You have no obligation to me whatsoever, Laura," he said quietly. Striking a match, he turned up the wick on the lamp next to the leather chair. "My betrothed," he continued, turning to face Laura in the full light, "will come to me a virgin, and remain faithful to our marriage vows all of her life."

Laura stared.

"What are you doing here?" she asked at last. Her soft disbelieving voice betrayed her puzzlement.

"To set your mind at rest," he answered gently, "I came to retrieve my favorite pipe and finding Melanie awake, have had a very necessary discussion."

They stood there in silence, gazing at each other. Then, with a last, wide-eyed look at Nat, Laura turned on her heel and left the cabin.

When the door closed behind her, Nat took Melanie in his arms. "Sleep well, my love," he whispered into her hair. As an afterthought, he added, "Have you any more questions, little moon goddess?"

"One more," she answered solemnly. "Do you always lie on silken sheets?"

Nat laughed aloud.

"The silken sheets were placed on my berth for the first time. I brought them from the Far East and once assured of your arrival, I ordered Mahmoud to prepare the bed with them. I thought you might enjoy sleeping thus."

"Nat," she answered, raising her lips to his, "you have a truly sinful effect upon me. I doubt not that you will cause the loss of my immortal soul!"

He kissed her then and she reveled in his touch and his tenderness. Even in his lovemaking, he made her feel like a delicate, porcelain doll.

It was only later, reclining alone in Nat's berth, that Melanie, staring out the porthole at the moonlit waters of the harbor, questioned the motive behind her sister-in-law's visit. With the memory of Nat's hands still haunting her flesh, Melanie tried to forget the yearning in Laura's eyes as she gazed at him.

What was behind Laura's visit? She and Melanie had ignored each other since the altercation in the carriage this afternoon. Was Laura aware that Nat had come here tonight? And had Nat planned seduction in order to guarantee their marriage? Melanie knew her hot and cold moods worried her fiancé these past weeks; and Laura, also, had been concerned that Melanie might withdraw from the betrothal agreement.

She shrugged off growing uneasiness.

I am so accustomed to doubting, she told herself, *that I have become a true cynic!*

Remembering Nat's arms about her, his lips on hers, and his vows of love, Melanie chose to believe in him. She sighed and settled down to sleep.

The moon shone full on her slumbering face and spread out over the satin pillow, thick dark hair framed her innocence and vulnerability.

The gentle rocking of the ship first insinuated itself upon Melanie's consciousness, quickly followed by the cry of gulls seeking scraps thrown overboard from the galley. Awakening slowly from a dream of Nat, she opened her eyes to a bright, beautiful morning. For some time she lay there listening to the sounds of water lapping at the sides of the vessel. Voices drifted, muted to her ears, as sailors called out to each other and the lilting tune of a sea chantey floated down from high in the rigging.

Melanie smiled. Closing her eyes again, she saw herself at the age of ten when her father had taken her on a short voyage up the coast of Maine. Melanie loved sailing and Ephraim, disappointed in Jared's fear of water, indulged her as often as her mother would allow, which was not often enough for Melanie.

Unlike wives of other whaling captains, Ephraim Hardy's wife had an aversion to the sea and refused to sail with him on voyages sometimes lasting two or three years. She loved her husband with all her soul and every ounce of her diminutive body, but love could not dispel her terror of the seething oceans. So Ephraim's crew, perhaps more than any other, were unaccustomed to women on shipboard, thus in the habit of saying whatever they pleased in whatever manner they chose. With Melanie aboard, however, the crew, grizzled whalers all, curbed their usually coarse language. Though the little girl was treated respectfully, their prime motivation was the captain's threat of keelhauling, should they forget themselves.

That first week at sea, Melanie listened with childish delight to the lilting words of a sea chantey wafting from the billowing sheets, each time sail was hoisted. One morning at breakfast, she parroted the rollicking words to her father. Ephraim, not a cowardly man, turned ashen at the thought of what his wife would say when they once again reached New Bedford. With dire threats, the worst of which was that she never could accompany him to sea again, Ephraim convinced his daughter to forget the abominable sailor's song.

Now, after all these years, lying in Nat's berth on the *Mirimar*, Melanie heard the same bawdy tune and with a light heart, sang along gleefully when the

seaman started the second time around. She began
with the innocently innocuous lines that gave nary a
hint of what was to come.

Oh, whiskey is the life of man, whiskey . . .
Johnnyyyy!
Oh, I'll drink whiskey while I can, whiskey
for my Johnnnnyyyy . . .

On the brink of the next verse, Melanie stopped,
astonished at her newfound knowledge of its meaning. Remembering her father's face, she now understood why he'd been so perturbed.

Lying on satin sheets in the bed of her betrothed,
Melanie was suddenly more than ever aware of the
change in herself since meeting Nat. His very
presence in her life cast an entirely different light
upon her existence. Joyfully, she now faced and embraced yearnings hidden from her consciousness overlong; but though she'd remained virginal, such
knowledge had cost her innocence. She realized, then,
that innocence ceases being a virtue when its time has
passed . . . and when too avidly held, becomes ig-
norance.

A knock at the cabin door interrupted her reverie.

"Melanie." Jared's low voice came clearly from beyond the threshold.

She answered, asking him to wait while she donned
her robe.

"You slept late this morning, Melanie," he greeted
her when she admitted him at last. "We are awaiting
you at breakfast, then must take the shallop to the
wharf. There is much shopping to be done for the
wedding and your time in Boston is short."

"Is Nat accompanying us?"

"He rides to Commercial Wharf, but has an ap-
pointment at his warehouse. We will meet him for a
late luncheon this afternoon."

Melanie brushed her hair back from her shoulders: "I shan't be long, Jared. I will join you within thirty minutes." She looked quizzically into her brother's face, realizing he was troubled. "Jared? Is something gone wrong?"

"I must speak with you, Melanie." His tone was serious as he settled in the mandarin chair.

Puzzled, Melanie took the peacock chair, with the small table between them.

"I understand you had an altercation with Laura while journeying here yesterday."

"It was the other way around, Jared."

"She tells me you accused her of lying to you."

"Did she say what the lie was about?"

Jared sighed: "Melanie, I know Laura and Nat are old acquaintances. I know they kept company for a short time before we met. But that is no reason for jealousy on your part! She is my wife and your sister-in-law. Nat sought you out because he loves you and for no other reason; he has told me enough times this past week of his feelings for you!"

Melanie sat in silence, astonished at the turn the conversation had taken. She stared at her brother through wide brown eyes as he continued.

"Laura loves you, Melanie. She wants only your happiness. She is doing everything she can, despite the fact that she is unwell, to see to it that you have a memorable wedding this next month. Yet, you persist in your antipathy toward her. I have never known you to be spiteful!"

"Jared!" Melanie could no longer resist telling her brother her true feelings. "It is Laura's antipathy toward me that is so galling! She sends little darts and jabs at me constantly. She does everything possible to keep me off balance and miserable; pointing out her superior ways, beauty, and knowledge! I am sick and tired of your wife, Jared! She is the spiteful one! I despise her flirtatious ways with Nat and her constant nagging at me for imagined slights and things of no consequence!"

Jared heard her out and was silent a long moment before answering.

"Melanie, I know at times Laura is difficult to abide. But I understand her better than you think. Each time she is with child, she becomes insecure, needing constant reassurance."

"Your reassurance, Jared, should be quite enough! She has no need to seek reassurance from other men! How can you overlook her flirtatious demeanor?"

"She is beautiful," Jared answered quietly. "During pregnancy, her beauty is threatened. That is her way. It means nothing. My wife loves me."

Jared dropped his eyes before his sister's searching gaze, and Melanie wondered if Jared's insecurities did not match those of his wife.

"Try to be patient with her awhile longer, Melanie," he said, reaching out to take her hand. "You will be married within the month, and no longer have to put up with Laura's vagaries . . ."

And you, my brother, will have to put up with them for the rest of your life! Melanie thought, with a surge of sympathy.

After Jared left, Melanie dismissed thoughts of Laura, telling herself she would soon be rid of her. All of life stretched ahead, long and thrilling . . . a life with Nat, whom she loved with her whole heart; a life free of Laura and the deteriorating happiness of her beloved brother.

Now, she looked forward to shopping for hats at LaBlond's Chapeaux; and for slippers and shoes, as well as boots to match the day dresses, morning wear, and ball gowns of her trousseau presently being completed at Goulet's.

Melanie dressed with care, choosing a pale pink dotted swiss with high neckline and tucked lace bodice. Matching lace edged long sleeves, as well as her

parasol and the wide-brimmed, soft, flouncy hat. The
mirror reflected a hitherto unknown beauty as she
gazed at her image through sparkling brown eyes
filled with happiness.

Melanie entered the ship's salon to breakfast, and
Nat and Jared arose, while Mahmoud pulled out her
chair.

"You are especially lovely this morning, my dear."

"Thank you, Nat."

Their eyes met, warm with shared memories of last
night.

Looking at the man she loved, Melanie was filled
with a glow of rapture. Suddenly cognizant of Laura's
piercing green eyes, she lowered her lashes and took
her place at table.

After breakfast, they entered the shallop and re-
traced the watery path over the harbor to Commercial Wharf. There, after reiterating once more the
time and place of their luncheon meeting, Nat gave
Melanie a quick peck on the cheek and departed.
Laura, Jared, and Melanie rode by open carriage into
the main part of Boston.

Time passed swiftly. After purchasing reticules and
shawls, parasols and lingerie, all of which were to be
sent to the ship, they descended upon the city's most
fashionable booterie. Nearly two hours later, Melanie
was close to exhaustion as they rode across town to
LaBlond's, their final destination.

After much protest, Jared gave in to Melanie's insistence and left her in the capable hands of the pro-
prietress, promising to return in time for luncheon
with Nat at the Union Boat Club.

At LaBlond's, Melanie's flagging energies revived.

"There is something about buying hats," Madame
LaBlond said with a toothy smile, "that does re-
juvenate a woman, even a harried bride-to-be!"

Melanie tried on some ready-to-wear millinery, but
mostly she sat still while Madame, with three

hovering assistants, created hats right on her head in colors, fabrics, and styles complementing trousseau sketches sent along by Goulet's.

Before the first hour had passed, Melanie learned that Madame LaBlond, true to her reputation, could be trusted to know exactly what was right for her. And aside from changing a feather from left side to right, or fastening a cluster of flowers low in the back on a bonnet instead of in front, Melanie made no suggestions whatsoever. By the time Jared and Laura arrived, Melanie had ordered more than two dozen hats and chosen her wedding veil; a floor-length creation of wispy chiffon and lace, falling from a tiara crown of seed pearls.

When the carriage drew up to the Union Boat Club at the foot of Beacon Hill, Nat awaited them. He'd reserved a table overlooking the Charles River and over lunch of quahogs, lobster, and steaming bowls of famed Boston clam chowder, they viewed small boats of assorted sizes skimming over the sunlit water.

Halfway through the meal, Melanie was surprised to see James Talbot enter the dining room. He followed the maitre' d to a table where two prosperous-looking gentlemen obviously expected him. Shrewd eyes, muttonchop whiskers, and an air of superiority gave them the mien of bankers or investors. They carried on an earnest conversation all through luncheon while Melanie's gaze strayed unconsciously toward their table. At one point, James's dark, brooding eyes met hers and he smiled warmly. Embarrassed to be caught staring, she smiled self-consciously and bent to her plate.

"James is desperately trying to make a deal for ships," Nat said in a tight, barely controlled voice, and Melanie realized he'd observed her interest in the presence of his half-brother.

"He is in dire straits due to the fact that he signed

contracts with southern plantation owners to deliver new shipments of slaves from Africa. Though well paid in advance for the venture, he has been unable to fulfill his promises."

"I understand he modified the whaler to carry slaves," Jared said. "Is that ship not enough?"

"The whaler Jonas gave him was lost to British patrols on a search and seizure warrant, off the coast of Africa. He has been here in Boston for over a week trying to lease-purchase a ship to accommodate large cargoes of captives."

"I cannot believe James is a slave trader!" Laura began.

"Believe!" Nat cut in abruptly.

But Laura was not to be put off.

"James is not a cruel man! Old Sadie, an ex-slave, took care of him since he was ten years old, when Jonas finally decided to provide for James and his mother. Surely, he would never deliver humans into bondage for profit!" she ended uncertainly.

"James Talbot would do anything for profit! And old Sadie has naught to do with his burning ambition! His determination to acquire riches impels him to utilize any method, no matter how debased. If it costs lives and the liberty of others, his needs must still take precedence."

Melanie was silent, but she was inclined to agree with Laura. Surely, James, with his charm and warmth, could not be a slaver! Then, she remembered the tension she'd recognized beneath his gaiety.

At James's table, the two businessmen arose. James stood also, and as the gentlemen left the dining room, he moved to Melanie's side. Taking her hand, he bowed and kissed it.

"It is good to see you again, Melanie," he said softly. Then, smiling at Laura, "You are radiant as ever, Mrs. Hardy."

Nat stood abruptly, nearly turning over his chair in so doing.

"I will thank you to leave quietly, Talbot; or I must embarrass the ladies by creating a scene!" His low voice held a menacing note.

As though nothing had been said, James stared into Melanie's wide, frightened eyes.

"I must see you, my dear . . . and soon!"

Then, before Nat could make another move, James strode rapidly toward the door. A frown appeared on Melanie's brow as she tried to absorb the meaning of his words.

Nat supplied the answer.

"James wants your ships, Melanie. And will leave no stone unturned until he accomplishes his purpose."

"I am in charge of Melanie's ships," Jared said in puzzlement. "And he has not approached me on the subject."

"He will, in time," Nat answered. "He sought Jonas's favored brigantine, the *Sea-Wind;* but only last week, the court turned down his bid to break the will. Though the brig was specifically left to me, James claimed it was given him verbally, shortly before Jonas's death. If so, Jonas failed to so state in his bequest."

Laura sighed, then spoke softly.

"Is it possible that your dislike of James colors your interpretation of his actions? Surely, so many people would not be sympathetic to James if he were the scoundrel you make him out to be."

Nat looked at his companions through hard eyes.

"You may not believe me now, but mark my words! James Talbot would sell his soul to acquire the riches he feels are due him." His tone indicated that the subject was dropped.

Suddenly weary from the strain of shopping, and the near catastrophe of a scene between Nat and his half-brother, Melanie made no protest when Jared insisted they rest before the long evening ahead.

The remarkable play, *Uncle Tom's Cabin*, was opening this night at the Howard Atheneum, and Nat had managed to obtain box seats for the occasion. There had been much discussion of the book, which had been a sensation this past season. And Laura and Melanie were delighted when Nat imparted the news that the author, Harriet Beecher Stowe, would be present in the balcony next to them. After the play, they were to have a late supper at one of Boston's renowned restaurants.

It was four o'clock when they once more reached Commercial Wharf where the shallop waited. Once in her cabin, Melanie removed her gown, then, lying across the berth in her petticoats, fell almost instantly into deep slumber.

Some time later, she was startled into wakefulness. Wondering at her precipitous exit from a troubled dream, she gazed through the large porthole at lengthening shadows over the water, where myriad, tiny whitecaps gave evidence of a freshening wind. A soft tapping came at the door, and Melanie knew this was the cause of her awakening.

The door opened and Nat stepped over the threshold. She watched him approach with a sense of relief. Melanie had awakened with a strange sense of loss. Fear clutched her heart with a cold hand, and she needed Nat's arms about her to dispel the effects of a threatening dream. She lifted her arms to him and he went into them, burying his face in her neck.

"I'm sorry to awaken you, my love," he whispered. "It grows late and curtain call is at half after eight."

Melanie was silent, clinging to him.

He held her close. Then, sensing her agitation, sat down beside her, looking into her eyes.

"Melanie? Are you feeling unwell?"

She shook her head and felt a tear leave the corner

of one eye, to dissolve itself on the satin pillow. Nat touched the wetness with one finger.

"Tears, my little one?"

"Oh, Nat! It was a dream ... a bad dream!"

He gathered her to him.

"My beloved! I cannot follow into your dreams, but know that I will protect you from harm to the best of my ability while your senses remain open to me."

He kissed her then, a long, deep kiss as the sadness in her heart retreated to the innermost corner.

He held her a moment longer and with an affectionate pat on her petticoated bottom stood grinning down at her.

"Come, my lovely! Time passes swiftly. Soon the shallop will be ready for departure!"

As she dressed for the evening, Melanie fought the strange despair nudging her with an insistence impossible to fathom. Try as she would, an eerie sense of foreboding settled over her shoulders like a cloak, dampening her former enthusiasm and worrying her like a dog with a bone.

I wonder how long I will find comfort in Nat's arms? The thought rose unbidden to her mind. *Why do I feel this will not last?*

With a final effort at shrugging off the haunting premonition, she picked up her jet evening bag and went to join the others in the salon.

CHAPTER SIX

The shallop left them at the foot of Commercial Street and they climbed the stairs to find an open victoria awaiting them. Though it was barely twilight, carriage lamps glowed at each side of the elegant vehicle. A silk-hatted coachman, whose livery exactly corresponded to the royal blue tufted upholstery, handed them into their seats with a flourish, before ascending his high perch. Obeying a slight flick of the reins, the matched pair of beautifully groomed horses marched sedately up the narrow, winding road. The polished metal on the fine leather harnesses reflected flickering lamplight and the last rays of the setting sun.

"We have an hour or so before curtain time, so we will take a fast tour of the town," Nat said.

As they rode through Boston's twisting thoroughfares, he pointed out the Public Garden, edging Boston harbor. "The original plans were based on the Gardens of Versailles," he told them when they passed the elaborate entrance.

Through the high iron gate and surrounding fence, they saw flower beds with buds and blooms in wild profusion. Wooden benches under ornamental trees and palms in green wooden tubs along the walls gave a tropical air to the scene.

"In winter," Nat said, "the pond becomes a popular skating rink for young and old alike."

They saw the train bridge and the Bunker Monu-

ment atop Breed's Hill. In the distance, Nat pointed
out Beacon Hill and said it was called Nigger Hill on
the other side, because freed blacks and fugitive slaves
had homes and hovels there.

They rode up Tremont Street past the Common,
where tree-lined paths and popular promenades or
Courting Walks were paved with brick. Elegant, ex-
pensive homes surrounded the Common. Tall, bow-
front town houses with large windows and classic iron
balconies nestled amidst tree-filled parks enclosed by
cast iron rails and adorned with one or two pedestal
fountains.

As they drove through the winding streets, the
clop-clop of horses' hooves was sometimes muffled,
sometimes hollow, on alternate pavement of brick
and blocks of granite.

They saw the Frog Pond Fountain, a French style
park basin surrounded by a stone curb. Seated in the
carriage, necks craned, they stared in astonishment at
water jetting eighty feet into the air to sparkle like diamonds at the very top as droplets caught the dying
rays of a sun now below the horizon.

"Four years ago," Nat explained, "water was
brought to Boston from Lake Cochituate, twenty
miles away. Bostonians are no longer dependent on
wells or cisterns. Water is brought directly to the
houses via a brick acqueduct, stone tunnel, and iron
pipes. By the mere twist of a handle, hotels, restaurants, and nearly every home in the city has water
gushing upon command. At any rate," he added, "every home of the upper and middle classes."

It was full darkness when they turned into the
crowded street leading to the theater. Huge flares lit
up the marquee and patrons clamored at the entrance. All types of private and public conveyances attempted to enter the teeming thoroughfare, but
uniformed police dispatched all except those attend-
ing the play. Theater boys in bright blue jackets

and tight yellow pants gentled skittish horses with a white-gloved hand on bridle, setting carriages into line for the slow movement up to the entrance. Then, saluting for a penny tip, they moved on to others in need of their services.

The house lights were dimming as Nat's party entered the theater and by the time they were ushered to plush, red-cushioned box seats, the play had begun.

At intermission, Melanie gazed about the theater from their elaborately carved and decorated private balcony. Alternate panels of carved mahogany and cherrywood, slit with large plate glass mirrors, captured her wandering eye. Glass chandeliers, dimmed during the play, had their wicks turned up. Light reflecting in the mirrors illuminated elegantly gowned women and impeccably turned out men.

On a private balcony close by, a lovely woman in dove-gray satin, resplendent in rubies and diamonds, smiled warmly at the entrance of a tall, frosty-haired Negro. She offered her hand and he took it, returning the smile with a flash of white teeth in an ebony face.

"Nat, look!" Melanie's eyes widened in surprise as she watched the group of seven other people greet the black man with warmth and respect. The women nodded and smiled. The men shook hands. All acknowledged his presence with enthusiasm. He accepted a proffered seat between an elderly man with sharp, piercing eyes and muttonchop whiskers, and a younger, esthetic-looking man in fawn-colored frock coat.

Leaning forward to let Jared and Laura hear, Nat explained in a low voice, "The black man is Lewis Hayden, a fugitive slave and one of the heads of the black Masonic Order. He is a well-respected member of the Abolitionist Vigilance Committee and a political leader of importance in Boston. He heads the Underground Railroad, conducting slaves in safety to

Canada. The man with muttonchop whiskers is William Lloyd Garrison, a fervent Abolitionist and publisher of the widely read paper, the *Liberator.* Garrison calls Hayden his staunchest ally."

"Who are the others?" Laura asked.

"The man on Hayden's left is Ralph Waldo Emerson, a man of letters whose fame is well known; particularly in connection with the now-deceased Margaret Fuller. The lady in gray satin is one of the foremost proponents of schools and education for the deaf, Julia Ward Howe. She is seated beside her husband, Dr. Samuel Gridley Howe, ardent reformer and promoter of education for the blind. Next to Howe is the Englishman, George Thompson, an antislavery orator of no little consequence. His inflammatory speeches have done more to convert do-nothing-dogoodists into active, meaningful Abolitionists than any other method of conversion, aside from the *Liberator.* The woman on the other side of Thompson is Harriet Beecher Stowe, whose play we enjoy tonight. Next to her is James Russell Lowell, the poet. The dark-haired beauty beside him is unknown to me."

During the rest of intermission, there was a great coming and going in the balcony nearby. Engrossed, Melanie felt she was watching subjects of an unknown kingdom pay their respects to royalty.

"Boston," Nat told them later, "is a city of teachers and reformers, notably Abolitionists; as well as religious zealots, such as Transcendentalists and Unitarians."

After the theater, they joined a milling crowd outside to await their carriage. As they passed through the theater lobby, the black man, accompanied by others in his party, greeted Nat with warm pleasure. It was apparent he had known this elite group well and for some time. Introductions were made and light conversation went on all about her as Melanie observed Nat at the fringe of the group speaking earnestly to Lewis Hayden, whose silver-gray head reached nearly the same height as Nat's.

The carriage wound through the streets and eventually stopped before an elegant porticoed entrance. A liveried doorman helped them alight and they walked over a plush red carpet, to enter the crowded main foyer. At a small curved podium, a maitre' d presided zealously over his reservation list.

"Mr. Larimore, you requested a private dining room on the second level," he stated imperiously.

Nat nodded and they followed in the wake of a white-coated waiter. Melanie took in the plush surroundings. Huge, many-faceted crystal chandeliers hung from the three-story ceiling to the second level, lighting the entire scene with the blazing brilliance of multichimneyed whale-oil lamps. On three sides of the large room, ornate frescoed balconies, alternating one between the other on the second and third levels, curved out over the main salon. Melanie counted eight on each side, four on each level. On the wall opposite them, a wide, gracefully curved staircase swept upward. People were ascending and descending the purple carpeted stairs; and a few elegantly bedecked ladies, apparently feeling this a prime place to search for friends and acquaintances, showed off stylish gowns while poised with one richly beringed hand on the golden banister. On a dais at one end of the dining room, a string quartet strove valiantly to be heard above the crowd.

Melanie, on Nat's arm, climbed the staircase in the wake of Laura and Jared. Halfway up, Laura paused to catch her breath.

"Perhaps we should have taken a table in the main dining room, my dear," Jared said worriedly. "You should not be climbing these long stairs in your condition."

"I'm fine, Jared." She brushed aside his concern. "I

will not sit like an old woman just because I am
enceinte!"

A group of people surged around them while
Laura leaned heavily on the rail, scanning the sea of
faces below.

"There is James Talbot, waving at us." Her voice
held a note of surprise. "After his reception at
luncheon today, I'm surprised he would acknowledge
our existence!" she added sharply.

Melanie gazed in the direction indicated and saw
James making his way through the crowd toward the
staircase.

"He'd better not thrust himself upon us this evening." Nat's tone was threatening.

"He certainly is a handsome man," Laura observed
in a low, musing voice, turning her head to throw a
taunting smile at Nat.

James had nearly reached the foot of the staircase
and Melanie raised pleading eyes to her fiancé.

"Nat, please do not make a scene."

"He will attempt to speak with you, Melanie. And
as your betrothed, I forbid it! He is of no account! I
resent his being seen in your company."

"Suppose I *want* to speak with him?" Melanie
raised her chin defiantly.

Nat's eyes narrowed and his jaw jutted stubbornly.
"I forbid it!" he repeated, taking her arm again to
urge her up the stairs.

Melanie wrenched her arm from his grasp.

"Nat, you are unreasonable! I have known James
Talbot for many years. It is my wish to speak with
him! I will join you in a few moments."

And she left him sharing astonishment with Jared
and Laura while she made her way down to James,
who climbed to meet her.

His searching gaze caressed her face, but despite
soft warmth in his eyes, Melanie recognized anxiety
lurking in their depths.

"I know this is awkward for you, my dear," he said, glancing up at Nat, who stood with blazing eyes and rage-reddened face. "But, I must tell you there are forces at work that will prove my sincerity when I admonish you to avoid marriage to Nathaniel. You will need a friend, very soon, I fear! And do not believe Nat's lies about me! He has his own reasons for turning you against me!"

"James, what are you saying? What is to happen?"

"There is no time now," he answered, noting his half-brother's descent. "I will be in Marblehead even before you arrive tomorrow. Meet me at the bottom of the cliff at Hazard's Bluff as soon as you can slip away unnoticed. I will be watching for you."

"But we are not going to Marblehead tomorrow—"

Before her words were out, James had kissed her hand and disappeared in the throng surging toward the stairs.

"Melanie, we are waiting!" Nat's tight, angry voice was at her shoulder. She allowed him to pull her arm through his and they turned to mount the steps once more.

On the second floor, they followed the waiter down a long hall through a dark paneled door into an elegantly furnished private dining room. Heavy purple velvet draperies, curved to fit the balcony rail, muffled sounds from the main dining salon below. The decor was opulent; done in plush reds, pale pinks with gold frieze and tassels, mirrored walls and plum-colored satin cushions. Blushing, Melanie recalled a passage in a forbidden novel perused while awaiting a fitting at Goulet's. It was the description of a brothel, and the comparison rose now, unbidden, to her mind.

As the waiter prepared libations for all, Melanie opened the draperies and stepped out on the tiny balcony. She searched the crowd for James, but he was nowhere to be found. A sea of laughing, chattering people were oblivious to eyes staring at them from above. Laura came to stand at her side.

"That was a foolish move on your part," Laura said in a low tone. "You couldn't possibly have done anything to make Nat more angry. The bad blood between the brothers is well known."

Melanie was about to respond heatedly, when Nat joined them.

"I would like to speak with Melanie alone, Laura," he said solemnly.

With a faint smile, Laura stepped back into the private dining room.

"I need not tell you, Melanie, there is no love lost between James and myself—" Nat began.

"That is none of my concern!" Melanie broke in. "The feud is between you and your brother! Why must the whole world side with you in this?"

Nat silenced her with a gentle hand on her lips.

"Melanie, I think only of you when I say that friendliness between you and James will give gossips a field day. Many are aware of his former intentions to court you, which he conveniently forgot when the Polynesian girl's dowry was a fortune in black pearls. Seeking you out in public when you are now betrothed to me, and while his wife lies dying in Marblehead, is a juicy morsel for wagging tongues!"

"If he has a fortune in black pearls, why is he crying poor and trying to borrow money for ships?"

"After the ceremonial wedding in the islands, he bought another ship. It, too, was confiscated with a cargo of slaves, just off the African coast. Then, mingling southern funds with money from the pearls, he lived with his new wife for nearly two years in royal splendor on the continent. When the plantation owners tracked him down, he had no money left to reimburse them. He arranged, somehow, to lease back his confiscated ship and convinced the plantation owners to give him more time. Then, he sailed to

New Bedford with his bride and tried to convince old friends to finance his dastardly venture. Obviously, he was unsuccessful. Now, the clock runs out . . . and he has neither ships nor money to fulfill his promises. He begins to panic."

"Will the southerners finance another ship for him?"

"They have put him on notice that he will fulfill his contract without further assistance from them, or he will forfeit his life."

Melanie gasped: "Nat, surely we must help him!"

Nat shook his head.

"James has ever been imprudent with money. Pouring good funds after bad is comparable to pouring sand through a sieve!" He placed his hand under her chin, forcing her to look at him. "He seeks your ships, Melanie. Do you want to befoul them with the stench of slaves? James cares naught for you, his wife, or anything in the world but himself!"

"But we cannot let him die!"

"He will find a way out of this as he has always done. James is a destroyer, Melanie. Were we to help him now, he would turn our very alms against us! He is obsessed with the acquiring of everything I own, telling himself it is rightfully his. He will pour more thought and energy into my undoing than using what he has to attain wealth on his own. The southern money and that realized from the pearls could have gone to make him wealthy the rest of his life. But, instead of investing it wisely, he had two extravagant years of high living and made two halfhearted attempts to fulfill his promises; which, had he succeeded, would have given him half again as much wealth. Dastardly though that mission may have been, had he accomplished it, he would have used the money to destroy—not to build—to ruin the reputation and empire built by Jonas Marfrey. All because he feels he was unjustly denied his birthright." Nat turned away. "I cannot help him, Melanie! I will not help him ruin me and all Jonas worked to achieve!"

"Nat! He is your brother . . ."

Nat's eyes were cold as he turned again to face her.

"Jonas denied fathering James, and I believe him. In any case, there is doubt as to whether or not Jonas fathered *me*!" He stared out over the balcony. "There is another consideration." He went on. "James is a slaver, and I, an Abolitionist! He represents all that I abhor! I fight to free slaves, and he hunts them down like animals!" He reached out, taking Melanie in his arms. "Surely we could not have the same blood in our veins, Melanie! We are at opposite ends of the pole!"

In the circle of his arms, staring up into his earnest blue eyes, Melanie dismissed all thoughts of James. She loved Nat with all her being, and at this moment, the love shared between them was all that mattered.

Nat smiled down at her.

"Come, my love. Let us sup and enjoy the rest of the evening."

The door to the private dining room had opened and a flurry of activity accompanied two white-coated waiters transferring plates from a table on wheels to the oval dining table.

"There is an extra place, Nat," Laura observed as they stepped back into the room. "Did I understand that your business manager, Paul Lanier, is to join us?"

Nat nodded, frowning: "He should have arrived by now," he said, taking out his gold pocket watch. "Perhaps some business matter has detained him."

Nat and Jared began to speak of the candle factory on Nantucket, and the women fell into silence. Melanie's thoughts were confused, and she tried to sort them out.

If she were to believe Nathaniel, James's attentions were not without purpose. He wanted her ships and,

were she not betrothed to Nat, would most likely woo
her for her dowry, upon his wife's death. Indeed,
upon speculation she realized that even her betrothal
did not seem to deter him from boldly speaking to
her as though she were an elderly and available spinster without masculine mentors to see to her best interests. For in this day and time, young women did
not have a say in controlling their own property. Fathers, brothers, guardians, or other male relatives administered their resources until marriage, at which
time females and their wealth were transferred and
subject to the authority of their husbands. Melanie's
ships were in the care and custody of her brother,
Jared, and when she married Nat, he would then control them; unless, perchance, she married a widowered
James Talbot, who, as her father had warned, coveted
the whaling vessels of her inheritance.

The waiters left the room and as the door closed, it
opened again. A tall, slender man of middle years appeared in the doorway. His hair was dark and an olive complexion emphasized distinguished gray at the
temples. Large, earnest brown eyes took in the occu-
pants of the dining room and came to rest, with an
expression of wonder, on Laura's dazzling beauty.

I have seen that look before! Melanie thought in
exasperation. *Apparently, here is another to fall under Laura's enchantment!*

"Paul!" Nat broke the spell. "You're just in time.
I'd about given you up!"

Tearing his eyes from Laura, Paul placed a flat,
square box into Nat's outstretched hand.

"Sorry to be tardy, Nathaniel," he said in a deep,
quiet voice. "It could not be helped."

They spoke confidentially for a moment or two,
then turned to the others in the room. Paul and
Jared shook hands in greeting and he was then
presented to the ladies.

Melanie judged him to be in his early or mid-forties. She was favorably impressed with his quiet, deep voice and keen, piercing eyes. She noted that when his gaze fell upon Laura, however, he seemed mesmerized and a smile hovered about the corners of his pleasant, full-lipped mouth.

Amazing! Melanie thought. *Men are like small boys in a toy shop when it comes to a beautiful woman!*

"Tell me, Mr. Lanier, where is Mrs. Lanier this evening?" Laura asked coyly.

"Mrs. Lanier passed away nearly seven years ago," Paul answered quietly. "I have not found another."

Laura dropped her eyes. "Oh," she murmured, "I am so sorry!"

She raised her gaze to him again, and Melanie was reminded of a cat observing a canary.

She realized then that Nat also observed Paul, and this little byplay. His eyes held a glint of amusement, and he too, had the trace of a smile hovering about his lips.

Jared, apparently enjoying his meal, carried on a conversation to which a bemused Paul Lanier gave only divided attention. Melanie recalled Jared's words that morning in her cabin. *During pregnancy, her beauty is threatened. It means nothing. My wife loves me.*

Looking at Jared now, Melanie realized she had been mistaken in believing him obtuse. Her brother, though giving no outward sign, was not insensible to the game being played out before him.

Paul was the epitome of a gentleman. Nothing was ever said that could possibly be interpreted in a disrespectful manner. He paid Laura no lavish compliments; he just worshipped quietly at the altar of her beauty. Many husbands would have resented his barely concealed, infatuated gaze; but since Jared chose to appear incognizant of the situation, it was simply a source of enjoyment to Laura, wonderment to Melanie, and amusement to Nat.

The main course, fowl stuffed with oysters and clams, had just been served when Paul turned to Nat. "Your first mate, Stokes, tells me morning fog should burn off well before midday. You will have a nice sail up the coast to Marblehead tomorrow."

Melanie looked at Nat in surprise. "Marblehead?" Her eyes widened. "James Talbot said we would sail there tomorrow!"

She did not miss the glances exchanged between Paul and Nat.

After a long moment, Nat turned to Melanie.

"Would you enjoy seeing your new home?"

"Oh, yes!" She clapped her hands in a sudden display of pleasure, then shyly reached out to touch his arm. "I would dearly enjoy seeing it. Thank you!" Her warm gaze met his and she felt a rush of love and happiness in that special moment.

Then, as a new thought occurred to her, she turned anxiously to Jared. "Have you agreed to sail?"

"Of course, Melanie! We are all going."

"But you have always avoided the sea—" She stopped, realizing she was embarrassing her brother.

Nat looked up in surprise.

"You have an aversion to the sea, Jared? I was unaware that it bothered you!"

"In bygone years, Nat," Jared hastened to assure him, "when I was a child! Father so loved the sea. I studiously avoided it because he wanted me to share his obsession! But that was long ago . . ." His eyes, earnestly gazing into Nat's face, seemed almost apologetic for his failing in the esteem of his friend. "Do not concern yourself, Nat. I am well able to oversee the candle factory on Nantucket!"

Only Melanie, knowing Jared so well, detected the faint hint of fear behind his eyes.

Nat gazed silently at him, weighing his words.

"Jared," he said quietly, "Paul can oversee, as well. It only means a trip or so a month and it falls naturally into his line of duty. As for tomorrow, we could take a carriage to Marblehead in much shorter time. I only thought the ladies might enjoy a sail . . ."

"I have had enough of carriages!" Laura put in petulantly. "The ride from New Bedford to Boston was the last I care to endure for some time!"

Jared smiled, patting her hand: "No need to fuss, Laura!" Then, turning to Nat, "I am looking forward to sailing up the coast. We are not crossing oceans! And since I insist on sailing to Nantucket on overseeing jaunts, I will begin now to accustom myself to the rolling sea!"

Regretting that she had begun a conversation causing her brother discomfort, Melanie changed the subject abruptly.

"Nat, is the house nearly finished?"

"There is some interior work yet to be done. However, it will be ready in time for our wedding next month."

"How long will it take us to get to Marblehead tomorrow?" Laura broke in, imperiously changing the subject once more. "I'm not certain an ocean voyage is the thing for me just now, either."

"Three, mayhap four hours at the outside, depending upon prevailing winds." Nat laughed. "And a trip up the coast is hardly an ocean voyage! You will be sailing on a longer voyage when we leave for New Bedford in another day or two. We sail along the coastline then also; around Cape Cod, through Nantucket Sound to Buzzard's Bay, then into New Bedford harbor."

They completed their repast. Dishes were cleared and the waiter brought in a chilled magnum of champagne in a large silver bucket. When the cork had been popped and glasses filled, Nat raised his glass in a toast.

"To my beautiful bride to be!" he said, gazing affectionately at Melanie.

Glasses were raised, then refilled, and raised again.

Nat reached for the flat black velvet box Paul had placed into his hands upon arrival, and turned to Melanie, taking her hands in one of his.

"Melanie, my dear," he said gravely, "I want to present your betrothal gift. I trust you will be pleased."

Solemnly, he placed the box in her hands and sat back to watch as she opened it. Melanie pressed the tiny gold clasp at the front and watched the lid rise on a hidden spring. There, on a background of white satin, blazed a necklace of breathtaking beauty; emeralds the size of robin's eggs were interspersed with round blue-white diamonds. Many-faceted gems caught the candlelight, reflecting their brilliance repeatedly; dissolving the incandescence only to pick it up again in another gleam, another blaze of glory. The perfection of each stone was obvious, even to one not versed in the symmetry of gems. Melanie's eyes were drawn in fascination beyond all willpower.

She gasped. "Oh, Nat! It is utterly sublime!"

She took the necklace from the box and held it at arm's length. It was impossible to define the strange, transcendental emotions brought into being by the exquisite magnificence of the green icy fire flashing from the emeralds and the blue-white lightning from the diamonds.

So fascinated was she with her betrothal gift, Melanie failed to notice the shadow passing over Laura's face at sight of the necklace. Thus, she was unprepared for her sister-in-law's sharp voice cutting into her reverie.

"The jewels should be mine, Nat! They perfectly match my eyes!"

Laura tried to sound coy, teasing, but the statement pierced Melanie's heart, for she saw, beneath the ban-

tering tone, that Laura harbored anger at the gift.
She realized then that her brother's wife had seen the
necklace before, and perhaps, laid claim to it. There
was also the possibility that Nat had indeed acquired
the necklace for Laura! The gems certainly did match
her seductive green eyes. Melanie placed the precious
jewels carefully back into their resting place in the
box.

"The necklace is for my wife," Nat answered
evenly, eyes fastened on Melanie. "The future mother
of my children."

But Nat's words did not penetrate Melanie's
thoughts. Rather, it was his tone as he spoke, without
looking at Laura; as if the matter had been previously discussed and he was reiterating his decision
once and for all, closing the subject.

The full moon cast a silver glow across Boston harbor when they left the open victoria. At the foot of
the steps, the shallop waited. Stokes, the first mate,
came immediately to speak in low tones to Nat.

"Yer friend, Talbot, were talkin' to th' crew early
on."

"What about the *Olympia*?" Nat asked quickly.
"Did he speak with her crew, also?"

"No, sor! She sailed a'fore he come. But I must tell
ye' . . ."

Melanie could hear no more as Nat bent his head
to listen to Stokes's barely whispered words. She saw
the sudden, calculating look in Nat's eyes.

A husky, swarthy seaman Melanie had heard called
Kreuger held the shallop steady, waiting for the captain's entrance. His little beady eyes followed Nat's
lips as he answered Stokes. And Melanie wondered if
the sailor could read his words.

Then Nat shrugged. "There is nothing to be done
about it," he said. "Get word to Hawkes; Paul is taking care of the rest."

With a nod, Nat joined his party in the shallop.
Stokes pushed off and signaled the swarthy crewman
to commence rowing with the others. He watched
them pull away, then mounted the stairs and faded
into the darkness of Commercial Street.

As they sped over the black, silver-streaked waters
of Boston harbor, a sudden wind sent wisps of cloud
scudding across the face of the moon and flicked droplets from the tips of waves into the boat. Spray, like
needles of ice, stung Melanie's cheeks before Nat
drew her into a warm, protective embrace. She
snuggled close, grateful for his concern. But she was
disheartened, and she knew the reason.

The betrothal gift, beautiful though it was, sad-
dened her. Convinced it was originally meant for
Laura, it would always be a reminder that it was her
brother's wife who first claimed Nat's love, and the
knowledge pained Melanie.

The wind died as they came alee of the ship. While
rowers maneuvered to come alongside, Nat tightened
his arms about Melanie and whispered into her ear.

"Are you happy with your betrothal gift, my love?"

"Yes, Nat," she lied. "I am very happy . . ."

CHAPTER SEVEN

Melanie lay wide awake staring out the large port-hole at slow, rolling swells in the bay. The wind had eased and a waning moon followed a rippling path across the water to throw a pale shaft of light over the foot of her bed.

A waning moon . . . a waning love . . . The words of an ancient saying crossed her mind. She was pensive, restless, fearful; and could not reason why. True, her happiness at sight of the betrothal gift had melted away with the realization of its original purpose, but it was hers now, as Nat would be hers this time next month.

Wooing sleep, she relaxed her muscles and gave herself over to the measured cradling of the waves. Sometime later, halfway between sleeping and waking, she sat up with a start. The cry of a child was carried on the wind! Fully awake, she waited, but heard only creaking timbers as the ship rocked gently on the water.

It was only a dream! she thought, then tried to persuade herself it was the sound of gulls crying in the night.

Moments later, she heard Stokes's voice in the companionway, and wondered if he had just now boarded.

Her mind, circling, wheeling, would not be stilled again. She thought of the evening in Boston. Nat had gone to a great deal of trouble to make this night as nearly perfect as possible. He had been kind, attentive, and concerned. It was exciting to see the politics and unrest of present day Boston through his eyes; to visit a theater far more grand than any she'd ever seen, and to dine at the lavish restaurant with the cream of New England society.

She remembered Laura's look of naked envy, anger, and shock when Nat presented the betrothal gift . . . and she saw James Talbot's soft brown eyes dimmed with anxiety, as he pleaded with her to disbelieve Nat's lies about him. She couldn't help wondering if indeed Nat belabored James's faults to turn her against his half-brother. James's admonishment about her pending marriage rang in Melanie's ears and she resolved to meet him at the foot of the cliff at Hazard's Bluff. Then, perhaps some of her questions would be answered.

A strange loneliness engulfed her as she stared out the porthole at the moonlit waters, and she felt a sudden yearning for Nat. She recalled their parting at her cabin door nearly two hours ago.

"Melanie," he'd said, "tell me what disturbs you. All I want is your happiness."

"I am tired, Nat. Nothing more. A good night's sleep is the best remedy."

He'd kissed her gently and held her close for a moment.

"Sleep well, my love. There is no need for early rising, since we sail with the tide."

We sail with the tide. The words should have thrilled her. They sailed to Marblehead where her life with Nathaniel would soon begin to unfold; a life of love, and children . . . and happiness.

I am just now beginning to live! she told herself crossly. *Why do I feel there are tears ahead? Why do I search for trouble?*

But deep in her heart, she knew there was no need to search. Trouble had entered Melanie's life the day her brother Jared married Laura. From that day forward, Melanie had been constantly undermined by Laura's assault upon her psyche. Laura's habit of "pointing out for your own good . . ." filled Melanie with nagging, tormenting doubts about herself; her abilities, her appearance, even her intelligence. And Melanie remembered a conversation with her father before he sailed on his last voyage.

"I am not certain now that Laura will make Jared happy," he'd said in a ruminative tone. "She needs a man stronger than your brother will ever be, to curb her overwhelming self-interest. She is enamored of herself to the exclusion of all else, even her son."

He'd turned to Melanie, speaking earnestly.

"Laura is jealous of you, for she recognizes in you qualities she does not possess. Watch her! And do not weaken; for little by little, she would take from you that which you most treasure."

And too the gypsy's words came back to her . . .
She will take from you, if she can! Be wary of her!

For Melanie, overtired and filled with a vague uneasiness, sleep was elusive. Try as she would, Melanie could not shake off the persistent sense of foreboding that engulfed her earlier as she dressed for the evening. Perhaps a breath of sea air would soothe ragged nerves and bring on the blessedness of sleep. She slipped out of bed and, donning a pale pink peignoir over her gown, silently left the cabin.

She paused in the dim recess of the companionway. Under a bright moon, the main deck lay white as snow. There was no one in sight. The fresh dew was cool and moist under her bare feet as she stepped into full moonlight. Then, speeding like a wraith across the vast whiteness, she flew into the shadows in the lee of the chart house. Breathless, heart pounding, she started in fear at the first stroke of the ship's clock striking three bells. When her pulse steadied,

Melanie made her way slowly around to the windward side and stood at the rail looking out to sea.

An incoming tide swelled the harbor waters. Riding at anchor, the *Mirimar* took the surging billows in stride, cresting the waves, then slipping easily down into shallow troughs. Enthralled with the moonlit magic of the scene before her, Melanie experienced a sudden sharp memory of a childhood voyage when she stood at the helm with her father on just such a night.

She raised her eyes to the star-filled sky.

"Help me, Father," she prayed, and was uncertain whether she spoke to Ephraim Hardy, or the Deity, Father of all. In that same moment, she questioned her reason for the prayer, ultimately deciding it came from some deep need hidden within her soul.

A barely audible sound startled her and she slipped into the dark recessed doorway of the chart house. A moment later, Nat passed so close she could almost touch him. He stopped at the rail, still within her vision, and stared out to sea as she, herself, had done at that very place. He looked so sad, so vulnerable, standing there in the moonlight, Melanie wanted to go comfort him—but in that instant, Laura appeared at his side.

"The necklace should have been mine, Nat! You implied as much when you showed it to me nearly five years ago!" Laura's voice was tense, as though continuing a conversation where it recently left off.

"I told you then, and I tell you now," his tone was exasperated. "The necklace was acquired for my wife; the mother of my children."

"When you made love to me in the berth where Melanie now sleeps, you led me to believe we would marry—"

"No, Laura!" Nat's cold voice cut into her words before she'd finished. "Until our last night together, marriage was never brought up between us."

"You said I was a fever in your blood . . ."

"So I did! But, I also said you are *not* the woman I want to wife!"

She turned to face him then. The wind tangled itself in her long red hair and pressed the filmy negligee against full breasts and the barely discernible mound of the child she carried. Slowly, sinuously, Laura's arms encircled Nat's neck. Her words came sharp and clear to Melanie's ears.

"And remember what *I* said, Nat! When you lie beside your wife each night, your loins will course with longing for *me*!"

Unmoving, he stared down at her.

Close as she was, Melanie saw his eyes searching Laura's beautiful face; then, praying this was a nightmare from which she would soon awaken, she saw him bend his head to her waiting lips. Mesmerized, Melanie watched with a pain so great she could not move.

Pinned between them and the wide expanse of deck, Melanie was a prisoner. From her dark hiding place, she looked on in shocked silence while the pantomime playing out before her eyes dealt a death blow to her hopes and dreams of a future with Nathaniel Larimore. And when his arms tightened about her sister-in-law, Melanie's love for Nat shriveled and died beneath the icy gale howling through her anguished soul.

A long moment later, Nat dropped his arms and, walking swiftly toward the companionway, left Laura standing there in the moonlight. Melanie heard her soft laughter as she turned to follow.

Melanie was numb, rooted to the spot. A vast coldness occupied the space where her heart had been. She would never know how long she remained in the shadowed doorway. It seemed hours before sluggish limbs carried her back across the moonlit deck to the relative comfort of her cabin. There, her dazed, befuddled mind, alternately vengeful and fearful, tried to sort out nebulous, fragmented wisps of thought in a vain attempt to bring order out of chaos.

The first pale streaks of dawn blended sea and sky at the easternmost edge of the world. Through the window of the master cabin, Melanie watched stars begin to dim while the pale moon, low on the same horizon, retreated slowly, hiding at last behind a puff of morning cloud.

Melanie's eyes were wide and dry. She lay naked on the bed, curled into a tight ball. Her muscles were tense and stiff. How long had she lain here? How many hours had passed since she stood in the deep, dark portal of the chart house witnessing a scene that turned her heart to ice and dealt her faith a tortuous death? In the space of a few moments, her world had shattered, dissolved before her eyes.

She writhed in agony as the scene repeated itself in her mind. The image of Nat's arms about Jared's pregnant wife was etched into the convolutions of her brain, and a thousand years could not erase the pain of watching all her worst suspicions and fears come to fruition.

When you made love to me in the berth where Melanie now sleeps . . . Laura had said.

Praying she was wrong, Melanie had sensed the succubus of Laura haunting this bed; now, she took no satisfaction in the accuracy of her perception.

Melanie's life had been sheltered, built on a foundation made firm by her father, her brother, and the far-flung ships of her family empire. Now she felt as though somewhere between dusk and dawn a hurricane had ripped away her moorings. She was helpless, bereft. There was no one to turn to in her torment. Her father was beyond reach . . . her ships belonged to the man who would claim her in marriage.

And what of Jared? To tell him of his faithless wife would destroy him. That her brother loved Laura, Melanie was certain. His wife and children were his life.

"We've been used, Jared!" she whispered into the pale dawn. "Laura married you to spite Nat, and now, Nat would use marriage to me as a cloak of innocence over their illicit love!"

Her brother's face, gentle, kind, and vulnerable, crossed her mind.

"My God!" The cry wrenched from her constricted throat. "What will I do?"

Her only answer was creaking timbers and lapping water as the tide cradled the ship.

Melanie's newfound knowledge brought with it a bitterness at her own stubborn refusal to recognize the truth earlier. Trying to follow the precepts she'd been taught, that some good is found in all souls, she'd made excuses for Laura; tried desperately to blind herself to the inherent evil of Laura's selfishness.

As a child, Melanie had felt a deep dislike for Laura. Perhaps, intuitively, she had understood the differences between Laura and other girls her age. Laura had developed a protective armor, a watchful, ever-alert awareness rarely found in one so young. Even as a child she stood apart, speculating, evaluating, making the best of any chance coming her way. Laura was always first in line to claim attention and approval, earned or not; and tireless in her efforts to elevate herself above her schoolmates. In short, Melanie had early recognized Laura's ruthless personal ambition: she would use any means to gratify her wishes with no conscience whatsoever regarding the rights of others.

Do not place all blame upon Laura! Melanie told

herself sternly. *What of Nat? His crime is worse! Making love to me; using me to get to Laura! And friend to Jared, the man whose wife he covets!*

For again, Melanie discounted Nat's words; all except his acknowledgment that Laura was a fever in his blood. Her sense of insecurity, planted and nurtured by her sister-in-law, blinded her to the possibility that the rest of his protestations might be true. Melanie was certain that Nat, though wounded by Laura's marriage to Jared, still loved her and sought this marriage to assuage his hurt. Later, Melanie believed, when Laura was delivered of her child, they would resume their affair under the very noses of Jared and Melanie.

"We've been fools, Jared! Fools!" she whispered into the fleeting shadows.

Then, rage arose within her and the sudden, blazing hatred she'd felt for Laura in the carriage on the way to Boston flared into being again.

If marriage to Nat under these circumstances was untenable, living unmarried at Halcyon House with Laura was utterly impossible! To watch Jared's increasing anxiety in the face of Laura's deception; to listen to his excuses for her while knowing the true state of things, would be too much for Melanie's endurance. Though cognizant of his hypocrisy, Melanie decided marriage to Nat was the lesser of two evils!

"I will marry Nathaniel Larimore!" she said aloud into the first light of dawn. "And I will make him sorry he ever thought he could use me for his own ends."

She wondered then if it was possible to change destiny. Her feelings of helplessness fluctuated with bitterness. *Perhaps I am not meant to marry Nat!* she thought suddenly. *Perhaps I am only an instrument in some predesigned plan to bring Laura and Nat together once more.*

Then, remembering her father's belief that all

things were possible if he so set his course, she made herself a promise. *Whatever happens,* she vowed, *I will never again be caught vulnerable and unprepared!*

Melanie's betrothal gift was on the table beside her berth. She reached for it now and opened the box. On its bed of white satin, the necklace glimmered in the pale dawn like some strange meteor from a far-off star. The cold, icy green fire and stark silver icicles seemed to stab at her heart, numbing the pain . . . taking away all feeling.

When the sun was fully over the horizon, Melanie slept, oblivious to the grating rumble of the anchor chain when it was pulled into place. And as the wind took the sails and the *Mirimar* skimmed through Boston harbor into the surging waters of Massachusetts Bay, she slept on.

It was nearly midmorning when a knock at the door awakened her. Struggling from deep slumber, Melanie heard the knock again, then Jared's voice, muffled, close to the door.

"Melanie? Are you still asleep?"

"A moment, Jared."

Reaching for her peignoir, she slipped into it and started across the rug. She stopped halfway to the door as the memory of predawn hours flooded over her.

"Melanie?"

She moved slowly toward the door and opened it.

Jared stared at her through startled eyes.

"Are you unwell?"

"Tired, Jared. Just tired."

"We are now at sea. Nat says we should arrive at Marblehead in two or three hours, if the winds prevail."

She stared at him through dull eyes.

He hesitated, waiting for a response.

"Please tell Mahmoud to bring black coffee—now!"

"Mahmoud?" Jared's tone was puzzled, questioning her sudden authoritative voice and apparent unconcern for her dishabille.

"Mahmoud! And tell him I want plenty of hot water for my bath!"

Jared's brown eyes were quizzical and his brow wrinkled in confusion. He shot her a strange, questioning look, then went to do her bidding.

Melanie stood before the mirror brushing her long brown hair. A stranger looked back at her. She searched her tired face. A milestone had been reached and taken its toll. Her chin had a determined lift, and when she looked deep into her own eyes, now she saw a subtle difference. Once, innocent dreams and illusions shone from their depths; now, weary sophistication dimmed her gaze.

Mahmoud knocked, and entered at her response. He placed a tray with steaming carafe and a wide-bottomed mug on the small bamboo table.

"May I bring the tub, missy?"

She nodded and he left.

She sat in the butterfly chair and poured a mug full of coffee. Sipping slowly, she tried to blank out her mind, concentrating on savoring the black brew. She tried not to think to the future, nor backward to hours preceding this moment. But she was only partially successful. Something pressed against the closed door of her consciousness; something persistent, to which she had not given credence because her attention had focused on all that subsequently occurred.

Why had James Talbot felt she would need a friend? Somewhat reluctantly, she had dismissed his words at the time, telling herself they were a ruse to speak with her alone; to enlist her aid in his need for a ship. Indeed, perhaps that was the case—but then again, perhaps not! His words: *You may need a friend in the near future* had been spoken urgently,

and at jeopardy to himself, since Nat stood threateningly nearby! Why? What did James Talbot know
that she did not? More questions arose in Melanie's
mind; unanswerable questions she'd never dreamed of
before this moment.

She left the chair and wandered restlessly about the
room. She picked up objects and put them down
again, vaguely aware of a transformation taking place
inside herself. It seemed she had two distinctly different personalities, each struggling to survive the other.

Mahmoud knocked again. This time he laboriously
dragged in the oval-shaped copper tub, high at one
end, where Melanie looked forward to resting her
aching head. He left again to bring bath water. It
took a long time to fill the tub. Melanie wanted it
brimful and hot. She intended to do more than soak;
she intended to relax and sort out her thinking before they reached Marblehead, where she'd be face-
to-face alone with James Talbot. Her resolve to see
him grew stronger with each passing moment.

Mahmoud placed a huge, fluffy Turkish towel on a
stool near the tub and left for the last time. Melanie
piled her hair atop her head, fastened it with hair-
pins, and stepped out of her garments. She stood
nude before the mirror looking objectively at herself.
Her skin glowed with the soft patina of ivory; her figure, petite, round, was every bit as seductive as
Laura's. And her breasts, though smaller, were full
and firm with enticing, pink-tipped nipples. Her tiny
waist, scarcely the span of a man's two hands, emphasized the gentle, pleasing curve of her hips, while
round, firm buttocks led gracefully to long, well-
shaped legs. She raised a slender arm, viewing herself
from all angles, under a merciless eye.

*The only difference between Laura's figure and
mine,* she decided, *is that I am petite. Also, she displays her charms to advantage, while heretofore, I
have always conformed to modesty!*

She met her own gaze in the mirror again, mimicking the bold, seductive look in her sister-in-law's eyes when in the presence of an attractive man.

"I must fight fire with fire!" she said aloud. "I will not live in Laura's house, spinster aunt to my brother's children; unappreciated helper, buffer, whipping post to my sister-in-law and burden to Jared! I will marry Nat Larimore . . . and make him forget he ever loved Laura!"

She walked to the tub and stepped inside. The water was hot. She lowered her body slowly into it and felt her tense muscles ease. Leaning her head against the high copper back, she relaxed her body while her mind went on sorting, sifting, seeking various avenues of attaining the goal she sought, wondering if indeed it was meant to be.

Reposing languidly in the warm water, Melanie lazily inhaled the scent of roses in her bath oil. Her skin felt silky, sensuous, as she slowly ran her hands over arms and shoulders, spreading the water over her smooth skin. She leaned back in the tub. Inert, exhausted from the inner battle of emotions, she closed her eyes, and dozed.

She was startled into wakefulness by a knock at the door.

"Melanie?" It was Nat's voice. "May I come in?"

"No!" she answered, without hesitation.

"Are you ill? May I get something for you?"

"No, thank you."

A moment's pause, then Nat opened the door and stepped inside.

Melanie lay quietly, gazing up at him.

"I told you not to enter!" Her voice was even and her eyes cold, blank.

"You're bathing!" He stared at her in astonishment.

"Obviously! That's why I told you not to enter."

He walked over and stood looking down at her.

The water barely covered her breasts. Small as she was, the tub was still too short to allow her legs to extend straight out, so one knee was slightly bent and the other leg half out of the water with her foot resting lightly on the edge of the tub. She had crossed her arms over her breasts and lay there staring up at him.

He bent to kiss her full lips, but the expression in her eyes gave him pause.

"I have seen you in moonlight with nothing to cover your beautiful body; does daylight make such a difference?"

"Daylight makes a great deal of difference, Nat!"

There was something baffling in her tone and Nat's eyes searched her face.

Was this the shy Melanie who, only yesterday, couldn't take a compliment without blushing? Where was the maidenly modesty? What had happened to make the girl a woman so aware of herself, her body, and a man's desires? For as surely as he looked into her eyes, Nat knew that somehow, somewhere, Melanie had lost her innocence. There was an appraising quality in her gaze, almost boldly inviting.

Unmoving and unmoved, lying in the same position as when he entered, Melanie said, "I think you'd better leave now. I want to be alone!"

Puzzled, angry at her commanding tone, Nat went to his knees beside the tub and, staring into her eyes, slowly took off his shirt.

"What are you doing?" Her voice had just a tinge of curiosity.

"I'm going to make love to you . . ."

Her eyes widened and she stared at him in alarm.

Plunging his arms into the water, he encircled her body at the waist and fastened his mouth on hers. Her lips, hard and tight, softened under his. Her bosom, slippery with soap, pressed sensuously against his hairy chest, and he slid one hand down her back while the other cupped one elusive breast.

Deep inside, some part of Melanie stood in appalled recrimination at the rapid numbing of her defenses; then, with a silent scream, died forever as Melanie's lips matched Nat's urgent desire.

When you give up control, you give up yourself! The words rose unbidden to her mind, but she didn't care. At that moment, she both *hated* Nat and *loved* him; but most of all, she wanted him! And the new Melanie was determined to take what she wanted.

He buried his face in her breasts, licking the soap and water from her skin. His rapidly moving tongue on her flesh sent Melanie into a frenzy of exquisite yearning. She writhed when his questing hands roamed her body; and his arms held her suspended in space and time, as well as in the warm water. His seeking mouth found one hard nipple and fastened greedily upon it while he explored her thighs.

When he again cradled her hips in his arms, drawing her up to him, she reveled in the smooth skin of his back under her skimming fingers; and the muscles of his shoulders, strong and rippling. He trailed his lips past her ribs, her waist, touching her in all the secret places, sending her into sweet, tormenting desire; a salacious appetite only Nat could assuage. Her longing for him bordered on delirium.

His mouth found hers again and she shuddered in wanton delight. She opened her own and his tongue sought its contours, corner to corner. He explored, tasted, inhaled her very essence, making her a part of him in a way she never thought possible.

In total abandonment, she gave over her body. And he played each tender nerve as a master musician senses the resonance in a beloved instrument. He swept her over mountains . . . crested clouds with peaks of desire. In the strange thrill of near fulfillment, Melanie's breath came in gasps and she quivered under his touch.

Nat reached for the large Turkish towel Mahmoud had placed nearby. Then, lifting Melanie, relaxed and pliable, out of the water, he wrapped her gently and sensuously in the soft fluffiness. When he had finished, she was bound loosely, her arms held within the folds, and he rained kisses on her face, her throat, her shoulders as he held her close.

Astonishment mingled with ecstasy when she realized that, despite Nat's ability to send her to heights of desire, she was still virginal. He somehow managed to keep her hungry, wanting him desperately, responding to each touch of his fingers, his mouth, and his tongue.

He swept her easily into his arms and carried her to the bed. Slowly, he uncovered her, cast the damp towel aside and stood looking down at her through eyes glazed with desire.

"You are a delicious, pagan nymph," he whispered feverishly. "And this is your wedding bed! Here and now! For I can wait no longer to claim you . . ."

Sweeping back the coverlet, he lifted her once more and placed her gently on the satin sheets, removing the pins and smoothing her long hair tenderly over the pillow.

Suddenly, all desire left Melanie. She tried to remind herself of her resolve to fight fire with fire . . . to make Nat forget Laura. But she would *not* share her wedding bed with a ghost!

"No, Nat!" A startling, icy look filled her eyes. "You will not claim me now . . . and most of all, you will *never* claim me in this bed!"

He stared in astonishment.

She is like a chameleon! he thought. *Changing moods with the slightest breeze!*

His perplexity was evident. He opened his mouth

to ask her what was wrong, but a knock at the door broke the tension of the moment.

"Ye're needed topside, cap'n! Marblehead Neck's on th' lee beam, 'bout two miles off . . ."

Nat stood a moment longer, staring down at Melanie. Lazily reclining, she regarded him calmly through eyes that only seconds before glowed with her yearning. She saw his bewilderment replaced by anger, but made no move to appease him; nor to give reason for her change of heart.

I will tell him only if he asks! she thought. *I will volunteer nothing!*

The knock came again.

"Cap'n?"

"I'll join you on the quarterdeck, Stokes!" Nat's voice was tight, controlled. He continued to stare, as if to discover an answer written across the pearly flesh of Melanie's nude body.

She was mentally preparing the order of her words; positive at any moment he would ask her reasons for rebuffing him.

But, instead, Nat turned and, scooping up his shirt from beside the tub, strode angrily to the door. He stopped there and sent Melanie one last blazing look.

"We will discuss the meaning of your extraordinary statement before the day is over!" he vowed, with barely controlled rage.

CHAPTER EIGHT

The sound of the door closing behind Nat echoed in Melanie's ears, but was soon replaced by shouts of the crew calling to each other from aloft. Stokes's crusty, New Englander accent flavored the forenoon air as he bellowed orders to recalcitrant sailors.

Melanie rushed frantically to the armoire. With impatience, she tossed her dresses over a chair one by one, realizing suddenly what a conventional little fool she'd been all her life. Now, she longed for gowns like Laura's, with low décolletage and daring back.

Her new pale yellow organdie, sprigged with tiny embroidered forget-me-nots, was lined with taffeta of the same color. It was her most brazen day dress. Indeed, it was a scandalously improper gown, pretending modesty under the guise of high neckline and demure little collar and cuffs. Melanie recalled the disagreement she'd had with the dressmaker when the dear lady insisted the lining cover no more than the full skirt and fitted bodice to just above the rounded contour of her bosom. The rest of the dress, the back and long tight sleeves, was bare beneath the sheer fabric. Even while yielding to arguments of both the dressmaker and Laura, Melanie had secretly determined she would never wear such a scandalous gown. Now, giving fervent thanks for having been dissuaded, she feverishly began her toilette.

Less than half an hour later, Melanie's mirrored image returned her gaze with complete confidence in her piquant beauty. Her soft, fawn-colored ankle boots with pearl side buttons had two-inch heels; and she had dressed her coiffure in a new manner, adding more inches to the illusion by lifting long, dark tresses high at the crown, to fall in a cascade of curls to the nape of her neck. The top half of her breasts, thrust upward by tight waist cincher and strapless brassiere, were tantalizingly exposed beneath sheer organdie. Her skin was creamy smooth beneath the see-through material. Innocence of design, combined with gossamer fabric, made the gown more enticing than one whose exposure of naked charms left nothing to be discovered by the questing eye.

"Am I wearing this frock to taunt Nat?" she asked herself. "Or am I preening for James Talbot?"

It was not, at the moment, a question she could answer.

Evaluating her mirrored reflection, Melanie marveled that she showed no visible sign of her inner torment at Nat's deception. Focusing her thoughts on James Talbot had helped. Scoundrel though he may be, she reasoned, the thought of James had brought her through that long, miserable night. Curiosity as to the meaning of his words, if nothing else, kept her from foundering; plus the fact that he was a potentially available, handsome man who once sought her hand.

Melanie stepped out on deck into the warm morning sun. Opening her ruffled yellow organdie parasol, she paused in the shaded circle to look about. Laura stood alone at the rail, gazing at the shoreline still some distance away. On the quarterdeck, Nat shouted to his men in the rigging. Melanie was about to inquire as to Jared's whereabouts when her brother appeared carrying a glass of water and a small medicine bottle.

"You are feeling unwell?" Melanie asked politely,

going to stand beside Laura. In almost the same moment, she despised the hypocrisy of her query, since actually, at this moment, she cared not a fig about the state of Laura's health.

Laura rudely put off answering. She took the glass from her husband and swallowed the proffered nostrum.

"I slept fitfully last night," she said at last.

Regarding her with a self-assured look from under the sunshade, Melanie's voice was enigmatic.

"Why ever so? We had an exhausting, though enjoyable day and evening. Surely, you must have been fatigued?"

Laura stared at her, noting her choice of gown and subtle change in demeanor. Then, in an apparent decision to defer comment, she looked away.

"I was indeed weary, but could not sleep. When you become *enceinte,* perhaps you will understand."

"I understand perfectly, Laura," Melanie said in a low voice, gazing out over the water. She felt her sister-in-law's stare and after a moment, turned to confront her. "I do not have to be with child to understand why you lost sleep last night."

Ignoring sudden wariness in Laura's eyes, and Jared's quizzical look, Melanie turned her back on them and moved up toward the bow to contemplate rapidly approaching land.

The picturesque rocky shore was uneven; deeply imbedded with little bays, coves and inlets cut between sheer cliffs and mountainous, craggy headlands rose abruptly from the sea. As if to take the brunt of storms and hurricanes and to knife the fury of winds and seas that slammed into the rugged coast with seasonal regularity, God had flung a handful of huge sentinel rocks along the offshore. The ship skirted them now, weaving in and out, seeking a channel that cut a deep, safe passage toward the harbor.

Slowly now, with sails eased, the shoreline became

more distinguishable. As they drew closer inland, Melanie saw rocks and high-rising bluffs covered with lichen and green moss. Gulls circled and dipped along the cliffs, rising swiftly to blend their snowy brilliance with matching fluffy clouds; manifesting again, starkly white, against bright blue skies.

They were passing a tiny coast town with a rise of thick, forested hills beyond and a little, timbered footbridge over a creek rushing down to the sea. Windmills and rooftops of barns and homes peeked out from behind trees bearing new apple and cherry blossoms. Clapboarded houses, silvered by salt air and weather, sat close by the shore, with sea-washed pebble beaches or little wharves in front, and gardens and fields spreading up the slopes behind them.

On a long sliver of a hill, low stone fences separated farms reaching up from the south, and in a clearing surrounded by birch and maple stood a little white church with bell tower sparkling in May sunshine and snowy spire tapering off into towering trees.

They passed a cove whose rocky beach swept the edge of a wide field where Indians hoed corn long before the arrival of white men's sailing ships. North of the field, halfway up a gentle hill and beyond a thick oak grove, a new house was taking shape. Raw and waiting, it stood with small square foundation and a chimney up the middle. The glassless windows stared over a riot of tangled grass, herbs, and weeds; and a thicket of blackberry vines sprawled to the half circle of woods beyond.

The winds carried them toward a double peninsula. Its southeastern projection was Marblehead Neck, where a lighthouse stood sentry. They sailed past the Neck and rounded the point. Ahead was the second peninsula, tall, forbidding, rising straight up from the sea, and crowned by a growth of soaring pines. Rushing waters broke over huge sharp boul-

ders, roiling, thrusting into little coves and inlets, then
retreating to leave a trail of seaweed and flotsam
strewn contemptuously over sand and rock beaches.
Turning shoreward, they sailed into sanctuary between the headlands toward the town of Marblehead.
The harbor waters were more calm, lapping with lei-
surely waves at the sides of the ship.

Melanie was suddenly aware of Nat standing at her
left and just behind her.

"There it is," he said, pointing to a spot high on
the headland as they passed. "That's Hazard's Bluff
. . . where our home now nears completion." There
was pride in his tone and Melanie realized there was
also hurt, at what had recently passed between them.

Instinctively, she reached out to touch him; then,
mindful of her own deep hurt, withdrew her hand
and stared in the direction he pointed.

She saw a spiral road leading uphill from the town,
disappearing into thick evergreen trees. Somewhere
beyond that forest was the house of which Nat spoke.
The home which might or might not be theirs to share.
For Melanie was not certain Nat would agree to the
terms she now felt compelled to impose upon their
union. She had formulated a speech in her head during
her long predawn ordeal, and now awaited only the
right moment to face him with her proposition.

Berthed at Marblehead were a few small fishing
craft, a packet boat, two Gloucester fishermen, and
two merchant vessels, one of which was Nat's *Olympia*. Hails went forth from the *Mirimar* as sailors
recognized their sister ship; and standing with Melanie near the bow, Nat returned the salutes and re-
spectful calls of his other crew. Beside the ship, men
toiled with ropes and pulleys, unloading cotton from
the southern states for the mills on the slopes beyond
the harbor.

A small group of Negroes with fearful eyes stood
close by the *Olympia;* four strong tall bucks and five

or six women with children, some suckling babes. Melanie had only a momentary glimpse before a burly sailor sent them scurrying into the gaping hole of the cargo hold.

"Nat!" Melanie turned in surprise. "Why are those blacks on your ship?"

"They are workers," Nat answered tersely.

"Workers? Women with infants?"

"Wives and children of the men. Those young bucks are strong. Loading and unloading cotton is something they know well. They don't want to leave their families behind on a long voyage."

"So, they live on the ship? Are they your slaves?"

"You know I am an Abolitionist!" Nat answered sharply. And his tone implied he had closed the subject.

There was a sound behind them and Melanie turned to see Kreuger, the swarthy sailor, standing close to Nat. His lips twisted as his mouth made a grunting sound.

"What is it, Kreuger?"

Nat watched as the man made signals with his hands.

"It is all right, Kreuger. I am aware of it."

"I have seen that man each time we rode the shallop," Melanie said when the man had gone. "But I never realized that he cannot speak."

"He is a good crewman," Nat answered. "Conversation is not necessary on a ship and though mute, Kreuger is not deaf. He understands orders."

The town of Marblehead had houses of stone and masonry, as well as weathered, silver-shingled homes rising on hills, one above the other. Most were two and three stories, multigabled, with ornate, gingerbread scrolls and round peaked towers crowned by the painted rails of widow's walks.

They are not dissimilar to the homes of New Bed-

ford, Melanie thought as the ship glided slowly into berth beside the *Olympia*.

As in most seacoast towns, the docks were lined with warehouses and fisheries, sailor's taverns, and hotels. Beyond those facilities, Melanie saw the smoke and smelled the stench of tanning factories just north of the harbor. Here, shoes and leather goods were produced and shipped out on trading vessels to all parts of the country, and foreign shores as well.

There was the odor of hemp and tallow, oil and turpentine, spirits, and new fitted yards and spars. Cables and ropes were left in tight circles, or snaked along the planks of the wharf. And a bonnetted old hawker, with seamy lined face, watched them tie up at the pier, crying, "Fish . . . and lavender . . . an' what'd'ye'lack; an' ribbons . . . an' needles . . . an' ask me!"

They left the *Mirimar* and waited in a nearby carriage while a short distance away Nat spoke intently to an obviously perturbed Captain Hawkes of the *Olympia*. Melanie tried to read Nat's face as his captain's earnest, sometimes forceful words were accompanied by quick, agitated gestures.

He is absolutely unreadable! Melanie thought. *He is an actor; capable of presenting only what places him in the best light, for whatever ends he pursues. He has,* she thought with a sudden stab in her heart, *a predilection for deviousness!*

Nat spoke solemnly for a few moments, then, with a quick slap on the man's shoulder, came toward the carriage.

The conversation in the restaurant was strained. Melanie was quiet, speaking when necessary but otherwise preoccupied with her own thoughts. Laura, pale, with a worried look deep in her green eyes, was not her usual, buoyant self; so Jared and Nat attempted to carry the conversation with a false effort at injecting a holiday spirit. Now and then, Melanie felt her brother's questioning gaze upon her, and she endured a pang of sudden sorrow to be causing him anxiety.

They lunched on fresh cod and lobster from a Gloucester fishing boat, then topped off the meal with melon, a rare delicacy just off a ship from the tropics.

When the meal ended, they entered the carriage once more and set off up the rocky spiral road above the town to Hazard's Bluff. Nat, obviously enamored of his house, kept the conversation going, giving the history and background of each of the outstanding features they would find there.

He had brought plate and silver from Spain. A huge stained-glass window from a cathedral high in the Basque mountains had been carefully wrapped in sheep's wool and cushioned in the hold with silks from the Orient, velvet tapestries from Arabia, and tiger skins from India. The carved ebony balustrades were acquired, he said, from a monastery deep in the Himalayas. Blocks of Carrara marble became the floor of the huge entrance hall, and parquet floors throughout the house had entailed months of work by Italian craftsmen brought to the country for this special purpose.

The carriage halted at the top of a narrow road leading up from the highway. Ahead, the way twisted downhill through thick, fragrant evergreens, around a wide inlet, then cut a constantly rising path the whole length of the crooked half-mile-long peninsula called Hazard's Bluff. The high cliff where the road ended fell sheer and steep to the sea. A spidery web of steps with flimsy handrails zigzagged down the side of the cliff to a small narrow beach facing the ocean.

Gazing across the inlet from their rocky height, they could see the U-shaped three-story house, made of stone and masonry with a fountain and neophyte garden in the center. Solid as the promontory upon which it stood, it was a beautiful mansion, spreading both wings like arms reaching toward the pine, spruce, and yellow birch trees sweeping up the peninsula from the mainland. Large bay windows, wide verandas, and great French doors assured that this would be a bright, sunny home; a cheerful place, inviting happiness, contentment, and love.

Melanie felt tears rush behind her eyes. She wanted to visualize her future with Nat as joyful and rich, but it was useless. There was no certainty that this home was built for her, or that she would ever occupy it as mistress.

They wound downhill past the wide inlet, then began the ascent to Hazard's Bluff. Her heart a heavy weight in her breast, even the bright blue sky and the lovely sight of wildflowers on the hillsides did nothing to cheer Melanie.

All at once, around a bend in the road, they came upon the entrance to Hazard's Bluff. A wrought iron fence divided the property from the mainland. Concrete pillars towered proudly, twelve feet tall. Imbedded into them was a curlicued, wrought iron double gate, tipped with sharp spearheads, matching the fence tops.

Nat left the carriage and turned a bell at the side of the pillar. The sound caused a frantic fluttering of birds and in the sudden silence that followed, they heard a man's answering shout.

Nat returned to the carriage and they waited. Sunlight filtered through the trees, dappling the earth with light and moving shadows. A soft wind swayed the branches and the loud cry of a seagull, floating on the breeze, underscored the peace and beauty of this place.

A man walked down the gentle slope toward them. Melanie saw that he was tall and lean and as he drew near she noticed his face was weathered from salt air and sun. His walk was rolling; doubtless more accustomed to an unsteady deck beneath his feet than solid land.

"Zeke Seavey," Nat said as the man opened the gate. "An old salt with sharp mind and keen eyes. A trustworthy caretaker, and a good one." He leaned over conspiratorially to Jared. "Ask his age and see what yarn he hands you! He longs impatiently to return to the sea and does all he can to impress me with the fact!"

The gates swung open and they rode through. At Nat's direction, the driver stopped just inside. Nat presented Zeke to his guests. Melanie was drawn to the old seaman, recognizing in him a zest for the seafaring life that her father shared.

"I'm nearin' seventy," Zeke answered Jared's query. "Though I don't rightly look it!" he added immodestly. "Th' sea-brine pickles a man . . . preserves 'im, to ta' speak; keeps 'im hale and hearty! Don't know how long I'll oblige ye, cap'n! I be needin' s git back ter th' sea. Here I feel a fish out o' water!"

Nat grinned, placing an arm about Melanie.

"It won't be long now, Zeke. As soon as I carry my bride over the threshold, you are free to take the next ship out." He squeezed her shoulder affectionately, and basked in the gleam of approval in Zeke's old eyes.

"*Yer* ship, cap'n!" Zeke said quickly. "Don' mind lookin' ter yer duskies! Don' want nuthin' else but yer cargo!"

Melanie felt Nat's muscles become rigid. A guarded look came into his eyes, and into Zeke Seavey's as well, though Zeke's were also tinged with remorse at his thoughtless words. Abruptly, the old man doffed his hat to the ladies and made tracks as rapidly as his seaman's gait would take him to close the entrance to Hazard's Bluff. Nat tapped the driver's shoulder and they were off up the tree-lined hill.

Circling under tall pines and spruce, they rode past

the fountain between the wings and stopped under a
broad porte cochere before the manse. The stonecut-
ters had done a truly magnificent job in the building.
Each window was set in sculpted blocks, forming a
pattern of white against the pale pink stone; and
above wide, double entrance doors, a stained glass
fanlight was framed in smaller, exquisitely cut stone
configurations.

They alighted from the carriage and went up
broad steps to the flagstone veranda. Heaped on either side of huge white pillars framing the entrance
were planks, laths, shingles, and clapboards; nails
stood in kegs and pieces of stone and colored rock
were scattered about amid oak timbers and every sort
of wood fitting.

"The house is not yet completed," Nat said again
lamely. "But it should be ready for habitation within
the next month or so . . ."

"Should you be carried over the threshold?" Jared
asked with an innocent half smile, looking at Melanie.

"She is not yet a bride!" Laura answered sharply.

Melanie smiled back at her brother, realizing he
had spoken in an effort to induce her to break her
long silence; and to ease the air, thick with hostility,
between Melanie and his wife.

Nat opened the double doors and they followed
him inside.

Melanie gasped.

The house did, indeed, live up to the promise of its
outward appearance. The vast entrance hall, floored
with pure white Carrara marble, had a ceiling that
ended three stories up, in a domed skylight on the
roof. On each of the two levels above the ground
floor, marble balconies formed a half-circle overlooking the entrance hall. Dominating the center of the
room, an enormous vermillion-carpeted staircase
swept grandly from the second floor landing, in ever-

broadening descent between the arms of magnificent ebony balustrades.

"Nat!" Laura's voice was filled with awe. "This is truly magnificent!"

Melanie felt Nat's quick glance as she raised her eyes, wide with admiration, to pale pink stone walls hung with priceless tapestries and oils.

She met his questioning gaze and knew he looked for her approval.

"Nat, it is the most beautiful house I have ever seen . . . beyond my wildest dreams!" she said without hesitation.

Taking heart at her warmth and the wonder in her tone, he moved quickly to her side and, without hesitation, placed his arms about her.

"I hoped you would approve, my love," he said.

Laura turned and walked through a wide archway beyond the staircase. Jared followed in her wake.

"Melanie!" Nat grasped her arm in sudden urgency. "Tell me what troubles you!"

"Now is not the time," she answered.

She pulled from his grip and walked rapidly in the direction of Jared's voice exclaiming over the view in the next room.

Nat followed close behind.

It was an enormous ballroom facing the ocean. Huge floor-to-ceiling windows took up two sides, joining with another three-story domed skylight to catch the moods of the restless sea. Sunlight and shadow reflecting on the muraled back wall gave life to seventeenth-century costumed personages bowing, dancing, and walking under huge balloonlike trees. Plush pale blue carpeting edged the dance floor.

Nat led them through the rest of the vast mansion.

In the east wing, the huge library had two walls of empty floor-to-ceiling shelves. In the center of the shelved third wall was a broad stone fireplace with wide hearth. But the fourth wall drew the eye, blotting out all else; a stained glass window, inset just above the baseboard, soared twelve feet high, with a width the span of a man's arms. Sunlight, pouring through many prisms, threw multicolored rainbows over plush red carpeting.

The large bright kitchen and servants' quarters beyond were not yet completed. The dining room facing the cliff side of the peninsula had one mirrored wall and the parquet floor was unfinished. Upstairs, the master bedroom had a large dressing room and enormous bathroom with commode and running water. Six other bedrooms shared a common convenience room, where a built-in copper tub stood next to a pile of metal pipes and stone, awaiting completion.

Wide windows . . . balconies . . . window seats screaming for cushions . . . gables and towers; all beautiful, breathtaking . . . and needing a woman's touch.

"It is a beautiful house, Nat," Melanie said again, when he led them outside to show the grounds.

It is a dream, she told herself. *Could I possibly be mistress of such a house?*

They stood looking over the side of the cliff. A waist-high rail curved protectively around its edge, for it was a sheer drop to the beach and the little clearing below. At the open end, the spiderweb stairs wound downward and Melanie wondered if she would trust the narrow steps and flimsy handrails. From this viewpoint, there was a truly breathtaking spectacle of the surrounding land. They could see the inlet and the summit where the carriage had stopped on the way to Hazard's Bluff. In the distance, Marblehead's spires and widow's walks were visible. Against the green hills at the south end of the harbor, masts pointed skyward from the shipyards, and when the wind was right, it carried the sounds of saws and hammers laboring to bring forth new vessels. Puffy white clouds were scattered across bright blue sky, and the flawless day was marred only by dark smoke that hung in clumps over the tanning factory.

"I see another house over the inlet," Laura said. "Not so grand as this, but it seems to be a nice house."

"It belongs to James Talbot," Nat answered shortly. "His land begins where mine ends—at the inlet."

They spoke of Nat's plans for the gardens and a gazebo, and the embellishment of several other vistas such as this on the peninsula, where a clear view of the ocean and surrounding land was enhanced by height.

Nat, Jared, and Laura moved on while Melanie hung back to study more closely the strange movement behind a tree in the clearing below. As she watched, James Talbot stepped out with a long cylindrical object in his hand. She fought down momentary annoyance as she realized that he'd been observing her through a glass while she'd been innocently unaware. He waved at her and motioned toward the spiderweb steps, urging her to join him. She waved back, starting toward the steps to begin a cautious descent. Before reaching her goal, however, she stopped as Nat called to her. Melanie looked about for Jared, then saw him talking to Zeke Seavey near the driveway gates.

"Melanie . . ." Nat said when he reached her side. "I am concerned about you. Have you tired of so much walking? Would you like to return to the house and rest awhile?"

Melanie tried to hide the fact that she'd been startled. So intent was she on joining James Talbot, who even now awaited her at the foot of the cliff, that she'd failed, until the last moment, to see Nat coming for her. She wondered if he'd seen her wave and nod at James.

Noting the distracted expression on her face, Nat shook her arm gently and peered down at her: "Are you unwell?"

"Nat, I am neither tired nor unwell. I just feel the need for solitude . . . in order to think . . ."

"We must talk of whatever is troubling you."

"Later, Nat! I am not up to it now!"

"We will discuss it *now*, Melanie! I will not continue to fight ghosts and shadows! We must face it lest it overwhelm us!"

"I also have some say in the matter!" Melanie said, raising her voice and standing tall, dark eyes blazing up at him. "I say I am not yet ready to discuss it! When I am ready, I will so inform you!"

For Melanie now realized that she must first talk to James Talbot, before speaking with Nat. She wanted to have all the facts before reaching a decision that would affect the rest of her life.

Nat stared, astonished at her fury.

With a final look of outrage, Melanie turned on her heel and set off in a direction different than she'd originally intended. She halted when Laura's voice, laden with sympathy, carried on the breeze.

"Let her go, Nat! She is often moody and unsociable. There is no accounting for it. If you *will* live with her, you must accustom yourself to these displays of childish pique!"

Laura took his arm possessively, and Melanie watched them walk off toward the house.

When they had disappeared into the trees, Melanie sped as fast as two-inch heels would allow to the steps leading down the cliff . . . and to James Talbot waiting patiently below.

She descended slowly, carefully, and saw James watching from the edge of a little grove of trees. Only the dull red of his waistcoat kept him from blending into the surrounding foliage. He beckoned and she sped toward him across the open space.

"Melanie!" He took both of her hands and looked her over with unfeigned admiration. "You are indeed more beautiful than I have ever seen you!"

The breathless impetus of her flight mixed with guilt at their illicit meeting made Melanie's eyes uncommonly bright and her cheeks flushed. But, she realized suddenly that James's eyes were not on her face; they had fastened on her low décolletage and the soft ivory flesh beneath the sheer fabric.

Then, quite unexpectedly, she was engulfed in his arms. Frightened, she tried to protest, but his hungry mouth claimed hers. Since her strength was no match for his and his embrace was not displeasing, she ceased her struggles after a moment. She waited to feel the warmth and rising passion she'd felt with Nat, but it did not come. With her eyes closed, enfolded in the circle of James's arms, she felt disappointment. His kiss atop the hill that long ago summer's day held the memory of more thrill and excitement than she felt now.

But it was my first kiss! she thought, *and I had not yet met Nat!*

James released her abruptly and with alarm in his eyes made a quick apology.

"Forgive me, Melanie! I am a beast! I have yearned for you and dreamed of you for so long, I could not help myself!" He stood away from her and his gaze was beseeching. "Please say you forgive me!"

She looked calmly at him. She was not at all insulted, and although she'd not relished his kiss, it had not repulsed her, either. As a matter of fact, she realized with a tinge of surprise, she'd felt absolutely nothing.

"I forgive you, James," she said solemnly. "Now, what is it you have to tell me?"

He folded his arms and leaned back against a tree.

"It is not a pretty tale I have to tell, Melanie," he said, with a sorrowful expression on his face. "But, 'tis better you hear it from me than those with less kind intentions. And that you learn it now, before you make the mistake of a marriage that will ruin your life . . . and mine, in the bargain."

"How could my marriage ruin your life, James?"

"Because I love you and I have loved you for a long time . . ."

Melanie ignored this statement: "James, please do get on with your story!"

He looked at her through tender, soulful eyes.

"Surely, Melanie, you know that Nat carries the torch for your brother's wife?"

Melanie's heart paused a moment, then resumed with a rapid beat. There it was! She could not reason why the words sent a chill through her bones. She'd been aware of the fact for a long time, and it had been confirmed when she witnessed the scene on deck in the early hours of this very day. Now, however, came confirmation from the lips of another.

Melanie looked carefully at James's face, wondering if the sincerity she read there was real, or feigned; for it crossed her mind that James, also, was an actor.

"How could you possibly know that?" she queried in a tone surprisingly calm.

"I have watched Nat for many years. I learned his habits, his companions . . . and most of all, I learned of his burning love for Laura. Sailors and landlubbers all spoke of the flaming-haired woman who held Jonas Marfrey's heir in her spell; of her visits to his ship—and their tempestuous romance.

"And I laughed, for I knew Laura. I was there on that memorable afternoon Laura met Nat." James leaned forward, speaking earnestly. "A group of New Bedford rakes, of whom, admittedly, I was one," he grinned, "challenged Margot Tilden and Laura to approach this Norse god, whose handsome looks and rough ways they had been extolling.

"We made bets that he would not tumble for either of them, and did not have to urge too much before the girls agreed to discover whether or not all they'd heard about Nat's penchant for pretty girls was correct. Laura won, of course! Laura always wins what she sets out for." He paused, looking closely at Melanie.

She returned his gaze with a cool, waiting air.

"We went to the wharf and watched while Laura, flirting and teasing like a dockside wench, invited herself aboard his ship. Later, after an uncommon length of time, we went off and left her to Nat's good graces."

"You are only telling me that Laura won your silly bet. You are not telling me that Nat was in love with her."

"Surely, you have heard the gossip?" James asked gently.

"Gossip is nothing upon which to base truth," Melanie answered, forgetting she'd said just the opposite to Laura in the carriage on the way to Boston.

"It is said they squabbled and he sailed away," James continued. "Laura's reputation left much to be desired among the eligible bachelors of the town, and Laura realized the fact; so she set her cap for your brother."

"Why was my brother not aware of her reputation?"

"Jared is of a different breed. He never bothered with the rest of us. Studious, sheltered, he was easy pickings for our wild Laura. When Nat returned after three years at sea, Laura was a respectable wife."

"You have told me nothing that would preclude my marriage," Melanie said coldly. "You have only told me of what you presume to be a love affair; and that, without any proof except hearsay!"

Looking her straight in the eye, James took a deep breath and plunged onward.

"When Nat returned to New Bedford after a three-year voyage, he went straight to Laura's former home, seeking to make contact again. When he was told she'd married Jared, he went to your father at the warehouse with some lame excuse for his visit. Your father assumed he came to ask for your hand, and Nat let him so assume . . ."

Melanie's eyes widened, and her breath came quickly.

"How could you possibly know this?"

James smiled faintly.

"New Bedford is a small town, Melanie! Old Benjamin Stubbs has been a close friend of Laura's family for years. Since the death of her uncle, he yearns to fill the vacancy as husband to the long-nosed widow, and, of course, to stuff his pockets with what is left of the estate. Laura's aunt told Stubbs of Nat's visit. He informed her of the warehouse call and what he'd overheard. She then spread word that Laura 'jilted' Nat—which many know is untrue."

Melanie turned her back on James. Her heart was pounding and her breath came quickly. Benjamin Stubbs had been inventory clerk and bookkeeper to her father since before she was born; and he still worked in the warehouse with Jared.

After a long silence, she turned once more to James, who waited patiently for her response.

"I will look into the truth of your statement, James," she said with outward calm, "but I still do not understand why you are so concerned with this matter."

"My concern, Melanie, is for you," he answered gravely. "Do you not see that you are being used by Nat—for your ships, and for Laura? Just as your brother has been used by Laura for so long?"

"What do you mean he uses me for my ships? Nat has enough ships of his own!"

"Nat uses your dowry through your brother, Jared, even before you are his bride! How else could he supply a spermaceti candle factory with oil? He entered into business with Jared so he could have early access to your whaling ships."

"He has whaling ships of his own!"

"He has *none* of his own! He traded all of Jonas's whalers for merchant vessels . . . and his profiteering in trade has yet to crest in order to meet his initial output in clipper ships. Despite his dealing in fugitive slaves, and the Abolitionist money pouring into his coffers, he overextended himself when he ordered the last clipper design from Sam Pook! She rolls down the ways within the month and Nat is sorely put to provide the necessary funds to send her on her maiden voyage!"

"But Nat has much wealth in his own right! He added a great deal to the wealth of Jonas Marfrey, through trading and various enterprises . . ." Her voice trailed off.

"Jonas Marfrey's wealth should not have gone totally to Nat," James said, bitterness creeping into his voice. "One month to the day before Jonas died, he stood on the bridge of the *Sea-Wind* and told me she would be mine! Apparently, he did not have time to change his testament, but when I told Nat of this, he should have honored Jonas's verbal agreement. Instead, he turned on me viciously and ordered me from my own father's favorite ship!"

Momentarily, Melanie felt sorry for him, but her mind had fastened on one phrase and she'd been so startled, she'd only half listened to what came after that.

Despite his dealing in fugitive slaves, James had said.

She put up a hand to stop him from continuing.

"James, what do you mean when you say Nat deals in fugitive slaves? I know he is an Abolitionist; but that does not mean he deals in fugitives!"

"He deals in fugitives, Melanie," James said softly. "He takes them in the holds of his merchant vessels and your whalers from various pick-up points along the southern coastline, and delivers them to safety in Canada." He paused, reaching out to take her hand. "That is why, my dear, I said you will need a friend in the near future. The authorities are aware of Nat's activities. Even now, his movements are being watched. He will be caught one day and if your brother, Jared, is in league with him, he too will suffer. Then, you will need someone who loves you as I do to see to your needs."

This confirmation of her nebulous fears frightened Melanie. Her eyes widened, and she swayed slightly at the impact of his words. His put his arms about her, gently pressing her head to his shoulder.

"Melanie, I dearly love you," he whispered. "Everything Nat has belongs to me . . . including you." His arms tightened and his lips sought hers.

Suddenly, Melanie wanted nothing more than to run from the shock of his revelations. His arms became constraining, and she was held in a viselike grip. With a sudden move, she jerked away and ran toward the clearing. But he was after her in an instant. He caught her halfway to the stairs, pleading with her to listen and trying to force her back into the trees. She fought him there in the little clearing, but he subdued her finally, by holding her close with her arms to her sides.

"Believe me, Melanie," he whispered, "Nat is not the man for you. I have loved you a long time. Soon, I will be free to make you happy. We belong together, my darling."

"James! Let me go!" she cried, but his mouth covered hers.

It was a long kiss.

She waited to be affected in some manner, but there was no sudden surging of hot-blooded desire . . . no tingling nerve ends, no palpitations . . . no languid, delicious, ever-gathering momentum of hunger, as she felt when Nat kissed her.

She told herself it was because of her deep hurt at Nat's betrayal and the sudden awareness that Nat, also, was not above flaunting the law while acquiring gain at the expense of others.

Suddenly, she was torn from James's arms to land, facedown, on the soft grass. Stunned, she shook her head to clear her vision and saw Nat send James Talbot sprawling to the ground with one blow of his fist.

"You filthy son of a devil's whore!" Nat shouted between clenched teeth. "Get up and fight!"

James, still reeling, rose unsteadily to his feet.

"I do not wish to fight you, Nat," he said in a slow voice. "It is not feasible in view of the fact that you have several inches and possibly fifty pounds to your advantage. It would be quite painful to engage in fisticuffs with you. However," he added, "to equalize the difference, I will be happy to fight you with whatever weapon you choose. Though dueling is against the law, I don't think either of us is averse to breaking rules."

Then, as Melanie rose to her feet, ignored by both men, she saw Nat stride up to James and grab him by the throat.

"Hear this, you sniveling dog! If I ever find you have been near Melanie again, I will kill you! There will be no time for excuses; no time lost! There will not even be one breath between the instant I see you and the time you meet your maker!" He thrust him contemptuously away.

James landed on his knees in the dirt.

"Crawl back to your house and stay there until we sail!" Nat snarled at him. "Get out of my sight before I change my mind and kill you now!"

Again, James rose to his feet, eyes blazing. Melanie held her breath. She realized that he was no match for Nat, but feared he was too angry to retreat. He took one step forward and bent his head to rush Nat, when the sound of horses' hooves going at a reckless pace gave them all pause. A horse and rider topped the summit over the inlet, racing at breakneck speed for the gates of Hazard's Bluff. Melanie was shocked to recognize Stokes, the first mate of the *Mirimar*.

Anger left James's eyes. With a slight bow and a half salute in Melanie's direction, James turned and started slowly up the hill toward his home, an odd, self-satisfied expression on his face.

Then, Nat came to stand beside Melanie.

"Divorce yourself from the thought of marrying Talbot!" he said, glowering at her. "His wife is not yet dead, and unless he hurries her along, she could linger on for some time to come!" He grasped her arm. "You will marry me—whether or not your wishes coincide with mine!"

His grip hurt as she was dragged along beside him toward the stairs climbing the side of the cliff.

"You will never again put me or yourself in such a position!" he continued, biting his words to keep from shouting at her. "If I hear you have seen Talbot again, or even spoken with him in greeting, I will thrash you within an inch of your life!"

Melanie, suffused with a burning rage of her own, opened her lips to retort to his outrageous threat, but seeing Nat's head raise and his eyes light up with mingled relief and gloating, she followed his gaze.

She was astonished to see the *Olympia*, in full sail, round the point at rushing speed, heading north toward Canada. Melanie glanced swiftly at the summit above the inlet. James Talbot stood there in brooding observation.

Then, she was forced to fasten her gaze on the ground to keep from stumbling; for Nat pulled her along in a cruel grip, toward the stairs.

CHAPTER NINE

"So Talbot didn't know about the *Olympia!*" Jared was saying as Melanie and Nat entered the house. "He filed against the *Mirimar!*"

"Aye, sor!" Stokes answered. " 'N by time they searched th' *Mirimar*, th' *Olympia* had th' stragglers aboard 'n was nearly half a' hour out on th' way ter Canader!"

Jared turned accusing eyes on Nat.

"You placed our women in jeopardy by taking slaves on the *Mirimar!*"

"Wait, Jared," Nat said calmly. "Let me explain. The *Olympia* carried fugitives, but a few stragglers arrived moments after she shipped out last night. We had to take them at the last minute. I sent word to Captain Hawkes to await us here at Marblehead in order to transfer them."

Melanie realized then that she had not been mistaken. It *was* a child's cry she'd heard in the night! And James had told the truth about Nat's involvement with fugitive slaves.

"How did Talbot know the *Mirimar* carried runaway slaves?" Jared asked.

"He was talkin' to th' crew at the wharf las' evenin'," Stokes volunteered. "Mayhap, some o' th' crew . . ."

Nat shot him a keen glance: "Look into it!"

"Aye, cap'n!"

"Then, Captain Hawkes's anxiety was because of

his order to wait at Marblehead instead of immediately putting out to Canada," Jared pursued.

Nathaniel nodded.

"Hawkes was fearful when a Marblehead sympathizer told him of the planned search and seizure of one of my ships. His receipt of my order to await the *Mirimar* was even more alarming.

"Paul Lanier was late to dine with us because of a meeting with our informer," Nat continued. "He told me Talbot filed against the *Mirimar*, but I was unconcerned, for I had no intention of shipping fugitives on our voyage up the coast. When we reached the shallop, Stokes told me of stragglers hidden aboard the *Mirimar*. Their very lives depended on reaching the *Olympia* and sailing to safety in Canada. I sent Stokes to alert Paul and order Hawkes to await our arrival."

"Were you not doubling your chance of discovery; endangering both ships by having the *Olympia* stand by?"

"Yes, Jared . . . in a sense. However, I knew Paul would see to it. Stokes went straight to him after seeing us off at the pier last night. Paul sent a message to our agent with Marblehead Harbor Patrol, who changed time on the search papers, allowing us well past the estimated time of arrival; time to transfer the stragglers and allow the *Olympia* another hour to set sail. The same messenger delivered my order to Captain Hawkes to await us, but failed to tell him it was the *Mirimar* a search claim had been filed against."

Nathaniel sat back in his chair and took a deep breath.

"Thus," he said with a grin, "favorable winds and no unforeseen circumstances gave us well over two hours at Marblehead before the search order became effective." He reached for his pipe. "I told Stokes to have a horse ready at the livery stable and when the

Olympia sailed and the *Mirimar* was searched and released, to ride like the wind and notify me. Talbot is
usually nearby observing the results of his treachery,
and he would then believe his plan was successful."

"Why so?" Jared's eyebrows went up.

"Merely to buy time for the *Olympia* to reach
Canada without further harassment. I'm certain Talbot assumed when he saw Stokes riding here that the
Mirimar had been searched and confiscated. Though
he saw the *Olympia* sail past Hazard's Bluff, I'm sure
he was unaware of the fact that she is now one of my
ships; else he would have filed against her also. I just
received her papers last week." He puffed his pipe
with a satisfied smile. "Now, Talbot is gloating in his
house, and will do so for the next hour or two, until
news reaches him that his plans for my undoing have
again been foiled. At the moment, however, he enjoys
what he believes to be a victory, thus forestalling any
immediate deviousness on his part. Until we reach
New Bedford again, I will rest easy. Once there, I
will have the ability to anticipate where he plans to
strike next."

Melanie was fuming. Nat sounded so satisfied; so
self-righteous! James's words still rang in her ears,
and she resented Nat's assumption that everyone
agreed James was in the wrong and Nat wore the
crown of innocence!

"Why would harassment of you and your ships
help Talbot?" Jared asked. "It does not line his pockets, nor enhance his position in any way."

"Were he successful in his plan to discredit me,"
Nathaniel answered, "it would prove that I am the
ne'er do well, and he the poor misabused son of
Jonas Marfrey. For in the event of my death or imprisonment, he is in line to take over my assets;
property, ships, and all that belongs to me, unless I
have a wife, legitimate issue, or both, at the moment
of my untimely incarceration or 'accidental' death.

Murder is out! For Jonas's will firmly lays down the rules of our warfare; irrevocably stating that death must come about by accident, or due process of law, meaning, of course, direct confrontation with the more serious aspects of the precepts of our country, which would then act as executioner."

Jared shook his head.

"It is a game you play between you! You and James Talbot!"

"A deadly game," Nat agreed, eyes narrowing. "A game where I am the quarry and James the hunter; and one that can only end with the death of one of us," he finished softly.

"Surely, Jonas was aware that would happen?"

Nathaniel nodded.

"I now believe so," he answered in a low voice. "Though he denied paternity of either of us, it is only recently I came to believe he knew the possibility existed that he fathered us both. He was not an unkind man," Nat continued, "but he was a competitive one. I learned quite early that everything Jonas gave must be earned. He left almost everything to me and provided James just enough to foster a taste for good living. Jonas's will pits us against each other; forces us to fight for survival! Upon my death or imprisonment, James stands to gain a fortune; upon James's death, I would gain peace of mind and security in my inheritance.

"Shortly before he died, Jonas set James afire by verbally conferring upon him his favorite brigantine, the *Sea-Wind*. Jonas failed to change his will to that effect, fanning James's existing hatred of me and strengthening his resolution to accomplish my undoing. Thus, I have no recourse but to fight, to defend myself from his attacks. I now believe this deadly game of matching wits was the ultimate bequest to us both. 'Fight, and let the best man win!' was Jonas's creed. He was a hard man who won many a battle in his struggle for survival. Remembering the man he was and his way of thinking, I revile myself for only now realizing this enmity between James and myself was planned to decide which of his sons is worthy of his beneficence."

"He must have been a diabolical man to conceive such a monstrous scheme! Setting his sons against each other!" Laura shuddered.

Nat shook his head.

"Not to Jonas's way of thinking! He obviously believed we must fight for the right to his legacy; I to retain it . . . and James to gain it. Ultimately, whoever wins is truly Jonas Marfrey's son! And the loser unworthy—unless he fought valiantly!" Nat relit his pipe, which had gone out. "I was puzzled at the closing of the will," he said, musing, "but after all this time, I now believe I have solved the riddle."

"What riddle?" Laura asked eagerly, after another long pause.

"The will ended with a saying: 'A worthy adversary is one of Life's greatest gifts!'" Nat looked out the window again, lost in thought.

"What does it mean?" Laura asked impatiently.

"I now recollect his words, oft' uttered when I was a boy: 'Bulls are fought in Spain; the whale in the world's oceans; in days of old, knights battled fierce dragons! Bulls, whales, dragons! All are Life's greatest gift to man: Worthy Adversaries to test his mettle!'" Nat's voice had dropped low, and the last words hung suspended in the silent room.

Melanie was stunned. She was appalled at the game Jonas Marfrey obviously played from the grave; and she had just learned of another reason behind Nat's desire for early wedlock. And James's urgent efforts to prevent this marriage caused her to wonder how much of his attempts to beguile her had to do with the fact that he planned Nat's downfall.

The long, drawn-out silence was unbroken. Nat

continued staring out the window. Laura had a faraway look in her eyes and Jared's face held a thoughtful expression.

"Is Marblehead a regular rendezvous for the Underground?" Jared said at last, changing the subject.

"No," Nat answered. "At the moment, Massachusetts has only two embarkation points on the way to Canada; Boston and an island off Cape Ann. There will be another soon." He glanced sharply at Jared. "Of course, the main part of the Underground Railroad is usually overland. We are concerned with coastline fugitives only."

"How is it, then, that the *Olympia* took slaves to Marblehead?"

"Normally, that would never happen! Several weeks ago, one of our ships became disabled offshore near Marblehead Neck, during a storm. Her cargo of fugitives was given refuge by an Abolitionist there. When another shipment of runaways was scheduled for Canada, the *Olympia,* loading cotton for Marblehead mills, was the only available vessel in the Charleston area. Captain Hawkes is unaccustomed to sailing with fugitives and," Nat smiled, "other explosives! So, I was concerned that his naturally nervous mien might give us away. But, thankfully, all went well; the stranded ones have been retrieved, the stragglers transferred, and all the fugitives are on their way to Canada. However, I doubt I will put Captain Hawkes to that test again soon. He does much better with silks, spices, and more benign cargo in his hold."

"Was that disabled ship a whaler?" Melanie asked sharply.

These were the first words she'd spoken directly to Nathaniel since his outrageous statement in the clearing below the cliff. They had climbed the stairs and made their way to the house in angry silence.

Nat fixed her with a piercing gaze.

"Did Talbot say we shipped slaves in whalers?"

"He said you shipped them in *my* whalers!" She met his gaze head on, and lifted her chin defiantly.

Jared answered for Nat: "Melanie! Your ships are in my control. Do you believe I would place them in danger of confiscation?"

"You are also using them to gather sperm oil for the Nantucket candle factory, are you not?"

"That does not jeopardize them!" Jared was obviously puzzled.

"I am not yet married to Nat, though my ships line his pockets!"

Astonishment was stamped on all their faces, and Stokes discreetly sidled out the nearest door.

"Melanie . . ." Jared said at last, in a voice carefully emphasizing each word, "it will take two, possibly three years before we realize any oil from your whalers." He came close and touched her hand. "You know how long ships must be out on a whaling voyage! Would you prefer them in dry-dock? They would do no good there!"

Realizing she had no answer to that particular question, Melanie turned to Nat.

"You must reap a rich reward from the Abolitionists, to take such chances for the sake of fugitives."

Nat's eyes were enigmatic.

"I *am* an Abolitionist! I neither take funds, nor pay myself for performance of a humane act."

"Then, your men must require more than ordinary mariners for placing themselves in jeopardy!" She looked him straight in the eye, remembering James's tale of Nat's Abolitionist money.

"My men are paid to do what I tell them; whether the cargo is cotton or fugitives, the pay is the same," he said coldly. "In the event of apprehension," he added, "it is the shipowner whose life and liberty, as well as property, are at stake. The captain may lose his papers and if he wishes to continue a seafaring life be forced to sail under command of another; while sailors merely seek another berth."

Melanie and Nat stared at each other with scarcely veiled hostility until Jared stepped into the breach.

"I am still not clear as to how it functions, Nat. Tell me how it comes about, this obtaining of fugitive cargo . . ."

"As I said before, most of the movements of runaways are conducted by the Underground Railroad on an overland route. We are concerned only with coastline fugitives. Abolitionists and sympathizers carefully plan our cargo in groups of anywhere between five and ten at a time. Their escape routes are studiously timed at each arrival point; necessarily so, for the outposts are usually cramped for space and larger movements would immediately become suspect.

"Oftentimes, we find stowaways in our holds; families mostly, or one or two runaways fleeing willy-nilly, a step or two ahead of the slave catchers. Many, upon reaching the docks, slip into the first available vessel, unaware it is manned by southern sympathizers, or men who would sell their grandmothers for a penny; in which case, when found, as usually happens, they are turned back into captivity for the bounty on their heads. In the case of strong young bucks, especially, the reward may reach hundreds of dollars. Most of the slaves who escape with no direction, or certain route, are caught and either crippled or killed as an example to other slaves."

Melanie shuddered. She had never understood the great schism that was manifesting itself in the land. Her father had forbidden her to accept or read Abolitionist pamphlets handed out freely along the docks and in the park. When she questioned him regarding the issue taking such hold upon the country, her father told her it was not "women's business" and to leave the running of the government to men.

Her brother followed the same pattern of thought

set down by Ephraim Hardy. Melanie's only information had come from a pamphlet smuggled into the house by Kate. After perusing it hurriedly, Melanie was frightened and appalled at the breaking up of families and other more specific stories of cruelty. She had thrown the paper into the grate and watched it burn.

Jared and Nat continued conversing, but Melanie's attention was distracted by pain that had been building just beneath the threshold of her consciousness. She folded her arms and felt feverish throbbing midway between shoulders and elbows.

"Melanie!" Jared's voice was concerned. "Whatever is the matter with your arms?"

She raised one arm and gazed blankly at the delicate flesh, red beneath the sheer fabric. A faint tinge of blue was beginning to show. She lifted the other, and saw the same angry bruises starting to manifest.

"Melanie?" Jared's voice came again.

She looked at him through suddenly tired eyes.

"It is nothing, Jared. Nothing!"

And turning, she fled through the archway and across the ballroom. There she opened one of the tall French doors and stepped out on a marble balcony facing the sea.

She stood at the rail staring down at the ocean, writhing and foaming among the rocks over a hundred feet below. Long past its zenith, the sun was still high enough to emblazon tiny droplets of salt water with the luster of diamonds. The swift sea wind carried flecks of spray and Melanie felt wetness on her face. Momentarily, she wondered whether it was sea spray or tears; but when moisture coursed down her cheeks, she knew they mingled, one with the other.

"Melanie?" It was Nat's voice behind her, soft, penitent.

Angry at herself for allowing her emotions to show, she turned and looked up at him through cold eyes.

"I am sorry," he said. "It was not my intent to injure you. I suppose, in my anger at seeing you with James, I held your arm too tightly." He looked at her other arm. "But I do not recall gripping your right arm!" he finished with surprise.

"You did not," she answered in a low voice.

"Who then?"

She stared at him.

His eyes widened as his brows gathered stormily.

"James? Do you mean that bastard laid rough hands on you?"

She continued to stare, moving not a muscle.

"He *forced* you to kiss him?"

"Did you believe I did so, willingly?"

She turned away, contemplating the sea again.

"You placed yourself at his mercy when you went to him!" Nat said bitterly. "You are betrothed to me, yet you went to see another man! You were in his arms, and whether or not you gave consent, his lips were on yours."

She continued to ignore him.

"Answer me!"

She winced when he angrily took her arm and turned her to face him. "What is there to say?"

"How could you do such a thing . . . when we are to marry within the month?" He placed his hands atop her shoulders, pressing her to look at him.

She raised flashing dark eyes to his.

"And how could *you,* Nat?" she asked, in a voice filled with all the hurt and anguish she'd felt since last night. "How could you so deceive, not only me, but Jared? Seeking my hand in marriage so that you could see Laura openly, in apparent innocence? How could you make love to Laura on a ship where her husband and your betrothed were in such close proximity . . . and when she is expecting her third child?"

Now it was Nat's turn to stare.

"I have not made love to Laura in such circumstances!" he said at last.

"I saw you, Nat! I was on deck last night when you kissed Laura. I heard your conversation, and I know now, the gossip was true!"

He searched her face, making no effort to reply.

"For the purpose of defeating James Talbot, you could have married any woman," she continued, "and there are many who would be only too happy to wed you! But you sought me out!" Her eyes blazed at him. "Deny it, Nat! Tell me you did not seek marriage to me in order to associate freely with the woman you love—my brother's wife!"

He shook his head slowly.

"I do not love Laura, Melanie! I never did! It is you I love."

He dropped his hands and turned to stare out to sea.

Melanie did the same.

"Have you told Jared?" Nat's voice was a low-pitched whisper.

"Have no worry, Nat. I would not . . . and will not, tell Jared. It would hurt him deeply to know you are using him. If he is to find out, it will be from some other source."

Silence again.

"I have thought long and hard on this," Melanie said at last, eyes focused on the surging waters below. "I *will* marry you, Nathaniel. Marriage, even under these circumstances, is better than living at Halcyon House as Laura's whipping post; watching my brother's increasing anxiety and listening to his excuses for his shameless wife." She turned then, to face him squarely. "But I will be your wife in name only,

Nat! I will share your name and your house, but *never* your bed!"

He turned to look at her again. His features were expressionless, his eyes fixed upon her face.

"My brother will one day be aware of why you chose me; but until then, your secret is safe so far as I am concerned." Melanie put out her small hand. "Is it a bargain, Mr. Larimore?"

He was silent. Neither did he take her hand.

"This is the only way you may see Laura in decency and decorum," Melanie urged with a sudden sinking of her heart. "And be near her always," she added weakly.

She feared then that her plan was not such a wise thing. Suppose he decided not to marry her?

"Is that not the reason you asked me to become your wife?" she pursued, withdrawing her hand, worried at his long silence.

"I asked you to become my wife because I loved you," he answered through his teeth.

"I doubt that, sir." She continued, despite misgivings, noting he had used love in the past tense. "You could have married any one of a dozen others, yet you chose me! And when I observed your charade on deck last night and watched Laura follow you through the companionway, I understood why I was the one honored by your proposal. All those questions that had formerly plagued me were then answered." She spoke with a bravado she did not feel.

"And what of you, Melanie!" Nat asked, watching her through narrowed eyes. "Are you not aiding your brother's 'shameless wife,' as you call her? Are you not equally shameless in offering to participate in a false marriage; assisting in the deceit of a loving brother for your own comfort? You give yourself the mien of a hypocrite! Do not look down upon Laura, Melanie, for your deception has no more valid reasoning than what you consider Laura's to have!"

Melanie gaped in astonishment. She had never considered her proposition in the light Nat now presented. It was true! Offering herself in a sham marriage and her brother as the sacrificial lamb on the altar of falsehood and duplicity was too high a price to pay for her release from Halcyon House. She could not answer Nat's charge, for she knew in her heart he was right!

With a quick intake of breath, Melanie turned away, hiding her face from his questing eyes. Sudden disgust flooded her soul as she recognized her own cunning, hidden so long even from herself!

What a sense of innocence we all have! she thought. *And how swiftly we attempt to exonerate ourselves by pointing to the faults of others!*

A sound startled her and she turned, along with Nat, to see Stokes peering around the edge of the French door.

"Are we settin' sail wi' th' ebbtide, as ye said?"

Nathaniel nodded.

"I must first speak with Zeke Seavey, then we will embark."

"I be off to th' docks now, Cap'n!" Stokes answered with a two-fingered salute.

As Stokes left, Laura and Jared came through the door to the balcony where they stood gazing at the breathtaking view. The conversation turned to mundane topics and Melanie, after excusing herself, went wandering through the house alone.

She found a little niche in the south tower; a curved window seat that looked out over the land and part of the sea. It was more secluded than any place she had yet come across, and she curled up there, nursing her sore arms and her broken dreams.

Nat had not agreed to her proposition! Suppose he decided not to marry her after all? How he must despise her now! She had shown herself agreeable to trickery and deceit of her own brother in order to satisfy personal, selfish ends! Perhaps, in confronting Nat, she had ruined forever her chance at happiness. For Melanie loved Nat, of that she was certain. She recalled James Talbot's kiss and wished she could have responded even a little to his touch. But deep in her heart, she knew there was one man, and one only, who could unlock her emotions—and that man loved another.

Fear engulfed her. Fear of a future that turned her into a maiden aunt, with empty arms and sterile heart; but most of all, fear of a future without Nat.

As she sat there in the home that might never be hers, she believed she had lost Nat forever. Though he was under the same roof at this moment, he might as well have been thousands of miles away, for she sensed his withdrawal from her as soon as she'd made her proposal.

Had I never felt his lips on mine . . . his hands on my body . . . or heard his amorous voice in my ears; had I never basked in his tenderness, or felt the longing . . . I would not miss him so much! she thought.

Tears welled up, spilling over her cheeks, and she gave in to them. After a time, she fell asleep.

She awakened to the sound of voices calling her name.

Jared's voice was very close and she realized he was climbing the tower stairs. Looking out the window, she saw Nat with Laura a short distance behind him; both of them calling her name into the trees surrounding the house.

"Jared?"

He was beside her in a moment.

"Melanie! We have been over an hour searching for you! We are all beside ourselves with worry! Nat thought perhaps you'd gone back to James Talbot, and is now on his way to find out!"

Melanie's eyes widened in surprise.

"I can't imagine why he would think such a thing!"

Then, looking out the window, she saw Nat sprinting toward the steps that led down the cliff.

"Stop him, Jared!"

Jared undid the casement and shouted to Nat that Melanie had been found. Then, seating himself beside her, he took her hand in his.

"Why are you so unhappy, little sister?" His voice was gentle and when he put his arms about her, she burst into tears.

How could she tell her beloved brother that she had willingly offered to aid in deceiving him?

She sobbed for a few moments, deep, heavy sobs that racked her body and left her empty and weak. Jared let her cry, patting her shoulder in consolation, hugging her to him and comforting her in every way he knew. When the sobbing was over, the handkerchief he'd given her was soaked with tears, and she leaned feebly against his shoulder.

"Are you so unhappy, Melanie? Is it that you don't want to marry Nat?" Jared's eyes were puzzled as he observed her face. "At times, I think you love him and other times, I believe you despise him! It is very confusing, Melanie, to be watching your actions these past days. I know Nat is also confused; he has told me so!"

He is no longer confused! she thought bitterly. But she remained silent. Wiping her eyes, she tried to pull herself into some semblance of propriety.

"Is it that you are in love with Talbot?" Jared's eyes widened at the thought. "James may be a pawn in Jonas Marfrey's game of chess, but it is my feeling that he looks only to your ships and your wealth! Besides, his wife may long linger to deter any plans you make for a future with him!"

"No, Jared! It is not James Talbot."

The moment the words were out, Melanie felt re-

gret. Better to let him believe James the cause of her
strange moods than to have him guess the truth!

"What, then?" Jared took the handkerchief from
her and began gently dabbing at her cheeks. "Melanie, we have always been close. We have spoken
honestly to each other since childhood! Tell me now,
what troubles you. Perhaps I may be of help. It
distresses me to see you so unhappy!"

Jared's solemn brown eyes searched her own and
Melanie, reminded of the honesty that had always
been between them, felt her wounds open afresh.
Now guilt, added to fear of hurting him, kept her
from confiding in her brother.

When he found no answer in her face, he continued.

"I know I am not perceptive, as was Father. I am
positive he would soon have ascertained the cause of
your uneasiness." He smiled engagingly. "Perhaps I am
slow in some respects, my dear sister, but eventually,
with what Father always called 'dogged persistence,' I
find the answer! Tell me, Melanie, or I shall have to
dig and scratch until the reason is found!"

As when they were children, he flashed a teasing
grin at her, unaware of the arrow he sent piercing
her heart.

Please, God! Melanie prayed. *Never let him find
out about Nat and Laura . . . or of my unconscionable offer of betrayal! He would be so gravely
wounded, I fear he would never recover!*

She smiled tremulously.

"Dear brother," she said, with a soft little laugh.
"You have not yet discerned the vagaries of feminine
wiles! It is necessary to keep Nat on his toes until the
ceremony! Else he will become so accustomed to my
affections before marriage that it will serve to make
him take me for granted afterward! Indeed, I cannot
but let him think I have doubts! Which, truly, I do;
as do all brides when the nuptials draw near."

She stood, patting her curls and straightening her skirts.

"I am fine now, Jared. Thank you for letting me spill my tears on your shoulders; and please, I implore you, forgive me for taking advantage of your dear, sweet nature!" She stood on tiptoe and kissed his cheek, and when his arms went around her, rested her head on his shoulder.

"Dear Jared!" she said softly. "I love you very much! I wish you the very same happiness you wish for me!" She leaned back and looked him directly in the eyes. "Please be happy, Jared! Please!"

They heard Laura's call as she and Nat entered the house. Melanie followed her brother down the winding tower stairs to join them.

Nat scarcely acknowledged Melanie's presence, but Laura launched immediately into a tirade, accusing her of inconsideration, as well as rudeness at causing them all such trouble. Jared silenced her then; and while Nat spoke with Zeke Seavey in the entrance hall, they went outside to the porte cochere, where the carriage waited to take them back to the ship.

CHAPTER TEN

They sailed with the ebb tide; a time when the sun had just disappeared behind the bluffs. Before they reached deep water, the western sky was streaked with the last fading color of a dying day.

They dined in the ship's salon on Maine lobster and quahogs, with curried vegetables, flaky Indian pastry prepared by Mahmoud, and a dry white wine Nat had procured from the vineyards of France.

"When will we arrive in New Bedford?" Laura asked listlessly.

Melanie sent a sharp glance at her sister-in-law. Her eyes were puffy, as were her hands. Noting that her eyes were at half-mast, as though she felt extreme malaise, Melanie knew a twinge of alarm. Laura was, after all, an expectant mother and an overabundance of excitement and exertion must have taken its toll. A glance at Jared told her that he also had noticed Laura's sudden fading.

"We should be rounding east of Cape Cod by dawn, and lunch on Nantucket Island," Nat answered. "Then, after a few hours of business, sail home while the sun is still high."

Jared's head came up.

"You did not say we were sailing to Nantucket!"

"If it is agreeable with you, of course, Jared!" Nat amended quickly. "I supposed, since we must sail in the vicinity, it would be wise to look to matters there, thus saving you a trip. If we do so now, your presence

will not be needed there until late next week . . .
or even the following, provided there is no urgency in
Charleston."

Nat's eyes held Jared's.

"Of course, you realize, Jared, it is unnecessary for
you to go to Nantucket at all while I am away.
Stokes will remain with the *Mirimar* in New Bedford,
and Paul will be arriving by coach within the week.
One or both of them can take the pinkie schooner to
Nantucket. It is only a matter of preparation for the
cargo of the *Sea-Wind* when she returns from Charleston. And in case of emergency, you would be notified."

"No, Nathaniel!" Jared shook his head stubbornly.
"It is my investment, as well as yours on the island.
Though I trust both men implicitly, I would be
failing in my duty to you, as well as myself, were I to
fall upon them to fulfill my obligations."

"In that case, when you sail to the island, Stokes
will man the schooner along with one other crewman.
It is only a matter of storing provisions at night after
the candle factory is closed." Nat paused, studying
Jared's face. "Are you certain you want to jeopardize
yourself in this manner?"

Melanie's ears sharpened.

"Jeopardize?"

"The candle factory is also a new outpost on the
escape route for the Underground," Laura answered, slanting tired eyes at Melanie, who felt
momentary hurt that Laura had knowledge while
she'd not had an inkling.

"Will many come there?" she asked, glancing at
Nathaniel.

"Probably not, at first," Nat answered, turning his
eyes to his glass. "Word is now being spread to sympathetic captains and shipowners that 'unauthorized
cargo' may be left at Nantucket for later shipment on
our voyages to Canada."

"Nat, you have made me an Abolitionist," Jared pursued. "As far as jeopardize myself, can I do less than any other man believing as we do?"

With a faint smile and nod of his head, Nat gave in and directed his conversation to Jared: "I will bring the first contingent of fugitives from our underground outpost in Charleston within the next two weeks, more or less. A coffle is being brought from Sumter for sale in Charleston. If all goes according to plan, that group will be wrested from the overseers and become our first consignment for Nantucket on the route to freedom." He paused to light his pipe. "I will send a message from Charleston," he continued, "via one of the clipper ships, giving our approximate time of return. It is important that Stokes and one other crewman await us on arrival night, ready for any eventuality."

"When do you leave?" Jared asked.

"The *Sea-Wind* awaits me at New Bedford. I will sail with the morning tide day after tomorrow." He read the unspoken question in Jared's eyes. "Returning, as I said, in two, possibly three weeks, barring unforeseen circumstances." He dropped his eyes to his plate and Melanie wondered if he would further add that he returned in time for their wedding, but he made no reference to it.

Nat had uttered not a word to her since they embarked; nor even glanced in her direction. He had made a studied effort to avoid acknowledgment of her presence.

You would believe, observing Nathaniel, she thought, *that I had wronged him, instead of the opposite!*

But Melanie took comfort in the fact that he had answered her question about the quantity of arrivals at Nantucket. Though now she thought on it, it was a cold explanation; one that could have been made to anyone. He had not called her by name, or even looked at her as he spoke.

Laura and Jared retired early. Nat conferred with his top crewmen in the chart house, and Melanie was left to her own devices.

Alone, beset with guilt and worry, she went out on deck and stood at the rail. The moon was gone and the black velvety sky filled with brilliant pinpricks of light. Searching the heavens for Orion, as her father had taught her long ago, Melanie noted that the stars were intermittently blotted out by thick, heavy clouds. The seas were running high, and a quickening wind carried, at first, drops whipped from the waves, then long streamers of spray.

"Smell the storm coming!" her father used to say. And now the daughter of the whaling captain braced for the storm without, as well as the tempest brewing within.

Sheet lightning flickered in the distance, outlining the scalloped edges of thunderheads racing before the line squall. Waves began to pile up and huge swells rose threateningly, bearing down on the *Mirimar*.

There was a rumble of thunder, increasing to a roar as the ship sailed into the edge of the storm. Melanie stood transfixed as jagged streaks of lightning and a loud, rolling thunderclap pierced the sky. For a moment, the waters lit up bright as day, then subsided, leaving inky blackness and burgeoning winds to strike terror to her heart.

She heard shouts from the men as they climbed into the rigging, and Nat's voice and Stokes's, barking orders over the rising gale.

Melanie clung tightly to the rail, mesmerized, unable to move. Then, Nat's arm went about her and she was swept roughly toward the companionway.

"See to Jared and Laura!" he shouted above the wild storm.

His words were barely out when a screeching, twist-

ing wind ripped through the shrouds. A tangle of
lines and canvas tumbled halfway down the mast. In
the bowlines high above the drenched and dangerous
deck, men's shouts were scarcely heard above the gale.

Nat gave Melanie a hard shove down the passageway and she watched dazedly as he fought to close the
door in the sudden blast. Then, she felt and heard a
huge wave hit the ship. A sudden gush of water
washed under the closed portal and rushed along the
floor toward her.

She turned and fled down the passageway to the
cabin where Jared and Laura were doubtless ill and
cowering before the storm.

She knocked, but it was impossible to hear above
the howling wind. As the ship lunged down the side
of another mountainous wave, Melanie was thrown
against the door, opening it precipitously. She was
flung to the cabin floor in a jarring fall. Shaking her
head to clear it, she slowly rose to her feet again.
Hanging on to the nearest secured chair, she gazed
about the room.

The pewter lamp swayed wildly from the overhead
beam. With each roll of the ship, flickering light
bounced off Jared's face, green with sickness of the
sea; and Laura's features, pale, with beads of moisture
on her forehead, convinced Melanie that she was
sorely needed here.

It was a small cabin and the stench of illness nearly
made Melanie nauseous. But she was not given to seasickness; the long voyages with her father had in-
ured her to the malady, for which she was extremely
grateful.

Half seated, half lying, Jared had tied himself to a
chair fastened securely to the floor next to Laura's
berth. When he raised his eyes to Melanie, they were
filled with a mixture of emotions; terror most of all,
mixed with shame, and regret that he could do nothing to assist himself, let alone his wife. Laura, fas-

tened to the bedpost by a sheet beneath her arms, retched violently into a chamberpot held in her shaking hands.

"Jared! Lean over with your head between your knees; it will ease the vomiting," Melanie told him, realizing his shirt and pants were befouled and he was weak and helpless in his present state.

Then, she saw to Laura, easing her back onto the pillows and lessening the tight hold of the sheet beneath her arms.

"You cannot remain here!" she said suddenly. "There is no convenience room, and it is vital now!"

She tucked the blankets about Laura, pulling them tightly under the mattress; then, leaving Jared doubled up, fled the cabin in search of Mahmoud.

She found him in the pantry next to the ship's salon. Precious china plates had been wrapped in cotton and secured with twine, and he placed them carefully in slots in the built-in cabinet.

"Mahmoud!" she cried above the howl of the wind. "You must help me! My brother and his wife are both ill and must needs be removed to the master cabin where the convenience room is handy!"

Mahmoud was unperturbed. During his years with Jonas Marfrey, and these past years with Nat, he had survived many storms at sea. His fatalistic belief kept him safe in the knowledge that this, too, would pass—and if not, he would calmly acquiesce to destiny. He nodded obsequiously and followed her down the passageway, hanging onto walls and doors when the ship rolled with battering waves.

Less than an hour later, after much attention by Melanie and Mahmoud, Laura, bathed and freshly gowned, slept in Nat's berth in the master cabin, oblivious to the storm raging beyond the large porthole.

Jared, washed and in clean nightshirt, lay resting on fresh linen in his own cabin; settled by the strange

East Indian potion Mahmoud had prepared and fed him, despite his violent protests.

Finally there was a lull in the storm. Melanie, exhausted and too tired to think, wearily prepared for sleep. She unfastened the pins from her hair, then realized her hairbrush must have been tossed from the bureau top by the rolling ship.

I will search for it tomorrow, she thought, and climbed into bed beside Laura, without even the faintest recognition of the irony of their closeness.

Melanie awakened once during the night, when the ship rolled sharply, throwing Laura against her. But resting under the influence of Mahmoud's mysterious potion, Laura only moaned softly and continued sleeping.

A pallid dawn slit a leaden sky when Melanie awakened again. She sat up, staring across her brother's wife through the large porthole where the first faint light of day fell over great, swelling waters of the Atlantic. Melanie's father had taught her well; she knew these were not the offshore waters of Cape Cod. Movement of the water and resulting roll of the ship told her they were in deep ocean, far from land. The storm had blown them off course, and she wondered just how far it had taken them.

A mixture of rain and high seas slapped against the porthole. Though the ship creaked and groaned with each huge wave, Melanie knew the storm was passing and the worst was over. She closed her eyes and slept again.

Several hours later, when a lowering sky cast dull light through the porthole, Laura moaned, opening her eyes with a sudden, startled expression. She cried out, then doubled up, and Melanie thought she was in for another bout of seasickness.

"Laura," she said, "wait! I will get the chamber

pot, then have Mahmoud make more of the seasickness potion."

"No, Melanie!" Laura answered between clenched teeth. "It is not that! I—I—am in labor!" she cried out again, more loudly this time. "Melanie! I am going to lose the child!" she gasped through her pain.

Melanie blanched. Never in her life had she been alone in an emergency of this nature! She had not the faintest idea of what to do.

"Stay here, Laura!" she cried unnecessarily. "Don't move! I will get Jared!"

Laura looked at her through agonized eyes.

"Jared . . ." she said with a twisted smile. "He can do nothing but become apprehensive! Get Mahmoud! He will know what to do!"

"Mahmoud!" Momentarily, Melanie was shocked. Then, remembering the little Hindu's unperturbed demeanor and wise, ancient eyes, she knew Laura spoke the truth.

All the rest of that day and on into the night, Mahmoud sat beside Laura's bed. Several times an hour, he spoon-fed her a thick, amber liquid from a miniature, ornately carved brass vessel. With long curved spout and elongated handle hung over a spirit lamp, it was a strange, alien decanter. Mahmoud, in his dark turban, wide, full pantaloons, and loose silk shirt under a sleeveless embroidered vest, reminded Melanie of a sinister drawing out of her childhood book of *Arabian Nights*.

Oftentimes, when he placed the spoon to Laura's unwilling lips, she made a face and complained.

"It is bitter, and leaves my mouth pursed," she whispered.

"You must drink it while it is hot!" Mahmoud would answer in his odd English accent. "It may, perhaps, save the child."

Shortly after midnight, returning to the cabin after

she had seen to Jared, Melanie overheard a brief conversation between Laura and Mahmoud.

"When we first met years ago, Mahmoud, I would not have believed you would attend me in a situation such as this."

"Life," he answered, "is an unread book, holding many surprises. We may have an idea of the story, but the pages turn slowly. Until the last one is read, the outcome is uncertain."

Despite a sudden surge of bitterness at this latest confirmation of Laura's duplicity, Melanie gave no outward sign of her feelings. It was Mahmoud who answered her query as to Laura's immediate state, while Laura closed her eyes, turning her face away in a gesture of hopelessness.

"I will remain with her throughout the night, missy," Mahmoud said quietly. "Properly administered, the potion should avert disaster for the child."

"Then I will retire to Jared's cabin," Melanie murmured softly. "Should you need me I will be immediately available."

"You will sleep in my cabin."

It was Nat's voice behind her, low, vibrant, filled with unquestionable command. Astonished, Melanie swung around to face him. She had not laid eyes on Nat since the previous evening when she'd been unceremoniously shoved through the companionway door.

"I will rest in a forecastle bunk," he added, looking down at her through hard eyes that belied the softness in his tone.

Melanie stood at the entrance while Nat had a word with Mahmoud and Laura. She hadn't the faintest idea where his temporary cabin was located and could only wait.

Then he was at her side.

With a hand at her elbow, Nat escorted her in silence through the dark passageway to steep, ladder-like stairs leading down to the next deck. A lantern swung at the top of the small square abyss. Motioning Melanie to wait, Nat lifted the flickering lamp off the hook and plunged rapidly downward. At the foot of the steps, he raised the light high and called her to follow.

For just an instant, Melanie stared down at him. His eyes looked sunken in the wavering light and they gleamed up at her out of the shadows. His broad shoulders seemed to rise and blend into the darkness, giving the odd appearance of a hump at his back. When he repeated his order for her to join him below, she felt a moment of fear.

Nat set the lantern on the floor, then reached a hand upward to aid in her descent. Tentatively, she placed one foot on the top step and gripped the rope strung like a balustrade the length of the stairs. She was nearly midway to the lower deck when, grasping her about the waist, Nat swung her down beside him.

Startled, she felt the involuntary tightening of his arms and her old yearning for him sprang full-blossomed into being. Breathless, caught off balance, she rested her cheek against his broad chest to regain equilibrium. Through the rough seaman's shirt, she heard the heavy pounding of his heart. Held fast in Nat's unrelenting custody, she felt the length of his body pressing against her. Lifting her gaze, she met his burning stare, then watched transfixed, as his head bent slowly toward her. His hungry eyes, narrowed with sudden, surging passion, fastened on her lips. Instinctively, as his mouth drew near, Melanie's tongue flicked, moistening full, slightly open curves, ready for his claim.

He was scarcely a breath away when she screamed.

Nat's arms dropped swiftly to his side and she swayed in the sudden withdrawal of support. Later she would recall that brief glimpse of his anger; for the moment, her mind was otherwise occupied. Some-

thing had run across her foot and scurrying noises
told her that wharf rats shared this voyage.

Nat turned abruptly and with long strides moved
on down the passageway. As darkness closed about
her, Melanie's astonishment gave way to fright. Lifting her skirts, she ran to catch up with him, while the
swaying lantern cast fearful shadows over closed doors
on either side, some of which were locked with
chains.

She reached his side when Nat paused before the
gunroom. The word *Explosives* had been neatly
painted in white on the dark, heavy door. Taking a
huge key ring from his pocket, he unfastened the pad-
locked chain and pushed the door open on silent
hinges. He lifted the lantern high and peered inside.
Standing slightly behind him, Melanie stared past his
upraised arm at one hundred or more rifles and small
weapons standing militantly in racks along one wall.
Neatly ranged on nearby shelves were large bags of
gunpowder, saltpeter, and boxes of bullets, while in
the center of the room, the yawning maw of a fair-
sized cannon aimed directly at them.

Melanie gasped.

"Surely it is illegal to carry such weapons?"

"The right to carry arms is one of the precepts of
the American Constitution," Nat answered coldly.

"But we are not at war! And this is an arsenal!"

"We are at war, Melanie. An undeclared war between North and South. It is only a matter of time
before open warfare is given credence."

Forgetting the mixed feelings of anger, guilt, and
confusion she had known these past few days, Melanie
touched his arm to draw attention to her earnest
question.

"But surely this ship cannot be in such danger that
it must carry this deadly cargo?"

"This ship often carries more dangerous cargo,"
Nat answered, stepping back into the passageway and

closing the door. "At some future time it may be necessary to defend it."

Melanie's eyes widened in the flickering lamplight. "You mean you would fight the patrol ships?"

"If necessary. The *Mirimar* has yet to battle for her life, but in the event there is no other way, she is prepared. As are all my ships."

Melanie withdrew her hand.

"Whalers are not fast enough for such service," she said musingly. Then, as revelation swept through her mind, she shot him a swift, discerning glance. "James was right! You disposed of your whalers for merchant vessels in order to run slaves to Canada! Surely there must be some profit in this madness?"

In the dim light, Nat's mouth hardened into a thin line.

"Do not befoul my ship by mentioning your lover's name while you are aboard!" he said in a low, deadly voice. "I have told you . . . I do not profit by transporting human beings to freedom. I am an Abolitionist! I live according to my beliefs. And will brook no questioning from you, or anyone else, as to my motives!"

Swinging the lantern angrily, he strode away from her again. She followed close behind him down the passageway. They passed a door labeled *Storeroom*. A short distance beyond, Nat stopped abruptly before a louvered door and, taking out the keys again, unlocked it. He stepped back, indicating silently that Melanie was to enter.

She stepped over the threshold into a cabin only slightly smaller than the first mate's cabin almost directly above where Jared now slept. Though not luxurious, the room was fairly comfortable. A small Persian rug had been placed upon the bare plank floor and Melanie recognized it as one usually seen in the ship's salon. A wide berth was situated beneath two small portholes on the curved wall amidships. A

long table and several chairs were bolted to the floor
and a rough seaman's chest served as chiffonier and
wardrobe. In one corner of the room, Melanie recognized her own two trunks and portmanteau. From the
lone dark beam that halved the ceiling, a lantern
swayed and creaked with the thrust of the ship, sending flickering shadows scurrying about the room.
Drops of spray struck intermittently against the porthole's dark glass.

"I have had your trunks moved here from the master cabin," Nat said in a cold, flat tone. "The berth is
made up with fresh linen and there is an extra blanket. I trust you will be comfortable."

Melanie stared up at him, recalling with pain in
her heart the devious twists of fate that had brought
them to this impasse. She noted the stubborn thrust
of his jaw; sensed barely leashed anger in the way he
bit words issuing from the full, sensuous mouth she
had come to love so much.

For a long moment, he gravely returned her
gaze. Then, Melanie was crushed in his embrace. Her
eyes widened in surprise as Nat's mouth, hard and
cruel, claimed hers . . . and his tongue thrust deep
while she went weak with astonishment and sudden,
flaming desire. She was swept up into his arms and
carried across the cabin to the bed, where Nat tossed
her roughly. Then, throwing himself beside her, he
covered her body with his own.

Melanie fought the weakness sweeping insidiously
through her entire being.

"Nat! No!"

"Melanie! Yes!" he mocked in bitter tones.

His face, close to hers, darkened in rage.

"If it's James Talbot you want, then it's him you'll
get! But I will be the first man to claim your body!"
His voice was hard and his breathing labored as he
pressed urgently against her.

He rolled to one side then, and holding her two

hands in one of his, pulled the pins from her hair. She strained to free herself, but Nat forced her to lie down again.

"No, Nat! Please!"

Her entreaties fell on deaf ears.

Slowly, deliberately, he ran his fingers through the long, heavy locks, spreading her dark brown hair over the pillow; smoothing, caressing . . . and Melanie realized his desire heightened with each stroke. Once again his weight pressed her slim body deep into the down mattress. He buried his face in her hair and she nearly smothered against his shoulder. She struggled frantically before he recognized her predicament and moved to free her breathing.

"You are in love with Talbot, are you not?" Nat's whisper was harsh in her ear and she felt the tension in his body as he waited for the answer.

Denial rose to her lips, but the sudden vision of Laura in Nat's arms filled her mind and she choked back the words. She could not explain, even to herself, the odd mixture of guilt, jealousy, and love flooding her thoughts and emotions at this moment.

Nat rolled on his side again and, inches away, stared deep into her eyes.

"I intend taking you, Melanie! You are promised to me and I will make you mine, with or without benefit of wedlock! There will be no excuses . . . no crying out. Nothing will save you now, from what is about to happen!"

Melanie stared up at him. She could not believe this was the same man whose lovemaking had sent her into delirium just a few days ago; the man to whom, at the outset of this misbegotten voyage, she'd given utterly and completely the very essence of her being. Willingly then, she would have given up her maidenhead, but he had not claimed it. Nobly, honorably, he'd postponed his own lustful appetite for loftier principles. Apparently now, believing his claim upon her to be threatened, he cared not a fig for ethics or propriety . . . or indeed, for her feelings in the matter under these altered circumstances.

Composing her features, she closed her eyes and tried to assume the appearance of a statue. She would not allow the slightest twitch nor softening of mien to betray her true feelings. Nat must never know what this outrage was doing to her; that his total disregard for her sensibilities shocked her to the very roots of her soul.

Melanie's confused thoughts ran in all directions, only to return to the harsh reality she prayed to blot out of her consciousness; the fact that the man she loved was about to take revenge upon her for a crime she had not committed, that of loving someone other than himself. And, she told herself, he would probably use her in the same manner he undoubtedly did doxies and tavern maids in ports all over the world!

There was silence in the room. Nat's breath came warm and steady close beside her; but his hands were quiet. Melanie opened her lids slightly to see what he was up to and found herself staring straight into his searching gaze. His eyes lowered to her bodice, fastened to the throat with myriad tiny buttons. When he looked up at her once more, she noted the piercing, stormy glint in his narrowed eyes as he began unfastening each button with maddening ineptitude. After a long moment, frustrated at the delay, he placed his hand at the collar and in one, sudden move, ripped the fragile material to her waist, including as he did so, her chemise. And Nat's eyes feasted on Melanie's full, rosy-tipped breasts as they stood free and beautiful in the pale lantern light. When his lips came into contact with the soft flesh, Melanie closed her eyes in sudden, all-consuming ecstasy. In that instant, she gave up her feeble effort to fight the swift, flaming desire that engulfed her.

Melanie didn't know when she was divested of her

clothing. She only knew that Nat's hands were on her body . . . moving over her breasts . . . her stomach . . . her thighs . . . and where his hands moved, his mouth followed.

When he settled heavily atop her again, she realized that he, too, was nude. And when his gently nursing mouth found hers, she opened her lips and felt his exploring tongue.

So caught up was she with her own passion that she did not immediately notice when his anger turned to tenderness; she only knew that she loved him. And when he entered her, the pain she'd expected never manifested. The gentleness with which he took her virginity . . . and the fusing of his body into hers . . . was a delirium beyond her wildest imaginings.

At last, languorous, filled with a heretofore unknown glow of contentment and love, she lay spent in his arms; and wondered that she ever thought she could have done otherwise.

There was silence between them when it was over. Nat held her gently, tenderly, and the warmth of his body warded off the chill of the cabin. Melanie heard rats scurrying in the passageway, but felt no fear. Nothing would dare harm her while she lay in the arms of her beloved. Nat's breathing slowed, became deeper, and she knew he slept. Fearful of waking him, she remained painfully still . . . dismissing the cramp in her leg as unimportant, compared with causing him a moment's discomfort. At last, she too fell asleep.

He awakened her just before dawn. His mouth sought hers again and she knew what he wanted without a word between them. This time their lovemaking was even more ecstatic . . . for she had learned to move as he liked . . . and he knew every inch of her body . . . every nerve . . . every tendon. His touch played over her masterfully, rousing her, bringing bittersweet hunger to every atom of her being.

And when he shifted his body to enter again the sweet wetness of her, she clung to him, moaning softly, until his lips took her yearning sounds into his mouth.

When they had both found release once more, they slept.

The sun was pouring through the two portholes above the berth when Melanie awakened again. And Nat was gone. For a long time she lay there remembering the feel of him in her arms; the contours of his body as he lay above her and close beside her. The pillow was indented with the stamp of his dear head, and she took it into her arms and rested her face in the still warm hollow. She recalled the sensuous clinging of his thick, sun-bleached hair as she ran her fingers through it . . . and her mouth was stamped with the phantom imprint of his lips. But most of all, she remembered the delirium they'd experienced together . . . the oneness . . . the love.

Then, with a sudden chill, she realized that not once on this bridal night just past had Nat told her he loved her. Many times over the months, he'd uttered those words—but on this night of nights, words of love had not issued from his lips! And the bitterness in his voice at the beginning of their lovemaking rang again in her ears.

If it's James Talbot you want, then it's him you'll get! But I will be the first man to claim your body!

By the time Melanie dressed and went to see about Laura in the master cabin, they had left the Elizabeth Islands far behind and were more than halfway across Buzzard's Bay, scarcely an hour out of home port. She left Laura's cabin and went looking for Nat, but he had disappeared into the chart house with Stokes. So she went to gather Laura's belongings, and her own, confident that she would see her beloved before they disembarked. But she was wrong.

At midmorning the third day out of Marblehead, the *Mirimar,* with one broken mast, limped into New Bedford harbor. The doctor was sent for the moment they tied up at the wharf. And so it was that Laura, accompanied only by Melanie and two attendants, arrived home pale and wan, in a lying-in-carriage; for she had lost her baby before the ship reached Nantucket Sound.

Melanie looked about her familiar room at Halcyon House. Here, in her childhood sanctuary, she had dreamed dreams . . . faced fears . . . and prayed for miracles.

Now, she looked through different eyes, and knew she would never again find comfort within these walls. For she had ventured forth into the world as a child, and come back a woman.

As Kate unpacked the trunks, her old eyes searched Melanie's face.

"Ye've changed much, in less than a week!" she said with a keen glance.

Less than a week!

Melanie was astonished. She had been so caught up in each hour of every day, she had failed to count their number! It seemed impossible so much could happen in so short a time! And she could feel so mature!

Where is the invisible line from youth to age? she wondered. *Can it be crossed in one moment of time? And if so, do we realize that instant, or is it only later, looking back, that we remember where . . . and when?*

CHAPTER ELEVEN

There was nothing to indicate, that bright, cheery morning, that it would be anything more than an ordinary day.

"Kate tells me she would like to be retained by Captain and Mrs. Larimore at Hazard's Bluff," Jared said with a teasing smile as he and Melanie sat at very early breakfast.

Melanie's heart skipped a beat at "Mrs. Larimore."

Since that fateful night over a week ago, she had neither seen nor heard from her betrothed. He was noticeably absent the morning she and Laura left the ship with the doctor in attendance. Jared, returning several hours later after a lengthy meeting with Nathaniel, had brought no message from him; and when the *Sea-Wind* rode the evening tide out of New Bedford harbor, Melanie watched from her window, filled with painful uncertainty, for Nat had sailed without saying good-bye.

It was with misgivings that Melanie went ahead with plans for her wedding. Indeed, she was swept along with the enthusiasm and energy of those town matrons who, because of Laura's indisposition, took over in her place.

"Poor dear," one of them had said last week at Goulet's, unaware of Melanie in a nearby fitting room, "she is without a mother to help her through this important time in her life. Now, her sister-in-law is languishing! We must do what we can to help!"

So Melanie had gone along with the fittings and plans for the wedding ball after the ceremony. With Mrs. Hoffman and Laura, she addressed invitations, and even endured the embarrassment and hesitancy of each woman as, one by one, they made furtive attempts to prepare her for the wedding night.

"Melanie?"

"Yes, Jared." She brought her mind back to their conversation quickly. "Kate and her brother have a small house at the Neck. He is at sea most of the time, and the close proximity to Hazard's Bluff would allow her to look after their property and enjoy her 'lilacs in the dooryard,' as she puts it." She reached out, touching her brother's hand. "Do you mind if Kate comes to live with me?"

"She has always loved you," he answered, smiling. "More than she ever did me, I'm afraid!" he added ruefully.

"She loves you, Jared. It's just that you were given to pulling her apron strings and bringing frogs into the nursery," Melanie said with a laugh.

"And you were a quiet, serious little thing, with your nose forever in a book; or staring into space, dreaming impossible dreams," he rejoined with an indulgent grin.

I am still dreaming impossible dreams! Melanie thought sadly.

"Have you had word from Nathaniel?" she asked, buttering a biscuit and trying to sound nonchalant.

"Paul Lanier received a message advising us to expect him on Nantucket within the next twenty-four hours . . ."

Melanie was astonished.

"But he said two weeks, more or less! It is barely over a week!"

"Apparently, it was less. He made proper connections with the Underground and we're to prepare for fugitives arriving with him." Jared took a gulp of his coffee. "So, little sister, Paul, Stokes, and I are off within the hour to Nantucket to make provision for our forbidden cargo. I shall return possibly day after tomorrow."

Melanie recalled the small valise she had passed without undue notice at the foot of the staircase.

Unaccountably, she felt a sudden chill.

"Be careful, Jared!" she whispered fearfully.

"Be not concerned, Melanie. All will go well," he said, gazing fondly at her. Then, changing the subject, "Your ship is not so bad off as we thought. The *Leviathan* should be off to the whaling grounds with tomorrow's ebb tide."

One of Melanie's whaling ships had been damaged off Nova Scotia at the entrance to the Bay of Fundy, during last week's storm, which had extended over a vast section of the coastline of Canada and New England. The *Leviathan* had returned, crippled, to home port for repairs.

But Melanie was unconcerned about the ship; she was more interested in further news of her betrothed.

"Did Paul say Nat would be coming to New Bedford?" she asked, trying to keep eagerness out of her voice.

"I'm sure, my dear, that your beloved will do everything in his power to join you as soon as possible," Jared said, smiling.

Rising from the table, he kissed her on the forehead.

"Do not look so worried, little one! Else your brow will be permanently creased before it is time!"

She too arose and followed him to the door.

"Is Laura aware you sail to Nantucket this morning?"

"I told her good-bye last evening. I do not wish to disturb her rest this early to do so again. In any case, so taken up is she with plans for your wedding, she will scarcely miss me."

Melanie watched him enter the carriage. When it disappeared around a bend in the winding downhill road, she went to her room to set plans for the day.

It was nearly ten o'clock when Melanie, ready to leave for a fitting at Goulet's, paused to tuck a stray lock beneath her bonnet. At that moment, Kate knocked, then entered hurriedly. Through the mirror, Melanie saw her frowning at a thick square of folded paper in her hand with a large "T" insignia imbedded in the outsized drop of sealing wax.

"Fer you," Kate said, holding out the missive. "From James Talbot."

Her troubled eyes met Melanie's startled ones in the glass.

" 'Tis beyond me," she said, shaking her head. " 'N I see no reason ta' fear 'im, but me bones say 'tis bad news!" She stood firmly in the center of the room waiting for Melanie to open the note. "A messenger waits below fer yer answer."

With swift resolution, Melanie broke the seal. At the top of the long page was a short, terse paragraph.

My Dear Melanie,
It is imperative, for the safety of your brother and Nathaniel, that you meet me at once at the Spouter Inn. With Paul Lanier gone from the mainland, no one but you can avert the disaster about to befall your loved ones. Their very lives are at stake! Make haste, I implore you! There is no time to lose! A messenger awaits your reply.
                                        Yrs. Resp.
                                (Signed) James T.

Melanie's heart pounded and her throat went dry as she held out the paper to Kate, who read with astonishment.

"Whut c'n it mean, dy'ye s'pose?" the old woman

asked, fear in her quavering voice. "James 'uld niver send news sich as this 'thout good reason!"

"I wonder, Kate," Melanie said, feeling a sudden cold chill creep up her back, "Is this 'good reason' for *James* . . . or is he sincere in wanting to help Jared and Nathaniel?"

Kate stared, uncomprehending.

"Are ye sayin' James Talbot'd do ye 'n yers inny harm? 'N fer 'is own sake?" she gaped wide-eyed at Melanie.

"I have not told you, Kate, of my encounters with James while in Boston and in Marblehead." Melanie reached for the letter once more. "James is devious. I do not trust him. And Nathaniel has forbidden me to even greet him in public, let alone meet him in private!"

"But whut if th' man's sincere in wantin' to aid ye? Whut . . . dear Lord, if there's somethin' sorely th' matter with Jared n' Nat? C'n ye take th' chance o' *not* meetin' 'im?"

Melanie tried to quell rising panic.

"What shall I do, Kate? I am frightened!"

"Meet 'im, child! See whut's amiss, 'n know where ye stand! 'Else, if somethin' 'appens ta' Jared 'n Nat, ye'd niver fergive yerself!"

"Meet him! At the Spouter Inn?" Melanie suppressed a shudder.

"Whut iver c'uld 'e be thinkin' of?" Kate murmured. "No gentleman 'uld ask a lady ta' meet 'im there! 'N James was always a gentleman!" She shook her head. "That den o' opium eaters, furrin sailors, 'n heathen cannibals!"

Despite fears engendered by James's note, Melanie smiled. All black sailors were "heathen cannibals" since one day at the marketplace when Kate had been accosted by a garish mariner with black filed teeth and gold circle earrings through pendulous lobes.

Melanie went to her desk and wrote on the bottom
of the note with her plumed pen.

James:
I cannot meet you at the Inn. I will be in the
park across from the theater within the hour.
                           (Signed) Melanie H.

She handed the note back to Kate, who left immediately to place it in the hands of the messenger who
lingered impatiently below stairs.

Alone in her room, Melanie tried to sort out scattered thoughts and prepare herself for the dread
meeting with James. Within five minutes, Kate reap-
peared.

"Th' carriage is waitin' fer ye," she said, moving
to the window. "An' it looks like fog rollin' in from
Buzzard's Bay. Mayhap ye'll fail to see James through
th' mist in th' park!"

"I trust Jared had no difficulty reaching Nantucket!" Melanie answered with an anxious note in
her voice.

"He sails with good men; an' a bit o' fog in Buzzard's Bay need not be reachin' ta' Nantucket Sound!
'Though, heaven help us, I pray 'tis not that sort a
news James be givin' ye!"

"I pray, also, Kate!" Melanie whispered, kissing
the woman's wrinkled cheek.

"I should go with ye, child! Ye have no business
meetin' a man alone in th' park, gentleman though
he be!"

"There is not time, Kate," Melanie said. "I will return as soon as possible with the news."

By the time Melanie's carriage reached midtown,
the mists had crept into New Bedford, blotting out
the sun. She alighted in front of the closed, empty

theater and, bidding the coachman to wait, crossed the street to the park.

Long tendrils of fog were tangling in the tops of tall trees, snaking in wisps down the trunks to creep insidiously over the ground, obscuring walks and benches. Sound was muffled in the town, and the blare of foghorns and ship's bells seemed far off. Sailors had withdrawn into vessels and taverns; and shops were empty, for patrons waited until they could see the sky again before venturing forth.

Melanie felt all alone in a ghostly world as she stood under a tree close by the empty thoroughfare. Now and then, a truant breeze cleared a path to show an occasional carriage or human making their way through the pale gloom; only to be swallowed up again in the engulfing mists.

"Melanie?"

Her heart beat a rapid tattoo in her breast and she froze at the sudden calling of her name. The voice seemed to fill the vaporous air and she could not tell the direction from which it came.

Turning, she saw James Talbot gradually appear through the swirling cloud. His footsteps gave no sound on the path, and she could make out only his head and shoulders, still some twenty feet away. Then, emerging suddenly, he was at her side.

"I am sorry for the fog," he said, as if it had manifested because of some oversight on his part. "But," he took her hand and raised it to his lips, "it was imperative that we meet."

"What is the urgency, James?" Melanie fought down the dread that suddenly swept over her, stronger than ever.

"There is little time, so without preamble I will come directly to the point!" The words tumbled rapidly from his lips.

Reaching into his pocket, he brought out a sheaf of papers.

"I have here some documents drawn up by Judge Lyons. I am offering you three thousand in cash, American dollars, to lease the *Leviathan* for a six-month period. Should my voyage extend beyond that measure, I will reimburse you accordingly."

Melanie was astounded.

"I do not have the authority to do this!"

"Yes, you do, Melanie! Your brother is away from the mainland, as is your betrothed and his business manager. Because this is a matter of extreme urgency, you, as owner of the ship, may affix your seal and signature showing you have leased the vessel to me for this length of time and amount of money. All is valid concerning our transaction, as Judge Lyons will assure you."

Taking her arm, he began leading her down the path toward the other side of the park. "I have a carriage waiting; and witnesses tarrying in Judge Lyons's office to assist us in sealing the bargain."

"Your note said it was a matter of life and death for my brother and Nat! This is no urgency of mine!"

James took a deep, exasperated breath.

"Melanie, my dear! It is only a matter of time before Nat is intercepted in his fugitive slave running; and Jared will be right beside him. Do you not see that I do this for us both? Who is to look after you when Jared and Nat are gone? Your ships will be tied up . . . and the courts can hold forever if they've a mind to. You and Laura will be fortunate if you are able to meet the daily, mundane necessities when the inevitable happens! As it will, Melanie! Mark me! Jared and Nat will be caught! The fines could wipe out your entire dowry, along with Jared's estate! I want to be able to step in then, and take care of you. I cannot help without the wherewithal to do so!"

"If Nathaniel is caught, you are due to take over his entire fortune, James! I am aware of that!"

"But it also would be tied up in courts for months,

perhaps years! And what would you do for funds in the meantime?"

"James, I disbelieve you! Why would the courts take my dowry and Jared's funds?"

"The fugitives shipped to Canada by Nat, and now Jared, are stolen property, Melanie! They belong to southerners just as surely as their land and horses belong to them. They have money invested in their property, and Nat robs them as certainly as if he lifted their purses! When caught, if he escapes with his life, his fortune will go toward reimbursement to the owners!"

Melanie gasped. Then, she tried to reason.

"When Nat and Jared return, I will present your proposition to them," she said, disengaging herself from his grasp. "But I cannot do what you ask at this time, James."

He stood back with a cold smile.

"If you do not abide with me in this, Melanie, I must allow the port authorities to act upon the charge that has just now been filed against the *Sea-Wind,* to search and confiscate cargo and ship when Nat reaches Nantucket Sound today or tomorrow. There is no specific time on the papers, so an ambush awaits his arrival. There is also a search and seizure order for the candle factory on Nantucket, and a warrant for Jared, should fugitives, or evidence that fugitives have been harbored there, be found."

Melanie's knees buckled, and, ignoring James's hand reached out to steady her, she leaned back against the nearest tree.

"The *Leviathan* is not yet ready to sail," she said weakly.

"That is what the shipfitters, who are loyal to me, were supposed to tell Jared. The ship is now ready, and so are my men. You may save Nat and your brother, if you will be reasonable and accompany me to Judge Lyons's office to sign this document."

"I cannot!"

"Then, should Nat and Jared escape death, to face incarceration, I will present this note to them, wherein you offer to meet me in the park, instead of the inn. Your brother and Nat should be interested in the implications in your own handwriting sent to me at my hotel . . ."

He held out the note, and Melanie recognized her answer to his written request for her meeting, which had been cut off. Her answer now became a separate sheet of paper, giving the impression she had summoned James for the purpose of an assignation.

She realized then what had been lurking in the back of her mind. Kate pointed it out, but Melanie, preoccupied with worry about the meaning of James's message, had not listened. "Of course! A gentleman does not repose at the Spouter Inn! And a lady does not meet him there. It was a trick!" she said. "For this very purpose!" Anger blazed from her eyes and she stood straight, glaring up at him.

He looked sadly at her.

"Melanie, someday you will realize that I do this for your good, as well as mine. Whether you realize it or not, I am still truly in love with you!"

"What sort of love is it that intimidates and bullies? And what of your wife, lying ill in Marblehead? How dare you speak to me of love! You have no idea of the meaning of the word!"

"You will realize soon, Melanie, that I speak the truth!" he said sorrowfully. "And you will then understand why I had to do this; though it pains you now, I will make it up to you, I promise!"

She felt suddenly helpless. It would do no good to rail at him. She realized her position and could only make the best of it.

But not before I worry him a little! she thought.

"I will see to it, James," she said with a bravado she certainly did not feel, "that you pay dearly for what you do today! I vow you will not get away with this!"

And she wondered if she could; then prayed that she would have the ability to follow through with her oath.

"There is nothing you can do, Melanie." He looked regretfully at her.

She stared at him through eyes filled with hatred.

"I did not realize you were such a formidable enemy!"

"Never *your* enemy, my dear! Just Nathaniel's!" he answered smoothly. "And I am not Nat's only enemy! There are others who sympathize with me in my plight!"

An errant breeze blew through the park, and the mist swirled about Melanie's feet.

"How do I know you will call off your dogs? It would be to your advantage to have Nat and Jared incarcerated, or killed!"

"On my word as a gentleman, I will call them off!"

"You are no gentleman, James; I am only now realizing that fact!"

He ignored the bitterness in her tone. "Sign these papers and I promise I will disturb you no more with my presence. I will no longer need the crumbs of Nat's inheritance; I will be wealthy in my own right!"

He spoke vehemently, and Melanie realized again the burning, driving urge that consumed him; the need to surpass Nat, the interloper in what James felt was his own true destiny. He craved power and wealth and was determined, despite his words, to wrest from Nathaniel what he believed rightfully his own. And beneath the anger and greed, Melanie recognized resentment that Jonas had chosen to endow these gifts in another direction.

"It is not as though I am stealing your ship, Melanie! I am merely leasing it; a business transaction between old friends. I am paying the normal rate to lease a seagoing vessel for the amount of time necessary. It is done every day, this leasing of ships!"

"If it is done every day, why must it be my ship?"

"Because there are no others available at the moment," he answered lamely.

"Or because no one else will lease a ship to befoul it with the stench of captive slaves!" A sense of helplessness came over her again.

"I have a crew standing by at this moment," he said, taking her limp hand and pulling it through his arm. "We could begin our voyage within the hour!" He urged her along the pathway toward the road, where a waiting carriage loomed eerily through the fog.

"Then," he continued in a lighter tone, helping her to enter, "you may happily spend the rest of your day with nuptial plans; for Nat will be free as a bird to make you his wife."

She was trapped, like a butterfly on a pin! She sat back dazedly in the carriage, and they set off across town to Judge Lyons's office.

All went as James had planned. The papers were signed before witnesses; none of whom Melanie had ever seen before.

Then, Judge Lyons raised cold, dispassionate eyes to Melanie.

"It is important, Melanie Hardy, that you swear these papers were signed of your own, free will; that the experience of this sudden leasing in the absence of your brother and your betrothed has only to do with accommodating Mr. Talbot, and not because you were coerced into this in any way! Do you so swear?"

She was silent for a long moment, staring at the Judge. He blinked not an eye at her. Surely, he knew better? Certainly he was aware she would not do this of her own free will? She recalled his presence in the receiving line beside his portly, good-natured wife at Mrs. Hoffman's soiree on her betrothal night. She had even danced with him!

Wondering how this man could be party to such an unconscionable act, Melanie closed her eyes, praying God's forgiveness for perjuring herself. Surely, God would look favorably upon her deviation from His commandment, in view of the peril her brother and Nathaniel would face had she not done this thing?

She took the oath, signed the receipt, and accepted the money. And when the Judge affixed the seal and placed custody of the *Leviathan* into James Talbot's hands, Melanie silently vowed once more to do whatever necessary to thwart him in his plan to use her ship for his diabolical purpose.

As they left the Judge's office, Melanie turned to James.

"Now we will go to the authorities to call off your charges!"

James smiled.

"I will send a man to do it," he said casually.

He waved a hand and Melanie saw a swarthy sailor coming toward them. With a start, she recognized the mute from Nat's ship.

"Dismiss the charges, Kreuger!" James said offhandedly.

The man nodded and disappeared in the thinning fog.

"James! You gave your word!" she cried in desperation. "And that man is mute! He cannot tell them anything; besides, it is you who must dismiss them! You promised as a gentleman!" She grasped his coat, shaking him feebly, tears running down her cheeks.

He put his arm about her, patting her shoulder in a gesture of consolation.

"So I did, my dear! And you told me I was not a gentleman!" He offered her his handkerchief. "Come, my lovely. Ride to the docks with me, then you may take the carriage wherever you wish!"

"James!" She thrust away his arm. "You gave your word you would drop the charges!"

"And you, my dear, gave your word that you signed the papers solely because you wanted to accommodate me." He patted her hand.

She looked at him through wide, terrified eyes.

"You had no intention of dropping the charges!" she said in a fearful whisper. "You are a monstrous cad!"

He laughed again.

"How do you know I filed charges? Perhaps I only said so to intimidate you—and accomplish my purpose." His voice softened. "Come, my love, accompany me in the carriage, and we will ease your mind."

He opened the carriage door and stood aside, extending a hand to assist her entrance.

With one wild look, she turned and fled into the mist. Her footsteps were muffled and she heard his shout behind her. But looking back, all she could see was thick, pea-soup fog. She was alone with her terror.

She thought of going to the authorities herself, and denouncing James's allegations against her brother and Nathaniel. Then, she realized that if he had *not* filed, her very presence would immediately make her loved ones suspect. And if James *had* filed, her fear of their apprehension would add fuel to their apparent guilt.

Forcing herself to walk calmly, she took deep breaths to quiet her rampant thoughts.

There is something! she told herself. *There is some way I can prevent this terrible thing from happening!*

Suddenly, her mind cleared and it came to her. She must go to Nantucket as quickly as possible and warn Jared. Then, perhaps, they could somehow divert

Nat before he brought the *Sea-Wind* into Nantucket Sound.

She quickened her steps and headed toward the park, where hopefully, her carriage still waited.

The little sloop Melanie had happily sailed each summer of her youthful life was tied to a small dock in a sheltered cove just off the Acushnet River. She considered sailing it to the island. But as she walked, she realized that though the fog was thinning, it still hung heavy in wide areas. Fog meant lack of wind! Melanie tried to recall what her father taught her of New England fog banks; how far they usually extended and the likelihood of spreading over wide areas beyond the coastline, but memory failed her.

At this moment, all of Nantucket Sound could be blotted out by mist. If she took the sloop, she might becalm for hours, or at least until it was too late to help Jared and Nathaniel. Besides, it was a long run to Nantucket—six, possibly seven hours, depending upon prevailing winds.

She glanced quickly at the little fob watch pinned to her bosom. It was barely half after eleven. The packet boat to Nantucket sailed at one o'clock . . . sharp!

She had reached the park. The carriage waited, a few yards away.

CHAPTER TWELVE

With a sigh of relief, Melanie, with Kate beside her, leaned against the rail of the little two-masted schooner as it hoisted sail and slid down the Acushnet River. On one side, New Bedford rose in terraced streets outlined by lush, green foliage and accented with bright, multicolored flowers spilling over gardens and outcroppings of rock.

On the other side, whaling ships and merchantmen, small craft and large, crowded the wharves, gathering about huge mountains of empty casks to pour the precious oil of whales; or nestled up to nearby warehouses for cargo on the docks.

Fog had lifted over the land, but still pressed low in spots, particularly over water where tops of masts disappeared into gloomy haze and long wisps snaked over the river like steam hovering above a nearly boiling saucepan.

"How long will we be puttin' up with this?" Kate asked disdainfully, nose in the air as she surveyed the motley group of passengers.

"With luck, we will arrive on Nantucket before sunset," Melanie answered, praying for speedy winds and a smooth passage in time to accomplish her mission.

"I must be sittin' 'fore we gain open water!" Kate said. "I'll find me a seat inside, if ye' be standin' here much longer! 'Else, we c'uld both rest easy from th' stares a' these lubbers, by steppin' within!"

Melanie lifted her small valise, as did Kate, and

they moved into the passenger room amidships, where long benches under wide windows were filling rapidly as the boat groped sluggishly toward the mouth of the harbor. Conversation buzzed all around and Melanie's thoughts subsided. The surrounding din exhausted her and she gave up a futile attempt to predict the outcome of this excursion. She stared out the window. An opaque, eerie mist hung over the world, pressing close, engulfing the little packet boat in dense, suffocating cloud. Melanie could scarcely see the rail a few yards beyond. All the world seemed swallowed up in mist and the sun was blotted out as if it had never been.

"I'm sure I missed somethin'!" Kate said. "I niver packed so hastily in me' life. Don't blame me if ye' don't have all ye' need!"

"We may not even stay the night, Kate," she replied tersely.

Kate had been shocked when Melanie arrived home in a flurry, and told her story while throwing clothes and toiletries out to be packed.

"I see no reason for you to go to Nantucket!" Laura had stormed. "What could Nat be thinking of, to send for you at a time like this? And if it was necessary to go, why did you not leave with Jared this morning?"

Laura assumed Nathaniel had sent for her when Melanie said she was leaving for Nantucket, and because of Laura's recent ordeal, Melanie had not wanted to confide the true reason.

"You are in the midst of preparations for the wedding!" Laura cried in a last-ditch effort to prevent her from leaving. "What on earth could you be doing in Nantucket that is more important?"

Aware that the only escape from Laura's questions, as well as her wrath, was to steadfastly remain true to her course, Melanie had made no response and, with Kate in tow, left the house as quickly as possible.

The packet boat sailed on through soupy gloom.
The passengers' voices rose and fell. Melanie leaned
her head against the window and dozed.

She was awakened suddenly as the little ship was
taken by a rising wind. Reeling, leaning precariously
sideways, the ship came to life from dull lethargy.
Tossing bright foam from her bow as sails filled, she
fairly skimmed over the water.

Melanie's heart pounded in elation. She had
prayed for this, and now it was here. At this pace, if
the wind was steady, they would reach Nantucket Island much sooner than she had expected.

When the ship regained itself, she stood up and
made her way outside to stand at the rail. More than
three hours out of New Bedford, they were entering
Nantucket Sound and Martha's Vineyard was just off
the starboard bow.

The fog had been swept away by a brisk ocean
wind. Crackling flashes of lightning outlined the bulk
and height of towering black thunderheads whose
threatening rumbles announced encroachment from
the northeast Atlantic, beyond Cape Cod.

The little schooner sailed on and before wind and
rain blotted out the horizon, Nantucket Island lay in
the distance; a long, low sandbar, pale and lifeless
against the creeping darkness.

Though it was well past mid-May, night fell before
six o'clock and waves rose threateningly, washing over
the deck, sending fearful passengers inside again to
pray for safety.

Nantucket harbor was calmer, though waters ran
more swift than usual. They disembarked at the pier
and found shelter from a driving rain inside the little
wooden building where passage was purchased and
travelers relieved themselves before crossing.

Most of their shipmates were met by friends and
relatives. Standing in the rain, Melanie was hard put
to find a carriage to take them to the candle factory

at the southeastern curve of Nantucket Island. Eventually, she flagged down a lorry loaded with boxes and various other items. For an outrageous price, the driver agreed to travel an uncertain road to the "Godforsaken outer anthills of Nantucket," as he, a Cape Codsman, called it; for naturally, no Nantucketer would ever so refer to their beloved island beach!

For well over an hour, they traveled through driving rain and wind while the drayman kept up a running narrative dialogue of how he came to live on this lonely offshore elbow of sand. His wife, it seemed, had been born here and here she would die; planting mushrooms for shade and endowing thistles with the qualities of great and venerable oaks.

At last, after what seemed an eternity, they drew up before a long, low building a stone's toss from the sea. The crash of waves against the dunes vied with wind and rain in raucous symphony as Kate and Melanie stepped from the vehicle into uncertain sand.

The driver was impatient to be off. With a sense of trepidation, Melanie paid him; then, with Kate at her heels, ran toward a wildly swinging lantern hung over a single door. The sign above the entrance read: Nantucket Spermaceti Candle Factory.

As they made their way across muddy sand, a sudden flash of lightning illuminated a horse and coach standing close by the building. Melanie's heart sank to her boots. Jared, Stokes, and Paul Lanier had come by pinkie schooner to this isolated place close by the sea. The sole purpose of this remote spot was to obviate the necessity of towns and townspeople. A few fishermen's wives worked here an hour or so a day; but they lived in scattered shanties along the beach, and there was not one among them rich enough to own a horse, let alone a carriage! The vehicle could mean only one thing; the nebulous "Authorities" had preceded her, and Melanie's rush to warn of their coming had been futile! The terror James's threat had engendered within her breast and the urgent need to warn Jared and Nathaniel would end when she stepped beyond that narrow door. Were all her efforts fruitless?

With Kate behind her, Melanie turned the knob and opened the door. The fact that it was unlocked frightened Melanie even more. Surely, if this was a hiding place for fugitives, Jared and Paul Lanier would have secured the building against easy access!

They found themselves immediately in a long, narrow room. A chain hung from the center of the ceiling, dangling a crude wooden chandelier, circled with a handful of candles. Flickering shadows leaped over the walls as a draft from their entrance set the peduncle swinging wildly, nearly extinguishing the tiny wavering flames.

Long rows of tables held candle molds of all shapes and sizes; and mingled with the smell of oil and wax were other, unfamiliar odors.

"Jared?" Melanie called. Her voice was loud in the empty room and faint echoes bounced off the white-washed walls.

Her only answer was another gust of wind and the rush of rain spattering against the windows.

There were two small doors, one at each end of the room, in the wall opposite the entrance. Melanie and Kate walked cautiously through one of them. They stepped into another room exactly matching the dimensions of the first. This, however, had a huge fireplace and scattered over the hearth were jugs and kettles, pots and utensils for melting wax and mixing with oil. Two large casks stood nearby and a crude plank table held molds of all sizes and shapes.

The flimsy back door rattled with each gust. When lightning flashed as Melanie gazed through the cracked window, she saw, momentarily, a stretch of beach and dunes, with the angry waves beyond.

Apparently, the small building was empty; two

rooms, back to back, with lighted candles, the door unlocked, and a mysterious horse and carriage tied up outside. Melanie drew her brows together in puzzlement.

"There's none here!" Kate said in a near whisper. "Who b'longs to th' horse an' buggy, d'ye s'pose?"

As if in answer, there was a faint sound, scarcely audible above the raging storm outside. A moan, that could have been the wind . . . or a human in pain.

Then, they heard a man's voice, low, rumbling, and a scraping sound, as of a footstep on the floor.

Melanie and Kate held on to each other fearfully. It came again. The muffled voice, mingled with moaning, filled the room in which they stood. Melanie's wide eyes searched each shadowed corner and found nothing; while Kate's fearful, darting glances also sought the origin of the terrifying, muted murmurs.

"Lord help us! Th' place is ha'nted!" she cried, crossing herself.

The two women clung to each other in fright, alone in a building miles from civilization, on a sand dune by the sea. Heaven only knew what ghostly inhabitant threatened them now . . .

Suddenly, before Melanie's bewildered eyes, the floor rose up and a man's head and shoulders appeared. She stared, momentarily stunned, before realization flooded over her that the man stood on a short flight of steps beneath a trapdoor leading to a cellar below.

The man, elderly, stooped, and with balding head, regarded Melanie through astonished eyes. With his startled gaze fixed upon the two women, he called over his shoulder.

"We have visitors!"

There was a scuffling sound as the man stepped up into the room. Then, immediately behind him,

Jared's head and shoulders appeared. Beyond Jared, came Paul . . . then Stokes.

Melanie felt suddenly weak with relief. She had won the race after all! Her taut nerves suddenly relaxed and she felt her knees give way. The balding man reached out a steadying hand as Kate slipped an old rickety chair up behind her. Melanie sank gratefully into it.

"Melanie!" Jared cried, going to his knees beside her. "Whatever are you doing here?" His voice was filled with astonishment and his bewildered gaze went from Melanie's blanched face to Kate's anxious features.

"Oh, Jared!" she exclaimed, throwing herself into his arms. "I am so thankful you are yet safe!"

"Safe?" His eyes searched hers and his tone was puzzled.

"Talbot has filed agin' ye!" Kate said, speaking rapidly. "An' agin' Nat, also! Ye best be quittin' here fast, a'fore they git to ye!" she finished breathlessly. "An' ye must gie th' alarm to Nat, a'fore he enters Nantucket Sound, fer they be'a waitin' fer 'im there!"

The four men in the room stared from Kate to Melanie, and in Jared's arms Melanie felt the tension that took over his body.

"Tell us, calmly, Melanie, exactly what happened?" Paul Lanier's voice, quiet and steady, eased rising anxiety.

So Melanie told her story and when she was finished, the men all looked to Paul for a decision.

"We must warn Nat, of course!" Paul said. He glanced quickly at Stokes. "Will the pinkie schooner take the open sea in this weather?"

Stokes nodded.

"She draws deep enough; though she'll bob like a cork when we hit offshore swells."

Paul looked sharply at the balding man who stood nearby rearranging instruments in a little black bag.

"What about him, Doctor?" Paul asked, with a nod of his head toward the still-open trapdoor.

"He'll be fine. I've drained the infection, sutured the wound, and bound it well. But he will have to remain fastened securely below deck; for a blow, or use of the leg in any way, could reopen the wound."

Jared turned to face the man.

"Doctor Prentice, this is my sister, Melanie," he said formally, if belatedly.

Melanie nodded.

The man smiled and, taking her wrist with a professional air, counted her pulse.

"If you and your companion," he said, nodding at Kate, "wish to return to New Bedford, I will be happy to drive you to the packet boat myself. However," he glanced at his watch, "there is not another boat out until morning. My wife and I will be happy to put you both up for the night."

Melanie shook her head.

"Thank you very much, Doctor. But I assure you, I am fine now. I am accustomed to the sea, and wish to accompany my brother to warn my betrothed of the danger. Then, I will sail back to New Bedford on the *Sea-Wind*."

Jared shook his head vigorously.

"No, Melanie! You will not go with us! Anything might happen. There is a storm out there and the schooner could be swamped! I will not allow you to endanger your life!"

Clenching her fists, Melanie stood straight and defiant before him.

"Let me remind you, Jared, that I have gone through a great deal to bring this news to you! I will not be put aside at the last moment! I have faced more danger before arriving here than I could possibly face from now on! The pinkie schooner is seaworthy; I know that to be a fact, and Stokes will back me up!" She turned her gaze upon Stokes, who stood near the back door.

He nodded.

"Nathaniel is my betrothed!" she continued. "And I must assure myself of his safety! Besides," she added, "it will take all three of you to sail the boat to a spot where Nat may be intercepted; then, there is the matter of signaling him . . . and who will look after whoever is in the cellar with an injured leg?" She turned again to Jared. "It does seem to me that Kate and I could be of great service when your hands are full with sails and weather!"

The eyes of the four men met.

The doctor smiled.

"Despite her size, she makes good sense. And she seems healthy enough," he stated professionally.

"And feisty enough!" Jared answered with a grin.

Ignoring Kate's fearful eyes, Melanie took her hand and they followed the doctor through the trapdoor to the cellar. In the dim light of a lantern, they saw a tall, thin black man with a bandaged leg, lying on a pallet of straw.

"How did he arrive here?" Melanie asked, gazing at the unconscious fugitive.

"He stowed in the hold of a Gloucester schooner berthed at Cape Cod. Eavesdropping, he thought they sailed to the Bay of Fundy, when in truth, they'd just left there. The captain, a sympathizer, notified me when his ship docked at Nantucket. I brought the man here to join Nat's fugitives." The doctor shook his head. "How he reached Cape Cod must be another story!"

"Will he awaken soon?"

"I've given him a potion that will keep him asleep for the next few hours. He was delirious with fever. The infection was deep, but I drained the wound and cut away a portion of gangrenous flesh. He will recover, but the pain will intensify when he fully

awakens." He pulled a bottle from his coat pocket.
"A sip of this five or six times an hour should keep
him quiet." He looked from Melanie to Kate and
back again. "Remember! The leg must remain perfectly still! If it is bumped, or used in any way, the
wound will reopen!"

Less than half an hour later, the doctor had driven
his horse and carriage off into the night and Melanie
and Kate, bundled in blankets, sat with the sleeping
fugitive in the low-beamed hold of the pinkie
schooner.

Two hours went by, according to Melanie's little
fob watch. They had sailed beyond the surging landswells into deep ocean. The seas were rough,
bouncing the little ship about like an inflated ball.
The rain had eased to an intermittent drizzle, and at
the foot of the short ladder, Melanie gazed up
through the glass of the small square hatch. A star or
two glimmered in the black sky. The storm had
nearly blown itself out. Melanie breathed a sigh of relief and went to sit beside Kate, who now and then
fed the injured fugitive a sip of whiskey from the
bottle the doctor had given her. Melanie suspected
Kate might be surreptitiously imbibing a few nips
herself, since her mien had mellowed considerably the
past hour, despite fierce rocking and rolling of the
little schooner.

No matter! Melanie thought. *It will help her survive this ordeal and keep from adding to our prob-
lems.*

The tiny lantern, fastened to the low beam above
their heads, swung crazily as the little boat, fighting
heavy seas, labored up each mountainous wave,
perched precariously for a moment, then plunged
downward. Melanie lay back on bundles of sacking
and gave herself up to the intermittent reeling of the
ship. Relaxing her muscles to prevent bruises, she

tried, without benefit of Kate's palliative, to subdue
raw nerves and keep imagination from running rampant. Now and then an outsize wave swamped the
deck and hit the hatch glass, startling her out of newfound lethargy. Then, as the storm eased, she slept.

Shouts from the deck overhead awakened her precipitously; Paul's voice and Stokes's, cursing and calling loudly above the wind and sea. Melanie sat
upright in startled fear. She was thrown back again as
the ship lurched sharply, and, taken broadside by a
cascading deluge, nearly capsized in a long, tumbling
roll.

Moments later, the ship righted itself again. Voices
on deck fell silent as the little boat sailed on through
the night.

In the dim light, Kate and the fugitive slept peace-
fully, unperturbed by trepidation of the elements;
numbed and succored by the tranquility found in the
doctor's bottle.

Seized with a sudden, paralyzing fear, Melanie
fought to reach the ladder and began climbing,
slowly, laboriously; not because of agitated seas, for
the waves had subsided and the wind and rain nearly
ceased entirely. It was the cold, fearsome knowledge
growing deep within that froze her limbs and
clutched her heart with dread.

At the top of the ladder, she fumbled with icy fingers at the hatch, opening it at last to a burst of cold
wind and a spattering of seafoam. Melanie climbed
out on the slippery deck, clutching at the handspike
windlass to keep from falling. Through the darkness,
she saw Stokes, fighting the lines, struggling to bring
the ship around again as full sails billowed noisily
overhead. Amidships, Paul strained slowly toward her
and the flapping sounds drowned out his words as he
reached her side.

"Jared?" she screamed, searching the deck through

frantic eyes. "Jared!" she cried again, the awful intui-
tion verified as she collapsed against Paul.

He held her tightly a moment, and beyond her
numbing paralysis, she sensed his deep sorrow and agitation. Scooping her into his arms, Paul swept her
down the ladder of the open hatch and into the hold
again.

"Kate!" Paul's voice was loud and, sleep still in her
eyes, Kate sprang up with alacrity.

"Whut's 'appened to 'er?" she cried in alarm.

"See to her, Kate. Her brother's been washed overboard!"

"Dear God!" Kate cried, clasping her hands in a
prayerful attitude.

"He was seasick," Paul continued. "We told him to
go below when the storm abated, but he refused.
While Jared retched at the rail, Stokes and I had our
hands full keeping afloat in heavy seas. Unexpectedly,
we were swamped by a huge wave and Jared was
gone before we could reach him!" Paul's voice broke
and the lines of his face were etched with grief.

Kate took Melanie in her arms.

"There, there, 'Cush'la . . ." she crooned. "Th'
good Lord's embracin' 'im now . . ." Tears coursed
down her cheeks and she rocked Melanie back and
forth as she'd done when she was a child. "E'en as a
wee lad, 'e hated the sea! Now, 'e's followed 'is father
into th' deep! May 'is soul rest in peace!"

Melanie would forever remember that night in the
hold of the little schooner. Lying on the sacking, she
prayed to cry, but could not. Her brother, whom she
loved deeply, was gone; and unaccountably, her eyes
were dry! He was the last of her family and she was
alone! Her chest ached with a frightful pain. She
prayed to die! She could not look into the future, and
tried to shove the past away from her cognizance.
Staring blankly at the little lantern swaying from the

overhead beam, she fought memories that rose insistent, and unbidden, to her mind.

She and Jared riding sleds downhill together in the winters of their childhood; Jared's laughter at her reluctance to mount a horse, and his pride and assurances when she succeeded. Her fright when he played boyish pranks on Kate, and their joint glee, with Kate oftentimes surprisingly amused at a harmless joke. Shared holidays . . . whispered secrets . . . and Christmas gifts. Jared's help when she was stymied with her lessons . . . and his defense of her when classmates teased her on the walk home from school. Long, solemn discussions, when their father hid in his study after their mother's death; and after word of Ephraim's demise, common sorrow and mutual comfort.

"A wee bit o' this, child, 'ull 'elp ye git through!" Kate urged, holding the bottle to Melanie's lips.

Melanie turned her head away. The smell of whisky flared her nostrils and her stomach churned.

With a comforting pat, Kate took her place again beside the sleeping fugitive.

Staring once more at the swaying lantern, Melanie suddenly recalled words spoken by her father, while she was still too young to comprehend . . .

She'd taken a short voyage with him down the coast to Norfolk and they'd been buffeted by a storm. She was eight then, and for the first time, her feet rested on an unsteady deck. Ephraim had taken his daughter to his cabin and tucked her into bed. But, as the berth rocked with each motion of the ship, Melanie cried out in fear; for the only security in that strange, rolling world was her father's calm gaze and steady hand on her trembling shoulders.

"I must leave you now, Melanie," he'd said. "I've work to do if we're to get through the storm."

She'd clung to him then, and begged him not to leave her.

"Melanie," Ephraim had said, smoothing her pillow and forcing her to look into his eyes. "Have faith! The Lord will bring you through many storms before He takes you to His side, and you must learn from all of them! Each time I bring my ship through a tempest, I learn what must be done and what must *not* be done the next time!"

He'd pointed to the ship's lantern swaying from the rafter.

"You believe that lantern to be unsteady, do you, child?"

She nodded.

"'Tis not!" Ephraim had stated positively. "'Tis the most steady object on the ship, 'sides the compass! That lamp," he'd pointed a sturdy finger, "rides with gravity, which is the center of the earth, and keeps all things keeled evenly. 'Tis the ship that's rocking! And if you watch the lantern, you will see how far off we are! When the storm eases, the lantern will be stilled, for the ship will be brought into line with gravity."

She'd stared at him, trying to understand.

His long middle finger tapped her flat little chest.

"Deep inside, you have a center of gravity! There is strength within you, and wisdom, if you but realize how to use it! Though storms rage all about you, the lamp in your soul remains steady. It is, truly, the only security in the world! Trust and believe in the lamp God has lit within, and you will always come through life's storms. . . ."

Through wide, dry eyes, Melanie now watched the slowly swaying lantern. It seemed her father's words had been repeated aloud inside her head, and his voice still rang in her ears. Her body rolled without resistance to each whimsical toss of the ship, and finally she slept.

CHAPTER THIRTEEN

When Melanie opened her eyes again, the lantern had stilled. The ship rolled gently with easy swells and Kate and the fugitive yet slumbered. The gentle movement of the boat told her they were far offshore, for there was no sound of surf or surging landswells rolling toward the beaches.

Melanie felt empty inside, with a deep sense of loss and an agony that only time and tears would ease. But the weighty fear she'd felt for so long had disappeared.

My premonition has come true! she thought, surprised to find a sense of relief mingled with the mourning.

She sat up in the dim light and looked at the little watch pinned to her bosom. It was shortly after midnight. Her mind went over the past six urgency-filled hours since their arrival on Nantucket. Each one stretched into infinity. Was it truly only yesterday that she had breakfasted with Jared and discussed wedding plans and Kate's wish to accompany her to Marblehead? She thought of her last moments with her brother; his final kiss on her forehead and his loving concern as he arranged sacking into the pallet on which she now rested. It seemed impossible that Jared, so intelligent, so matter-of-fact, and in his quiet way, so vital, could be gone forever.

Numb from the shock of Jared's death, she was only dimly aware of the stiff soreness caused by hard boards beneath her slumbering bones. Smoothing her hair, she rose painfully to her feet.

There was no sound from the deck overhead. Though her senses were dulled, curiosity sent her climbing the ladder slowly, remembering the terror that accompanied her the last time.

When she opened the hatch, she was greeted by a gentle wind and a dark blue sky, pierced with bright stars. Paul and Stokes were in the bow of the boat, deep in conversation. As Melanie stepped out on deck, they both turned and motioned her to join them. She stood a moment at the rail in an attempt to get her bearings.

The furled sails and motionless aspect of the ship told Melanie they were at anchor. Where? And for how long? These questions arose in her mind demanding answers.

"We're 'bout five mile' offshore from th' candle fact'ry," Stokes said, coming up beside her. "Cap'n Larimore will be comin' straight in, 's'way I figger it, 'n we sh'uld be able t' warn 'im off!"

"But James said they would watch for the *Sea-Wind* at the mouth of Nantucket Sound!" Melanie said, bewildered.

"As they most likely are doing," Paul interjected. "Apparently James was uncertain which course Nat would take. In any case, they will take no chances. By now they are probably searching the factory—in vain, for we left no trace of fugitives ever having been there. They are, doubtless, awaiting the arrival of the *Sea-Wind* on Nantucket, as well as at the mouth of Nantucket Sound; for if Nat sailed directly to Canada, that would be the most likely place to intercept him, just before rounding Cape Cod."

"Suppose he misses us in the darkness?" Melanie asked, as she felt fear once more reaching for her.

"It is somewhat like finding a needle in the haystack!" Paul agreed. "Except that, figuring the charts, the angle from which Nat would be approaching Nantucket leaves little likelihood of missing us. He will have his running lights, as we have ours. When we spot him and he is close enough, we will send up a flare."

"He will think it is the authorities!" Melanie said worriedly.

"The flare will light our schooner also. He will then recognize us and heave to."

"We will have to be mighty close before we set off the flare," she said, with anxiety in her voice.

Stokes nodded.

"Only whin we know fer sure it's the *Sea-Wind* will we set it off."

An hour went by, and another, during which time Melanie stood at the rail on deck, searching the darkness for Nat's ship; and praying that Jared's death was swift and without pain or fear.

She looked out over the water beyond the soft glow of their running lights. From the shining stars, horizon to horizon, there was nothing in sight but surging, swelling water. The sea had been her livelihood and that of her family. The sea had given them sustenance, but it had taken away the lives of the two people in the world she had loved deeply, without reservation or hesitation. Ephraim Hardy's body had sunk below waves such as these; and now, just a few short hours ago, Jared's body had disappeared into the same watery grave.

To what purpose? Her question went unanswered.

Would this same, surging ocean claim Nathaniel's life as well?

Nat! Melanie had not given much thought to him these past turbulent hours. How would he greet her when she went aboard to tell him her grim story? Had he indeed given her up forever since their confrontation at Marblehead? And, having later claimed her body, had he put her out of his mind and heart, consigning her, defiled, to James Talbot? The wedding would have to be put off in any case, because of Jared's death. Was this the release Nat sought? The excuse to nullify any hold she might have upon him now that Jared was gone and Laura a widow? Nathaniel would now be handling the Hardy funds for the widow, as well as the sister; for as Jared's business partner, and with no other male family member to see to their welfare, Nat was bound now, more than ever, to Laura and Melanie.

What would Nathaniel be, now that Jared was gone? Would he be her husband . . . or would he, when the mourning period was over, be husband to Laura? When he found she would not be wife to James, would her ships and fortune be handled by Nat only because of her relationship to Jared's children?

No! she decided. *In such circumstances, I will make other arrangements!*

But try as she might, she had no idea in which direction to look for assistance. She thought of James Talbot, and his last words to her before she fled into the mists . . .

How do you know I filed charges? Perhaps I only said so to intimidate you and accomplish my purpose.

What if he had not really filed with the authorities? Suppose, in his desperate need for a ship, he had merely used her fears for Nathaniel and Jared to coerce her into signing the papers? Suppose, dear God, Jared had died for naught?

But then certainty flooded through her being. Melanie knew as surely as if she'd been there that James had indeed filed against her loved ones. Looking back over the past, she realized that in every instance, she'd made excuses for James's actions. Though deeply hurt, she'd secretly forgiven him for the anguish and embarrassment he'd caused her when, after asking her father for her hand, he sailed home with a foreign wife; blithely ignoring the fact that the whole town knew she'd been jilted. And his flamboyant insistence upon seeing her, even after her engagement had been announced, and in plain view of her family and fiancé! And then, using deviousness to lure her to see him alone in Marblehead.

Though, in all fairness, she thought, *I was willing enough to meet him after observing Nathaniel's rendezvous with Laura the previous night.*

And she felt again her fear and trepidation as his intimidating message sent her flying through the fog to meet him in the park.

Standing there under a midnight sky, awaiting a ship that sailed unaware into peril, she realized many things.

A searing anger then arose within her breast; at Nathaniel, at James, and herself, as well. She'd been weak; allowing herself to be used, pulled in opposite directions, for whatever purpose, by two strong men who obviously cared not a whit for her tender feelings.

Then she, who had never permitted the turbulence and disquietude of the world to cause her to vent her bile, or strike back in kind, found at this moment that she could not but abhor and revile James Talbot; a hard, calloused creature who had caused the loss of her beloved brother. From the depths of her soul, that deep, calm well of certitude and endurance, she felt an outrage so burning, so intolerable, that she cried out in vengeance and the freshening winds carried her words over a stygian sea.

"James! You are a cad and a murderer! I will never forgive you to my dying day! And I pray, that as you draw your last gasp, you may suffer for the irreparable damage you have done in order to achieve your own selfish ends!"

Unaccustomed rage exhausted her and the underlying worry about her relationship with Nat added to her depression. Her mind ran in circles and the more she tried to make sense out of chaos, the more confused she became.

Then, suddenly she found herself taken over by a strange peace. It was as though a soothing hand were laid upon her sorrowing heart and she leaned against the rail, giving herself up to the roll of the ship while a quickening wind caressed her unpinned hair.

There was naught to be done, she decided, until she confronted Nathaniel and they passed this crisis. When she was able to see which way the wind blew, she would know what to do. Until that time, she could only watch . . . and pray.

Another hour went by.

Having consigned her worries to God and cleared her mind of all except sorrow for her brother's sudden demise, Melanie waited patiently for Nathaniel's ship to make its appearance out of the darkness.

It was nearly three o'clock, and clouds had been steadily creeping across the starlit sky, blotting out the light and bringing with it wisps of fog low over the water once more. Melanie saw the ship first—far off, just a glimmer between the waves. She called to Paul and together they watched the lights draw closer. Fifteen minutes later, they made out the lines of the *Sea-Wind*.

"It is! It is!" Melanie cried. "Send up the flares before they pass us by!"

Stokes and Paul decided to wait another long ten minutes; and the flare was sent up just when Melanie was almost certain the *Sea-Wind* would run them down.

There was shouting from the large vessel, but the words were unintelligible, having lost their meaning in the misty distance between. Answering shouts came from the throats of Paul, Melanie, and Stokes. Kate rushed up on deck and added her cry to the din. The

Sea-Wind dropped anchor, and a short time later, a shallop was lowered over the side to meet them.

Nat was the first one aboard. As he climbed over the rail, he raised his lantern high to see Melanie standing nearby, bedraggled, soaked, her eyes wide and dry; and the dark circles beneath them told him there was deep trouble in her heart.

He went straight to her and took her in his arms. She buried her head on his chest and trembled, though she said not a word, nor did she sob.

Nat held her thus while Paul told the story, and when he had finished, Melanie realized Nat's arms had tightened about her and one hand stroked her shoulder and back in consolation.

"Come, my love," he said. "You will rest aboard my ship and we will take you home." He kissed her cheek and brushed it with his hand, tenderly caressing the soft skin, telling her in the only way he knew that his love remained unchanged.

It was decided then and there that the nine slaves aboard the *Sea-Wind* would be transferred immediately to the pinkie schooner for transportation to New Bedford. There, they would be hidden until it was safe to ship them out to freedom in Canada.

"When the fugitives have boarded," Nathaniel told Stokes, "sail west around the vineyard and Elizabeth Islands, then up Buzzard's Bay to New Bedford. I will leave three men to sail with you. Paul will board the *Sea-Wind* with us. The authorities will not be looking for a schooner; nor will they think of watching that route. When you are safely launched, I will take the *Sea-Wind* to the mouth of Nantucket Sound, as though I sail to Canada. Then, when they have sent shot across my bow, and only then, will I heave to. When they have searched and found no evidence of fugitives, they will assume, as usual, that James is taking his spleen out upon me and my ships again."

And so it was that Melanie was once more ensconced in Nat's master cabin on one of his ships. Truly, this cabin had not the luxury nor the elegant appointments of Nat's favorite ship, the *Mirimar,* but it was heaven to Melanie's battered body and aching head.

Kate occupied the berth in the cabin next to hers and considering her state after imbibing the doctor's prescription for the fugitive, Melanie doubted she would come to bid her good night.

Melanie washed her face and brushed her hair with Nat's stiff hairbrush; then, shedding her clothes, she slipped between muslin sheets and allowed the berth to cradle her aching limbs. She sighed, remembering those satin bedclothes and the blissful days in Boston, which now, in retrospect, seemed long years ago.

With the intention of extinguishing the whale-oil lamp affixed firmly to the table beside the berth, Melanie fell asleep as her hand reached out to it. When the ship again bestirred itself, Melanie was slumbering soundly.

Nat awakened her.

He'd come quietly into the cabin carrying a tray with a steaming bowl of chowder and some hunks of soft white bread.

Opening her eyes, Melanie saw him staring down at her with warmth and tenderness in his blue gaze. His eyes had been hard when he looked at her in Marblehead and before he claimed her aboard the *Mirimar.* She wondered if his anger had only now dissolved, in view of Jared's death, or if he had forgiven her earlier, as she'd prayed he would before he sailed to Charleston.

The aroma of chowder reached her nostrils as Nat placed the tray on the bedside table.

"I thought you might be hungry, my love," he said. "A little food will help you rest better; at least until we reach New Bedford again."

She sat up, drawing the sheet and blanket about

her, leaving bare shoulders and arms exposed. She reached eagerly for the chowder and Nat buttered her bread while she ate.

"It was brave of you, Melanie, to do what you did to save us!" Nat averred, watching her eat and fighting himself to keep his hands from her.

"There was naught else to do," she answered simply. Then, sighing. "But it did not help Jared," she said woefully, still without a rise of tears. "It killed him!"

"It was an accident, Melanie! Jared should never have gone to Nantucket. He feared the sea too much to be a good sailor. Paul and Stokes tried to keep him from going, but he insisted." Nat shook his head regretfully.

Melanie made no response. At this moment, she concentrated on her food. She had not eaten since early the previous day and felt suddenly famished.

"I have some wine that might go well with your meal," Nat offered, rising to go to the little cupboard above his desk.

Moments later, Melanie leaned back upon her pillows sipping a glass of dry white wine. The meal finished, she was now satisfied. Nat sat quietly for a time, watching her slowly relax from her recent ordeal.

Then, taking the glass from her hand, he seated himself on the bed and took her in his arms.

"Will you forgive me, Melanie, for my abominable treatment of you in Marblehead . . . and on the *Mirimar*? I have reviled myself many times for such brutish behavior. My only excuse is that I was consumed with jealousy when I saw you in James's embrace at Hazard's Bluff. I was angry, fearful that you loved him still; and might leave me for him upon the death of his wife."

"I forgive you, Nat." She answered him simply. "Because it is you I love."

"I know that now." He raised her hand to his lips. "When you willingly gave yourself to me on the *Miri-mar*, I should have known. It was only in retrospect that I came to realize you truly return my love. I have dreamed often of that night. I've yearned to hold you and say what I stubbornly refused to say that blissful night . . . that I love you with all my heart and soul."

His lips claimed hers and for the first time since this nightmare began, Melanie was at ease. The muscles of her body had been rigid for many hours.

She felt the warmth of Nat's flesh through his shirt and returned his kiss with all the yearning she'd felt through the long, cold night and the weeks since their estrangement.

When his mouth released hers at last, she drew back to look up into his eyes.

"One question, Nat," she murmured. "Why did you leave for Charleston without saying good-bye?"

"It was not my intent to do so, my love. As you know, we were late arriving in New Bedford. The news awaiting me there barely left time to provision and sail away again. As a sea captain's daughter, I hoped you would understand. At the same time, I had not yet settled my mind as to your feelings for Talbot. As well, I hesitated to give Jared a message for you since he assumed we'd made our good-byes before you left the ship." He kissed the tip of her nose. "I had such a beautiful speech prepared when next we met," he whispered. "And I fear the words have just come tumbling out with no sense of order!"

He held her so close for a moment, she could scarcely breathe.

"You addle my thinking, my lovely! And delight my soul!" He released her then, and with a gentle kiss on her forehead, stood up.

Suddenly, lassitude overcame Melanie. With the assurance that Nat still loved her, she was too fatigued to think beyond.

"We will be at the Sound by dawn," he said, sensing her exhaustion. "Sleep, my love. Soon you will be home in New Bedford and need all your resources to comfort Laura in her sorrow."

Melanie was asleep before Nat left the cabin.

A loud noise precipitated her from slumber. She opened her eyes to the gray dawn and heard the scurrying of many feet, mingled with shouting and the blare of a foghorn. Mist pressed intermittently against the porthole, dispersing when recurring ocean breezes sent the wisps twisting to clear a space some distance away. During one of those intervals, Melanie momentarily glimpsed a ship some five hundred yards from where she gazed.

Melanie dressed quickly and met Kate in the companionway as she left the cabin.

"Whut is it now?" poor Kate asked, as her sleep-addled brain tried to absorb not only where she was, but how she got here; for Doctor Prentice's bottle had enabled her to glide through the night's ordeal with less pain than she would have otherwise.

Melanie didn't answer, but beckoned her to follow. She found Nat on the quarterdeck, having just given orders to lower the anchor.

"What is it?" she asked, quietly tense. "Is it the authorities? Have they shot at us?"

Nathaniel nodded.

"They sent a volley over our bow. Apparently, there was a ship on the other side, which we were unable to see in the fog. I've sent a boat for survivors. If you look closely, you will see there is a ship afire at the mouth of Nantucket Sound."

Melanie stared in the direction he pointed. A solid fog bank covered the sea now, but where Nat had indicated, the cloud hung, pink-tinged and frightening.

"Are the authorities coming aboard?"

"I'm certain they are," Nat answered. "However, they will find nothing and we will not be detained long. At the moment, I am more concerned about the survivors of that innocent ship! It is possible that we will miss some sailors in the fog."

As he spoke, the mist cleared momentarily and Melanie gasped . . .

"Nat!" she cried, clutching his arm. "I do believe that is my ship, the *Leviathan!*"

Nat stared at her a moment, then, raising his glass, he remained unmoving for what seemed to Melanie an eternity.

"It is the *Leviathan*, Melanie," he said at last. His voice was low and filled with regret. "James, as usual, wanted to see the results of his handiwork."

In a resurgence of anger and frustration, Melanie followed Kate back to the cabin. She paced restlessly while voices, anchor chains, and other sounds of activity from the deck above filled her ears.

"Damn James!" she said bitterly to Kate. "His insatiable greed has not only caused Jared's death, but destroyed my ship and perhaps caused the death of others as well!" She stared out the porthole at swirling mist beyond. "I hope he pays dearly for this!" Her voice was heavy with rancor and she clenched her fist, banging it on the double thickness of the tiny round window. "I intend to see to it!" she vowed in a rush of tears.

Kate stared in surprise at the usually subdued, gentle lass she'd known all these years.

"I niver before heard ye curse, child! An' let me tell ye it don't become a lady ter do sich as thet! Ye cannot know what drove James ter do whut 'e did; ye' niver had th' miserable life e' did!"

"I don't care about his miserable life! There is no excuse for this . . . this . . . mayhem he has caused these last twenty-four hours!"

"Let me remind ye, th' good book says 'judge not yest ye be judged'!" Kate rejoined.

Melanie turned on her.

"He is the cause of my brother's death, Kate! Can you not see that? And look out there where my ship is ablaze in the water, and sailors are jumping, swimming for their lives! Are you saying that is not James's fault?"

" 'Tis true," Kate sighed. " 'E 'as done thet!" Then, after a short silence, she went on. "Unlike ye, child, I pray 'e is not hurt! Fer I always sorrowed fer 'im, an' wished 'im well in 'is stormy sail through life."

Melanie turned hard eyes on Kate and her look spoke more than a thousand words.

Moments later, Kate, not to be intimidated, spoke again in singsong reminiscence.

"I 'member James as he was a'fore Jonas died. 'E was a smilin' carefree youth; 'andsome, filled with a joy o' livin'." She lapsed into silence again.

And Melanie, wrathful at the picture Kate conjured up in her mind, pushed away the memory of James that summer's day atop the hill with the wind ruffling his hair, and his sailor's shirt slit to the waist . . .

Nearly an hour passed before Nat sent for Melanie.

"Th' cap'n wishes to see you on deck, miss," a young sailor said, doffing his cap. "He says come quick!"

She stared at Kate in puzzlement.

"Why would he want me?"

"I dunno, child," Kate said, shrugging her shoulders. "But ye best go runnin'! Th' cap'n ain't one ta' call fer quick, 'thout meanin' it!"

With Kate behind her, Melanie ran through the companionway and emerged onto a deck just clearing of fog. Nat and a group of men were on the quarterdeck, bending over a prone body.

Dear God! she thought. *They've found Jared!*

But it was not Jared she saw as the men stepped back to make way for her. It was James Talbot!

She went rigid standing over him as, propped up by Nat, he reached out a bloody hand to her and gazed through dimming eyes filled with the old warmth and tenderness. His head was bloody and a makeshift bandage had been applied to stem the flow, but Melanie saw instantly it was useless. His other hand, holding his side, was covered with gore pulsing from internal wounds and Melanie knew his time was short.

"Melanie . . ." His voice was barely a whisper. "I am sorry for it all . . . but, one thing! I have loved you . . . and I die loving you! In that, if nothing else, I have told the truth!"

He turned to Nathaniel.

"I could not best you, brother," he croaked. "Our father knew you were the superior man." He coughed a little. "But I take consolation in dying on his ship . . . his favored ship; the one he gave me, Nat! He truly did!" he finished breathlessly.

Nathaniel went to one knee beside James and took his hand.

"I know he did, James," he said softly, and Melanie was astonished to see tears in his eyes. "And you, my brother, have been a worthy adversary!" he finished. "You tested my mettle and strengthened my resolve, through all the years."

James eyes lighted.

"You mean it, Nat? I was a worthy adversary?"

"A very worthy adversary, James. Father would be proud!"

James's eyes remained on Nat's face and a brilliant smile lit up his features forever; for with his hand in his brother's, James Talbot gave up his soul.

Melanie turned away sobbing in Kate's arms. She could not cry for her own brother and now, despite her bitterness, she cried for Nat's! The thought

shamed her, until Kate's assurance that it was for
Jared as well that she mourned.

"Th' tears were shocked dry whin Jared went as he
did!" Kate told her. "It 'appens to many! Thin, seein'
others sorrow, th' well is tapped, 'n th' healin' tears
come . . ." Kate brushed tears from her own eyes,
for she was remembering James, the wee lad who
came often to her door begging supper—and Jared,
the happy-go-lucky boy who delighted in teasing her
with childish pranks.

"There's bin' too much o' death th' past hours!"
Kate said, leading Melanie back to the cabin.

Just before entering the companionway, Melanie
looked back. Nat remained on one knee in an attitude of prayer over his brother's body. His head was
bowed, and he still held James's hand; as if in death,
he would make up for what he could not give him in
life.

"Ye both lost brothers this awful time," Kate said,
tucking Melanie into bed. "Ye'er each o' ye sorely
needin' comfort now an' 'ave much in common t'
bind ye."

But Melanie, exhausted from the shock of two
deaths in a short span of time, and the strain of all
that had occurred the past twenty-four hours, had al-
ready slipped into sleep. For only through oblivion
could she recover from the sorrow and the wounds
that had been inflicted upon her gentle soul.

CHAPTER FOURTEEN

When Melanie awakened, they had docked in New Bedford and the familiar sounds of the wharves rose all about the ship. Kate came in to help her dress. Clucking over her like a mother hen, she said Paul and Nat had gone on ahead to break the news of Laura's widowhood.

When they left the ship, sympathetic townspeople had gathered about the gangplank to offer condolences. With murmured thanks and lowered eyes, Melanie entered the carriage with Kate, but her thoughts were of rushing uphill to Halycon House where she would be comforted by Nat. For only his solace could ease the pain in her heart.

As the carriage pulled up the driveway to the house, she saw many carriages had preceded them. They were met by friends and sympathizers who assisted her to alight and guided her inside. Numb, with no will of her own, Melanie allowed herself to be seated in the parlor and given hot tea and brandy to ease her sorrow. Bewildered, she looked at the faces about her; some familiar, some only vaguely remembered.

It was Kate who, despite her fear of "gentry," rescued her.

"Sure she's exhausted, th' little one!" she said brusquely. "See 'ow pale she is! 'Tis bed will be doin' her more good than lollygaggin' about with tea and brandy!"

So saying, she took Melanie's arm firmly and led her upstairs, while voices buzzed on in the parlor and plans were made for bringing food and supervising the Halcyon House servants during the sorrowing of Jared's wife and sister.

Melanie and Kate had barely reached the landing when they were confronted by Laura's Aunt Judith, who was on her way downstairs. She embraced Melanie silently, then with handkerchief to the corner of her eyes, descended to "represent the family," as she later put it, during their terrible shock. For Judith Callaghan was not one to allow others to usurp what she felt her rightful place. She was Laura's only relative; and with Melanie the only member left of the Hardy family, aside from her infant niece and nephew, Judith felt powerfully important. So, whatever plans the matrons of the town were formulating would need Judith Callaghan's blessing before becoming reality.

Paul met Melanie outside Laura's open bedroom door and led her inside.

"Melanie!" Laura's voice was pathetic, filled with shock.

Her arms opened and Melanie went into them. The two women embraced, sobbing; for they had lost a beloved man. It was the first time in their lives that Melanie and Laura shared the same emotion.

Nat stood beside the bed patting Laura's shoulder with one hand and Melanie's with the other. Once more, Melanie felt that he was torn between them. Now, as Jared's business partner; guardian of his estate as well as Ephraim's, she wondered again, despite his assurances of last night, whether, when it was all over, he would belong to Laura, or to herself.

Several days later, memorial services were held in the small Sailor's Chapel for Jared Hardy—and for James Talbot, who was also buried at sea. Laura, stunningly beautiful in somber black, sat between Nat and Melanie. Now and then she dabbed at her eyes beneath the heavy veiling, while the minister intoned the service.

"At times like this," he said, "we are grateful for the closeness and love of family and friends; for love is all we take with us when our travail here is over . . ."

Laura sobbed and hid her face on Nat's shoulder while Melanie's tears ran over her cheeks beneath her own black veil.

Jared, my brother, my friend. She spoke silently to him from her heart. *All my life, whatever happened, you were at my side to comfort me. When Father was at sea . . . when Mother sickened and died; and when word came of Father's death, I had you to lean upon. Now, I am truly alone.*

She bowed her head in desolation.

Then, a hand squeezed her shoulder. There was a rustle as Paul Lanier seated himself beside her and took her into his embrace. The gentle gesture renewed her tears. She rested against him; accepting consolation with mute thanks for his kind thoughtfulness.

When James Talbot was extolled in the memorial service, his face rose in her memory and she recalled his last words to her: *I loved you, Melanie.* But remembering that James's greed caused her brother's needless death, she could not find it in her heart to forgive him, much less to mourn him. His dying wife had been unable to attend services and old Sadie had told Kate she preferred to remember James as the young boy he was when she took him to raise, not as the bitter man he had become.

Melanie sobbed for her father and Jared; the two men who had once been her whole world. And she sobbed for herself, isolated, abandoned by those who had gone before and, she was beginning to believe, by the fiancé to whom she had looked in vain for comfort.

When they left the chapel a soft rain was falling and there was room only for Laura under Nat's umbrella. Melanie accepted Paul's offer of protection as, moving slowly, they followed Nat and the widow to the carriage for the ride back to Halcyon House.

The next days were most difficult. Laura languished in her room, alternately crying and staring out the window in deep depression.

"She has been through so much these past few weeks!" Mrs. Hoffman said to Melanie. "Losing her baby and now her husband! We must be very kind and thoughtful of her, for it will take a long time to recover from such cruel blows."

Melanie looked at the gentle woman through sad, tear-filled eyes and agreed that Laura had indeed been through a great ordeal.

"And you also, my dear!" Mrs. Hoffman crushed Melanie to her ample bosom. "The loss of your brother and postponement of your wedding . . ." She patted the girl's shoulder. "Believe me, Melanie, this will pass! The sun will shine again."

But platitudes were not what Melanie wanted at that moment. She yearned for Nat's arms; his care and concern. And as each day went by she came to realize more and more that it was Laura who was the recipient of his attentions to the exclusion of all else. Frustrated, helpless, she watched with growing alarm as the time Nat devoted to Laura increased; and Laura's dependence upon Nat became all-consuming.

She tried to believe that her basic insecurity where Laura was concerned blinded her to the true situation. It was possible, she told herself, that she only imagined the closeness between Nathaniel and Laura. Trying desperately to rationalize his behavior, Melanie questioned her own motives of possible jealousy or, perhaps, petulance.

Since Jared's death Melanie thought Nat had been treating her like a spoiled child. His concern for her resembled impatience. When he admonished her to get some rest, she felt he wanted her out of the way; that her presence bothered his conscience since he was at Laura's beck and call.

In the weeks that followed, Nat and Paul Lanier came daily to Halcyon House, arriving usually in midmorning and often remaining until late afternoon or early evening. While Nat was above stairs with Laura, Melanie and Paul held many long conversations as they sat together in the parlor.

"Paul," Melanie said quietly one day, "I believe I will go away for a time. This house depresses me and Laura will never recover at this rate."

"You feel Nat's attentions are keeping Laura from recovering?" Paul's shrewd eyes surveyed her across the small table separating them.

"Are you not of the same opinion?" she asked, for she had not been blind to Paul's continuing interest in her sister-in-law.

"I believe Nat does not realize what is happening," he answered haltingly. "When a woman grieves, she renders a man helpless to refuse her needs."

"I also grieve, Paul," Melanie answered softly, raising sad eyes to his.

"But you are not demanding!" Paul answered. "You ask nothing of him; you only wait. ' 'Tis the squeaking hinge, gets the notice.' " He smiled gently. "Melanie, why have you not conversed with Nat as to your true feelings in this matter? The smartest man can be obtuse at times when it comes to the needs of those closest to him. Speak with him, Melanie, before another day is gone! I am certain he would be astonished to know you feel second to Laura in his attentions." Reaching over, he took her hand and his earnest brown eyes searched hers. "But surely, my dear, you know Nathaniel loves you? There can be no doubt that you are the woman of his heart!"

Melanie lowered her head.

"I pray you are right, Paul," she answered softly.

Despite Paul's assurances, she missed the warmth and concern she'd become accustomed to from her fiancé. Now, he was preoccupied and when they did enter into discourse, it seemed an effort for him to absorb what she said.

On a bright, sunny morning several days later, Melanie was cutting flowers in the garden when she heard Nat's carriage topping the hill to Halcyon House. With an armful of roses and her heart in her throat, she made her way swiftly down the garden path to the gate. She reached it just in time to see Nat and Paul descend from the carriage.

"Nat," she called, with an uncertain smile, "please come into the garden. I would have a word with you."

She waved at Paul, who waved back.

"What's amiss, my love?" Nat said with a grin as he walked rapidly toward her. "Has a weevil attacked your roses?"

He came up to her and with an indulgent smile, placed his hand over hers on the gatepost. Then, entering the garden, he took her hand and drew it through his arm.

"You are like a little dark sparrow in a bower of blossoms." He spoke softly. "But despite your somber garb, you are the loveliest bloom of all." Bending his head, he kissed her gently on the lips.

And all her frustration and confusion seemed to melt away in the June breeze.

As they strolled slowly down the garden path, Melanie suddenly went quiet. There was so much to say and she'd prepared herself for his immediate decline of her invitation. When she could not force the issue as planned, she was left speechless.

Nat stopped beneath the rose arbor and placed one arm about her waist. With his other hand he tilted her chin upward, forcing her to meet his gaze.

"What troubles you, my Melanie?" he asked then, searching her eyes earnestly. "I know these past several weeks have been difficult for you; sorrowing for your brother and putting off our nuptial plans. These have been sad days for us all. Jared was my friend and future brother-in-law as well as my partner. At times, I fear you and Laura may come to despise me for his death. Then, I pray you will understand. Had I realized such a thing could happen I would have gladly given my own life! Melanie, can you ever forgive me?"

She reached a hand up to caress his face.

"Nat! It never dawned upon me to place the blame on your head!"

"You are kinder than Laura, my love. She has placed the entire fault upon me and though I had no intent at any time to jeopardize Jared's life, I cannot but feel guilty that my safety and that of the fugitives was bought at such an exorbitant price!"

"It is James who caused the untimely death of my brother!" Melanie said vehemently. "His greed drove him to Jared's murder and his own death! And in truth, I am not sorry that I am unable to find it in my heart to forgive him his dark deed!"

"James was what he was because of Jonas," Nathaniel said regretfully. "As I am. And as we are all products of our origin. Had Jonas not plotted and planned to set us against each other, none of this would have happened; and Jared would not have been caught in the cross fire of Jonas's diabolical game of chess. Though heaven knows that does not relieve me one whit of my own guilt in this terrible loss! I should never have introduced Jared to my

Abolitionist beliefs! Now, as Laura has so often pointed out, because of me she is widowed and two children are sorrowing and bereft."

Melanie's eyes widened: "Nat! Can you not see that Laura is binding you to her with guilt? She would stop at nothing—"

He silenced her with a gentle hand on her lips.

"Laura is right, my love. I am guilty, and must do my best to make it up to her for the loss of her husband. Soon, her grief will pass and she will begin to make a new life for herself. As for James, he is gone now, along with whatever demons that drove him. Demons that Jonas Marfrey placed upon his back. God rest his soul!"

"Jonas is long dead, Nat. And naught can be blamed upon the parenting when a man has far passed his majority and become such a one as James Talbot. He was devious . . . a liar . . . a cheat." She broke off as bitterness in her words caused like bitterness in her throat.

"Be not so hard on James, Melanie. None of us has suffered as my brother must have done. None of us has ever starved . . . nor been without kindness and concern; or, God help him, lacked a roof to hide from the rain and cold!"

Melanie was silenced then, realizing that Nathaniel had taken on an entirely different view of his half-brother since his death. But grief was still too much a part of them both to belabor the issue; so she held her tongue, reluctant to point out Nat's own suffering under his brother's vengeance.

"In any case," Melanie ended quietly, "placing guilt cannot bring Jared back!"

Nat took her in his arms then and she raised her lips to his in a long, passionate kiss. Still embracing, they sank to the wide slatted seat in the rose arbor. There, amid flowers and greenery, with only the birds to spy, they became immersed in each other and the ecstasy of the moment.

Melanie's body was pliable, like soft wax in her fiancé's hands as he pressed her to him. His lips sought her throat, her bosom, and his hands fumbled at tiny buttons at the neck of her black mourning dress.

All Melanie's fears and doubts vanished. She gave herself over to her senses as, eyes closed, the touch and feel of Nathaniel's hands and lips . . . and his rapid breathing as passion mounted became her only reality.

Then, a cold wind blew through her heart, as there came a tapping on the glass and Laura's plaintive voice shattered her dreams.

"Nat! I saw you enter the garden! I am waiting for you . . ."

Nat jumped to his feet with alacrity, pulling Melanie with him. Instantly his eyes, filled with guilt like those of an errant schoolboy, went to the window of the master bedroom overlooking the garden. Melanie followed his gaze. Laura stood there, wide-eyed, staring down at them. Her flaming red hair was in captivating disarray and the pale green negligee she wore barely covered her firm, full breasts.

"Come, Melanie." Nat's voice was hoarse with embarrassment and he would not meet her gaze. "I am sorry, my beloved! I should not have subjected you to my lustful nature; especially at a time like this!"

She looked him full in the face.

"At a time like what, Nathaniel?" she pursued. "At a time when we are both grieving? I am your betrothed! Is it wrong for us to take comfort from each other?"

He looked distractedly at her. Then, taking her hand, drew her after him at a rapid pace down the garden path toward the gate.

*   *   *

"He is bound to her by guilt for the widow and fatherless children he has created," Melanie told Paul after lunch that day when Laura and Nat had once more disappeared into the upper regions of the house.

Paul was astounded.

"But I wonder," Melanie continued, "if it is truly his guilt, or the fact that he realizes his love for Laura never died."

"No, Melanie!" Paul protested, recovering from the shock of her revelation. "Nathaniel loves you, of that I am certain! But," he shook his head, "guilt! Surely, Nat knows he is not guilty of Jared's death!"

"Laura has apparently made him so believe. She states that Jared would be alive today had he not been recruited to save Nathaniel and the fugitives."

"But that is conjecture only!" Paul answered in a puzzled tone. "Jared should never have been topside on a boat . . . any boat, in a storm! He was terrified of the sea and of all the men I have known, he was one who would never grow sea legs! Nat knows this! The fact that we were on an urgent mission to warn Nathaniel of apprehension has nothing to do with the fact that Jared should never have been aboard! But, at his insistence, Stokes and I acquiesed, to our sorrow! In no manner whatsoever is Nathaniel Larimore responsible for your brother's death! Stokes and I are more responsible than is Nat!"

"Then why is Nat accepting the guilt Laura places upon him?"

Paul shrugged: "I disbelieve he accepts it!"

"And why was he so abashed that Laura saw us together in the garden?"

Paul was silent for a long moment, then slowly he sought to answer Melanie's question.

"Perhaps," he said haltingly, "Nat feels guilty that Laura is now alone while he has you . . . and your love."

"I hope you are right, Paul," Melanie answered in a low tone. "I pray you are right! But I know Laura! She will bind him to her by whatever method necessary!"

Paul's eyes hardened. His voice took on a brusque tone.

"I will not allow that to happen, Melanie! You may count on it!"

It was full dusk when Paul and Nathaniel left Halcyon House. Melanie, having opened her window over the front lawn, heard their departure.

"I must discuss something with you, Nat. It is of utmost importance to us both!"

Melanie saw Nat's tall figure pause at the carriage post. She drew back behind the curtains and deliberately eavesdropped on the two men below.

"You have consoled Laura enough, Nathaniel!" Paul's low voice was stern. "Now it is time to step back and let her try her wings—alone! She will never do so as long as you remain a willing prop for her flagging courage."

"What are you saying, Paul? It has been scarce a month since she was widowed! Would you have me desert her?"

"I would have you pay more attention to your betrothed!" Paul answered vehemently. "She too needs consoling. Melanie feels abandoned and I can't say I blame her! I have watched Laura totally absorb your attention. Now, I believe it is quite enough. There is nothing more you can do except see to her financial welfare. Unless . . ." he said slowly, "you find yourself in the unenviable position of being torn between love of two women!"

Angrily, Nat opened the carriage door and swung himself inside. Melanie heard his voice, loud and argumentative when Paul, ducking his head, also entered the vehicle. The driver slapped the reins and the horses started downhill, leaving Melanie to wonder at the outcome of the conversation that had begun beneath her window.

The next day Nat came to Halcyon House alone. When Melanie questioned him as to Paul's whereabouts, he would only say that Paul "had business in Boston."

The days dragged slowly onward. The first month anniversary of Jared's death came and went. Though she waited hopefully, there was no change in Nathaniel's attitude toward her. Melanie sank deeper into depression. She missed Paul Lanier and their daily conversations and felt that he too had abandoned her.

Nathaniel spent less and less time at Halcyon House. When he did arrive, he disappeared into Laura's room and Melanie heard his deep, rumbling voice as they carried on long conversations.

Oftentimes, as he came and went, Nat would seek Melanie out to hold her close a moment or two, kiss her in a distracted manner, and tell her, in words sounding as though he recited by rote, that he loved her. But she felt his withdrawal. Something seemed to weigh heavily upon his shoulders; something more than the two deaths that had occurred almost simultaneously the previous month.

Perhaps, she told herself, *he is easing himself out of our relationship. Possibly he is unwilling to wound me afresh when my brother's death has only just occurred. What if, dear God, he has declared himself to Laura and now bides his time before telling me!* She drew a deep, tremulous breath and convinced herself she was right in her assumption. *It is over!* she thought. *He will ask at any time for the betrothal necklace; and I will mourn him forever, for I could never love another! Then, I will become what I feared—an old maiden aunt to my brother's children!*

Though in the same house, Melanie saw little of Laura. On days Nathaniel visited the house, she took her midday meal with Melanie and Nat. On the days he was absent, Laura remained in her room and trays were sent up to her. A few times Melanie knocked at the door and made an attempt to speak with her, for company alone, if nothing else, but Laura turned her away saying she was tired, or had a headache.

As one day blended into another, Melanie became aware that Paul's absence bothered her more than she'd initially realized. Why had he suddenly disappeared from Halcyon House? "Business in Boston" was not an adequate explanation and Melanie felt that Nat hid the true reason for Paul's departure. She wondered if the conversation overheard that evening over a week ago had caused a rift between her betrothed and his business manager. She wondered also what was behind the long, serious discussions Nat held with Laura beyond closed doors.

Perhaps, she thought, *realizing Nat's feeling for Laura, Paul's hopes have been dashed and he has withdrawn from further attendance upon us.*

Unable to contain her worried imaginings, Melanie insisted, more urgently this time, that Laura speak with her; but her questions were ignored and she was rudely asked to leave Laura's room.

Kate, noticing Melanie's brooding, tried in myriad ways to comfort her.

"I be goin' ter market terday, 'stid o' Marquerite," she told Melanie one bright morning. "Come wi' me an' we'll have a spot o' seafood at th' Lobster Pot. 'Tis none c'n criticise ye fer dinin' wi' yer old nurse, e'en tho' ye be grievin'."

Melanie hesitated. It had been long since she'd ventured into town. Aside from a few visits to Goulet's for fittings on her black mourning dresses, she'd not been outside the confines of Halcyon House since her brother's memorial service. Jared's widow and his sister must spend the year quietly sorrowing and, though a few sober visitors were allowed, the mores of the times demanded there be no outward surcease of lamentation.

Sensing her uncertainty, Kate continued.

"I mind when ye begged ter go ter market wi' me! Yer big eyes'd git bigger n' ye c'uld barely wait 'til market day . . ."

Melanie had forgotten her childish excitement as, hand held firmly in Kate's, they'd shopped amid sailors, housewives, and a motley mixture of humanity milling about a large open area opposite the midtown park. Twice a week, for as long as she could remember, farmers from the surrounding countryside brought produce, meat-on-the-hoof, and poultry to the marketplace while from dark, cool holds of newly docked ships came sweet southern fruits and fresh-caught fish along with other, more exotic foods for sophisticated palates. Often, in those bygone days, she'd watched her feisty companion choose fresh fruits, vegetables, and plump, squawking chickens. She'd listened to haggling over prices and came away sharing a flushed Kate's triumph over an argument; gloating along with her because of bargains safely tucked away in the shopping basket, or sent to the carriage with Lawrence, who was then coachman and ever-present attendant. A new, younger coachman guided the carriage these days, for Lawrence's feet were not up to standing about on hard cobblestones and his old eyes were unable to see more than a few feet distant.

Kate's voice brought Melanie back to the present . . .

" 'T'ain't as tho' th' Lobster Pot was fer mixed comp'ny! Ye know th' eatin' place wuz opened special fer Boston ladies n' other gentry cumin' nex' door ter Goulet's fer fittin's! 'Tis a proper place, 'n rare whin a man comes ter th' premises! Naught c'n be said if ye come there wi' me! 'Sides," she grinned, "I bin' wantin' ter see th' place; an' th' likes o' me canna' go there 'thout th' likes o' you!"

Melanie smiled. She knew Kate's powers of persuasion. When she made up her mind to something, she was not easily put off. Melanie's gratitude went out to her also, for she knew the reason for Kate's sudden "marketing" pact with the cook. Today, June twenty-first, was to have been her wedding day.

"You remember what day this is, don't you, Kate?" she asked, smiling sadly.

"Aye . . . 'n by this time next year, ye'll have all this a'hind ye! Yer weddin' day'll be all th' sweeter thin, fer havin' gone through these times tergether!"

As the carriage set off downhill, Melanie breathed deep of sweet morning air. A gentle breeze carried the scent of blossoms and an intermittent sea wind from the harbor added a refreshing salt tang that was at once poignant and invigorating to her flagging spirits. A brilliant blue sky was dotted here and there with tiny puffs of cloud and birdsong filled the air, a soothing balm to Melanie's aching heart.

When they reached the marketplace, Melanie felt she'd stepped backward in time. Sights, smells, and the milling crowd were the same as she remembered from childhood. Only the new hotel, perched on the side of the hill where old Ezra Martin's estate used to be, marked the passage of years.

Flocks of geese, slender ropes fastened loosely about their long necks, were tied to the sides of booths. Honking incessantly, their strident notes rose in concert with the cries of vendors and the rise and fall of many voices. And goats, hobbled by rope about one foot, circled the grassy area around the pole to which they were leashed; their plaintive bleating rose above the shouts of raucous, bartering customers. The sounds of horses' hooves blended with the rumble of carriages, lorries, and hansom cabs rolling over the cobblestones.

An increasingly hot sun poured down over the teeming market where vegetables and rotting fruit mingled their aromas. The air reeked of fish, unwashed humanity, animal manure, and pungent cheeses, along with a conglomeration of cooked foods, as hawkers sold boiled shrimp, sizzling sausages, and assorted pastries of all kinds to the swarming multitude.

As she followed Kate from stall to stall, Melanie realized that of all those in her personal world, only Kate remained constant. Her fighting Irish nature reveled in the tense contest between vendor and purchaser. Her blood surged and her eyes brightened as, voice rasping like a fishwife, she argued for the best price and the choicest wares.

Caught up in the bustling energy of the market, the girl forgot her melancholy. In the midst of life pressing about her, Melanie's youthful heart responded with sudden long-forgotten joy to the mood of the moment.

Shopping over at last, purchases were loaded in the carriage and immediately sent back uphill to Halcyon House. The coachman had orders to return and wait beside the park for Melanie and Kate.

The heat was steadily intensifying. Melanie, unaccustomed to standing so long, was only too happy when she and Kate left the square and ambled slowly past Goulet's to the Lobster Pot.

It took a moment for the two women to accustom their eyes from blazing noonday sun to the refreshingly cool restaurant. The stone building, naturally insulated against summer heat and frigid winter winds, had mullioned windows shaded by opaque curtains and edged with dark, heavy draperies. Lush potted palms and greenery of every shape and size gave Melanie the impression they'd entered a charming oasis in the midst of a burning desert. The proper eating hour had barely begun and the place was sparsely peopled. Here and there, a few well-dressed matrons sipped cool drinks and gossiped or discussed the latest fashions. Soon, Goulet's fitting rooms would discharge women by the score. Melanie was glad they'd arrived early enough to find a quiet corner table behind a long row of flowers and tall boxed shrubs.

" 'Tis a nice enuff place," Kate commented, craning her short neck to see over the plants.

"It's hard to believe this was once a bakery," Melanie said. "Remember funny old Mr. Schultz?"

Kate nodded.

"Th' one thet run off wi' th' parson's wife?" she asked drily. " 'Pears 'e weren't *too* old!"

Melanie broke into barely restrained laughter and realized suddenly that it felt good. These past weeks she'd forgotten how to smile, let alone laugh.

Kate looked appreciatively at her.

"It done ye good, child, ta' come wi' me. I ain't seen ye laugh fer many a day!"

They ordered a light repast, then, sipping cool drinks, they watched strollers on the walk beyond their window and talked of Kate's home at Marblehead Neck and of her brother, who'd been at sea these past two years.

Melanie's back was to the room. Opposite her, Kate faced the planters and the tables beyond. It wasn't until Minnie Carstairs's piercing voice floated over the greenery that Melanie realized the conversation just a few feet away deeply concerned her.

"I hear Laura's ordered the books combed clear back to Ephraim's time; to be certain Jared did not allot too much of his inheritance and proceeds from the whalers to his sister."

"Yes," came Judith Callaghan's quieter tones, "Nathaniel and Paul have been tied up with Boston attorneys and accountants for over a week now. When Jared's will was read, Laura declined to accept one iota until the books were thoroughly gone over. And Ephraim's will as well . . ."

"But surely she would not leave the Hardy girl destitute?"

"Of course not, Minnie!" Judith's voice was edged with impatience. "But naturally Laura would lay claim to that which is rightfully hers. ᵗWhen old Ephraim died, Jared told my niece that one half of the whaling ships were left as dowry for Melanie. Laura was content with his explanation then. Now, however, he is gone and she wishes only to make certain the ships are truly Melanie's. After all, Laura has two children to look after—and she is alone!"

"Not for long, I'll wager! The way is now clear for Nat Larimore to rectify the mistake he made five years ago."

"The mourning year must be gone through," Judith murmured.

"Has Laura said anything to you? Surely, the captain's daily visits to Halcyon House have been for more reason than consolation? The servants whisper he spends his time in Laura's boudoir while his business manager and Melanie wait below stairs."

"Laura has said not a word." Judith's voice rose with underlying excitement. "It does seem, though, that Nathaniel finds it difficult to remain long from her side."

"Has he broken off yet with the Hardy girl? Poor thing! Imagine being jilted twice!"

"Naturally, he cannot do such a thing at this time," Judith rushed to say. "How would it look? No," she clanged her spoon against the side of her glass, "he will have to wait an appropriate length of time before that happens. Meanwhile, things will go along in as seemly a manner as possible."

A rushing sound in Melanie's ears drowned out the

rest of the conversation taking place beyond the foliage at her back.

"Pay 'em no mind!" Kate's words, loud and sharp, seemed to come from a long way off. "They be two squawkin' hens wi' nuthin' better ta do thin' gossip!" Her voice carried through the room and there was sudden silence beyond the greenery.

"Kate . . ." Melanie's voice sounded hollow to her own ears, "let us be off home!" She made an attempt to rise, but sat down again abruptly. Her weak knees left her wondering if she could indeed stand, let alone walk.

Bustling energetically to her side, Kate scooped up Melanie's reticule and with a strong hand on her arm, pulled her up from the chair. Buoyed by Kate's firm grip, Melanie lifted her head high and walked swiftly toward the door; then outside into shimmering heat. But despite the broiling sun and ovenlike radiation rising from hot cobblestones, Melanie felt chilled. She shivered slightly and folded her arms to hold warmth as Kate guided her across the street to the park. There, beneath a tall elm near the curb, the Halcyon House carriage waited.

They were silent riding uphill to the house. Dry-eyed, Melanie gazed out the window at trees, lush and heavy with summer foliage. Heat rose in waves above rock gardens along the way and on the distant horizon, beyond the nearest edge of Cape Cod, a line of towering white cumulus would, in all likelihood, turn black and stormy before day's end.

Melanie observed these outward manifestations of the world objectively, without emotion or concern; for her own private world was truly shattered now.

In the space of a few moments, through the mouths of gossiping women, Melanie's darkest nightmare became reality. They had put into words what she feared to acknowledge. It had been so clear all along! How could she have been so stupid as to believe Nat's blandishments? Obviously, with Laura out of reach, Nat would have married into the family just to be near her.

I've known all along! Melanie told herself. *But because I desperately wanted it to be so, I was duped into believing that Nat loved me for myself alone!*

He'd deflowered her; taken her heart and her maidenhead! Without qualm or conscience he'd ruined her forever for any other man; though she knew in her soul there could never be another.

With Laura now free, Melanie told herself, Nathaniel Larimore would pursue his heart's desire. His love for Laura had never died. It simmered and smoldered deep in his soul where he'd buried it the day Judith Callaghan told him of her niece's marriage. And his love for Laura had still burned when Nat asked Melanie for her hand in marriage on a March night in Mrs. Hoffman's garden.

And added to that, she thought, *he has deliberately, deviously, kept from me the knowledge that Laura seeks not only my intended, but my very inheritance!*

A searing anger burned away the pain. A white-hot rage consumed her and set her muscles flexing, ready for physical violence if need be. Once before, she'd felt this wrath; the night on the *Mirimar,* when she'd watched Laura go into Nat's arms. But it had subsided then, more into sorrow than anger. This time, there would be no softening, she vowed. She longed to strike back at Nathaniel . . . at Laura . . . and at the witless gossips who had precipitated her uncontrollable yearning for vengeance.

He has gone too far! she told herself. *There is no going back to the way we were! I will not be jilted again! This time, loudly and vindictively, I will do the honors!*

The carriage drew up before the wide doors of Halcyon House and Melanie saw that a hired cab had preceded them. Her heart leaped into her throat. She prayed that it was Paul and not Nathaniel who called; Paul, whose steady, quiet presence was truly what she needed now.

"Be not concerned wi' gossip, child!" Kate admonished as they mounted the steps to the veranda. "Be'times, wimmen speak whut they be wishin', 'stid o' what be certin!"

Still shaken with anger, Melanie entered the house to find Nat coming downstairs toward her. Their eyes met. She wanted to turn away and run, but her limbs, weak at sight of him, refused to move from the spot. He came up beside her then and, taking her into his arms, kissed her gently on the forehead.

"I had to see you today, my beloved," he said softly. "For this would have been our wedding day and I had to be with you, if only for a short space of time . . ."

With a slight smile and a glance at Melanie that said "I told you so" as plain as any words, Kate disappeared beyond the entrance hall toward the kitchen at the back of the house.

Melanie looked up at Nat. Her cold eyes searched his face and beyond deep blue eyes into his very soul. As he gazed back at her, a puzzled expression came over his features. He frowned.

"Melanie? What troubles you?"

She released herself abruptly from his arms, and walked rapidly across the marble hall toward the staircase.

"It troubles me, Nat, that there are secrets between you and Laura and I am the last to know of them."

"Secrets?"

Melanie turned on the second step. His eyes were guileless as they met hers; startled, and above all, innocent.

"Nat," she said in a deliberate voice, "why did you not inform me that Laura believes my father left me

penniless and dependent upon my brother's good will
for my very livelihood?"

"The fact that Laura wishfully believed so, did not
make it a fact."

"Why was I not informed that the books were
being audited and my father's will questioned?"

"Because it would have distressed you to no avail.
The audit is finished; all is in order. And the lawyers
have reiterated the fact that your father's will is valid
and he did, indeed, bequeath you the legacy in question."

He strode toward her. In sudden panic, she swiftly
mounted the stairs.

"Melanie! Where are you going? I must speak with
you further!"

"I am going to my room, Nathaniel," she answered.
"There is something there I wish to return to you!"

He caught up with her on the landing. Taking her
arm, he turned her roughly toward him.

"Melanie! Why are you behaving this way? What
have I done to hurt you?"

"Unhand me, Nathaniel! If you wish to speak with
me, then follow and I will show my intent!"

Pushing him roughly away from her, she once more
began ascending the stairs. Nat followed close behind.
On the third floor, she moved swiftly down the hall
and, with Nat at her heels, entered her bedroom. In
silence, she went to her dressing table and, taking a
key from the locket worn beneath her dress, she
opened the jewel box where the betrothal necklace
was kept. Looking coldly into his eyes, she held the
jewels out to him.

"Laura is now free!" she said in an icy voice. "And
so are you!"

Nat tore the necklace roughly from her hand and
tossed it back on the dressing table.

"Never again will I listen to such nonsense flow
from your lips! I do not love Laura! I have never

loved Laura . . . and I never will, other than as a dutiful brother-in-law! It is you I love, Melanie, and you alone!"

"Lies!" Melanie said bitterly.

The words overheard less than an hour ago came back to her . . .

Meanwhile, things will go along in as seemly a manner as possible.

"You have not the courage to free yourself of commitment to me now!" she continued. "You cannot face the judgment of friends and business associates by admitting your love for Laura has never died. You would use me to place the cloak of innocence on your relationship with my brother's widow until the mourning period is over. Then, when judgment of others would be less harsh, you would, with proper regret, inform me of your change of heart!"

Nat shook his head in disbelief: "Melanie! Where have you conceived this idea?"

She turned away from him and walked to the window.

He came to stand beside her.

"Melanie! You must listen to me! I have no idea what you are saying and cannot understand what I have done to make you believe I would treat you in such a manner!"

"I have listened to you before, Nat!" she said, turning to face him. "And believing you, I have only been wounded the more!"

"Melanie . . ." His voice softened.

Despite her resolution, she did not fight him when he took her into his arms, where she promptly dissolved into tears. He kissed them away with soothing words and tender caresses. Then, leading her gently to the bed, he pressed her tenderly back upon the counterpane.

"You are distraught, my love," he whispered. "I am sorry you learned of Laura's silly assumptions. I forbade her telling you, for I knew all was in order and only went through the audit to appease her. When did she tell you of her investigation?"

"It was not Laura, but her aunt, who inadvertently let me in on your secrets."

"I have no secrets from you, my Melanie. And because I knew the futility of Laura's decision, there was no reason to distress you!"

She looked up at him from her pillow. Her wide eyes, still moist with tears, held an iciness in their depths.

"You conspire with Laura to cosset me with lies and dreams, until the time comes to abandon me for her. Judith Callaghan told Minnie Carstairs that very thing less than an hour ago! She said that during this year of mourning, you and Laura would see things went along in as seemly a manner as possible."

Nat's jaw tensed and his fists clenched.

"Apparently, there are many things to be set aright!" he said softly. "I will see to it immediately."

Ignoring her frigid stare, he bent down and kissed her cheek when she turned away her lips.

"Rest, my love. All will be made right before long!"

As she watched him leave her room, Melanie knew only that she'd had enough of uncertainty. How often had she succumbed to Nat's blandishments; his lies? She could not bear another wounding.

But she was unaware of one, final blow, yet to be endured.

Nat went straight to Laura's room.

"Why did you advise your aunt of the investigation of Melanie's inheritance?" he asked abruptly, upon entering.

"Nat . . ." Laura said, pouting, "Aunt Judith is all I have left in the world, except the children and you. Naturally, I would discuss my fears with her, since you have abandoned me these past few days."

"I explicitly told you I did not want Melanie worried with this madness of yours! Now, she is severely disturbed by your aunt's tattling tongue!"

"I am certain she meant no harm to Melanie, Nat!" Laura protested. "She has a certain fondness for the girl."

"Deliberate or not, I will not have Melanie upset. Knowing Judith's affinity for gossip, you should have been more discreet."

"I did as you asked, Nat! Even when Melanie insisted upon plying me with questions, I made excuses for not speaking with her! Why do you beleaguer me like this? I have done nothing wrong!" Laura, near tears, looked beseechingly at him. "This is the first time I've seen you in days and you storm accusingly into my room, angry about something of which I know nothing! I have been through enough, Nat! Stop it, please!"

She burst into tears and for the second time in less than five minutes, Nathaniel Larimore was confronted with the helplessness of a wounded female.

Wringing her hands, Laura stood rooted to the spot while tears ran over her cheeks. Placing an arm about her, Nat led her toward the bed. Laura swayed and would have fallen, had not Nat caught her with both arms. Then, leaning off balance, supported by his embrace, Laura's arms fastened about Nat's neck and she raised her lips to his.

On her way downstairs to find Kate, Melanie glanced through Laura's open door. Her anguished eyes saw, in that split second, Laura enveloped in Nat's arms, while his mouth was close to her waiting lips.

Despite Nat's protestations only moments ago, Melanie felt that nothing had changed.

Nat loves her! she thought. *And there is naught to be done about it!*

Her heart broke into little pieces at that moment and all anger fled. Only sorrow and hurt remained. She could no longer bear to be a hindrance to a love that had endured all these years.

At least, she thought, *if I cannot have happiness, I can see to it that Nat does! I love him too much to deny his heart's desire.*

So she went to find Kate and present her with a plan that she only now realized had been formulating in her mind these past few weeks.

CHAPTER FIFTEEN

Melanie and Kate left Halcyon House before dawn the next morning . . .

"Where in th' world 'uld we go?" Kate had asked in astonishment when Melanie went to her with the plan late the previous afternoon.

"To your house, Kate! At the Neck! It is the perfect place for rest and to contemplate the future with no obligations or interruptions."

"My place!" Kate's astonishment grew. "Child, my house is fine fer *me*! But, yer used ter grander livin'! 'Tis no place for a lady to bide!"

"Does it have a roof?" Melanie asked. "Does it have a bed? And a kitchen? And an outhouse . . . or necessary room?"

At each question, Kate nodded and her brows went up even further toward her hairline.

"But, 'tis a crude house," she said solemnly. "An' nothin' grand 'bout it!"

"Grand is not what I need at the moment," Melanie answered. "For the next few months, I would enjoy the simple life. I want none to know my identity; and especially important, you are to tell no one here at Halcyon House that we are leaving! We will slip away before dawn tomorrow and leave them with their woes . . ." Melanie's voice trailed off, and Kate glanced sharply at her.

"So that's th' way th' wind blows!" Kate said

musingly. "I knew that one wanted 'im—an' now she's
usin' poor Jared's drownin' ta' gain 'is eye!"

"They are in love, Kate," Melanie said forlornly.
"They have been for a long time!"

"Oh, pooh!" Kate scoffed. "Laura Callaghan cannot truly love 'inny but herself! An' whin' it's a man,
'e must carry 'er image in 'is eyes, as yer brother did
. . . an', as Paul Lanier does now!" She shook her
head vehemently. "No, child! Yer mistaken! Nat
Larimore does not carry 'er image with 'im. 'Tis yers
'e carries in 'is heart!"

"You don't know, Kate!"

"I know all that's needed! Ye' mustn't run off 'n gie
Laura a clear field, child! Else, beggin' yer pardon
. . . yer a fool!"

"You just said Laura and Nat aren't in love."

"Love doesn't come inta' anythin'! She *wants* 'im!
An' men bein' whut they are, she'll git 'im if ye' bow
out!"

"I can do nothing else, Kate! I cannot bear to see
them together as they have been since Jared's death!"

Kate bowed her head.

"I'll go along wi' ye, child! But I'm not likin' it!"

Melanie packed lightly; a few simple dresses she'd
worn about the house when not expecting callers;
several pairs of sturdy shoes for walking in the hills
and forests, and a few ordinary toiletries, but none of
her jewels except the priceless emerald and diamond
necklace that was her betrothal gift. Having offered it
to Nat and having it declined, Melanie decided that
this, at least, Laura would not have!

I will be a simple country girl! she told herself. *I
will be Kate's niece; her brother's daughter visiting
from the woodsy country of Ohio.*

When Nat left that evening, he kissed her and held
her close; but she stifled her yearning and listened
with mute pain when he admonished her to wait,
have faith, and all would be well. She watched him

walk out into the night and bade him a silent good-
bye while her heart cried out in longing for the love
she'd thought they'd once shared. Then, she went
quietly to the nursery and kissed Jared's sleeping children a tearful farewell.

The sun was just breaking over the horizon as Melanie and Kate trudged downhill toward the livery
stable. Melanie glanced back at Halcyon House,
bright in the first rays of the sun.

Good-bye house! she bid silently. *I take all the
good memories with me from the past. But my days
within your walls are gone. I have no place there
now.*

While Kate bought passage for two on a hired
coach to Boston, Melanie waited in the shadows, fearfully watching for a familiar face who might recognize her and remember.

The money James had paid her that terrifying afternoon more than a month ago was all Melanie had
to see her through the time ahead. When that was
gone, she could not fathom what to do. With her
funds tied up in ships and banks, she knew she would
have to go to Nathaniel, who held her purse strings.

I will not do so! she promised herself. *I will die
first!*

The carriage took the Post Road toward Boston;
the same road Melanie had traveled with Laura,
barely six weeks ago. Only this time, it was Kate who
sat beside her and Melanie's simple cotton gown and
worn slippers were a far cry from the smart traveling
outfit the newly betrothed girl had worn to meet her
intended in Boston that long ago day.

"It seems years ago, Kate," Melanie said, in a voice
near breaking, "that Laura and I traveled this same
road to meet Jared and Nat."

"An' look at all thet's 'appened since!" Kate ex-

claimed, clucking her tongue sympathetically. "Laura
lost 'er baby . . . Jared's drownin' . . . an'
James's death . . ." Her voice trailed off.

And my eyes were opened to Nat's deception! Melanie added silently. *At least, I am not obliged to remain at Halcyon House watching him grow closer to
Laura each passing hour!*

They talked of that day when the authorities came
aboard the *Sea-Wind.* Melanie had been asleep and
missed their searching. Indeed, they had not even
come to her cabin because of the tragedy their shot
caused the sinking ship that had been waiting beyond
the mist.

"They were aware of James's antipathy toward his
brother; and in fact, had searched that very ship
many times before at James's instigation," Melanie
told Kate. "Paul informed me they could do nothing
else but clear Nat's name, since there was no evidence
of fugitives aboard ship, or at the factory."

"Whut iver 'appened ta' th' fugitives?" Kate asked.
"Did they git ta' Canader? 'N whut of the man wi' th'
sore leg we tuk frum th' candle fact'ry? Wuz e' healed
proper, d'ye' s'pose?"

Melanie nodded.

"Paul said the fugitives remained in New Bedford
harbor only one night. The *Mirimar* took them to
Canada the following day. And he assured me your
special patient must be well healed by now."

The sun's heat became more oppressive with each
passing hour. In the last days of June, with July an-
nouncing its imminent arrival by casting a hot breath
over the land, the scenery had changed. The new
green grass of six weeks ago had matured and was
now lush, and dark-thick; the fields that had been
fresh-turned held tall rows of corn and other vegetables. The blossoms of May had become ripening cher-
ries and pears, and small green apples. Yellow

dandelions, past their season, had turned to soft white fuzz and a summer breeze carried their spores to seed far places, while another generation dotting the hills and valleys awaited their turn for proliferation.

Only churches, weathervanes, and graveyards remained the same; unaffected by passing seasons though grass was longer over the headstones, and the angle of the sun on the stained glass windows differed slightly from the second week in May.

It was nearly noon when they reached the Toll House. Melanie, accustomed to the deference given her station, was astonished to find herself pushed back by the maitre' d, while a well-dressed matron and her entourage swept into the dining room.

She was about to humiliate the man haughtily, when she realized her mode of attire was against her. She had demeaned herself by hiding behind the appearance of a simple country girl; now she must grit her teeth and accept the consequences.

Kate, observing Melanie's discomfiture, hid a sudden grin behind her hand, while at the same time she felt a stab of pain at the offense rendered her beloved charge.

When they crested the blue hills of Milton, Melanie tried not to look at Boston harbor in the distance, where her gaze had eagerly sought Nat's ship from this same height, barely six weeks before.

As they followed the coastline, Melanie observed how rapidly the shoreline coves and bays had been filled. Now, where water once stood, warehouses and other buildings stood stark and half-built in the blazing sunshine. But the smell of the sea still rose rank and strong to their nostrils.

Only Commercial Street remained the same. Crowds of sailors, workers, hawkers, and merchants swarmed the narrow way. The shouts of vendors rose above the street. Pushing, shouting, the mass of humanity struggled for survival; for a few pennies to ward off the pangs of hunger; or to grasp at momentary freedom from want, by snatching the purses of the rich.

Melanie turned her eyes away when they passed Commercial Wharf. She could not bear to look and remember. She did not want to see that short flight of steps where the shallop used to deposit them from the *Mirimar* and pick them up again after happy excursions shopping for her trousseau and enjoying the best of the town. Melanie realized now just how privileged she'd been in those golden days. With regret, she decided to close her eyes to the past and look only to the future, whatever limited future she might have at this time in her life.

At the far end of Commercial Street, the carriage pulled into the terminal yard and deposited their luggage on crude, wooden planks.

"Where to, missus?" the stationmaster asked Kate, since the girl with her was obviously addled, with her far-off stare and uncertain movements.

Kate smiled at the man engagingly.

"Two fer' th' Neck," she said simply. " 'N I know th' coach goes on ta' Marblehead! But, 'tis th' Neck where we wanta' go, 'n we'd be 'bliged if 'e'd stop at th' road leadin' to it!"

" 'Long as ya' pay full fare, I don't rightly care where ya' git off!" the man answered testily.

Kate shrugged and laid out the money. She'd been trying to get a decent word from that man each time she arrived here, but he always acted as though she had the plague!

"No matter!" she said later to Melanie, in the coach on the road to Marblehead. "I'll find me a man better'n 'im some day! 'N whin 'e finds I've me own 'ouse, 'e'll regret 'is manners!"

Melanie looked at Kate in surprise.

"I was unaware that you were man hunting, Kate!" she said, looking at the woman with new eyes.

"I'm barely fifty-five," Kate answered. " 'T'ain't too late fer me if me' mither's any marker! She lived into 'er late seventies an' married four times. They was all sailors an' left 'er wid'ered now an' agin!"

"You've never married, Kate, yet the man called you missus."

Kate nodded: "Most do! They niver b'lieve a woman my age ain't b'in wed!"

"You spent most of your life in Halcyon House with us," Melanie said in astonishment. "And you must have been young when you came there. I cannot recall being without you."

"I was thirty-one whin I came there," Kate said quietly. " 'N yer mither was expectin' you. Jared was jist a babe whin I first saw 'im, an' th' two o'you 'er all the children I'll iver have!" She took Melanie's hand in her own. "That's why, child, yer happiness is all that's meanin'ful ter me!"

Melanie smiled affectionately at her.

"I love you, Kate! And I know Jared did also. But surely, in your youth, there must have been someone...?"

Kate nodded.

" 'E, too, was a sailor! I loved 'im wi' all me 'eart! But, 'e sailed away one fine day, 'n niver returned. I niver knew what 'appened to 'im! Whither th' sea ... or another woman, I'll go ta' me grave wonderin'. An' now, 'tis too late to worry 'bout it! If th' good Lords wants ta' find me a man, E'll send 'im my way. There's nuthin' I c'n do ta' hurry 'im up, neither. 'E knows I'm growin' old, 'n if 'E wants me ter wed, 'E knows what ta' do!"

Melanie smiled at Kate's simple faith, and wished she had some of it herself.

North of Boston, the highway rose higher each mile, and trees grew thicker and closer together. The road wound through forests and circled around hills, sometimes coming within reach of the coast where the deep blue Atlantic stretched as far as the eye could see. They passed through tiny towns whose only claim to the name was a small general store and livery stable, with an inn beside it. This was farm country, where soil was tilled on the sides of hills and those who were not farming sailed into the oceans for their living.

The carriage stopped abruptly in the middle of nowhere. Amid trees and thick underbrush on both sides of the road, only the sounds of birds and other creatures gave any sign of life. They had not passed a house or farmland for some time and Melanie was suddenly concerned. Then, just a short distance ahead, she saw a narrow, rutted lane leading off east of the main route.

" 'Tis th' way to th' Neck," Kate said, scanning the view from the window. "We must walk fer a mile or two, thin' left at th' path ter th' house."

The driver had left his high perch and opened the door. He helped Kate and Melanie with their baggage and placed them at the corner of the roadside. Then, in a cloud of dust, he left them, choking and coughing with sand in their throat and nostrils.

"We'll take th' time," Kate said efficiently. "Bein's yer unused ta' walkin' sich distances, ye' best change yer slippers ter those old flat ones ye' used ter wear 'bout th' house."

So saying, she opened Melanie's valise and fetched the shoes from the middle of it.

" 'Ere," she said. "Sit yerself down 'pon me' box, 'n change, 'else yer tender feet'll git blisters!"

Melanie did as she was told. Then, carrying her baggage, she followed Kate up the road toward Marblehead Neck.

Nearly an hour later, after several stops when Melanie sat breathless and perspiring at the side of the lane, they came to the path that led to Kate's house.

An apple orchard grew up the gentle slope of the hill to the northwest and on the other side of the twisting lane, the hill swept down to a narrow sand and rock beach fringed with witchgrass; beyond which rolled the bright, blue waters of the ocean. Breakers tipped with white foam surged gently and an azure sky was dotted with tiny puffs of cloud. The hand of summer lay heavy upon the land. Melanie took deep breaths of fresh salt air, rejuvenating her spirits and her soul.

Salt air and sea is good fer' what ails you! Ephraim always said.

Melanie smiled that even after all that had happened, her father's words and influence could reach her here, miles from home. Now she desperately needed his sage wisdom and the security of his love. For his love reached beyond a watery grave, she knew. His teachings and beliefs had guided her through these past agonizing weeks . . . and even before that, when the realization that she'd given her heart to a man who loved another, had nearly caused her to succumb to depression and defeat.

A wise and loving parent, someone had once written, *is one of life's greatest gifts!*

Melanie bowed her head and gave thanks that she had been the daughter of Ephraim Hardy, whose love and wisdom still guided her life. For now, she had chosen to make her own way, and she was alone.

Kate's house stood halfway up the slope; small and square with one lean-to shed attached to its western extremity. A wide rock chimney ran up one wall, narrowing as it reached the roof, and windows sparkled in welcome, reflecting late afternoon sunshine. The cleared land on the downward slope was a riot of unplowed tangled grass and weeds. Behind the house, a thicket of blackberry vines sprawled to the circling pine wood, heavy with the smell of ripening berries in the sweet summer air.

They entered the house through a curved lattice over the door, where honeysuckle and ivy twined. The house had one large room which served as kitchen and sitting room. On the east side, facing the sea, was a bedroom; at the back, surveying the forest, was a smaller sleeping room. Beyond that was the outhouse, the nearest thing to a convenience room that could be found.

"I told ye, 'tis not grand!" Kate said disconsolately, suddenly realizing what it must seem to Melanie's eyes. "But," she said, quickly brightening, "I'll have it shinin' spic 'n span within th' hour! I'll be sleepin' in me brither's room. 'N if ye'll take yer valise inter me room, ye should be fair cosy there. Th' bed is new 'n soft fer yer ladylike bones!"

Kate meant no sarcasm in her words, for her station in life taught her that ladies could endure much less than those of her own hardy stock and lifestyle.

Melanie did as she was told.

Aside from dust over the scarred dresser and mirror, as well as the bedstead, it was indeed a cozy room. One wide window facing the sea and another facing south over the field brightened the little bedchamber. Kate's efforts at decorating had included sheer white curtains to soften the sun, though their starch had long ago disappeared and they now hung limp and dusty from string rods atop the glass.

She changed her traveling clothes and donned a sheer blue dotted swiss that had seen better days. After washing her face and accepting a glass of cool spring water Kate drew from the hand pump, Melanie took dust cloth and broom and attacked the grime with a vengeance.

"I'll be goin' ter market in Marblehead," Kate told Melanie. "We've naught fer supper 'n th' days ahead. I've onions in th' root cellar, 'n some 'taters; but naught else. Rest yer bones. I won't be gone much more'n a' hour, takin' th' short way over th' hill."

"Kate, wait a moment," Melanie said, reaching into her purse. She took out twenty dollars and extended it to her. "This will care for us for a time. When you run out, I have more."

Kate's eyes widened at the vast amount, and she shoved it back at Melanie.

"No, child! I'd be a'frighted ta' carry sich a vast sum in me pocket! Keep it, child, 'n gie me jist enuff fer food these next days. Whin needed, I'll ask fer more!"

Melanie smiled and did as she asked.

Later, when she had finished her room and Kate had been gone for some time, Melanie sat outside on a broken fence rail enjoying the peace and quiet of the countryside. Though it was nearly six in the evening, the sun was still high and the warm, late June afternoon had a lazy quality about it. A honeybee buzzed happily about rhododendrons along the fence line and the cooing sound of doves wafted down to her from woods behind the house. She looked downslope to the little beach and saw gulls running in the wake of an ebb tide; picking at the sand with their sharp beaks, enjoying the meal obligingly deposited by surging waters.

Melanie loved forests and hills; but most of all, she loved the sea. She knew an inland life was not for her. As long as she could look out over the ocean to see wind on the water and tides ebbing and flowing with the currents of her life, she would be happy the rest of her days. For the sea was her father . . . and now, her brother. Their lives had blended with those waters, and she felt a kinship to swirling eddies and the ceaseless, mercurial waves.

She thought sadly of the house at Hazard's Bluff, not too far from where she sat, and wondered if Laura would be happy there. For that Nat would marry Laura now, Melanie never thought to doubt. All impediments had been removed with Melanie's retreat from Halcyon House. Nat, without care or conscience, could now claim his heart's desire without a twinge; for he had not deliberately caused Melanie's wounding by voicing his love for Laura. Melanie had taken care of that chore for him, by disappearing, never to see him again.

She recalled her devastating agony the night she watched Laura in Nat's arms aboard the *Mirimar*. And just yesterday her dull pain. Now, Melanie felt guilt at her deep anger and resentment.

Love is not something that can be avoided . . . or killed! she thought. *It is a spontaneous thing, and dies only from lack of nurturing. Or from a hurt so deep that it withers away.*

And Melanie prayed that having withdrawn from Nathaniel to soothe her wounds, she would one day realize love for him had died. That he was forever gone from her heart and her memory.

These were her thoughts, and so she reasoned as she sat atop the fence rail on her first day at Kate's house on Marblehead Neck. She had no way of knowing that warm summer afternoon, that though she'd taken a devious route to numb her pain, Fate had still more devious turnings ahead before her destiny was fulfilled.

CHAPTER SIXTEEN

July passed and the days of August flew swiftly as Kate and Melanie tended their little garden behind the house and the flowers lining the narrow path from the lane. Melanie had enjoyed Kate's "lilacs in the dooryard" and as the blossoms faded, the heavy, sweet scent did also, leaving only the memory of their flowering in Melanie's mind.

Oftentimes, she wondered while hoeing or gathering the fruits of their labors, whether Laura and Nat were planning their wedding, or, due to Laura's malaise, they had rushed precipitately into marriage, ignoring the usual mourning period.

Deliberately at times, she invoked the image of Nat and Laura on the deck of the *Mirimar,* and again on her last day at Halcyon House, telling herself that it was necessary pain, in order to exorcise the longing she still felt for Nat, and the agony at her self-imposed separation from him.

But then she would shrug and fall more eagerly to the tasks at hand. Exhausted at the end of a long day which began at sunup, she would throw herself into bed to sleep soundly; arising rested, refreshed and determined to face another day with less pain and less agonizing over the past.

Now and then, working in the garden, she would gaze at the sea beyond the field and watch a ship's sails just above the horizon; wondering if it was Nat's ship bringing his bride to Hazard's Bluff.

Oftentimes, she would walk the long few miles past Marblehead. She would stand on the road above the little inlet, where James Talbot's house now stood vacant and haunted since the death of his wife and old Sadie's ensconcement with another family in the town.

Looking across at Hazard's Bluff, Melanie would wonder how much longer Nat's house would stand empty. For though Zeke Seavey was still in residence in the little caretaker's cottage there, the driveway had become overgrown with weeds and there was no sign of life. At first, Melanie doubted that even Zeke lived there, but on one of her excursions, she had seen him come slowly downhill with his rolling sailor's gait, to stand gazing across the distance to where she stood. She had stared solemnly back at him, for she knew that in Kate's old sunbonnet and faded cotton dress, he would never recognize her as Nathaniel Larimore's betrothed. And in truth, he would probably not have recognized her had she been in more elegant attire; for he had seen her only once on the day Nat brought her to the home that could never be hers.

Kate had happily settled into her little house. It was what she had wanted for many a year, to live here under her own roof, with no worry about how she was to care for it and keep food in her belly for the long winter. She had not heard from her brother for over two years now, and with pain in her heart, she wondered if the last of her kin, along with Melanie's, had disappeared beneath the sea's hungry waves.

She'd carefully watched Melanie, who was as dear to her as though she were her own. She'd seen the effort the girl made to cast aside her feelings and build a life for herself here on this lonely hill beside the Atlantic. Kate had left her to her own devices, for in her wise soul, she knew that only Melanie could find the way to peace within herself.

She's eatin' 'er heart out fer 'im! Th' rotten man! Kate thought to herself, feeling her temper rise. *I'd luv' ta' tell 'im whut I think o' 'im fer not lookin' fer 'er afore now!*

For though few knew of Kate's home in Marblehead Neck, the old butler, Lawrence, did know. And if Nat had wanted to search for Melanie, Lawrence would be the first one questioned.

Many times, Kate had been tempted to drop a clue in the town about the true identity of her "niece from Ohio"! But she had given her oath to Melanie; and Kate, religious and superstitious, could not break a vow.

September came. Kate and Melanie busily made preserves and hoarded vegetables in the root cellar for the long winter ahead. Jams and jellies wafted their delicious aromas through the little house, and Kate's hot vegetable soups nourished them in the evenings that grew cooler with each passing day.

As the leaves began to turn, Melanie became restless. Her love for Nat refused to die. Despite all efforts to refrain from so doing, her thoughts were filled with memories of him; his arms about her . . . his kiss . . . his ardent passion when he made love to her in the rough cabin on the *Mirimar.* In vain, she tried to turn away the vivid images that flashed across her mind and burdened her heavy heart with haunting recollections she had run all these miles to forget.

With summer's heavy work finished, Melanie could no longer find escape in pushing tired muscles beyond normal capacity. The light chores necessary each day were completed long before she was ready for them to be, and she sought out countless insignificant little duties to keep hands and mind busy.

The few books she'd brought with her in early summer had been read and reread these past months. Now, on long nights, she would sit with Kate before the hearth and stare into the fire envisioning scenes of the past . . . and weaving golden fancies of what might have been.

Then it was Melanie began to realize no matter what she did she would never forget Nat. She would love him until she died, and prayed that day was not far off. For looking ahead, she knew life without him was, for her, no life at all.

It's a healin' time ye're havin'! Kate had said over and over when she saw misery behind Melanie's eyes.

"But I have not healed, Kate!" Melanie would later whisper into her tear-damp pillow.

By mid-October, all was in readiness for winter. Kate and Melanie now spent their time gathering wood for the fireplace; for the garden had been picked clean and the food, as much as possible, preserved or stored in readiness for the coming cold season.

Time now weighed heavily on Melanie's shoulders. Midnight would find her tossing restlessly, staring out at a harvest moon and listening to hoot owls calling eerily in the woods behind the house. And when the wind came in from the sea, the sound of surf crashing on the rocky beach below the field filled her ears. Then, her dreams were of that night on the *Mirimar*, when Nat took her into his arms at last; and they turned into nightmares when she found herself suddenly with Kate and the fugitive under a swaying lantern, rocking in the hold of the pinkie schooner while Jared was swept overboard from the deck above her head.

On those nights, Melanie would awaken sobbing. Then, recovering her senses, she would leave her lonely bed to sit on the floor by the window, watching the moon shine white on dead cornstalks and cast a silver glow over foam-tipped breakers rolling onto the beach.

On just such a night, Melanie gave up at last.

There is naught to be done! she reasoned to herself. *I cannot spend a lifetime mourning over Nathaniel, and I will never love another. I cannot go back to Halcyon House and when my funds are depleted, what will I do? Dear God! Please! Please give me the courage to walk into the sea and join Jared and my father . . .*

In the depths of despair, Melanie could see no future. Nothing but blackness arose in her mind when she thought of the years ahead. She prayed for oblivion, and with each passing day, she grew paler, and thinner, and weaker.

On a morning during the last days of October, Melanie awakened to dull, leaden skies. She'd heard rain on the roof throughout the night, while the wind howled about the little house with a mournful, eerie sound. She'd slept fitfully and the weather befitted her mood this cold, damp day.

When she came out to the fire, Kate had a pot of coffee brewing on the stove. Her hand was at her back, massaging the pain.

"I'll go to market for provisions, Kate," Melanie said. "Your rheumatism will only get worse if you go in this rain."

"I shoulda' done it yis'ta'dy!" the old woman said peevishly. "I knew we was low on sugar, 'n coffee . . . but agin' I put off goin'!" She had seated herself in the rocker beside the hearth and rubbed her swollen knuckles.

"I'll get some liniment for your bones." Melanie forced a smile. "You rest today," she said, kissing her forehead.

" 'Tis no day fer a wee thing like ye' t' be gaddin'

about!" Kate scolded. "Ye'll ketch yer death! We c'n make do 'til th' rain passes . . ."

"We're near out of candles," Melanie said listlessly. "We'll have only the fire to see by tonight. Besides," she brightened, "it will do me good to go into town. It's been two weeks since I've seen a human face other than yours." She patted the woman's hand reassuringly. "I'll be fine, Kate! Have no fear."

For Melanie felt a compulsion to see the house at Hazard's Bluff once more. She wanted to see for herself whether, during the past two weeks, it had welcomed Nat . . . and, perhaps, his bride.

"Yer too weak fer trudgin' sich a distance! Ye've lost so much flesh, th' slightest breeze 'uld blow ye' away!" Kate rejoined. "Ter'morra t'won't be a'rainin', 'n I'll make me usual trip fer necessaries!"

But Melanie was determined.

"No, Kate! It will most likely rain tomorrow, also. Then, we will have no breakfast coffee, no candles, and no sugar for an additional day. Besides," she added, with an attempt at lightness, "I am not so sweet that I will melt in the rain! I am going!"

This last sentence was said with more strength behind it than she felt, but her determination to see Hazard's Bluff once more gave her a momentary surge of energy.

Kate, preoccupied with her sore joints, could argue no more.

"Ye' don't know th' merchants in Marblehead!" she finished weakly. "They'll charge ye' outlandish prices whin they think yer gentry."

Melanie's face broke into a startled grin.

"Kate! Can you honestly look at me in these rags and think of me as gentry?" She tried a halfhearted pirouette, then flared out her skirt and made a low curtsy.

Kate looked her over.

"Nay! I don't see how," she said, with a brief,

answering smile. "Git sum flour 'n a few eggs 'n I'll
bake ye' a marmsey cake . . ." she added, watching
Melanie don her old woolen hooded cape.

Melanie smiled, pulling on her overshoes. Kate's
"marmsey cake" was a childhood treat. Melanie and
Jared would dig in with relish when Kate presented
them with a huge hunk as reward for being "specially
good" or as bribery to behave themselves while their
mother entertained her sewing circle or church group.
The name, she'd told them when questioned, came
out of her childhood, when her own mother would
bake them on rare occasions as a treat for her hungry
brood.

" 'Wish't we had a bumbershoot fer ye ta' carry in
this rain," Kate said anxiously.

"No matter. I have the cape hood, and it is not
raining so hard now. I'll be fine, Kate."

So saying, Melanie kissed her on the cheek and set
off down the lane. Her brief attempt at lightening
Kate's mood as well as her own had passed, and her
spirits were as dampened as the weather.

Autumn is beautiful in sunshine, sparkling bright
and blazing; but autumn in the rain is stark, dreary,
with vibrant colors dimmed. Then, the sham that is
Indian summer disappears, revealing the real truth of
the season at last—the year is dying.

A cold wind was beginning to manifest and dead
leaves swirled, rustling on the lane in front of her.
The drizzle lightened as Melanie took the slippery
path downslope on the other side of the hill beyond
the house. Branches, some with a few stubborn leaves
clinging in a death grip, others stark, barren, began
to whip in gusts. Melanie ducked her head often to
avoid being stunned by a blow from an erratic, buffet-
ing limb. Summer birds had long flown the advancing
winter, but stubborn little brown sparrows dotted
lowering skies. They funneled up now from the twist-

ing way ahead, just out of Melanie's vision, and their
startled cries filtered through the lament of a rising
wind.

Melanie knew she would be gone longer than Kate
expected, but she was reluctant to tell of her many
jaunts past Marblehead to view Hazard's Bluff from a
safe distance; when Kate believed she was merely
roaming the woods, communing with her thoughts.

I will use weather as an excuse! she told herself,
feeling a twinge of guilt for fibbing to her childhood
mentor. But Melanie could not bear to share her
secret; that she lived with the ghost of Nathaniel at
her side each hour of every day . . . and if, perchance, she could but have a glimpse of him from a
distance, her yearning might be eased.

Melanie walked on, remembering last autumn in
New Bedford. Nat had not yet come into her life,
though she'd thought of him often since the day in
the tobacconist's shop. She recalled despairing that he
would ever come to court her as her father had
promised.

And after James Talbot brought home his Polynesian wife, she'd almost resigned herself to becoming
maiden aunt to Jared's children. There were none
others in her circle of acquaintances that interested
her; or who had shown any predeliction toward her
redemption from the status of old maid.

But despite Laura's constant nagging, life at Halcyon House had been comfortable, familiar, and, Melanie now realized, even exciting. The stifling
sameness of her days these past months gilded
memories of her New Bedford world of church pic-
nics, choir practices, dress fittings, and soirees. Then,
she recalled that painful shyness made most of these
activities trying at times; indeed, she'd often forced
herself to join the ranks of humanity.

I should be happy in solitude! she thought ruefully. *Were I of another persuasion, I should most likely have joined a nunnery!*

Then, she blushingly dismissed that thought, recalling the cabin shared with Nat on the *Mirimar* the last night of their voyage from Marblehead. Nat's lovemaking had sent her into a world of ecstasy she'd never dreamed of in her sheltered, pristine existence. She tried to subdue her thoughts; to forget the touch of his hands on her body . . . his lips on hers . . . and his whispering, seductive voice in her ears. But Nat's passion was engraved upon her soul, and the feel of his arms about her could never be forgotten.

At the bottom of the hill, she walked across a sparsely wooded marshland, picking her way carefully to keep from slipping into bogs that held a thin film of ice over stagnant water. Here, reeds moaned in a rising gale, and bits of dead grass and leaves swirled in little eddies across the flat, desolate swamp. Stepping out from the lee of a rise, she was smitten by a cold wind blowing in from the harbor. She pulled her cape tighter, and dug her hands deep into voluminous pockets, hunching her shoulders to hold in the warmth and keep from shivering.

She stood a moment on the cleared rock path that led down to the docks, searching tall ships berthed there with sails furled. Not one of Nat's vessels was among them. Her heart sank. She'd been almost certain that he came these past days to the house at Hazard's Bluff; something deep inside signaled his nearness.

Dejection took over once more.

Why am I doing this? What would it serve if I did see him? It would only shred my heart afresh, and since I have no intention of ever facing him again, why punish myself in this manner?

She could not find the answer. She only knew she

was driven to place one foot before the other and follow her urging.

She decided to go straight to the Talbot house on the inlet, which was her favorite watching place. On the way back, she would do the marketing. So she circled the harbor well above the wharves and took the tannery road rounding the hills over the town to meet the narrow highway rising toward Hazard's Bluff.

Nearly half an hour later, climbing the smooth, well-worn route, her footsteps began to falter. The little turnoff to the inlet was just ahead, but Melanie felt suddenly weak. Breath came in short, quick gasps, and she went to lean against a tree at the roadside. She remembered then that she had not breakfasted. In truth, she'd been having these spells more frequently lately, due to a diminished interest in food.

I will buy something at the market upon which to nibble while I make my way back to the Neck, she told herself.

As she was about to step out onto the road again, she heard a horse and carriage coming fast. There was only one possible place that carriage could be going, aside from the old Talbot mansion, and that was Nat's house!

Terrified that she might be seen and recognized, Melanie ran downhill. A broad, flat shelf, whose rim overlooked the town, broke the cliff's sharp descent, just ten or fifteen feet below the highway. She hid in a little copse of trees while the carriage rumbled past on the road above. In her haste to run for cover, she had failed to notice that the trees stood in swampy marshland. Now, sloshing through ankle-deep water, hurrying up to the road once more, Melanie realized her feet were soaking and the bottom of her skirts, as well.

Despite squishing boots and the cold seeping through her bones, she ran the rest of the way to the

Talbot house. The carriage must circle the inlet before reaching the gates to Hazard's Bluff and she
wanted to see who would ring the bell at the portal.

Melanie barely made it in time, for Nat was hurrying back toward the carriage to await Zeke Seavey's
answer to his summons. Her heart raced, recognizing
his broad shoulders in a wide, heavy cape and the
movement of his long legs as he ran through rain that
had now begun to fall again. Melanie wondered if
Laura accompanied him, but peering through the
drizzle, she could not tell if anyone else occupied the
carriage.

Zeke Seavey came downhill to open the gates.
When he swung the second gate wide, his sharp,
seaman's eyes pierced the distance between them, en-
veloping her forlorn figure standing in the trees next
to the Talbot house. Zeke stood there a long moment,
a silent sentinel, never moving a muscle as his fixed
gaze studied her from afar. With her heart in her
mouth, Melanie saw Nat leave the carriage and speak
to the caretaker, then follow his pointing finger to
where she stood.

She was fearful of moving. Perhaps they would
think her a specter, haunting James's house . . . or
a vagrant gypsy seeking shelter in an empty old mansion. After a few long minutes that seemed like hours,
Melanie saw Nat turn the horse and carriage around
and head back down the road toward the inlet. She
knew then, too late, that he'd seen her and possibly
recognized her silent form observing from afar. It was
only a matter of moments before he would reach the
spot where she stood.

In panic, she searched about for a hiding place.
The house was locked, she knew from experience; for
on several of her excursions to this place, she'd tested
the doors and windows and found them securely fastened.

A pathway led uphill through the woods behind

the house. Melanie ran from tree to tree, hiding behind each one, then peering out to see if the carriage
had yet reached the Talbot drive.

Rain fell harder now and by the time Melanie
crested the hill, she could barely see Nat stop the vehicle before James's old home. From her hiding place
behind thick brush and fir trees, she peeked through
the thicket to watch him walk halfway up the hill
which had been her escape route. His eyes were steady,
relentless in their search as his piercing gaze swept
the bushes and trees on the slope above. At long last,
Nat turned away and walked down toward his waiting
carriage.

With a deep sigh of relief, Melanie took a path
downhill toward Marblehead and the market.

In years to come, Melanie would try to remember
that long walk home through teeming rain. Her
mind, befuddled, confused, carried the image of Nat,
and all the months between were as though they had
never been. Her heart broke again, and she realized
once more that it had never healed.

By the time she reached Kate's house at the Neck,
the little basket of provisions she carried was half-
filled with rainwater and she'd been drenched to her
skin on the homeward journey.

Kate, forgetting her rheumatism, cried out frantically over Melanie's state and the length of time her
venture had taken.

Tired, feverish, Melanie allowed herself to be
undressed and dried, then wrapped in one of Kate's
voluminous flannel nightgowns.

Her scattered thoughts had a nightmarish quality.
Though she knew she was at home in Kate's house,
seated before the fire and wrapped in blankets to ease
the chill, she was uncertain of everything else going
on about her.

Kate placed a warm pottery mug in her hands, and

when Melanie raised it up to sip, it had the taste of whiskey and herbs.

"Drink it, child! 'T'will ward off th' lung fever 'n bring ye' ter yer'self agin'! 'Tis me mither's own herbal posset. She brought us all, now n' agin, thru' th' fever, 'twixt 'er possets 'n 'er poultices. . . ."

Kate's voice droned on incessantly, as, oblivious to Melanie's true condition, she launched into an excited tale of the visitor she'd had while Melanie was absent.

CHAPTER SEVENTEEN

"'E left th' carriage in th' lane and come runnin' through th' storm!" Kate was saying. "I was niver so s'prised in me life ta' see sich a grand gen'lman as Paul Lanier standin' in me' very own doorway . . ."

Kate had risen painfully from her chair when she heard the unaccustomed sound of horses' hooves pounding up the rutted lane. Peeking from her window, she was astonished to see a hired carriage stop before her little cottage.

Brushing her skirts and smoothing her hair, she waited anxiously for the knock at the door. When she opened it, her mouth gaped in astonishment.

"Mr. Lanier, sor! Beggin' yer pardon, whut's 'appened? Is't th' wee one?" Kate's hand went to her breast, for she thought for just a moment that Melanie had been discovered drowned in some bog between here and Marblehead, or worse, had thrown herself into the sea.

"May I come in, Kate?" Paul asked, rain streaming from his oilskins.

Kate stepped aside and, ducking his head, Paul entered the little dwelling. He stood a moment looking about, feeling a twinge of guilt at the length of time he'd allowed Melanie to abide here.

But in the end, she will be happy that I did so! he consoled himself silently.

"Miss Melanie is not at home?" he asked politely.

Kate shook her head.

"Nay. She went 'bout a' hour ago fer necessaries in Marblehead. I be worried 'bout 'er, bein' so frail an' all, goin' in th' storm, but she would do't!" Kate said, seating herself in her rocker again, and with a sweep of the hand, inviting Paul to take a seat on the settle near the fire.

Paul removed his oilskins and gingerly placed them over an old scarred wooden trunk next to the hearth. Then, taking a seat, he reached for his pipe and looked about the rustic room.

"How is she, Kate?" he asked, lighting a match and puffing slowly.

Kate shrugged her shoulders.

" 'S well as inny girl'd be whin fergotten by th' man she loves . . . 'n the rest o' 'er fam'ly 'n friends as well!" she said in biting tones.

"She has not been forgotten, Kate. Nat loves Melanie."

"Is a strange way o' showin' it, 'e has! Leavin' 'er be all th' summer, 'n niver a word out o' 'im; nor a 'how be ye'! Carin' not that she' de bournin' 'er 'eart out fer 'im!"

"Nat was unaware of Melanie's whereabouts," Paul said quietly.

"Ya' mean, ye jist found out now, after all th' months?"

"No . . . I knew where Melanie was all along."

Kate stared at him.

"If'n ye knew, why didn't ye do somethin' 'bout it?"

"I couldn't, Kate. I first had a game to play with Nat and Laura . . ."

"Ye didn't tell th' cap'n where she was at?"

Paul shook his head.

"Hummmp!" Kate snorted. "If'n 'e wanted ter know, 'e'd a' found out from Lawrence."

"He questioned the man, but I paid Lawrence well

not to tell Nat where you live. Lawrence and Jared
were the only ones in Halcyon House who knew of
this place at the Neck. So, with Jared gone, and
Lawrence apparently ignorant of your whereabouts,
Nat had to search blindly for Melanie, all the summer and fall. He started at the livery stable, but no
one remembered a lady of Melanie's description leaving there on the morning in question. He sent detec-
tives throughout Boston, then down the coast to
Rhode Island, Connecticut, and finally, New York
City, itself . . ."

Kate looked at him through puzzled eyes.

"Why did ye' not want 'im ter find 'er?"

"Because, Kate, the situation Melanie ran away from
had to be changed before she could return to New
Bedford . . ."

Kate closed her eyes and shook her head.

"Fer th' life o' me, I be hearin' ye, but make no
sense out o' yer words!"

Paul leaned back against the faded pillow of the
settle and puffed his pipe.

"Nat went crazy when Melanie disappeared," he
said with a slight smile. "He tore the town apart looking for her, then realizing she was not there, he
checked every ship that had sailed that day, sending
his fastest clippers in search of them; trailing them
into harbors and ports all up and down the coast. He
sailed a clipper himself seeking Melanie, and returned each time, frustrated and angered that such a
thing could happen to him. He went to New York
and hired all the men he could find to seek her out;
he offered rewards and every sheriff and constable up
and down the coast of the United States has a likeness
of Melanie . . . and you, as well, Kate!" Paul
laughed.

Kate's eyes bugged.

"An' ye still didn' tell 'im?"

"No." Paul puffed his pipe again. "I needed time,

Kate. I needed Nat out of the way, so I could plead my suit to Laura. When Jared died, Laura and Nat, in their grief, became involved in a situation that belonged in the past. They took comfort from each other, but they were not really in love. They were friends . . . and I wanted to make certain that they remained just that. When Melanie played into my hands by leaving, I decided to make the best of my chances. I sent Nat off on wild goose chases—kept him gone for weeks. And all the while, knowing with him out of the way, Laura would turn to me for comfort."

Kate gasped.

"Ye put that sweet lil' gurl thru' all o' that, fer yer own sake?" She stood up, angered beyond belief, Irish blood boiling.

"I knew Melanie was safe with you, Kate. I had a man check periodically and he reported seeing her hoeing in the field, walking through the woods, and shopping in Marblehead."

Kate sat down again, but her eyes still blazed at the man seated opposite her calmly puffing his pipe.

"Melanie left because Laura was coming between Nat and herself. Since I knew he loved Melanie, and that Laura's sorrowing and clinging helplessness were all that held Nat to her, I wanted to make him realize sooner than later, that he was forsaking Melanie," Paul continued. "So, by sending him on fruitless jaunts in frantic search of his betrothed, I had a clear field to Laura, whom I have loved since we met," he ended simply.

Kate's eyes had bugged again.

"Laura and I are to wed in the spring," he told her quietly. "When the mourning period is over."

"So, now ye've told th' cap'n?"

Paul shook his head.

"No. Apparently, Melanie has been going to the old Talbot house across from Hazard's Bluff, to stare at Nat's house across the little inlet. Zeke Seavey's sharp old eyes spotted her a few weeks ago, and told Nat of the girl who haunts the trees there . . ."

Kate's features held surprise.

"I'd no idee . . ." she murmured. Then, suddenly, "Who be Zeke Seavey?"

"The sailor-caretaker at Hazard's Bluff," Paul answered. "Nat and I came by carriage to Marblehead today," he continued. "And while he went to question Zeke, Nat thought I was going to Marblehead to interrogate the inhabitants there. However, since I knew where to find Melanie, I came straight here to bring her to him."

"I ain' sure she'll go . . ." Kate said, shaking her head and trying to absorb this lengthy tale and the meaning of it to her charge.

"When will she return, do you think?" Paul asked, standing up to retrieve his oilskins.

"C'uld be soon; 'n thin, 'cause o' the' rain, she may bide some'eres, 'til it passes."

Paul nodded.

"Kate, I will go fetch Nathaniel and bring him back here. Do not mention the story I've told you just yet. It is enough to know that he loves Melanie and she loves him; as I truly believe she does."

Kate nodded.

"Then, they will be happy together, with all other impediments removed."

When Kate stood, Paul placed a hand on her drooping shoulder.

"You're a good woman, Kate, and I know you only want the best for that sweet, lovely little lady. I regret that she had to suffer through these past months, but it was the only way to make Nat realize quickly just how much she means to him."

Kate's smile was bright. Now she understood the meaning of Paul's lengthy tale!

"God bless ye', sor!" she said. " 'N I cain't wait ter see th' angel's pritty face whin I tell 'er."

With a reassuring pat, Paul walked to the door. Then, he turned . . .

"Nathaniel and I should return within an hour or two, Kate," he said. "And remember, you know the true story, but for now, that is our secret!"

And with a smile, he'd run through the rain to the carriage.

" 'Seems 'e's loved 'er since th' day 'e set eyes on 'er, tho' fer th' life o' me, I can't tell why!"

Kate's words had rambled on and Melanie's brain had stumbled and run with them, trying to understand, trying to comprehend; but they seemed to melt together sometimes, and fell upon her ears with no meaning.

The fire was unbearably hot and as she stared, it grew larger! It seemed that the flames enveloped her body, and the heat was all consuming.

" 'E's gone ter git th' cap'n now, n' bring 'em 'ere!" Kate finished. " 'N I'm feared ye got yerself inta turrible shape fur meetin' 'im after all this time!"

Those were the only words that truly dented Melanie's consciousness. With a wide-eyed cry of alarm, Melanie stood up, staring at Kate. Then, slowly, silently, she closed her eyes and slid to the floor.

The sea was cool and blue-green. Melanie could look up through the water and see a yellow sun shining just above the surface. She rose to the top and floated on the tide. The water was soothing. Her skin, that only moments ago encountered the boiling ocean, now reveled in the soft caress of temperate waves.

She went underwater again, wondering that it was so easy. She did not have to breathe here; there was no struggling, no gasping for air. There was no icy water, no boiling waves. It was just cool . . . and calm . . . and quiet. And she was so sleepy . . .

"Melanie!"

It seemed Nat's voice called to her from somewhere, and she felt a sharp stab of pain, for she knew she must be dreaming. Nat was at Hazard's Bluff now, preparing the house for his bride, Laura.

"Melanie! I love you! Can you hear me, Melanie?"

But his words faded away as her body was jabbed by sharp pieces of ice. She was in arctic waters now and she shivered, teeth chattering with cold.

The icy seas turned black and the sun disappeared behind low, threatening snow clouds. Melanie dove deep to escape the cold, but it was useless. She stiffened and then, slowly, inexorably, her body was encased forever in a huge block of ice. Powerless to move, eyes staring, fixed on glacial wilderness, she felt surprise that her emotions were not deadened also. For deep inside, the wounding of her lost love still throbbed; the ache remained. She tried to resign herself to the fearful knowledge that, throughout eternity, she would be denied healing.

"I tried me' onion n' garlic poultice wi' hot mustard!" Kate's voice came with strange echoes from far away. "On 'er back, 'n on 'er chest. It sh'uld work t' break th' fever ..."

Melanie wondered vaguely how Kate's voice could reach her here in the frigid depths of Limbo ...

Suddenly, the ice melted from around her body and she was freed. With surprise, she moved her limbs, and swam swift and deep toward warmer climes.

Floating lazily on the waves, Melanie tried to recall how she'd arrived in midocean. She had prayed for courage to join Jared and her father ... and she must have been granted her request.

The foam-tipped waves grew higher and hotter; then, beyond a boiling whirlpool, the iceberg appeared once more. She tried to swim away again, but her body was a dead weight. Something held her up,

to pour scalding seawater down her throat. She
choked, near drowning.

Let me be! she tried to cry. *It was so nice floating
on the waves, waiting for Jared and Father. . . .
Please, let me go in peace!*

But it seemed that in this strange, hot and cold
green world, she was mute, for no matter how she
strained, no sound issued from her lips.

"She cannot be moved," an unfamiliar voice said.
"If she passes the crisis in a few more hours . . ."

"Will she make it, Doctor?" It seemed that she
heard Nat's voice again, and Melanie was puzzled.

"She has not the will to fight," the unknown voice
replied. "She is giving in . . ."

What was a doctor doing in midocean? And she
was moving just fine . . . floating free . . . and
easy . . . with the sun on her face; while each wave
sent her speeding farther out into the deep blue-green
seas.

She floated for a long time in the silence . . . in
the deep green, pleasantly cool silence. Then, suddenly, came the whirlpool again . . . hot . . .
hot . . . drawing her down into the depths. She
opened her mouth . . . tried to scream . . . tried
to breathe . . . but an octopus had its tentacles
wrapped tightly about her chest . . . and she gave
up.

"Melanie!" It was Jared's voice. "Father said to
come up from there, immediately!"

Melanie opened her eyes and saw Jared, perched
on the tip of a wave. He looked so like himself when
they were children in Halcyon House—before
Laura—before Nat—before . . .

She felt the tentacles loosen, and she floated free
. . . up . . . up . . . the sides of the whirlpool
into the cool greenness . . . and she laughed aloud
at Jared, doing a jig on top of the water . . .

"Melanie! Come to me, child!" It was her father,

Ephraim Hardy, riding the waves as he would a horse. "You heard me, my girl! Come here, this moment!"

Effortlessly, with daring she'd never before possessed, Melanie extended her arms and soared straight up the side of an enormous breaker, then down the other side to be engulfed in her father's arms. . . .

"Ye're a good girl, Melanie!" her father said, looking tenderly into her eyes. "But, 'tis not yet time! Ye must go back!"

"No, Father! I cannot! Now that I've found you again, I must stay . . ."

But suddenly, there was no water . . . no Jared . . . and no Father—just blackness, settling over Melanie's eyes, numbing her body . . . and her erratic, spasmodic thoughts. And the sound of Ephraim Hardy's voice was in her ears, repeating over and over . . .

"Go back! Go back . . . go . . . back . . ."

Melanie opened her eyes slowly. The late afternoon sun poured across her bed and she heard voices in the next room near the hearth. She tried to make out the words, but she was so tired, so listless. She tried to lift her head and gaze out the window toward the sea, but after a moment gave in to helplessness.

She knew she was in her little room at Kate's house. It seemed she had occupied this room for a hundred years, watching the afternoon sun fall across the foot of her bed as it was doing now; changing its path only slightly with the seasons. Why was she in bed in late afternoon? There was work to be done . . . wood to be gathered . . . and food to be preserved for the winter.

"Kate . . ." she called weakly.

But the low voices in the next room droned on.

Who would be visiting? she wondered, with just a faint tinge of curiosity.

She called again, but there was no response. Then, tired from her efforts, she closed her eyes and fell asleep again.

When she next awakened, the room was dark. Her door was open and the flickering fire on the hearth sent leaping shadows across the bedroom floor. Listlessly, she turned her head. A man sat beside her with his head in his hands. She studied him without fear. Indeed, she was too exhausted to feel anything except curiosity.

In the half light, she saw that he was a big man. Wavering firelight bounced off thick hair, sunstreaked, golden blond—and his hands were as big as Nat's . . .

"Nat!" Her voice, explosive to her own ears, was, in reality, barely a whisper.

His head came up. With a tremulous sigh, he gathered her gently into his arms and buried his face in her long brown hair.

"Melanie!" His voice broke. "Thank God, Melanie . . ."

He smothered her with kisses and she was too weak to protest . . . and too happy to try.

A candle appeared in the doorway and Kate and Paul stood behind it.

"She'd out o' it; praise th' Lord!" Kate whispered.

And Paul bowed his head.

One week later, on a windy November day when a cold sun shone over the first snow of the season, Melanie, wrapped in fur robes, was carried by Nathaniel over the threshold of the house at Hazard's Bluff. There, she was ensconced in the master suite on feather mattress and pillows, with satin coverings, and her slightest whim obeyed.

Paul left the first week of Melanie's residence there.

Still suffering from the weakness of her illness, Melanie was surprised when he kissed her hand and placed it gently back on the satin coverlet.

"I cannot leave my betrothed much longer, Melanie," he said with a warm smile. "Laura is recovering nicely, but she is a woman who must have a man at her side, and I am delighted to be that man."

As the days and weeks passed, Melanie learned the story of Paul's coming marriage to Laura . . . and Nat's ceaseless search during their long months of separation . . .

Nat was at Melanie's side nearly every moment; watching her eat; watching her sleep; watching . . . and loving her.

For a long time she languished thus. And it seemed she was just awakening from a protracted nightmare where she saw her brother's wife and Nat embrace . . . and Jared and James dead; where she hoed in a strange field far from home while searching the horizon for Nat's sails . . . and in darkness and despair, gazed across the little inlet when Laura and Nat rode through the gates to occupy the house at Hazard's Bluff.

Kate was in and out, fussing over her and giving orders to a surprisingly meek Zeke Seavey, who hastened to do her bidding.

It took several months of tender, constant care before Melanie began to come to herself again. The lung fever had weakened her severely, but with the first breath of spring, a faint bloom came into her cheeks and the weakness that enveloped her all through the long winter began to leave her slender body. The doctor came often to Hazard's Bluff and Kate followed his orders implicitly, insisting, regular as clockwork, that Melanie imbibe the bitter, thick "tonic" that would bring back her strength.

The first week in April, Kate nervously approached Melanie in her room.

"I've somethin' ter ask ye . . ." she began hesitantly.

Melanie looked at her with surprise. Kate's face was flushed. Despite bright eyes and an irrepressible smile, she seemed reluctant to continue.

"Kate," Melanie asked, "is something gone wrong?"

"Nay! Niver wrong!" She grinned again. " 'Tis that I'm fearin' ye might think me daft!" She looked searchingly at Melanie.

Melanie smiled and shook her head. Suddenly, she knew what it was that Kate wanted to say.

"D'ye 'member me tellin' ye thet th' good Lord 'uld send me a man if'n 'E felt 'E sh'uld?"

Melanie grinned: "Zeke?"

Kate nodded.

" 'E's wantin' ta' marry me 'n gie up th' sea. We wan' ta' settle down in th' gatehouse. 'E's takin' a fancy ta' th' place 'n ye'll be needin' care whin ye 'n th' cap'n come home frum yer South Sea honeymoon this summer."

Melanie threw her arms about Kate and kissed her.

"Kate! I can't tell you how happy I am for you!"

"T'will be foine, thin? If Zeke 'n me set up 'ousekeepin' in th' gatehouse whin' we wed?"

"It will be wonderful, Kate!" It was Nat's voice behind them. "Zeke just told me the news. It appears you will be married before us, but I insist the wedding take place here. We'll have a party as soon as Melanie is strong enough."

"In a few weeks, Nat! I'm getting stronger every day, with Kate's care!"

Kate was beside herself with joy.

" 'N I'll niver 'ave ta' leave ye! I'll be 'ere ta' take care o' ye, same as always!"

Later that spring afternoon, Melanie curled up on the cushions of the window seat and with Nat's arms about her, watched the trees send lengthening shadows across the new-green lawn. She rested her head against his shoulder and listened to his dear voice as he told her of his love.

"Then . . . you never loved Laura?"

"Never," Nat answered positively. "Laura was beautiful, desirable, but I never loved her, nor did I ever tell her so! I would not wed her, for there was a nebulous something lacking. I did not recognize what it was until I saw you standing beautiful and innocent on the staircase that first night in Halcyon House."

He kissed her gently.

"With all that Laura has been given since birth," he continued, "she yearned for what she could not easily gain. Laura did not love me. It was just that she knew I could not be ordered about like one of her courtiers; and I refused to dance to her tune. The challenge made me desirable to her. Now, Paul has become her challenge. Paul does love Laura. But he is his own man, and it is Laura who will acquiesce to his wishes and be happy in so doing!"

Melanie smiled, and felt a happiness she never dreamed possible until this moment.

"Though self-centered," Nat continued, "Laura is not an unfeeling person, Melanie. And though devious, she is not evil. She was much concerned about your absence, and regrets over her treatment of Jared have spilled over to include her abuse of you. I believe, after she and Paul are wed . . . and," he raised her face to his, gazing deeply into her eyes, "after our wedding in June, you will see that things are now changed. Despite Laura's failings, she does care what happens to you, and, without any impediment," he added. "You can now be a warm, loving aunt to your brother's children."

His hold tightened about her.

"I have a fondness for Laura, Melanie," he said. "But only as a friend! My love belongs solely to you!

I have loved you since the first day I set eyes on you in the tobacconist's shop—but I didn't know it then."

"I knew I loved you then," she said simply, raising her head to look at him.

"You are so much wiser than I, my love," he answered.

Then, after a long kiss, he took her face in his hands and searched her eyes tenderly.

"The first night I came to call at Halcyon House, I sought something in Laura's face, then turned back to you. Do you remember?"

"Yes," Melanie whispered, trying to quell a pang at the memory. "She was so beautiful."

"Not nearly so beautiful as you, my love! In that moment, I studied Laura for the quality I'd found in you. A quality so rare, so precious, that it is seldom found among women of today. You are guileless, my Melanie! Incapable of deception in even the smallest things. Honesty and genuine soul beauty make you envied by women like Laura, for they recognize in you what they could never possess." He smoothed her hair back from her face. "You have a beauty that will never fade. Soul beauty, my Melanie, grows brighter with passing years . . ."

"I want to be so for your sake, Nat," she sighed, nestling against him. "This is where I belong! I am home at last."

Nat held her close, kissing her forehead with gentle lips.

"My fears were so real!" she whispered. "I suffered much, believing them true!"

He raised her chin. Their eyes met and souls blended.

"Your fears, my love," he murmured, "were but shadows on the wind . . ."

Danielle *Steel*

AMERICA'S LEADING LADY OF ROMANCE REIGNS OVER ANOTHER BESTSELLER

A Perfect Stranger

A flawless mix of glamour and love by Danielle Steel, the bestselling author of *The Ring, Palomino* and *Loving.*

A DELL BOOK $3.50   #17221-7